IN THE LAND OF LITTLE STICKS

North-Western Stories

Other Five Star Titles
by Les Savage, Jr.:

The Shadow in Renegade Basin
The Bloody Quarter
Phantoms in the Night
Coffin Gap
Medicine Wheel
Fire Dance at Spider Rock

IN THE LAND
OF LITTLE STICKS

North-Western Stories

LES SAVAGE, JR.

Five Star
Unity, Maine

Five Star First Edition Western Series.

Published in 2000 in conjunction with
Golden West Literary Agency.

Set in 11 pt. Plantin by Rick Gundberg.

Printed in the United States on permanent paper.

Library of Congress Cataloging-in-Publication Data

Savage, Les.
  In the land of little sticks : North-Western stories / by Less
Savage, Jr.
    p. cm.
  ISBN 0-7862-2111-9 (hc : alk. paper)
  1. Northwestern States — Fiction. 2. Western stories.
I. Title.
PS3569.A826 I5 2000
  813'.54—dc21   00-037178

TABLE OF CONTENTS

ACKNOWLEDGMENTS

FOREWORD

Dan Cushman

The town that should have appreciated writers the most, and did so the least, was Los Angeles, particularly the motion picture area that we call Hollywood. The motion picture industry has changed over the years. Hollywood no longer has a monopoly, for the industry has spread to New York and Florida. Writers are very big now. But back when Hollywood was younger and even big name actors were seven-year contract slaves that a vengeful studio could ruin on whim, any observant moviegoer must have thought it strange when the writer, who might be and probably was the real creator of the film, was belatedly remembered and listed almost as an afterthought late in the credits.

I was thinking along these lines when I sat down to write about Les Savage, Jr., because he was that particularly rare creature, a Hollywood native, born in the bosom of the industry, to a craft it so sorely needed, but little honored. He got his start writing for the pulp magazines, as did I. For those too young to remember, the pulps were magazines 7x9 inches in size, about 130 pages, with rough paper of heavier but lower quality than newsprint, manufactured from pulped wood. These usually contained ten stories of varying lengths. Twenty to forty pages was a novel; short stories ran about ten, with a picture page added; and the in-betweens were novelettes. Payment was by the word, so the big pulpers wrote mainly novels, because all three categories required a plot and a set of characters. So a novel, being longer, paid better and you got your name on the cover.

All of the pulps were published in New York City because that's where the agents and editorial offices were, although the authors could be found in spare rooms, attics, and even regular offices scattered across America. Matthews's A DICTIONARY OF AMERICANISMS, published by the University of Chicago Press, defines a "Pulp" as "a magazine printed on cheap paper made of pulpwood and usually containing matter of a cheap, sensational nature." The same entry quotes *The Saturday Evening Post* as saying that "the downfall of the old dime novel was started by the cheap movies and was completed by the pulp paper magazines." Turning to "Dime Novel," we find it was "a novel, often of a trashy, ephemeral sort, costing ten cents or less; cheap, sensational literature in general." The first one published was Ann S. Stephens's MALAESKA: THE INDIAN WIFE OF THE WHITE HUNTER in 1860.

On with the logic! If the downfall of the dime novel was completed by cheap movies and pulp magazines, the pulps must have been on the scene by 1908 when the first New York "film factories" were active, supplying the nickelodeons (movie theaters that charged a nickel and were set up and running in unused showrooms). Alva Johnston, an authority of such things, in his THE LEGENDARY MIZNERS has news correspondent Bronson Howard, returning from the Russo-Japanese War, "write adventure fiction for half a cent a word, and known to turn out 20,000 words at a sitting to become a mainstay at *Popular* and other action magazines." That war ended in 1905. Probably it was only a coincidence that the pulps and film rose together. There was little but action in the early films, and they required *scenarios,* not scripts like plays. "Is it true you wrote the scenario by telephone?" the judge in a lawsuit asked Wilson Mizner, New York playwright and playboy, who answered: "Yes, and I was paid by telephone."

The fiction writers? There was no great fortune to be had in an industry that tended to compose its next day's turns of plot the night before. However, good plotters could make money, and the fiction writers mailed their stories to New York agents and editors at low postage rates and, in an emergency, by night telegraph. Writers had been coming to California since the Gold Rush days. Bret Harte and Mark Twain, Jack London, a native son, and Henryk Sienkiewicz of Poland who authored QUO VADIS? Les Savage, Jr. was one of the few true Los Angeles writers. It was his real name, and it was a good one. For some reason, it always popped right out at you from the magazine. Not only was he an L.A. native son (well, he was *actually* born in Alhambra, a western outpost of the Greater Los Angeles—almost nobody is actually born in Los Angeles), but he had a heritage deep in the town and in the picture industry. His mother was a minor player in the silents, and his father was a studio still photographer.

Even though his roots were in the film industry, he hoped for an art career and enrolled in Los Angeles City College. In his second year he signed up for a course in writing, did a story on submarines, researched from an encyclopedia, and sold it. He quickly tested the water with a second, a Western called "Bullets and Bullwhips," that he sent to New York and sold to editor John Burr of Street & Smith's *Western Story Magazine,* the top Western market of its day, and his career was off and running. (Street & Smith really was a tough market to crack. It was an old New York pulp house that printed its own and had rolls of heavy newsprint blocking the

11

halls. Dan Cushman was never able to sell a line to them, neither Sydney A. Sanders, his agent, nor after Sanders's death, Captain Joseph T. Shaw who had once edited *Black Mask* and helped create the hard-boiled school of detectives, nurturing such lights as Dashiell Hammett and Raymond Chandler.) While Burr was praising the new author, Les Savage, Jr., was trying out his stories on Popular Publications, another pulp house, selling to *Dime Western*, the top of its line, and to *Star Western* and *10 Story Western*, and to Larabie Cunningham for *Frontier Stories* at Fiction House.

Meanwhile, working for a newspaper and doing advertising for the Fox Intermountain Amusement Corporation, with an office (or at least a desk) in its flagship theater in Great Falls, Montana, I spent my spare time, which was extensive, writing stories on Fox Intermountain's new machines, and I was in a position to talk by phone or in person to more Hollywood types than would otherwise be the case.

"Who is this Les Savage, Jr.?" I would ask. We were writing for many of the same magazines. We might appear on the same full-color jacket, in an almost fluorescent ink, and it was that **Les Savage, Jr.** that drew the eye. Max Brand was then the premier name, but it seemed concocted. Les Savage, Jr.—*Les* was friendly, common as soap, yet *Savage* had strength. Like the Savage rifle, a thing of beauty, only more friendly to the hand (it did have the reputation of freezing up in the fifty-belows of the North, but that's splitting hairs). And the *Jr.*—it implied youth, modesty, respect for Les Savage, Sr. For whatever reason, it was a name to be noticed, and to be at ease with. It was a great name. I know, having shared a number of covers with him, that my **Dan Cushman** was always upstaged.

Writing is a lonely business, far scattered across the land. I asked the writers I met about Les Savage, Jr., and was told that he was a young fellow, as writers go. Poetry, not prose, is the domain of youth. Few prose writers work out a mature style before the age of forty, while poets beyond forty are deemed peculiar, and somehow immoral. He was a doomed genius. He was a diabetic, writing against time, a sort of Keats of the action magazines.

I've often heard that writers write from their own frustrations. He wrote action stories, of the barren, wind-swept North, the snows, and rocks of granite. His North was unrelenting and did not yield to the men and women who contended with it. The North did not, like Iowa, or even Wyoming, yield before the horse and plow. The North was a fixed obstruction, too vast to be crossed without a recognition of the odds. In his short story, "Lunatic Patrol," Savage made it the terrible barrier to be crossed by a policeman, sent out to deliver a madman, alive; and the conflict between them was unique and terrifying, because the prisoner can win by escape, as a matter of course, but also by being delivered dead. A two-man conflict, it is linear and unrelenting, as were the snows they crossed. But there were other aspects: an old love, and something unexpected to tie the *babiche* of unity around the frigid tale, a warm homecoming, people with a past who knew their own humanity in a land where the odds were always against them. And a surprise at the end.

"The Lobstick of Charlie Giroux" was another of his superior tales, but one with more of the North's rough and typically French native society, a rogue with human qualities, and with the wild rivers rather than the endless snows as an enemy and friend. From far off Los Angeles he learned from reading, as most writers do, and brought man against nature to a unique, but gratifying, conclusion.

Savage's struggles, in his short pieces such as "Hard-Rock Man," never let nature be forgotten. His hard granite and snow are as much characters as the men who contend with them. Nature, which in the cold is unyielding, is always waiting for one to forget. It was all a long, long way from Bel Air, but Savage did it as few others. Mark Twain said, if you want a description of a steamboat trip, don't go to an old captain, go to somebody who has made the trip for the first time. He will notice all the sounds, smells, and vibrations too familiar and forgotten by the old steamboat hand. A Les Savage, Jr., story is linear to a remarkable degree. Too often, the flashback is a crutch for writers who can't or haven't planned how to work complexities of plot into the steady flow. As far as I know, Savage did not until later try the 60,000-word standard book form, or the book club's favorite, half again or double that length. His longer stories for pulps such as *North-West Romances* stayed with one storyline, starting from the beginning and continuing to the end, without forgetting the escape-hungry audience for which he was writing. He wrote for a special audience, generally male, those who wanted to escape the tedium of a job and at that time, perhaps, also shut away the screeching attention-getters on the radio. Yet a surprising number of magazines were read by professional men who used their minds rather than their hands at work, and sought a few hours of rest in the adventures of people who solved their problems through action in the outdoors.

Comparing the pulps to the big, smooth-paper magazines, one has to wonder which really could claim the greater literary quality. The pulp was designed for people who wanted to escape through reading, while the slick magazine sought to attract a similar audience, mainly female and middle-class, who were most likely to be buying washers, new foods, drapes, carpets, and cars. Writers, often female, might turn out a thousand stories for the *Post*, *Collier's*, and *Cosmopol-*

itan, mostly forgotten today. The chief advantage lay in the name writers, whose reputations came from genuine literary merit, lured by money to sell a novel in serial form, or write a short story.

The long North-Westerns Savage wrote were mainly found in *North-West Romances,* as were this writer's. It was rather restful writing. It was what you wanted to write, without having to worry about offending some advertiser or this or that social-betterment group. The author of this piece once wrote a raucous story about a bunch of Indians welcoming their hero home from the Korean War who had proved to have no—ugh!—nobility about him. It was published by the Viking Press, hardly a bivouac of trash, but prior to that it had been sent to *The Saturday Evening Post* for consideration. The editor rejected it as non-*Post*ian in content or tone. He was, however, kind enough to write me saying as much, with obvious regret. Some of the best Western writers of the day, Ernest Haycox and Luke Short, appeared in *The Saturday Evening Post* but were always careful to observe its editorial restrictions. One of our leading Western writers, A.B. Guthrie, Jr., of *The Big Sky* fame, once wrote a 5,000-word travel piece about going down the Missouri River to Fort Peak Dam and was nonplused when he saw it in print, rewritten and edited to the *Post*-style. Ever after that he maintained they employed a *dull-maker* at the magazine's editorial offices in Philadelphia, and the *Post* saw Guthrie's polished, although often angry, locutions no more.

One of Savage's best and longest efforts for *North-West Romances* was "Death Rules the Wilderness." It was a novel of some 25,000 words (a real book novel runs more than twice that), but even at this length it was long for *North-West Romances.* This story is laid in Savage's favorite North-Western terrain, the Athabaska country of Canada, full of ca-

noes, sled dogs, and rifles, catering to the male love of calibers and ballistics, and women of this land, fresh-air French-
Canadian and more darkly subtle whorehouse types (whore
was a word not allowed by even pulp magazine editors). We
have to settle for the suggestion without the act. Even pulp
stories were typically pure, with care taken not to offend the
most fastidious—except for homicide, which was acceptable,
if properly revenged. I occasionally took a perverse pleasure
in slipping in a torrid encounter here and there, just to test
how carefully I was edited. They always came out, but I had
the last laugh. The pulps paid by the word, and Fiction
House, which published *North-West Romances*, generally took
an author's word count. However, I was never absolutely and
positively sure they *all* were removed because, being generally behind in my commitments, I did not always read my
printed stories.

Whatever his experience, Savage had certainly done research on rifles, and, in including the many calibers and their
ballistics, he was giving what many in his predominantly male
audience liked to read. One might quibble and point out that
finding any but .30-30, .30-06, and .303 ammunition was not
to be counted on in the region's trading posts of that time, but
it was a pleasure for a man of outdoor proclivities to read
about guns and scopes, by someone who had the real dope
and talked of calibers fashionable in *Outdoor Life*, or in his
own dreams of the wilds.

"After many a summer dies the swan," or did it? Eventually, no longer was there a pulp magazine for which returning war correspondents, such a Bronson Howard in
1905, could turn out a rapid 20,000 words per sitting at the
then-valuable cent per word. Mr. Ian Ballantine, his company now a portion of Random House, later owned to having
invented the paperback book single-handedly. This was, even

more than today, a neat, standardized, hard-pulp book, half the size and with none of the smell of the pulp magazines (whose loose sulphide aroma tended to ripen with age) selling at 25 cents each.

New racks appeared. Many established pulpers had their horses shot from under them. Hard times were felt by even the *true* and *confession* magazines. Publishers, with rack space unused, rushed to print new books of the neater size, and even expanded the comic books into new fields. Dell found a bonanza in Walt Disney comics.

Les Savage, Jr., with no place for his name more prominent than the title, wrote original, not reprint, paperback books and wrote for television and motion pictures. He worked on THE WHITE SQUAW for Columbia in 1956 and RETURN TO WARBOW for Universal in 1958—his last screen credit. He died at Santa Monica Hospital, May 26, 1958. He was only thirty-five years old, an age when H.L. Mencken had his prose writers just finding their style. This volume contains every story Les Savage, Jr. wrote set in the Northwest, in Canada, Alaska, or the Arctic. In every case, the original manuscripts have been consulted in the preparation of this book so that, where necessary, the author's text has been restored to what he had originally written. It is splendid to have them altogether in one place, and as he would have wanted them to be.

MUSH FAST OR DIE!

I

Eddie Kopernick jumped up and back from the fire and snapped open the lever on his Winchester, all with one startled motion, and then stood there, peering covertly into the dark poplars filling the air with their heady spring scent all around his camp. It had been this way the past three years. It was how a man got. Jumping at every sound within a mile of him, the butt of his carbine slick and oily from the constant contact with his hands.

In place of a coat he wore a tattered Hudson's Bay blanket, a hole cut in the center poncho-style for his head, the four ends dangling like tails beneath his belt. His corduroy trousers were patched all over with greasy buckskin, and his moccasins consisted more of the rawhide whangs he had sewn on them for repairs than the original moose hide. Black snow glasses hid his eyes, and his shaggy mane of unkempt black hair and hoary curling beard gave his head a massive, leonine look.

"Eddie?" said the man who staggered out of the trees.

"Hell, Smoky," said Kopernick, and moved angrily toward the old sourdough. "I wish you'd make some sign before you bust in like that. Where are they?"

Smoky's gray hair fell over his pouched, dissolute face like the frizzled ends of a mop from beneath a battered black hat that had seen the inside of every saloon from Edmonton to Yukon. He tried to say something, but only smacked toothless gums, and took another step before he fell forward. Still holding his Winchester in one hand, Kopernick caught the man before he went clear down.

"Where'd you get the money?" he said caustically. "I told you. . . ."

"Lissen, Kopernick, lissen . . ."—Smoky's hand on Kopernick's arm was a gnarled claw—"I ain't drunk. Fust time in my life. I swear, I ain't drunk. He's right behind me, Eddie. Thought he done me in for sure, but I got away. . . ."

"What are you babbling about?" snarled Kopernick, shaking Smoky's hand off his arm and standing up over the crouched man. "You've had some red-eye. Ten beaver pelts against a sour bannock you talked while you were swilling. I'm getting out, Smoky. Andover's around here, and, if he gets word I am near Resolution, he'll be on my trail like a bear after honey."

"No, Eddie." Smoky threw his arms around Kopernick's legs, holding him there, sobbing like a baby now. "Lissen. I'm not drunk. You've got to. I went into town to meet 'em like I promised. They weren't there, and he cornered me in the Alaska Light before they came. . . ."

"Who cornered you?" asked Kopernick, trying to kick free. "Let go, you old *moonyass*. You're drunk, and I'm through. I don't know what you're talking about. I don't know why I came down here in the first place. Putting my head in a jump trap, that's all."

"For your own good, Eddie," bawled Smoky, puffy cheeks gleaming with his tears. "I told you. Meet me here and I'd have something that would clear you of that murder charge. You're the only man ever treated me decent, Eddie. I'd do anything for you, Eddie. . . ." Smoky broke off to cough

19

weakly, and Kopernick suddenly quit trying to free himself of the sourdough's grasp, and looked down at him with a strange, taut expression on his face. "Lissen, Eddie, I'm not drunk. Maybe I was when he cornered me in the Alaska Light, but I'm not now. A man couldn't be, the way I am now. It ain't lignite, see. It ain't lignite or bituminous or anthracite. They think it is, but it ain't. I know. I got the map to prove it. Not really a map. They think it's a map, but it ain't really a map. In my shirt, Eddie. He's right behind me."

Kopernick was on his knees now, catching the old man as Smoky started to cough again. "Will you make sense, Smoky? Lignite? What are you talking about? What map? I. . . ."

Kopernick broke off, stiffening to stare across the old man's bent head toward the trees. Another man stood there. Maybe six feet tall, the singular bulk of his upper body set grotesquely on a pair of short, bandy legs, like a pot of tea propped up on snubbed ski poles. In the Northwest Territories, fat on a man, as on a dog, was considered a weakness, and to anyone who didn't know him the evident avoirdupois on this man's belly might have been taken for that weakness. Kopernick knew him.

"Well, Caribou?" he said.

When Caribou Carnes chuckled, it puffed his fat cheeks up till they almost hit his eyes, giving his face a sly, puckish look. *"Si-tzel-twi,"* he said in Chippewayan.

"I haven't got any tobacco," said Kopernick, and he was watching the man warily now, still holding up Smoky.

"Then how about the horns of a deer in velvet?" chuckled Caribou, coming out of the trees like a great, awkward Cupid. "I would give my right arm for the horns of a deer in velvet."

He was born of a white father and a Chippewayan mother, this Caribou Carnes, and some of the heft of his upper body came from hauling York boats up the Athabaska, and the rest had come from eating. Where most men only wore leggings during the winter to keep their pants dry, he wore them all year around. Dog Rib leggings of soft, embroidered caribou hide, tied on his buckskin pants as high as the knees. He rubbed his heavy jowls, gleaming and blue with an unshaven stubble, and grinned enigmatically at Kopernick.

"Sort of dangerous for you to be this near Fort Resolution, isn't it, Eddie? Couple of Mounted Police here last Tuesday. Andover was one. He hasn't given up, Eddie."

Then it was both of them, turning to the rattle of rabbit brush on the opposite side of the clearing from which Caribou had come. Kopernick had one of his hands on his Winchester when the man showed. He wore a gray suit, the pants stuffed into muddy, laced boots, and the brush tearing at his clothes must have irritated him, because his narrow, dark face was flushed. Seeing Caribou and Kopernick seemed to surprise him; he stopped abruptly, and his hand slid spasmodically beneath his coat. Then he pulled it out again, and his forced grin showed chalky white teeth beneath a small black mustache.

"Ah, *m'sieurs,* I hope you are the ones."

"That's Smoky," said the girl, coming up behind the man. "They *must* be the ones."

"Ah, yes, Smoky," grinned Caribou Carnes. "Poor, poor Smoky. Always drinking. He must be having the d.t.'s again, eh, Eddie?"

Smoky was a dead weight against Kopernick's arm now, and he suddenly realized how wet his palm was. He pulled his hand from beneath Smoky, and looked at the viscid red blood on it.

"No," he said, "Smoky isn't having the d.t.'s, Caribou."

After Kopernick had pulled his other four point blanket over the body, he squatted there with his hand still holding

21

one corner, eyeing the girl. It had been a long time since he had seen a beautiful woman, and he couldn't help a certain sullen appreciation of the way her honey blonde hair swept down about cheeks colored high by the winds. Big blue eyes, too, that could do things with a man if he would let them. Body like the neat, trim frame of a racing *odabaggan,* with curves in all the right places to shed the snow. The breeze caught at her thin yellow skirt, whipping it about the curving lines of her legs, and he grabbed his Winchester and stood up suddenly. The hell with that.

"You with Caribou?" he asked the man in the gray suit.

"Caribou?" the man looked blankly at Kopernick. Then he looked toward Caribou Carnes. "Oh, him. *Non, m'sieu,* Miss Burdette and I are alone."

"Burdette!" Kopernick whirled to face the girl squarely, that taut look crossing the cracked, chapped skin of his cheeks.

"Yes." She was frowning at him, puzzled. "Arlis Burdette. And this is Jacques Brazeau. We are trying to get a man to guide us into the Barrens. You undoubtedly heard of William Burdette, who was supposed to have been murdered up north of Slave Lake three years ago. He was my father, and last month I received irrefutable proof that he is not dead. This Smoky . . ."—she stopped, looking at the blanket-covered body, and bit her lip, forcing the rest out—"Smoky contacted us at Edmonton. He said he'd lead us to the only white man living who had been to the Barren Grounds. Smoky was to meet us today in Fort Resolution with this man. We saw Smoky about half an hour ago, but he was acting strangely and wouldn't even stop to talk. We followed him out here."

"Acting strangely?" Caribou Carnes chuckled and pulled a hunk of dried backfat from his pocket, taking out his *besshath.* With this wickedly crooked knife of the Chippewayans, he began to pare off a piece of the meat. "I should think so. You know, Eddie, next to beaver tail there is nothing better than *doupille*. This backfat, now, is from a yearling caribou, and as succulent as when I first stripped it off." Smacking his thick, sensuous lips, Caribou turned with an affected innocence to Arlis Burdette. "Did Smoky tell you the name of this man he was going to show you?"

"Shut up, Caribou," said Kopernick.

The girl's face held a growing speculation as she stared at Kopernick. "No, Smoky didn't tell us any names. Only that this fellow was the only white man living who had been into the Barren Grounds."

"He-he . . ."—laughing like a sly old squaw, Caribou licked his plump finger—"he-he. I should think so. What about you, Eddie? Did Smoky tell you what he wanted to see you about here?"

"Will you shut up?" snarled Kopernick, leaping across Smoky's body to belly up against Caribou Carnes, one hand bunching the man's plaid shirt.

The grin on Caribou's face didn't fade, but it had suddenly lost its mirth. Carefully he put away the chunk of *doupille,* and his little eyes, almost hidden by fat cheeks, were focused on Eddie Kopernick's hand.

"I think you better let go, Eddie," he grinned, staring at the hand almost cross-eyed. "You seem to forget how many men have spilled their brains over my moccasins. Do you wish to add your gray matter to the list? I could kick your head off your neck from where I stand, Eddie. You wouldn't have to remove your hand from my shirt, even. I could. . . ."

"I'm asking you to shut up." Kopernick's voice was flat. "I'm leaving here now without any more hot air being blown out. I'm asking. . . ."

Only Caribou could have done it. Without having moved

his upper body a fraction of an inch, he brought his right leg out and up and around in a kick that would have felled a musk ox. Kopernick jumped back with a grunt, released his hold on the huge half-breed's shirt with his left hand, using his right hand to slash downward viciously with the Winchester. Caribou's kick met the gun with a sharp, bony thud, and Caribou screamed in pain, lurching sideways, and then falling over on his face. He twisted around and was up to his knees almost before he had hit, but the pain in his leg caused him to fall over on his other side. Kopernick stood there with his Winchester held across his belly, cocked, watching the half-breed without much expression showing on his face beneath the black snow glasses. Breathing heavily, Caribou rubbed his leg, the pain still contorting his mouth. It was a long moment before he could bring back that grin.

"I will kill you for that someday, Eddie." Chuckling, he stood up, putting his great weight on the leg gingerly.

"Why not now?" said Kopernick.

Caribou looked at the gun, then pulled the fat from his pocket, still chuckling. "*Kompay*, maybe. Tomorrow. Or the next day. It doesn't matter. Someday. I am the king of savate on the Slave Lake, and nobody can do that to me and live. Someday I will get you without that gun and kick your brains out."

"*M'sieu*," said the man the girl had called Jacques Brazeau, "am I to take it that you are the fellow this Smoky was leading us to?"

"You better not take anything," said Kopernick.

Caribou was licking his fingers with a loud smacking sound, watching Kopernick with sly little eyes. "How else could you construe it, Brazeau? You are looking at the only white man living who has entered the Barren Grounds. Other white men have been there, but they are no longer alive."

24

The girl was staring at Kopernick. "Then . . . who are you?"

"He-he . . ."—Caribou sliced off another piece of backfat—"he-he. It would seem Smoky was playing a joke on all parties concerned. Smoky didn't tell you the name of the man he was bringing you to, Miss Burdette? Smoky didn't tell you he was bringing Miss Burdette here to meet you, Eddie? You ask who this is, Miss Burdette? I want you to meet. . . ."

"Caribou!"

Kopernick's voice turned Caribou. The huge man swallowed the last of his *doupille*, grinning down the bore of the Winchester pointed at his belly. With a chuckle, he deliberately went on. "He is Eddie Kopernick."

The girl's face went dead white, and for a moment she tried to speak without any success, and, when it did come finally, it had a hoarse, strained sound. "Eddie Kopernick! Then you're . . . you're . . . ?"

"Yes," chuckled Caribou Carnes. "The man who murdered your father."

II

The Indians called it *tud-de-theh-cho*, which was Great Slave Lake, and its shores were still swampy and green with late summer, the conies and suckers so thick along the inlets that the latter could be scooped out with a dip net.

The calendar of the Territories was divided into dog season and canoe season, and, with the snow yet weeks away, the two Peterboro canoes were drawn up on the strip of white beach below the timber, tattered and patched with birch bark from their long haul north of Fort Resolution. Eddie Kopernick squatted with his head in the swirling gray smoke of the campfire to escape the maddening swarms of bulldog flies, cutting a ten-pound sucker into strips and hanging the strips on a spit above the flames. Caribou Carnes sat with his back against a tree, as oblivious to the flies as only a man with Indian blood in him could be, smoking a cutty pipe full of the Indian tobacco called *kinnikinnick,* made from the inner bark of the willow.

"You still thinking about Arlis Burdette, Eddie?" Caribou asked, chuckling pinguidly. "You shouldn't have left in such a hurry, after I told her who you were."

"What point in staying?"

"Maybe she would have told you what that irrefutable proof was of her father being alive."

"Don't be crazy. How could William Burdette be alive, when I . . . ?" Kopernick broke off, dark head jerking from side to side in a bitter, frustrated way.

"When you saw him dead three years ago?" grinned Caribou. "You should know, Eddie. I imagine it would be hard to believe a man was alive again after one had killed him. I never did get the whole story, Eddie. William Burdette was a research engineer for Anacosta Coal, wasn't he?"

"Let it go," said Kopernick stiffly.

"Yes," grinned Caribou. "As I understand it, Anacosta had sent Burdette up here to locate coal fields comparable to those estimated by geologists in Alaska."

"You use a lot of big words for an Indian."

"I am white, Eddie," pouted Caribou, holding the same dislike of most half-breeds for their Indian blood. "My father was Peter Carnes. At least almost white. How can I have any Indian blood when I am so erudite? I should have a Ph.D."

Kopernick scratched his black beard. "A man can get too smart for himself."

"I have begun to reach that conclusion, too, Eddie,"

chuckled Caribou. "It is much easier to sit on one's hams and eat beaver tail than to read all the books in the Athabaska library. You wouldn't believe it, Eddie, but I have read all the books in the H.B.C. library at Athabaska. I am a scholar and the king of savate on *tud-de-theh-cho*, and I can consume more unborn caribou calves than any ten men along the Slave River. I'll bet William Burdette never ate an unborn caribou calf." Caribou looked up under his bushy brows at Kopernick, little eyes sly. "As for discovering the coal fields up here, I understand Anacosta was interested in finding a practical way of exploiting what they found. With snow up here eight months of the year and the Indians so lazy they wouldn't even look at a coal shovel, much less pick it up, that would constitute a major problem for any corporation, wouldn't it? I imagine that's why the Alaskan coal fields haven't been utilized. There are also problems of transportation. Is that the fuss you had with William Burdette, Eddie? Over a problem of transportation?"

"Don't ride your sled too hard," said Kopernick.

"Is my *beth-chinny* going pretty fast now, Eddie?" grinned Caribou, using the Chippewayan word for sled. "I never did hear your side of the story, Eddie. Only what Constable Andover told. William Burdette and Nils Glenister hired you to guide them into the Barren Grounds? Smoky went along to pack for you over Pike's Portage. You made your base camp at Sithor's village on McLeod Bay. Nils Glenister and Smoky stayed at the Indian village while you and Burdette made your dashes into the Barrens. There had been trouble with poachers south of the Land of Little Sticks, and Constable Andover had come to Sithor's village investigating. Andover was there when you came back after the third run into the Barrens and had that row with Burdette about more pay for another trip."

"It wasn't that. He. . . ." Kopernick stopped suddenly, his mouth twisting bitterly. "Will you shut up? I don't want to talk about it."

Caribou chuckled. "So, you did have a fight with Burdette. And the next morning they heard a shot behind Sithor's lodge, and Constable Andover and Nils Glenister found you bent over the body of William Burdette. Your Forty-Four-Forty had several fired shells in its magazine. You claimed you'd been hunting. . . ."

"I had, I had!" exploded Kopernick. Then, cursing, he stuck his head back in the smoke and began working viciously at the fish again.

Caribou's chuckle was satisfied. "You're touchier about it than you like to admit, aren't you, Eddie?" The half-breed got out his inevitable hunk of backfat and began paring off a slice with his crooked-bladed *bess-hath*. "There's a lot of queer angles to that business, Eddie. Whatever became of Glenister, for instance?"

Kopernick spat it out. "How should I know?"

"Glenister was Burdette's partner. You'd think he would have gone with Andover and you when the constable started back to put you on trial at Edmonton. Yet Glenister stayed at Sithor's village, and, the day before you and Andover left, Glenister left, telling Sithor he was heading for Resolution. They never saw him anywhere. He just disappeared." Caribou took a succulent bite of backfat. "How did you get away from Andover, Eddie? He won't ever tell. I guess he's ashamed."

"I got away."

"He-he." Caribou's laugh seemed always to be sly. "You sure did. I guess nobody will ever know except you and the constable. I guess nobody will ever know what happened to William Burdette's body, either."

28

Kopernick whirled, still squatting. "Will you get off that sled? I told you I don't want to talk about it."

"Just disappeared. Like Glenister . . . disappeared. Is that why you're going north, Eddie? Because you don't know what happened to the body of William Burdette? Why not admit it?" Caribou sucked the grease off one plump finger with a loud, smacking sound. "The body disappeared sometime between the morning you were found with it and the following evening. Sithor's bucks took it to one of their lodges, and that's the last they saw of it. And now, when Burdette's daughter comes, claiming she has positive proof her father is alive. . . ."

"But I saw him, damn you, I saw him!"

"Yes, didn't you," grinned Caribou. "That's what you can't get over, isn't it, Eddie? You want to believe the girl, because Burdette being alive would clear you of a murder charge. Yet you can't believe her because you did the killing yourself. And yet, you can't stop yourself from going north to make sure, because you don't really know what happened to Burdette. It's ironic, isn't it? Of all the men in the Territories, you should know. And you don't. One thing I don't see, though, Eddie. If you used a gun on Burdette, how is it Smoky was killed with a knife?"

Kopernick rose slowly from the fire, his hands closing into fists. "You're going too fast now, Caribou. You better jump off that sled, before it tips over with you."

"I never tipped a *beth-chinny* in my life," chuckled Caribou. "Did you get what you wanted off Smoky . . . ?"

"You've tipped this one, Caribou!" Kopernick jumped to where Caribou sat, standing above him with his bearded face turned dark by rage. "When Smoky came to me, he was running from whoever had put that blade through him, and he told me that they were right behind. Next minute you showed

29

up on one side of the clearing, and that Arlis Burdette came on the other side with Brazeau."

"And we found you bent over Smoky, the same way Glenister found you bent over Burdette," said Caribou, getting ponderously to his feet. "My sled's still going first rate. You ain't got that gun, Eddie. Remember what I told you I'd do, when you didn't have it? My *beth-chinny*'s still going, but, if you want to try and turn it over, go ahead. Now, who were you intimating put that blade through Smoky?"

"Caribou . . . !"

Kopernick broke off, seeing Caribou's little eyes go past him toward the timber behind. For a moment, the snapping fire was the only sound. Then Caribou's voice came, a hoarse shout.

"*Ma-a-rche,* Eddie!" yelled Caribou. "It's Constable Andover!"

It was all confused to Eddie Kopernick after that, a running, shouting, brawling insanity of those two scarlet-coated Mounties looming at him from behind, Andover in the lead, a big, red-faced man in his early thirties with a thick blond mustache riding his bleak mouth like hoarfrost on a ridge of muskeg. He had his gun out, its thong flapping from the weapon's butt to where it was attached around his neck. Nine out of ten men would have tried to escape Andover's rush like that, but Kopernick's jump toward the constable was the thoughtless jump of a man who had been hunted till his reactions were those of a wild animal, and the very unexpectedness of it must have been what made Andover miss his first shot. With the roar of the gun deafening him, Kopernick went into the constable's solid bulk. They made a thick, fleshy sound, meeting, and then the ground was hard against Kopernick's back, and he was rolling beneath Andover. He sprawled into the fire, scattering smoked fish and burning brands everywhere, the sudden heat giving his struggles a spasmodic violence. He twisted Andover's gun around and, with it still in the man's hand, beat at Andover's face.

"Damn you, Kopernick . . . !"

Andover's desperate curse was cut off by his own shout of pain as the gun butt smashed into his brow. Kopernick got to his knees, straddling the man, shaking the burning sticks and coals off his back as he fought to tear the revolver completely free of Andover's desperate grip. The second constable had been blocked off from firing by Andover's running body, and now he was moving to get the two struggling men from between him and Caribou so he could shoot without fear of hitting Andover.

"Myers!" yelled Andover, struggling to keep Kopernick from hitting him again. "Don't let that man get at you with his feet. Keep away from Caribou's feet!"

Caribou caught Myers off guard by jumping directly across Andover and Kopernick, one foot striking Kopernick's head. Constable Myers tried to whirl toward Caribou as the huge half-breed came down on one foot. That left his other foot free to swing, and Kopernick knew what was coming. Even as Myers got his gun around that way, Caribou's first kick flashed out. It knocked the revolver up as it went off. With an amazing agility, Caribou followed up, dropping his kicking leg and throwing his weight on it and lashing out with the opposite foot all in one smooth swift motion, so fast Kopernick couldn't follow it. The second kick caught Myers in the belly and sent him crashing back into a tree, doubled over.

All this time Kopernick had been wrenching desperately at the gun to get it free of Andover's grip. Finally he tore it completely out of the constable's hand, and hit him again in the face with the butt.

31

"I am the king of savate on *tud-de-theh-cho,*" roared Caribou Carnes, "and I have spattered the brains of men with more guns than you"—he had his third kick coming—"all over my moccasins"—and it smashed Myers's head back against the tree trunk.

Caribou then executed an amazing follow-up, kicking the Mountie's gun out of his hand, and then caught the constable with a head-high kick that sent him slamming sideways from the tree trunk to roll over and over like a birled log till he came up against a spruce tree farther away and stopped and lay still.

The Mounties tied their guns on that way for good reason, and the best Kopernick could do was empty Andover's weapon into the sky before he got up. "Let's mush, Caribou."

Caribou was standing with his *bess-hath* in his hand, looking mournfully down at the constable he had kicked into unconsciousness. "I am tempted to take out his tripe with my crooked knife. But, then, I would be running like the little *nakee* all the rest of my life, just like you are, and sooner or later the little red fox gets caught, doesn't he?"

Kopernick grabbed him by the arm, and they were running when they reached the two Peterboro canoes. Kopernick jerked the towline attached to the lead canoe to test it, then shoved the craft into the water, and Caribou had the second one out after it. They both jumped into the lead craft, Kopernick in the stern.

"Pull that paddle, you big *moonyass!*" shouted Kopernick. "Andover's got his own canoe somewhere."

There was nothing a caribou-eater hated worse than to be called a tenderfoot in Cree, and, smarting under the gibe, Caribou bent over his paddle. "Don't talk to me, you Athabaska *teotenny*. I'll be pulling this canoe when you're dead in its bottom from exhaustion."

"Don't put that in my cariole," laughed Kopernick harshly. "You've got the streak of fat, Caribou. Big dogs, big men, it's the same thing. Packing or sledding or canoeing, the big one goes down first."

"You're a dirty Klincha liar!" shouted Caribou apoplectically. "I'll take twice your load on my packing board and reach the finish an hour ahead of you on an hour's run. I'll drive dogs three times as big as any *kli* in your team and beat you in a snowstorm with my mittens tied to my snowshoes. And I'll be paddling this canoe up here when they've given you a scow to tow on the Styx. I'm no caribou-eater that can't go in a straight line. I was pulling a paddle when you were riding around on your mother's back in a moss bag."

It was true. One of the paradoxes of the Territories was that, although the Chippewayans had for untold generations utilized the water for their transportation during every canoe season, they were still execrable boatmen. The Chippewayan paddles were clumsy things, thick and broad, and the caribou-eaters themselves had apparently never conceived the idea of learning to paddle so dexterously on one side that the canoe would be driven in a straight line, preferring to paddle two or three times on one side, and then shift sides, sending the boat in endless zigzags. But Caribou Carnes, as he so willingly admitted, was not a common Indian, and Kopernick felt the boat surge forward under the huge man's drive and saw their wake streak out behind them, white and gurgling and straight.

Back on the beach, Andover had risen to his knees, pawing the blood feebly from his eyes as he sought to reload his gun. He must have realized he could never do this in time, for he raised his hand suddenly, lowering the weapon, and his shout came over the rapidly widening breach of water to Kopernick.

"I'm not through, Kopernick. You can't find a pushup in

33

any river far enough away to hide from me. I'm after you on two counts now. I'm after you for Smoky. I'll get you, Kopernick. I'll get you if I have to follow you to hell!"

III

They belonged to the Dene nation, the Indians native to the Canadian Northwest Territories, and their origin was as mysterious as the origin of the winds they worshipped. The tribes speaking Chippewayan roamed the region north of Resolution, and those living near the Barrens had come to be called the caribou-eaters because their very existence depended upon the caribou to which they looked for their main source of food. Caribou Carnes had been born in Sithor's village, on McLeod Bay, and he had come north with Kopernick, returning to his people. Chippewayan was harsh and caustic to the ear compared with Cree, and it was this guttural tongue that filled the lodge of Sithor, punctuated by the lonely yap of a wolf dog from outside, or the snap of a spruce bough in the fire.

The encounter with Constable Andover was two weeks behind them, and Kopernick and Caribou sat among the fetid, greasy Indians, listening to Sithor.

"Your affair with the one called William Burdette is of no concern to us," he told Kopernick. "When one of our men is killed in a personal feud, we don't want the whites to interfere. Our only concern is that Constable Andover is known to be on your trail, and, if he found you here, we might be deprived of our treaty money this year for harboring you."

"Forget the constable," said Caribou Carnes. "Am I not in the lodge of my brothers? Kopernick comes with me. All we ask is that you sell him a good sled and enough dogs to run with."

Sithor was dressed in a caribou-hide coat, embroidered with porcupine quills down the front, epaulets fringed with musk ox hair. His face was seamed and wrinkled, and his eyes held the narrow, wind-marked look of a man who had spent his life staring across vast distances. "You aren't going into the Barren Grounds?"

The words caused the bucks to shift around Kopernick, murmuring and grunting darkly, and he felt cold suddenly. "You never did find William Burdette's body?"

Sithor shook his head, braids of gray hair bobbing against his shoulders. "Nobody knows what happened to it."

Kopernick bent forward, that intense look drawing the chapped, reddened skin taut across his cheeks. "Sithor, you were with Nils Glenister when he came on me and Burdette. Could you swear Burdette was dead?"

Sithor's brow wrinkled in a frown. "You should be the one to know that."

"Could you swear he was dead?"

"We carried him back to the village." Sithor took a sharp breath. "He *is* dead, isn't he?"

Caribou chuckled. "Are you asking us, Uncle Sithor?"

Sithor waved a grizzled hand impatiently. "But even if he were not dead, a man in that condition does not just rise and walk off of his own accord."

"Perhaps he had something to hide," smiled Caribou. "We have never heard the whole story of what happened between Kopernick and Burdette. Glenister might have told it, but he disappeared three years ago. Smoky might have told it, but he is dead. Burdette, alive or dead, is, at the present, in no condition to tell it. Kopernick. . . ."

"If Burdette is alive somewhere in the Barrens . . . ," said Kopernick, and stopped, because that ominous muttering had risen among the bucks around him again. He stared at their dark faces. "What is it?"

"You aren't going into the Barren Grounds," said Sithor. "For your own good, Kopernick. Don't go."

"Why do you speak like that?" asked Kopernick. "If Burdette is there, he can clear me. Your own hunters have been there."

"For the last two years," said Sithor, "the men who have sought caribou in the Barren Grounds have not returned. Seven of our bravest warriors left the village, at one time or another. We never saw them again. If you seek Burdette beyond the Land of Little Sticks, you will find nothing but death."

The braves muttered and nodded, and then they all began talking and shouting at once. A buck slipped in from outside and whispered in Sithor's ear. The caribou-hide tom-tom they called a *hali-gali* was sitting in front of him, and he beat on it for silence.

"There is another *teotenny* outside," he told Kopernick, "another white man."

"You mean white *woman*," she said, coming toward Kopernick through the crowd.

It was Arlis Burdette.

From the swamps north of camp came the low *kick-kick* of a secretive yellow rail, and somewhere a partridge was drumming on a balsam poplar. These were the only sounds Kopernick heard as he stood there at the door of the lodge, holding the skin flap back with one hand, gripping his Winchester with the other. The minute Arlis Burdette had spoken, he had been on his feet, jumping past her to the door.

"Did I surprise you that much?" she said.

"Where's Andover?" he asked, tight-lipped, peering out the door.

"What do you mean?" Then she must have understood, and she flushed angrily. "Oh, don't be a fool. I didn't bring the Mounted Police. I never saw such a suspicious man."

He stepped out the door and moved down the wall to stop there with his back against the hair-cap chinking the undressed spruce logs, sweeping the camp from behind his black snow glasses. Arlis Burdette followed, dropping the skin flap behind her, and from inside the lodge the Indians began shouting and talking among themselves.

"Look," said Arlis, coming up to Kopernick, "Brazeau and I have been trying to find a guide all the way from Fort Resolution up here. None of the Indians will go into the Barrens, and it looks as if what they say about you is true . . . you're the only white man living who's been past the Land of Little Sticks. We were a day's trek south of here when we passed a caribou-eater who said you were in his camp. . . ."

He was looking at her now, and she must have seen the puzzled expression crossing his face, for she suddenly grabbed him by both arms, something desperate in her voice.

"Oh, don't you see? I can't help it if you tried to kill my father. . . ."

"*Tried* to kill?"

"Yes, *yes*," she said swiftly, almost crying. "If there was anyone else who could take me into the Barrens, do you think I'd ask you? I'd do my best to see the Mounties get you. But there isn't anyone else. I despise you for what you did, but I need you. What you did can't have any significance. All I care about now is finding my father. If you guide me to him, I'll do anything for you. I'll even help you escape the Mounties. I've got money. Enough money to take you to China if you want."

He was rigid against the wall, painfully aware of her nearness, not wanting to look at those wide blue eyes. "You really believe your father's alive, don't you?"

"I've got to believe it. He isn't dead, I tell you. This letter proves it."

She fumbled a tattered piece of paper from the front of her Mackinaw, shoving it into his hand. Automatically he took it; then he shook his head, thrusting the paper back to her. She looked at his snow glasses.

"Andover was on my trail last winter," he said uncomfortably. "He had me running across the ice too long without glasses. The glare. . . ." He shrugged, indicating the paper. "You do it."

Her eyes remained on his face another moment, something indefinable passing through them, then lowered to the letter. "It's dated August First, Nineteen Twenty-Eight. Not much of a note, really. 'Dear Arlis . . . I've found it at last. Something big. Something bigger than Anacosta ever dreamed, or I ever dreamed, or any of us. As you know, I've duplicated all the data I collected up here during the last months, and sent the extra copies to you. Somehow, all the originals disappeared, and I can't make any official reports till I've corroborated my findings. I'll need that data to do it. Please get Anacosta to send those duplicates as soon as possible. If you need any help, look to Jacques. Your loving father . . . William Burdette.' "

It had been hard for Kopernick to concentrate on the letter. She was standing so close to him her honey-colored hair was almost brushing his beard—like the perfume poplars give off in the spring. It was hard to concentrate on anything. He swallowed something in his throat and edged down the wall to get away from the scent of her hair.

"That data . . . ?" He made a vague gesture with a hand. "That data . . . ?"

"Maps, charts, weather reports, geological findings," she said. "You know. Dad made this his base camp, and, whenever he returned here from a run into the Barrens, he compiled everything he'd found into reports, sending duplicate copies of each one to Anacosta. He is a scientist, primarily. Whatever coal deposits he found would have to be cross checked with all those other reports, before he could make any final, official report to the company. He couldn't locate his discovery exactly enough for the company, in the first place, without the maps he'd made. You can see how necessary all this data was to him."

"Three years. Then up he pops and writes you a short little note, with no explanation of where he's been or what's happened." Kopernick shook his head. "I can't eat those bannocks. Would there be any reason for someone else . . . ?"

"No, no." She had his arms again, looking up at him. "I had the handwriting checked by experts. It's his. He wrote this letter three months ago. You can see the date." Suddenly she was pleading with him like a child. "Tell me he's alive, Kopernick. Tell me you aren't sure you killed him. There could have been a chance, couldn't there? Nobody knows what happened to him, really. There could be a chance he's still alive. You of all people should know that."

"Everybody takes it I'm the authority on the subject," said Kopernick bitterly. "Suppose I'm not. Suppose I don't know any more about it than you? Suppose I didn't shoot him?"

"Oh, don't joke with me."

"That's what Andover said," muttered Kopernick.

Yes, that's what they all had said. *Don't make me laugh. You were bent over him with fired shells in your .44-40 and a bullet the same caliber in him. Out hunting? That's a little thick to swallow, isn't it? Out hunting? That's funny. Or unfortunate. Or don't make me laugh. Or don't joke with me.* Until he had quit telling them he was out hunting. Until he had quit telling them anything. Until he had just run like a wolf runs, without any particular goal except to avoid human beings and to keep one jump ahead of Andover.

"It's not so funny he should write a note like that." Arlis was talking more to herself than him now. "Dad is a scientist. You don't know men like that, Kopernick. They get so wrapped up in their work they forget time or space or life. Probably wasn't even thinking how funny it would seem for the note to pop up like that when he wrote it. He'll explain when we find him. Very logically. He's alive. Tell me he's alive. Some Indian must have taken him away. Sithor and his bucks carried Dad to the lodge, and then one of them took him away. That's how it happened, isn't it, Kopernick?"

She was crying against his shoulder, and his arms were around her somehow, and he was surprised at how small and soft she was. Like a snowshoe hare. Yes, small and soft and trembling against him like a little snowshoe hare. Then he became aware of how many Indians had come out the door after him, and of how long they must have been standing there, watching them.

"Maybe you'll take her into the Barrens now, Eddie?" chuckled Caribou Carnes. "I would take her into the Barrens, if she cried on my shoulder like that."

Kopernick pulled his arms from around the girl. "Shut up."

"He-he." Caribou's giggle drew his fat cheeks up till they almost hid his little eyes. "Sithor tells me he has a nice long Cree toboggan he got from Athabaska last year. That would make a good sled for you. And his *klis,* Eddie, the dogs. He has a spitz leader that makes you wish it was winter already."

Kopernick looked at the girl for a long minute, then jerked his head toward Caribou. "Let's go see the dogs."

In the summer, the Indians treated their dogs as carelessly as they treated their canoes in the winter, and the dozen Huskies lying around behind Sithor's lodge were gaunt and ner-

40

vous, rising to their feet and bristling as Kopernick came toward them. Caribou pointed out the spitz leader, a black male with the wolf showing in his prick ears and sharp nose.

"Maybe goes eighty pounds now," grinned Caribou. "But he'll run a hundred easy as soon as you start feeding him regular. Sithor says he led the team that won the races in Athabaska last year."

"Too big," said Kopernick. "How about that gray bitch? She looks like she'll make eighty at her top."

"Too big?" scoffed Caribou. "The bigger the better, I say. I already got my team picked out. Not a one will weigh under a hundred after I feed them up."

"And a smaller team will wear them out on the long run every time," said Kopernick, studying the gray female. "Streak of fat, Caribou, men and dogs."

Caribou's laugh shook his belly. "Wait till we get to running. I'll show you. I'll lead you all the way and have your dogs so gaunted up they look like the wrong end of a hard winter. Streak of fat. He-he. I didn't see any streak of fat in that canoe race with Andover."

"What's her name?"

Caribou looked at the lean, wolfish bitch. "Kachesy. It means Little Hare. Because she runs like one, I guess."

"Kachesy," said Kopernick, squatting down and holding out one hand. "Kachesy"—and the sudden velvet of his voice made Arlis Burdette look down at him in a certain surprise.

"You don't think she'll come to you?" said Arlis. "A strange dog."

"He-he," chuckled Caribou. "Down in Athabaska they say Eddie Kopernick is part dog. He doesn't drive them in a sled. He gets in the harness and pulls with them."

"Don't be fantastic," said Arlis.

41

"He doesn't sleep in a bag at night like ordinary men. He digs himself a *cabane* in the snow, just like the dogs. It wouldn't surprise me if he hid a tail down one leg of those corduroys."

"Oh, stop it."

"Kachesy." The female had come in slowly, hesitantly, snarling softly and bristling, but now Kopernick had his hand on her ruff. "Kachesy. I think I'm going to like you. Little Hare? How would you like to run in a toboggan? None of this gang hitch these caribou-eaters have been using on you. Nome-style, Kachesy."

"Nome-style," laughed Caribou. "Tandem hitch. I wouldn't drive my dogs that way if the horns of a deer in velvet depended on it. You do everything wrong, Kopernick. I don't see how you ever kept ahead of Andover last winter. Half dog, and you still do everything wrong."

Kopernick felt the gray's forelegs, and she relaxed under his touch. Straight and not too long, with a light spring in the pasterns that was good. He pursed his lips, nodding slightly, and ran his sensitive fingers down her hindquarters, a faint smile catching momentarily at his mouth as he felt the singular development of the thigh, and second thigh.

"This is my king dog," he said finally. "Sithor got a price?"

"My God!" Caribou threw up his hands in mock despair. "A female for a king dog. I've seen everything. He-he. I suppose Sithor has a price. He would sell his grandmother for two years' worth of treaty money."

"Pick out the best you can get," said Arlis Burdette. "It's on me. While you're looking, I'm going down to get Brazeau. He's unpacking our canoes."

The two men watched Arlis go off, the lilt of her walk tapping her wool skirt against bare legs with each step, and finally Caribou looked down at Kopernick, chuckling. "I guess

42

I'd go north, too, if a girl like that asked me."

Kopernick turned back to the dog abruptly, lips tight. "If I can find Burdette alive, it'll clear me of the murder."

"I'd go north, too, if a girl like that asked me," repeated Caribou, grinning slyly, and turned to go after Arlis.

It was dark before Kopernick had finished picking his team. Tying the five dogs apart from the main group, he turned toward the lodges. A bunch of gray jays came wailing through the gloom, heading south before a chill wind that presaged early snow. A silent squaw passed Kopernick, papoose carried in a moss bag on her back, caribou-hide skirt rustling softly against her bright red stroud leggings. Most of the Indians had gone into their lodges, and Kopernick could see streaks of light showing through the crack in the walls of Sithor's lodge where the hair-cap chinking had come out from between the logs.

The silence that descended over an Indian village after dark had always oppressed him, somehow, and Kopernick shivered a little, pulling the Hudson's Bay blanket closer around him. He'd have to get a parka out of the stake the girl was putting up for an outfit. First snow come, and this damned blanket wouldn't provide any more protection than a caribou hide with bot holes in it.

He was going down the narrow lane between Sithor's lodge and the next one when the scraping sound across the roof made him look up. There was a black shadow above him, and he hadn't even jerked up his gun when the weight struck his face, hot and resilient and stunning.

Kopernick went down with a shout that was muffled against the man's body, his head rocking to a blow. He tried to get his feet under him, but the passage was too narrow to straighten his twisted legs, and the man's weight held him down. He grabbed his Winchester with both hands, jamming it upward viciously. The man on top grunted, shifted violently, lifted an arm. Kopernick tried to roll aside from the blow. But he was jammed in too tightly. Something hard struck his head, knocking it back against the log wall, and he heard his own yell of pain.

He jammed the rifle up again, spasmodically, but it was a feeble thrust, and the man tore it from his hands, striking again. Kopernick threw up one hand, and the blow caught him there, knocking the fingers back into his face and smashing them against his jaw. The third blow struck him full across the forehead, and after that whatever sensation remained was dim and unreal in the whirling vortex of pain screaming through his brain. He felt the man's hands go beneath his blanket, feeling around on the inside of his belt against his skin, then he sensed the pockets of his corduroys being pulled out, tobacco and rawhide whangs spilling onto the ground.

"Damn you," he heard the man say, and felt his body jerk as he was rolled over. At first he thought he was struggling again, then realized it was only the desire to struggle in his mind. His body refused to answer that desire. He tried to sob in a sort of frustrated anger, and couldn't even do that.

"Kopernick?" It came from somewhere far away, hardly intelligible at first. "Kopernick, is that you? Where are you?"

The man crouching by Kopernick cursed again, and rose to slip down the alley way and disappear. The girl came from the opposite direction, and it must have been her calling. She knelt beside him, and he could hear her saying something fearful and compassionate, and her hands were soft against his face. He was coming out of it now, the pain growing more intense as his consciousness returned.

"Stunned me," he mumbled, shaking his head. "Stunned

me." He tried to sit up.

"Why?" she said. "Who was it?"

He fumbled beneath the broad belt which held in the four corners of his blanket, and pulled out a piece of paper. "I think they were after this. When Smoky first contacted me on Slave Lake, he told me if I met him at the poplar grove north of Resolution on the Tenth, he'd have something that might help clear me of the murder charge. You know what happened when he did meet me at the grove. Before he died, he babbled a lot of trash I couldn't understand about lignite and bituminous and how they thought it was a map, but it wasn't really a map."

"Lignite," she said. "That's coal. Who thought it was a map?"

"I don't know who he meant by *they*." Kopernick unfolded the paper. "Smoky said he had it in his shirt. I got it out without you or Caribou seeing me. This."

She squinted her eyes in the darkness to see what was drawn on the paper. "Looks like a picture of a tree."

"Lobstick."

"Lobstick?"

"You find them all over the Territories," said Kopernick. "Whenever something noteworthy happens along the trial, the men cut a lobstick to commemorate it. They choose a good-size tree and shave the branches off the trunk in a pattern. Like Commander Webb's lobstick on Caribou Island. You must have seen it if you came up Slave Lake. Webb saved a whole boatload of caribou-eaters from drowning, and they chose a pine growing near the water and shaved all the branches off one side about halfway up to mark the event."

"And you found this drawing of a lobstick inside Smoky's shirt?"

He nodded. "The only paper there. It must be what he was talking about. No two lobsticks are alike. If you ever saw the real one this picture represents, you couldn't miss it."

"But Kopernick," she said, "what could it mean?"

IV

Pike's Portage between Sithor's village on Great Slave Lake and Artillery Lake was thirty miles of packing for Kopernick and the others, wooded land interspersed by nine smaller lakes. Even the dogs carried a load, thirty-five or forty pounds packed into the panniers formed by a strip of canvas slung over the animal's back, held on by a breast strap and belly band. The men's packing boards were carried on their backs in such a way that the two hundred and fifty pounds of weight rested on the body's center of gravity, the board itself held by a broad strap around the head. Before the first day was over, Jacques Brazeau had lightened his load by half, and every few minutes he had to stop and rest his back. They reached Weeso Lake in early afternoon, but there he squatted down with his board, slipping the strap off his head with a bitter curse.

"*Sacre,*" he panted, "don't you beasts know the meaning of fatigue? I can't go any farther."

"We'll go until it's dark," said Kopernick. "Andover's behind us somewhere, and he'll be traveling lighter than we are."

"Oh, let the poor *moonyass* rest, Eddie," chuckled Caribou Carnes, setting down his load and rubbing the great smooth muscles of his neck, developed from countless portages like this.

"You wearing out already?"

"Wearing out?" Caribou bridled. "I'll pack you to the

MacKenzie Delta and be carrying both our loads when you're crawling along behind on your hands and knees."

"Streak of fat," said Kopernick.

"Streak of fat, my grandmother's moss bag. I'll outlast you on any portage from here to the Yukon. You can't. . . ."

"Oh, put on your mukluks and go after the sled. We'll leave Brazeau here, and maybe he'll be rested up by the time we get back."

They hadn't been able to carry everything in one trip, and had left the dismantled sleds and canoes in a cache three miles back. Caribou unloaded the panniers on his huge black Siberians and started off before Kopernick was finished unloading the last of his own smaller sled dogs.

"Do you and Caribou always have to fight?" Arlis Burdette asked Eddie Kopernick.

"I don't particularly like him," said Kopernick. "I don't particularly trust him. I wish you'd hired one of the other Indians at the camp."

"I didn't hire Caribou."

He looked up from his butt dog. "I thought you did."

"I thought he was with you," she said.

Kopernick turned to Brazeau. "Did you sign on Caribou?"

The Frenchman rubbed the stubble beard on his lean pale face, sloe-eyes not meeting Kopernick's. "He seemed to know the country. We needed another man. *Bon Dieu,* why make so much of it?"

"Sort of a private deal, wasn't it? Not even consulting Miss Burdette."

Brazeau flushed. "I was William Burdette's best friend, *m'sieu.* I have been his daughter's confidante and advisor since his disappearance. I do what I think best for her interests."

"Then you must know a lot about William Burdette," said

Kopernick, "and what he was doing. Maybe even more than Arlis knows. Nils Glenister, for instance."

Something passed through Brazeau's dark eyes. "Nils?"

"You knew him that well? What happened to him?"

The Frenchman shrugged narrow shoulders in his plaid Mackinaw. "How should I know? You should know better. Nils was with you and William on that last trip, wasn't he?"

"And Smoky," said Kopernick. "Smoky's dead because he knew something. What about Nils Glenister? Nils was supposed to have disappeared right after Burdette was . . ."—he stopped, glancing at the girl—"after what happened to Burdette. The general consensus of opinion seems to be that Glenister is dead, too. How about that, Brazeau? Smoky died because he knew something. How about Glenister?"

"Will you stop asking me? How should I know? All I know is Glenister was last seen in Sithor's village, the day after Andover started out to take you down to Fort Resolution. Glenister left the village then and never showed up at Resolution or any of the other posts farther south." Brazeau was fumbling in his pack for something. "What are you driving at, Kopernick? I. . . ."

"Don't pull that out with the dogs free!"

But Kopernick's shout was too late. Brazeau had pulled a big chunk of smoked whitefish out of the pack, and the five dogs leaped forward in a howling, snarling bunch. The Frenchman went down beneath them with a loud cry, rolling over beneath their bodies as they tore at him to get the meat. He came to his feet among them, fighting to stand up in the mad, yapping tangle, and Kopernick saw the big Grant-Hammond automatic in his hand.

"Pour l'amour du bon Dieu!" screamed Brazeau, and whirled about to bring the .45 to bear on Kachesy.

"Brazeau!" shouted Kopernick, and scooped up a loaded

48

pannier from where he had dumped it on the ground, and slung the whole pack saddle at the Frenchman, blankets and stroud wrappings falling out of the pockets as the pack saddle flew through the air.

The pannier struck Brazeau as the Grant-Hammond exploded, knocking the gun upward. Staggering backward under the impact, Brazeau was unable to keep his balance under the whirling turbulence of the fighting dogs, and he went down again. Grabbing a heavy tent pole from another pannier, Kopernick leaped among the animals, beating at them viciously.

"Kachesy," he swore, "get back, damn you, get out of here . . . !"

It was brutal, but most of them were half wolf anyhow, and the only way a man could control them when they were maddened and fighting like this was to beat them almost insensible. Kopernick laid about him with the clubbed tent pole until the dogs fell back, so Brazeau could roll over and get his feet under him. He still had his Grant-Hammond, and, while he was yet on his knees, he turned, cursing viciously.

"I'll kill them!" Brazeau shouted frenziedly. "I'll kill them all."

His first shot went above the head of Kopernick's butt dog. Kopernick quit beating the dogs and turned to slug Brazeau across the back of the neck. The Frenchman went forward with a hoarse cry, rolling over on one shoulder and onto his back. He pulled his gun arm from beneath him, and Kopernick saw the intent stamped in his rage-twisted face.

"Don't . . . Jacques!" cried the girl.

Kopernick threw the tent pole fully in Brazeau's face, and jumped after it, kicking at the man's gun while he was in midair. He heard the weapon go off and felt the hot leap of it against his foot, and then he was on Brazeau. The dogs were back in again, fighting each other for the shredded piece of whitefish and tearing at the two men to find more. Kopernick lurched up beneath their furry bodies, surprised to see the gun still gripped desperately in Brazeau's hand. He caught the .45 and twisted it around sharply, hitting Brazeau in the face with his free fist.

Kachesy and another dog crashed into Kopernick, knocking him off Brazeau. Partly freed of Kopernick's weight, the Frenchman got to his knees, throwing Kopernick over onto his back. The dogs rolled across Kopernick's face, hot and furry, claws ripping him, and another spitz jumped in. Kopernick tore at them, swinging his leg around in a blind kick at Brazeau. He heard the man grunt, and kicked again, and then he had the dogs off and could see, and still lying on his back that way he lashed out with his foot a third time, catching Brazeau fully in the face.

It knocked the Frenchman backward almost off his knees, and, while he was still twisted over, Kopernick shoved the last dog off his arm and rolled over and jumped Brazeau, snarling like one of the Huskies. He hit Brazeau in the mouth, knocking him flat, and tore the gun from his hand, and hit him again in the face when he tried to rise, and kept hitting him, sprawled across his body, until the man ceased to move. Then he staggered to his feet, finding the tent pole, and belayed the dogs till they were scattered about him in a circle, snarling sullenly and licking their wounds. Brazeau groaned feebly, and Kopernick turned to him, standing there with his face clawed and bleeding, his black hair down in a matted tangle over his snow glasses.

"You aren't doing any killing, Brazeau," he gasped. "Next time you try to use that gun on those dogs, it's you who'll be killed, I swear!"

They were on Aylmer Lake when the first snow fell, and they cached the canoes on the shore and bolted the runners on their sleds. Driving the heavy sledge called a *komatic* by the Eskimos, Caribou Carnes started right off at the five-mile pace adopted by the trippers over a good run.

"Hold them down, Caribou," Kopernick called to him. "They've been starving all summer. You'll run their legs off the first day."

"He-he." Caribou's laugh shook his belly against the bright red L'Assumption sash he had tied around his waist. "No wonder you want to go slow, with that crazy toboggan you picked. All it's good for is the woods, Kopernick. All my friends tell me the same thing. A man's crazy to ride a toboggan past Last Wood. All prairies up there, hard-packed snow, just like the Eskimos ride."

"Your friends never hunted as far as I took Burdette." Kopernick was jogging beside the woodland sled called a toboggan by the Indians, from the Algonquin word *odabaggan,* and he caught the tail line to steady it as the nose struck a rock. "There's more muskeg up there than you ever saw in your life. You need a toboggan for that."

"Muskeg, my grandfather's moss bag," laughed Caribou, lashing his dogs. "*Ma-a-arche,* you *klis, marche!* I'll be coasting over that muskeg like a beaver down a slide while you're all tangled up in your broken runners. And when we're on the level, you'll see how good that damn' ski of yours is against a decent pair of runners."

Kopernick spat disgustedly. Well, maybe the toboggan did look like a ski. Instead of runners, it had two flat strips of birch bolted together and curved up at the nose. The cariole, where the load was stowed, looked like a canvas bathtub, extending the whole eight feet of the sled and held in place by a sling extending from the curved nose to the backboard.

"Try climbing a hill with that *komatic*," said Kopernick. "You'd spill the whole load right in your lap."

"*Chanipson,*" shouted Caribou, using the Chippewayan to turn his dogs right around a tree. "*Chanipson,* you crazy *klis, chanipson!* Listen, Kopernick, my dogs are big enough to climb any hill with any load."

"And wear out before they reach the top."

"*Unipson!*" bellowed Caribou, turning the dogs left this time, his voice growing louder as his irritation increased. "They won't ever wear out. You never proved that streak of fat on me yet. I wore you out on the lake, didn't I? I packed you out on the portage."

"You didn't wear me out."

"Will you two stop fighting?" panted Arlis Burdette. "I don't see how you have enough breath left to speak a word."

Jacques Brazeau jogged sullenly beside her, narrow chest heaving, face covered with perspiration. The fight with Kopernick was a week behind, but the Frenchman still eyed him with a vindictive anger.

They settled down to a steady trot now, and the toboggan made a soft crunching sound through the hoarfrost coating the reindeer moss atop the rises. They crossed the tracks of a marten, made in neat little pairs across the trail, each set oblique to the other. Then they broke through a narrow passage in the brush, knocking frozen clusters of cranberries off either side, and entered a long open stretch.

"Kopernick," called Arlis suddenly, and he saw where she was pointing.

Caribou Carnes looked around from up ahead, chuckling. "A lobstick, Miss Burdette. You must have seen them on the way up from Athabaska. Not truly a natural phenomenon."

"Is that the one?"

"Is which the one?" asked Caribou.

"She wasn't talking to you," said Kopernick.

"Oh," said Caribou, a sly grin crossing his face as he slowed his stride to drop back toward them, "are you interested in a particular lobstick?"

V

It was then the shot came—sharp and clear on the cold air—followed almost instantly by Brazeau's shout. The Frenchman was running beside Kopernick's toboggan, and he lurched over, smashing into it. The sled swung sideways beneath his weight. He clawed at it to keep from falling, dragging for a few feet, one of his long Seauteaux shoes ripping out of its footstrap. Kopernick caught the tail line, but Brazeau's weight had already tilted the sled too far over.

"Whoa!" shouted Kopernick. "Kachesy, whoa . . . !"

But the frightened dogs had speeded up, the overturned sled bouncing and bumping along behind them, blankets and food dumping out of it with every foot. The second shot came just as Kopernick's steer dog rammed into Caribou's sled. Caribou yelled something, and stumbled, and rolled forward into the snow. Kachesy got mixed up in the flapping tail line of Caribou's traces, and the number two dog rammed into her, tangling the moose-hide traces, and Caribou's sled went over on them. With the whole team in a yapping, baying tangle, the third shot rang out. Kopernick felt the hood of his parka jerk, and heard the thud of the bullet going into the packed snow at his feet, and knew how it had to be now.

"Dive for that brush!" he screamed at the girl, and bent to reach inside the overturned cariole of his sled, still bouncing over the ground, pulled by the frenzied, tangled dogs. But

Arlis Burdette continued to run by his side, face twisted in a puzzled, frightened way. "Dive for the brush, damn you, dive for it . . . !"

With a bitter curse he yanked his .44-40 out of the cariole and jumped for her, catching her around the waist just as the fourth shot barked. The two of them rolled into the snow with the bullet of a high-caliber rifle making its mordant whine above them. Then Kopernick half lifted Arlis onto her feet and shoved her ahead of him toward the rabbit brush and stunted spruce trees at their right. He pumped two shots in the direction he thought would do the most good, and then threw himself after the girl into the cover.

They lay there, panting, Kopernick levering his rifle for a third try. Then the girl caught his arm, and he saw Caribou dragging Brazeau in from where the Frenchman had gone down.

"Cover me, Kopernick," called Caribou. "He's in that timber on the rise ahead of us. Cover me."

His voice was drowned out by Kopernick's .44-40. Kopernick raked the trees methodically until his magazine was empty, and by that time Caribou was in beside them.

"You're one up on me, Caribou," said Kopernick ironically. "I didn't think you had it in you."

"Oh, don't be like that now." The girl's face was flushed with anger. "He might have been killed, stopping to drag in Brazeau that way."

"He-he." Caribou's face was bathed in sweat. "I couldn't leave him out there, could I? Sniper got me in the arm somewhere. I think Brazeau's worse."

Kopernick had Brazeau's coat opened, and saw how thick and viscid the blood was blotting the man's plaid shirt, and Brazeau reached up to paw feebly at Kopernick's arm, nodding dully.

"*Oui, oui, c'est fini,* eh? All right. I don't complain. Listen, Kopernick. It isn't lignite or bituminous, *comprende?* I studied all the data William sent back to us, and I've been checking the geological formations as we came north, and I know. It can't be lignite or bituminous. He thought it was, but he must have realized he was wrong even when he was sending the data down. Not lignite, or bi . . . bi . . . tumi. . . ."

"That's the same thing Smoky said," urged Kopernick, catching at Brazeau's hand. "What do you mean? Brazeau?"

They hunkered there a long silent moment after that, and then Kopernick took off the Frenchman's bloody coat and put it over his dead face. Caribou was sitting, holding his thick arm, but his eyes were on Kopernick. That strange feral expression had come into Kopernick's gaunt face, the little muscles along his bony jaw bunching up and drawing the flesh so taut across his flat cheek bones that faint cracks began to show in the chapped, reddened skin.

"The same thing Smoky said down at Resolution," he muttered, almost inaudibly. Then he searched for his rifle. "You stay here."

"Kopernick . . . ?"

With the girl's call following him, he crouched out onto the flats. The dogs had dragged the sleds almost to the fringe of trees ahead, and were snarling and fighting among themselves. One of Caribou's black Huskies had broken free and was running toward timber. Kopernick reached his overturned toboggan and began rummaging for a box of .44-40s, throwing things heedlessly out on the snow till he found it. He snapped open his lever and began jamming the centerfires home, then moved in a swift run toward the stunted spruces. He had on a pair of Ungava shoes, shorter and broader than most men liked to wear for any speed, but more wieldy in thick timber where a longer shoe would have kept

55

running into the close-set trees.

Almost immediately he found where the man had crouched, and the tracks leading away through the trees. They had been made by the triangular shoe used farther north. Andover? Following the prints in a wary crouch, Kopernick shook his head. The constable wouldn't wear Eskimo snowshoes, or do the thing from ambush like that.

The timber showed the effect of the short summers up here. They had passed from the Canadian zone down around Resolution, and these trees were stunted and scrubby, most of them standing less than fifteen feet tall. For a while, the only sound was the soft *sluff-sluff* of Kopernick's shoes in the snow, barely audible even to him. His breath fogged before his face in the chill air, and he moved like a tense, wary animal, head never still. He was rising on a gentle slope when he heard the dim yap of a dog from ahead. He speeded up, reaching the crest, then stopped. Below the crest was an open field of tundra, stretching northward as far as he could see. The sled was a mile or so ahead of him, barely visible now. Kopernick whirled suddenly to a sound from behind him, jerking up his rifle.

"You're the most nervous man I've ever seen," said Arlis.

"He-he," chuckled Caribou. "You get that way when the Mounties have been after you three years."

"I thought I told you to stay back there." Kopernick's voice held impatient anger.

"We couldn't do any more . . . back there." The girl's face darkened a moment, but she was looking after the sled. "You're not going to follow it?"

"He's riding the runners," said Kopernick, almost sullenly. "We'd never catch a ridden sled on snowshoes."

"Kopernick." Her big eyes were wide and frightened on him. "Kopernick, who could it be?"

★ ★ ★ ★ ★

It was the real Barrens now, the Land of Little Sticks, where spruce trees over three hundred years old grew only eight or nine feet high, the timber spread in straggling groves, each grove separated by miles of treeless, empty prairie.

The girl was weakening under the trip, hardly having the strength to mutter one word during the whole day, stumbling doggedly behind Kopernick when the country became too rough for the dogs to pull her extra weight. Kopernick himself was running like some hunted animal, the gaunt lines of his face accentuated by exhaustion, haunted by the knowledge that the inexorable Andover was somewhere on their back trail, keyed up every moment of each long run for that rifle to begin crashing from some ambush again.

Only Caribou seemed unaffected. He had an incredible endurance, and seemed as fresh and strong after a twelve-hour run as when he had begun it, still full of that sly, chuckling humor, laughing even when he lashed his huge dogs unmercifully. Kopernick didn't know exactly when that day he first began to notice that Arlis was limping. They were crossing a stretch of swampland the Crees called muskeg, its brooding hummocks and ridges frozen over now to form a corrugated madness for sledding, and the girl in the sled would have been too hard on the dogs, so she was jogging along behind Kopernick.

"*Marche,* you stupid *klis,*" shouted Caribou, sending his rawhide lash cracking across the back of his steer dog. "You won't get any whitefish tonight, if you don't do any better than this."

"What's the matter, Caribou?" said Kopernick. "I thought that Eskimo sledge could take the muskeg."

"Who said I'm not taking it," laughed Caribou. "I just

have to touch my dogs once in a while so they don't forget I'm here."

"Put that lash on them much more and they won't have any hides left," said Kopernick. The girl cried out behind him, and he whirled around in time to catch her before she went clear down. She gasped a thanks, and tried to start running again.

"How long have you been limping like that?" he asked.

"I don't know," she panted. "It isn't anything."

"You wearing duffels?" he said. She nodded dully, and he turned to call after Caribou. "We're stopping here a minute."

"What's the matter? Those *klis* of yours wearing out already? Streak of fat, Kopernick, streak of fat."

Kopernick hardly heard him. He had set the girl down on the side of his toboggan and was removing her snowshoes. Caribou had turned his big sledge around and brought it back broadside to the toboggan so he could hunker down against it facing the girl. His big black dogs lay down in the snow, and Caribou took off the mitten over his right glove, and then the glove itself, reaching inside his parka for his big *bess-hath* and a piece of backfat. With the crooked knife, he pared off a chunk for himself.

"No wonder you've got foot trouble," he said, smacking his lips. "Your duffels are all the same size. You get them all too large that way and your socks wrinkle and the wrinkles freeze and then your snowshoe strings freeze and begin to cut into your toes and instep, and you're crippled up good."

Kopernick was holding one of her small, pale feet in his hands, and he saw how deeply the flesh had been impressed by the frozen wrinkles of the duffels. "How long have they been like this?"

"I don't know. I didn't think it was worth bothering you about. I didn't want to complain."

He was looking up at her, and a strange, new emotion welled up in him. He hadn't expected that from a girl, somehow. Then, with a jerk, he reached into the cariole for some fresh duffel, and began to cut it into strips.

"Oh, no, Kopernick," groaned Caribou, stuffing the last of the *doupille* into his mouth. "You aren't going to give her Indian duffels. That's only for some dirty Klincha. Make socks for her, at least. Do it like my squaw does and you never get wrinkles. Four pairs, each pair smaller than the next, so they fit inside each other. Snug as a papoose in a moss bag."

Kopernick began winding the strip of duffel he had cut around her foot. "We haven't got time to sew socks. This is better than any duffel you ever wore, anyway. If you'd admit a little more of your Indian blood, you might learn something. You can thaw these strips out at night twice as fast as socks. I've seen you put on wet socks more than one morning."

"I haven't got any Indian blood," pouted Caribou. "My father was Peter Carnes."

It had begun to snow before they were started again, and soon they were mushing through a soft white swirl. Kopernick began hunting for a sheltered spot to pitch camp before they lost their direction completely. It was then he heard the dog yap from somewhere on their left flank.

"Caribou?" he shouted.

"What is it now?" answered Caribou from the white snowfall, and it came from ahead.

"Whoa!" shouted Kopernick, and his dogs came to a stifflegged halt, and he turned to catch Arlis. "Crouch down in the lee of the sled. Don't move no matter what happens."

He had his .44-40 whirling toward the flank, head cocked for that yapping again. Andover? Kopernick began moving away from the toboggan. The snow beat softly against his face, and he kept pawing it off his dark glasses with a mitten. It seemed he was climbing a rise, and he began to breathe harder and to sweat inside his heavy parka of caribou hide. Then it was the yapping again, so much nearer this time that it startled him, and, even as he was stiffening, he heard the shout of a man.

"Andover?" Kopernick yelled into the snow, and then had his rifle up and going, because the other man was shooting.

The .44-40 jerked in his hands with the first shot, and, when he levered it, the empty shell flew out and hit the snow with a soft sizzle, and that was drowned out by the soft clattering of the other man's gun, and then Kopernick felt the blow in his belly, like someone hitting him there with all their weight behind the punch, and after that, just before he fell, the awful pain shooting through him. He felt himself rolling back down the slope toward the sled, and then he brought up against something hard, and stopped.

It seemed an eternity that he lay there in a stupor of pain, but it couldn't have been very long, because, when he could move again, he brushed dazedly at the snow on his glasses and then made out the man standing above him, holding a rifle. Through the pain flooding his body came the surprise, so strong it was like a physical shock. Kopernick raised up spasmodically, and his voice had a hoarse, incredulous sound.

"Nils Glenister!" he said.

The dogs stood with their brushes down like wolves, huddled together in their moose-hide traces, staring owlishly into the falling snow. Caribou was still on the runners of his sledge, face blank with surprise. The girl squatted pale and tense beside Kopernick, looking up at the man above him. It was his own toboggan Kopernick had rolled into off the hill. Caribou had come back about the same time Glenister had come down off the rise after Kopernick, and now they were all held by Glenister's rifle.

He was almost as big as Caribou—Nils Glenister—the slope of his great shoulders thrusting his whole body forward slightly, his moose-hide parka tattered and patched, strips of duffel wound about his legs as high as the knee in place of regular leggings. Ice had frozen on his beard and was breaking off in chunks, and his eyes had a feverish burn beneath the fox-fur lining of his hood. Kopernick saw the Eskimo snowshoes he wore, shorter than the Chippewayan, triangular.

"It was you sniping us the other day, then," muttered Kopernick.

"Did you find my tracks?" asked Glenister. "I tried to get you all at once, but you dove for timber too soon. I knew I'd get you sooner or later. When it started snowing today, it gave me just as good an ambush as that timber. If my damn' dogs hadn't yapped, I could have finished you before you knew what happened. Nobody'll find what's up here, Kopernick. Not even the Indians. They wonder what happened to their hunters who came into the Barrens. They should wonder. Seven of them, Kopernick. I kept count. And now you. All I want is the girl. She knows where it is."

"Where what is?" Kopernick could hardly speak with the pain in his stomach.

Glenister jerked his gun toward Caribou Carnes. "You stand still!"

"I wasn't doing anything," chuckled Caribou fatuously, and then his eyes were on Glenister's rifle. "Well, a Forty-Four-Forty. That's the same caliber Kopernick packs. How coincidental."

Glenister's feverish eyes seemed to glitter a little, and Kopernick stared at him, beginning to sense something in the man. He had seen the Barrens do that to other men before,

61

the utter desolation, the loneliness. Three years? That was long enough for the strongest mind.

"Glenister," he said slowly. "Who killed Burdette?"

Glenister turned toward him, grinning thinly. "I knew Burdette had found it on that last dash you and he took into the Barrens, Kopernick."

"Found what?" said Caribou.

"Burdette wasn't going to let me in on it," said Glenister. "His own partner . . . and he wasn't going to let me in on it. I took all the data he'd kept and tried to find it on the maps, but it wasn't there."

"So that's what happened to the originals." Arlis's voice was strained, as if she had begun to sense the implication of it now.

"Yes," smiled Glenister mirthlessly. "That's why William sent to you for the duplicates. After I couldn't find it in the data, I caught him out behind Sithor's lodge and tried to force it from him. The old fool put up a fight and grabbed at my gun. It was his own fault. Then I heard you coming, Kopernick, and ran down that alley between the two lodges. Sithor and Andover had heard the shot, though, and met me before I was completely through the alley. I tried to head them off, but they wouldn't take that. But when we came back, you were crouching over Burdette."

"He-he." Caribou's chuckle drew his fat cheeks up until they almost hid his eyes. "So you really were out hunting, Kopernick. How ironic."

"You. . . ." Arlis had one small hand up to her mouth, eyes wide and horrified on Glenister. "You killed Dad. Nils. You. . . ."

62

VI

A sudden virulent anger swept Glenister. "Yes, me. Who else? He was holding out on me, wasn't he? I was his own partner, and he wouldn't share it with me. I got his body out of the lodge they had taken it to that night, loaded him on a sled, and headed for the Barrens. I thought he'd have the map on him. But all he had was a letter he'd written to you and hadn't sent."

"Letter?" Arlis fumbled in her parka. "You sent . . . ?"

"Yes," snarled Glenister, his eyes blazing fanatically now. "I found it on William's body. But when I'd taken him away from Sithor's, I didn't have a chance to load my sled up for any extended trip. I'd only carried him a day's run north of camp, so I could search his body without the Indians finding me, but the snow caught me up there, and I got turned around. I would have frozen to death if a band of Dog Ribs hadn't found me up north of the Land of Little Sticks. It took them the better part of that year to nurse me into health again, and they didn't let me go till summer. I guess I was still delirious. There are blank spots. I don't remember much. I do remember killing every Indian who set foot past the Land of Little Sticks. I guess I must have spent the whole three years out in the Barrens, hunting for it."

"For what?" said Caribou, grinning slyly.

"Only last January did I come out of the fog finally, and piece things together. I still had the letter, and I realized I would never find it hunting blind like that. It was easy enough to change the Nineteen Twenty-Five to Nineteen Twenty-Eight on the date of the letter so nobody would notice it. Your father always made his fives like an 'S' anyway. As for the month, all I had to do was wait till August to send it so

63

that postal date on the envelope would match the one on the letter."

"But why send the letter at all?" The girl's voice was hollow.

"Isn't it obvious?" snapped Glenister. "In this letter William asked you to send the duplicates of all that data. But after his being thought dead for three years, I knew you'd come personally, when you got the note. And I knew you'd bring what he asked you. William didn't have the map with the other charts and data he'd kept . . . didn't have it on his person. He must have sent it to you with those duplicates. Now tell me where it is, Arlis."

"I don't have any map," she told him, frightened tears welling up in her eyes. "Are you crazy, Nils? We can't just sit and talk like this while Kopernick is. . . ."

Glenister took a vicious step to grab her shoulder, tearing her away from Kopernick and forcing her to remain on her knees. "Don't lie to me, Arlis. Your father must have made a map when he found it. He couldn't have come back to it any other way in the Barrens. Where is it?"

Caribou Carnes's complacent chuckle made Glenister raise his head. "Mister Glenister, has it ever occurred to you that William Burdette might have entrusted this map you speak of to someone besides his daughter?"

Glenister's face darkened. "How could you know? You weren't even with us."

"Smoky was," grinned Caribou. "Smoky packed over Pike's Portage for you, remember? Smoky stayed with you at Sithor's camp while Kopernick and Burdette made their trips into the Barrens. I met Smoky in the Alaska Light at Fort Resolution a month ago. He was drunk. I guess he was always drunk. Things spilled out of him, like they usually spill out of a drunk man. He told me how he had heard Arlis was at

Athabaska with proof that her father was alive. He told me he had effected a meeting between Arlis and Kopernick at the poplar grove south of Resolution. Kopernick was the only man who had ever treated Smoky decently. I guess Smoky wanted to help Kopernick clear himself.

"Ah, friendship. Smoky didn't tell Arlis he was taking her to Kopernick, and didn't tell Kopernick he would be meeting Arlis. I guess he realized neither of them would come if they knew who they were going to see. Smoky was waiting in the Alaska Light to take Arlis to the poplar grove, when I found him."

Kopernick tried to roll over on an elbow and raise himself, and groaned with the pain that it caused him. "It was you put that blade through Smoky. . . ."

Caribou took out his keen-edged *bess-hath* and began slicing at a portion of backfat, chuckling. "There is nothing like *doupille,* Kopernick, unless it is the horns of a deer in velvet. But it takes a sharp knife to cut it right. I had always thought William Burdette was going into the Barrens after something more than coal. . . ."

"But he wasn't," flamed the girl. "He was a scientist."

"And Smoky corroborated my opinion," went on Caribou, ignoring her. "He didn't tell me in so many words, but the way he was acting and talking whetted my dormant curiosity. I got him in the back room, but he turned sly. I guess my *bess-hath* wasn't as sharp as it should have been. He escaped me. That must have been when you and Brazeau saw him, Arlis. He was running down Dog Rib Row toward the poplar grove. He must have given it to you before he died, didn't he, Kopernick?"

"Given what?" said Glenister. "I think you're stalling. I'm going to kill you."

Caribou's chuckle was unperturbed. "I tried to get it off

65

Kopernick down at Sithor's village. Were you surprised when I came down off the roof on top of you, Kopernick? Arlis came before I could search you thoroughly. You don't think I know where the map is, Glenister? Why don't you look in Kopernick's parka?"

It was instinctive for Kopernick to try and roll away from Glenister, and that was what caused the big man to jump at him, a savage eagerness crossing his face. That eagerness took Glenister's attention from Caribou.

"Nezon!" roared Caribou, *"savate!"* He leaped across Kopernick's sled to crash boldly into Glenister before the man could jerk straight. The two of them went to the ground, and Kopernick screamed with the pain of Glenister's weight on his wound. Caribou was on his feet like a rubber ball, and, as Glenister lifted himself off Kopernick, whirling with the rifle coming up, Carnes launched a kick from the hips that smashed the weapon out of Glenister's hands, and brought his kicking leg down with a thump and pivoted on it and lashed out with the opposite one to catch Glenister in the belly, doubling him over, and recovered that kick while the man was still bent, and had another one smashing into Glenister's chin.

Glenister went over backward with a shout of pain, but rolled over and caught the toboggan as Caribou rushed him. He leaped up and took Caribou's next kick full in the face and went right on in, screaming insanely. He got Caribou around the waist, trying to jam a knee into his groin. Caribou jerked sideways, blocking the knee with his own knee. Face twisted savagely, Glenister clawed at the half-breed with broken, dirty nails. Caribou got his weight beneath him and brought his leg up in a circular swing to kick Glenister in the ribs. Snarling like a wild animal, Glenister let go with one arm to slug at Caribou's face.

66

"Nezon!" shouted Caribou gleefully, "he's crazy!" He caught Glenister's fist, straightening the man's arm and levering him back that way. Screaming fanatically, Glenister tried to keep his hold on Caribou with his other arm, but he finally had to let go. He kicked wildly at Caribou. Caribou avoided the foot nimbly and caught it while it was still in midair, heaving Glenister over with it. The man went onto his back, and Caribou jumped after him.

"Damn you!" howled Glenister. "I'll kill you. I've killed them all. Nobody finds out where it is. . . ."

Caribou kicked him back down as he tried to rise. Glenister rolled over on his belly, and Caribou jumped after him, kicking him in the head and face with a thick, drumming sound. Bawling with the pain, Glenister turned fully into the kicks and rose deliberately to his knees, his face a bloody mess. He caught Caribou about the knees. Caribou tried to twist away, jerking Glenister's head back with a blow to the chin. But Glenister clung to him with the bestial strength of a madman, snarling and cursing, tears of pain and rage streaking his mashed cheeks. Glenister was trying to climb up Caribou and gain his feet, arms twined desperately about Caribou's legs to keep him from kicking. But Caribou bent to jam the heel of one hand under Glenister's chin, forcing his head back. Glenister grunted spasmodically, bent backward like a bow under the strain, and Kopernick thought the man's back would break before he finally let go of Caribou's legs. The very instant Glenister released his hold, Caribou snapped all his weight onto one leg and lashed out with the other. Still on his knees, Glenister took the kick in his face.

"Oh, Caribou," screamed the girl, "stop it, for God's sake, stop it!"

But Caribou jumped on in, pivoting to kick again, dropping that leg back and shifting his weight onto it and lashing

67

out with the other. Pivoting and shifting and spinning so fast Kopernick couldn't follow each separate movement, Caribou kept Glenister rolling and jerking over so he couldn't rise, raining brutal kicks into him. Glenister tried to get up a last time, his face an unrecognizable blur, inarticulate, animal sounds escaping his pulped lips, bloody hands pawing at his eyes.

"Savate!" shouted Caribou, *"nezon!"* He jumped in again, and this time Glenister went down for good. Huge chest heaving, Caribou bent over and rolled the body over onto its back. He stopped to peer at the wreckage of Glenister's face, then he pulled open the parka and thrust his hand in to put it against Glenister's chest. Finally he straightened up.

"He was crazy, wasn't he?" chuckled Caribou. "I guess he's better off dead."

He turned to pick up Glenister's rifle, wiping the snow off it. Then he shuffled around in the white drifts till he uncovered the paper Glenister had taken out of Kopernick's parka. Caribou stared at it.

"So you were interested in lobsticks," he said, and glared at the girl. "What does this mean?"

She bit her lip, barely able to speak. "I don't know."

"This what Smoky gave you, Kopernick?" Caribou waited for an answer and, when it didn't come, said it again without the question. "This is what Smoky gave you. What does it mean, Arlis?"

"I don't know, I tell you."

"I think you do," he said, and the sly jollity of his chuckle only made it more evil. He went to his big Eskimo sledge and began unloading the extra blankets and spare gear; then he took the food in Kopernick's sled and loaded it into the space left on his own. After that he took out his *bess-hath* and walked toward Kopernick's team. Kachesy's ruff stiffened, and she snarled softly. Kopernick jerked spasmodically, trying to roll over and get to his hands and knees, but the agony that it caused him was too much. Arlis crouched over him, watching Caribou in a fascinated horror.

"Come here, Kachesy," chuckled the half-breed, holding out his hand. "Come here, Little Hare."

"Caribou . . . !" Kopernick gasped.

"Oh, I'm not going to kill your *klis,* Kopernick," said Caribou. "Just cut them loose. No food, no dogs. If that bullet in your belly doesn't kill you, starvation will. I sort of hate to do it, Kopernick, old friend. I've grown so fond of you during this trip. I guess there really isn't anyone up here quite like you. It will be the passing of an era. Come here, Little Hare."

With a sudden, vicious snarl, Kachesy leaped at him. Caribou jumped to one side, caught the dog about its thick neck as the traces brought it up short, and with two skillful slashes of his *bess-hath* had the moose-hide harness cut. He leaped away as Kachesy whirled. The dog stood there stiff-legged, fangs bared, brush up. Then she became aware that she was free, and moved to one side experimentally. Caribou cut the other dogs loose the same way, then turned to the girl.

"All right, Arlis, get into the sled."

She rose, trying to comprehend. "In . . . the sled . . . ?"

"Yes, my little green-winged teal. You and I are going to find that lobstick and you're going to tell me what it means. It's a singular lobstick. I know we haven't passed it on the way up. See it and I'd know it. It must be somewhere in the Land of Little Sticks. Get into the sled."

"No." A wild look widened Arlis's big eyes. "No, no. . . ."

She turned frantically and started to run, then stopped, looking back at Kopernick. Caribou jumped after her, and she turned again, breaking into a stumbling run. He caught up with her, catching her arm and spinning her around.

69

Kopernick saw the kick coming, and cried out with his inability to rise. Caribou did it as neatly as a man would with his fist, his moccasin catching Arlis on the point of her chin. He recovered and caught her even before she fell, carrying her to the sledge. Then he slipped his big Yukon snowshoes back on, uncurling his dog whip.

"Caribou," groaned Kopernick. "Don't be a fool. That lobstick doesn't mean anything."

"Oh, yes, it does," chuckled Caribou Carnes. "Everything. Burdette wouldn't trust it to the mails, because by that time he was beginning to suspect Glenister of intercepting everything he sent down and examining it before sending it on. So Burdette gave it to Smoky to take to his daughter. Burdette had meant to include the letter with it, asking her to send up the duplicates of that data. But Smoky got drunk and left too soon. I guess Smoky sincerely intended taking the paper with the lobstick on it to Arlis, but you know how that is. He got drunk and forgot about it for a while. Then, when he was sober enough to remember and start out again, he needed another little drink to fortify himself, and that drink led to a second, and so on. He never did get any farther south than Edmonton. Lucky he was sober when he heard Arlis had come north with proof her father was alive. Smoky wanted to help clear you, Kopernick. Ah, friendship. When Smoky spoke to me down at the Alaska Light, I thought he was talking about a map. I guess this is sort of a map, all right. A map only Burdette and his daughter would know how to decipher."

"But what good will it do you?" asked Kopernick, fighting for consciousness. "Coal? What can you do with that?"

"Not coal, Kopernick, don't you remember? Not lignite or bituminous. It's the old story, Kopernick, but it's always new, every time it's told." Laughing, Caribou lashed his dogs into a run, and shouted it back over his shoulder as they swept away: "Gold, Kopernick. Gold!"

VII

Kopernick didn't know how long he lay there, his spirit hovering in an agonized stupor, the blood on his belly congealing and freezing. Crazy things kept spinning dimly through his head. Arlis, mostly—soft and small and trembling like a snowshoe hare he had held once. The things he had felt when she was near. The softness in him that had come after so many years of hardness and bitterness and loneliness.

"Kopernick?"

He didn't know whether he opened his eyes, or they had been opened. The man had a lean, adamantine face, burned a reddish hue by the sun and the wind, eyes as cold and blue and humorless as the glacial ice on Caribou Island. It came to Kopernick suddenly that this wasn't in his mind, and he reached up to grasp at the man's leggings.

"Andover?" he said.

"Just wondered if you were still with us," said the constable, and nodded at Glenister, lying in the snow farther off. "You really messed up his face. Was that after he put the bullet through your belly?"

"Andover?"

"Yeah. I guess you're groggy." Andover took off his mittens and began to open Kopernick's parka away from the wound. "I came on ahead, Kopernick. Constable Myers stayed back in timber with the sled. We hit Sithor's village about a day after you left. This isn't as bad as all the blood indicates. Didn't hit you dead center. You'll make it back to Resolution for trial with some to spare. I've put some

71

whitefish out for your dogs. Looks like somebody cut them loose. That other fellow? They'll be back for him soon."

He found the flask of whisky down in the bottom of the cariole on Kopernick's sled and gave Kopernick a drink. It was pain, at first, but Kopernick reached up for another drink, feeling lucidity return.

"Andover?"

"Yeah." The constable was working at his wound now, swabbing the blood away with the whisky. He nodded at Glenister. "Who is he?"

"Listen, Andover," said Kopernick, the whisky having given him strength enough to sit up part way, hanging onto the constable's arm. "Listen. Caribou got away with Arlis. Gotta go after him. The lobstick was the only thing they had to go by, see? Burdette had lost his original maps, and he sent Smoky south with the lobstick to give his daughter. She had duplicate maps. You know the Barrens. Helluva time trying to find where you've been a second time. Even the Indians can't. Burdette couldn't without the maps he'd made. All he had to go on was the lobstick. Man could spend his life hunting that alone up here. . . ."

"You're raving like a lunatic. I'd better put these on you before you start something else."

Kopernick looked dazedly at the handcuffs on his wrists, jerked his hands too late, then he reached up to catch Andover's parka in both hands. "Andover. Don't be a fool. You can't let Caribou get away with Arlis. He'll kill her as soon as he finds that lobstick. He's got all the maps now and the drawing. He'll kill her. Damn you, Andover, listen. Let me at least get them. I'll do anything for you after that. I'll go back and stand trial. Just let me stop Caribou. She's with him, I tell you!"

"You're in no condition to stop anybody. Shut up now

while I bandage you. You're out of your head, Kopernick. Get back to Myers and we'll build a fire and make you some tea and bannocks. Wrap you up good."

"No." Kopernick tried to rise against the man's hands, the whisky burning a false strength through him. "I swear, Andover, you aren't going to stop me now."

Andover tried to jerk free, pawing beneath his parka for his revolver. "Kopernick, cause me any trouble and I'll put you out. Without compunction. I know you, Kopernick, and I'll knock you out."

Kopernick had him around the waist, trying to rise. He got his knees under him with his face buried in the acrid pithy smell of the wolverine fur lining the hood of Andover's parka. He felt Andover's right arm jerk outward with the gun. With a desperate gasp, he let go of the constable and drew back both hands, the chain on the cuffs rattling. Andover saw it coming and tried to throw himself backward and use his gun butt and shout all at the same time.

"Kopernick . . . !"

Kopernick crouched there on his hands and knees a long time after he had done it, shaking his head, trying to find the strength to move. Finally he crawled over till he was straddling the unconscious constable, fishing inside his parka for the key. The chain of the cuffs had made an ugly welt across Andover's forehead, and blood was starting to seep through the contusions. Kopernick unlocked the cuffs and snapped them open; then he put them on the constable. The hardest thing was to drag Andover to the sled and lift him in.

He didn't want to take a chance of Andover's using the cuffs on him the way he had on Andover, and he lashed the constable into the cariole with *babiche,* the untanned strips of caribou hide the Indians used for rope. Kopernick slumped over the sled, clinging to the lazy-board with numb hands.

Funny. They used *babiche* for everything. Toboggan was lashed with it. Dog's harness. Moss bags. Snowshoe straps. Everything.

He jerked his head up, realizing he had started to wander. Not knowing he was groaning with each movement, he turned away from the sled, one hand across his belly. How could anything hurt so much? Kopernick didn't remember when it had stopped snowing, but on the chill, clear air the dogs could scent things an amazing distance, and the whitefish Andover had put out had drawn Kachesy back first, and now the butt dog was slinking in, sniffing the air.

"Kachesy? Come here, Kachesy. Good dog, good *kli*. Little Hare. Put you in the moose hide. We'll make this last run a good one."

Harnessing each dog was a separate agony. He had to tie the sliced ends of the smoked moose-hide traces together and then place the saddle on the dog, slipping the traces through the loops on either side of the saddle, then hitching them up to the withy collar that was lined with caribou hide and packed with moss to bring the weight of pull on the dog's shoulders without galling. Finally he had them harnessed. He cut the lanyard on Andover's revolver, and stuffed the gun into his parka. Then he drank the last of the whisky, slipped his mittens on.

"All right." He grabbed the lazy-board to keep from falling. "I'm going to have to ride the runners, understand? Kachesy? Not much running. All riding. Think you can do it. All right. Mush!"

Their legs stiffened and the enormous muscles of their hindquarters stood out through the master hair and then the toboggan moved beneath Kopernick, and the snow began its soft *phlutt-phlutt* beneath the spruce runners.

Most of it was hazy and unreal after that. Most of it was

pain. Sometimes there would be the stunted clumps of trees passing by in a frightened black pattern against the white drifts of snow. Jack pine, maybe, or dappled spruce, or birches, standing like slim, pale Indian maidens awaiting the return of their bucks. More than the trees, though, was the snow. *Phlutt-phlutt* all the time. Fluffing up behind and sprawling out on either side. The tail line tapping across a bare spot of rock. The spruce runners crunching through hoarfrost covering the caribou moss on a rise.

Funny. Caribou moss. Caribou Carnes. I'm not an Indian. Trees like Indian maidens. Pain. Oh, God, the pain. Funny. Phlutt-phlutt. *Funny.* . . .

He jerked himself up, realizing it would be fatal to let it get him like that. He was so sleepy, though. He wanted to lie down in the white snow and go to sleep. Sleep in the white snow and forget pain and bitterness. Sleep.

Arlis?

It brought lucidity back in a shocking flash, and his whole body trembled to it. Arlis. It was what drove him on, through the pain, through the terrible lethargy. He swept past another bunch of stunted grandfather trees, limbs bearded white with dripping icicles. The dogs were running stretched out now, each with shoulders whitened by snow kicked up by the animal in front.

"Are you crazy, Kopernick. Let me go. Untie me, you fool."

"Caribou Carnes, Andover. You can't stop me. He's got Arlis."

For the first time, Andover must have realized Kopernick wasn't raving. The constable tried to twist his head around, still groggy with having just recovered consciousness.

"You mean you're actually trying to catch Caribou Carnes?" he asked, stupefied. "Kopernick, even you can't do that. Not with a bullet through your belly. You couldn't catch him under normal circumstances. I've seen those dogs of his."

"Streak of fat."

"What?" he asked. "Listen, Kopernick, you'll kill yourself. You won't last another mile. Look, you're bleeding again. Let me up, Kopernick. Let me run it for you."

"I don't trust you, Andover. I don't trust anybody."

Bleeding again. As long as he stayed quiet, the cold would have congealed his blood, but it was flowing out with his sweat now, darkening the front of his parka, wet and sticky against his belly. He had been following Carnes's trail in the fresh white snow almost since the beginning. Now his eyes wouldn't focus on the tracks, and, whenever he bent to see better, he almost fell from the runners. The dogs were running with the down brush of exhaustion, tails sagging like wolves, flanks heaving.

"Come on, Kachesy. Last run. *Unipson,* you *klis, unipson . . . !*"

The wheel dog steadied down with his forefeet to check the momentum of the toboggan, and Kachesy started the left turn around the snow-covered rise. They rounded the hill and passed another clump of trees, and Kopernick realized what was in Caribou's mind. Every time a grove appeared ahead, the trail immediately turned and pointed directly toward it.

"See what he's doing," babbled Kopernick dazedly. "Hunting for that lobstick. Hitting every bunch of trees he sights."

"What?" asked Andover. Then the sled jerked as he tried to sit up, staring ahead. "Kopernick!"

It took a long time for Kopernick to see it. He pawed at his snow glasses, thinking they were dirty. Then his eyes finally focused on that black dot moving so slowly across the snow field ahead of them. Miles ahead. No telling how far. Distances were deceptive. Funny. Miles ahead. . . .

Arlis!

Sobbing with his pain and exhaustion, he shouted hoarsely at the dogs: "Mush, you *klis,* mush!"

He didn't know exactly when Caribou began shooting at him. The sound of the shots began to come dimly through the fog, then more sharply. He heard something whine past his head, and Andover was shouting and writhing from side to side in the cariole, trying to break free, the sled tilting dangerously with his struggles. Kopernick began pawing for the revolver he had taken from the constable. Then he realized he couldn't return Caribou's fire for fear of hitting the girl, and he sobbed in a bitter frustration, cursing Caribou Carnes.

Caribou must have emptied his rifle, because he was running along all humped over and his elbow kept jerking as if he were reloading it. But it slowed him down, and without his lash over them the dogs weren't running so fast; and, when he looked around and saw how Kopernick had closed in on him, he quit trying to reload and jumped on the runners of his own sledge.

"*Ma-a-a-arche,* you Klincha *klis,* you Dog Rib dogs, you sons-of-wolf-bitches and pileated woodpecker fathers, you execrable crosses between an albino musk ox and a purple caribou. *Ma-a-a-arche,* or I'll stuff you in my rogan and drown you in the Slave!"

They topped a rise. Kopernick was beyond any sane reasoning, and he hardly heard his own mad screams as he clung to the lazy-board with the snow pluming up on either side of him. "Streak of fat, Caribou, streak of fat! Fat man with fat dogs, and I've run you down."

"Streak of fat, my grandfather's moss bag," roared Car-

77

ibou. *"Ma-a-a-arche,* you *tel-ky-lay-azzy*s. . . ."

He broke off to twist around on his runners as Kopernick's toboggan swept up beside the huge *komatic.* They had started down the other side of the rise and were running into a long sloping field, jagged rocks thrusting up through the snow on every side. Kopernick knew if he jumped Caribou, the dogs would run away down that field and eventually tip over the sleds.

"Jump before we get going too fast," he shouted hoarsely at Arlis, and then bent to cut the lashings on Andover.

The constable must have realized what Kopernick intended, for, as soon as his bindings were cut, he rolled over the side of the toboggan and bounced through the hard-packed snow, shouting hoarsely with the pain of coming up against a rock. The girl rose in the *komatic,* but Caribou reached forward and struck her down with the butt end of his empty rifle. The excited dogs were galloping faster and faster down the field, and Kopernick could hardly stay on his bouncing, switching toboggan.

"Jump," he screamed, "jump . . . !"

Arlis tried it again, but once more Caribou beat her about the head with his rifle, and she sank back, sobbing. "I can't, Eddie, I can't."

With a savage curse, Kopernick yelled at his dogs—*"Cha, cha!"*—and they swerved to the right, bringing the toboggan up beside the *komatic,* and Kopernick jumped.

Caribou tried to catch him with the rifle, but Kopernick had leaped for the cariole instead of the man, landing sprawled out over the girl, hands clawing for holds on the *babiche* lashing the slides. Caribou's gun butt thudded into Kopernick's head, but Kopernick caught the girl and got his weight beneath her and heaved.

"Eddie!" she cried, and then was gone, rolling away out of

78

his sight through the snow. The dogs were baying with their wild run, and the sled was moving faster and faster down the slope, equipment flying from its cariole every time it bounced across the rocks. Kopernick tried to stand erect to jump at Caribou, clinging to the sides. Then he saw the huge man climbing over the jerking, swaying lazy-board. Caribou had dropped his rifle and his dog whip, and he was chuckling.

"Now," he said, and Kopernick could barely hear him over the whipping snow and rattling, crashing sled, "we'll see about that streak of fat."

Kopernick ducked to meet the man's jump, throwing himself to one side from that first kick. The *komatic* lurched over with his weight, tilting dangerously.

Kopernick was almost thrown out, but Caribou retained his balance with an amazing agility, riding the sledge as if birling a log, leaning toward the opposite side to compensate for the *komatic*'s tilt and keeping his feet under him enough to jump on toward Kopernick and launch another kick. Kopernick was off balance, and he couldn't duck it. The foot caught him in the stomach, and he doubled over it with all the air exploding from him. The *komatic* was racing madly down the slope now and whoever was thrown out at this speed would stand little chance of living. Caribou jerked his leg out from beneath Kopernick's bent torso and pivoted to kick again.

"Savate!" he roared, and it came.

Gasping, Kopernick threw himself on that leg before it had gained its full momentum, and the aborted kick made a dull, fleshy sound against his chest, and he carried Caribou backward with both his arms twined around the man's thick leg. Caribou was down on the tarp-covered pile of supplies in the back end of the cariole, with Kopernick sprawled on top of him, the sledge leaping and jumping beneath them, snow puffing in a cloud from beneath the runners. Kopernick drew back his fist and slugged at Caribou's heavy middle, and heard the man's air explode from him with the blow.

"Streak of fat," he said, and his voice was muffled against the fetid heat of Caribou's parka, and he slugged again.

Caribou tried to thrust Kopernick off him, but the smaller man hung on with one arm, his other arm pistoning into Caribou's belly. Grunting sickly with each blow, Caribou finally twisted over to one side so he could ram his knee into Kopernick's belly. It caught Kopernick in his bullet wound, and the sudden shock of pain blinded him. Caribou levered a forearm across his neck and shoved him up and back. Kopernick caught at the sides of the cariole to keep from falling completely over and saw the huge man rise above him, swaying and lurching with the sled, shifting his weight for another kick. Kopernick tried to twist his legs beneath him and get onto his knees, but he had no strength left. He tried to shout something, and only a hoarse, animal sound escaped his numb lips. He didn't even see the kick when it came.

It felt as if his head had been jerked off, and he heard the sharp crackle of his broken snow glasses. He knew his body was dangling over the edge of the cariole, the snow shooting all over his face, and he felt the dull shudder of the sledge as Caribou brought his leg down and shifted his weight over to free his opposite foot for that last kick. With a guttural cry, Kopernick caught the sides of the cariole, fighting up through the terrible lethargy of pain. He saw Caribou's face above him, swaying back and forth, thick, sensuous lips spread back from his white teeth in a puckish grin, little eyes almost hidden by his fat cheeks. He saw the big man's body sway as he launched that last kick.

Without knowing how, Kopernick threw himself beneath the lashing foot, his body responding spasmodically to his will, carrying him up against Caribou's pivot leg. And before Caribou could recover his kick, Kopernick twined his arms about that pivot leg and, with the man's other leg still caught in the air above his body, heaved.

Caribou Carnes shouted something as he tumbled out of the racing sledge, but it was drowned in the din of baying dogs and clattering runners and rattling canvas, then he was gone, lost behind the sledge in the white snow and jagged black rocks.

Kopernick hauled himself weakly erect, panting, calling feebly to the dogs—"Whoa, whoa."—and then he saw it up ahead, through his cracked snow glasses, what Caribou must have seen from the top of that first rise before he realized Kopernick was behind, what he must have been going toward when Kopernick caught him. The lobstick.

Andover had kneaded the flour and water and grease for the bannocks and shaped the dough an inch deep inside the frying pan, and now they stood browning before the crackling fire. Kopernick sat with his back against the oddly shaped lobstick, the pain of his wound soothed, somehow, by the nearness of Arlis Burdette. On one of the maps included in the data she had brought her father, they found the lobstick labeled. No one could have told what it meant on the map itself, for Burdette had labeled many landmarks, but now that they knew its significance, they had been able to follow a line charted from the lobstick northward for a quarter mile to an outcropping of rock on the slope of a line of rocky hills. Andover held one of the samples he had taken, turning it over and over so the firelight caught on the streaks of yellow in the rock.

"I'd say a hundred dollars to the ton at the least," he muttered. "Soon's we get back to Resolution, we can have it assayed. I wouldn't have believed anyone who told me they'd found gold in the Barrens. The geological formations are all against it.”

“The sourdoughs have an old saying,” grinned Kopernick. “Gold is where you find it.”

Arlis smiled tremulously. “Constable, don’t you think it would be better to start back with Eddie tonight?”

“Rest’ll do him good,” said Andover, shifting the teapot above the flames. “That wound isn’t as serious as it might be, and, if we wait till morning, the snow’ll be frozen over for better running. You don’t have to worry about Eddie Kopernick, Arlis. If he can run down Caribou Carnes over a twenty-mile stretch with a hole in his belly, he can do a simple little thing like riding back to Resolution over smooth ice all wrapped up in four-point blankets.”

He turned to the bannocks, and Kopernick slid his hand out of the blanket to catch the girl’s fingers. “I know I must have seemed sort of wild to you, but a man gets that way, I guess, after three years of running and hiding. I used to be respectable enough, up here. I had a string of trading posts started, and an idea going for organizing the rivermen. Maybe this isn’t exactly your country, but, if you lived here a while, you’d learn to love it. What I mean is . . . if you had something that you wanted to stay for.”

“I’ve got something to stay for.”

“I wasn’t talking about the gold.”

“I know you weren’t,” she said, and her face was so close her hair brushed his cheek like spun honey.

“Tea?” said Andover, turning with the pot and a collapsible tin cup. Then he looked up and saw what they were doing, and turned his back on them uncomfortably, pouring the cup full. “No, I guess not. I’ll drink it myself.”

LUNATIC PATROL

Waiting for him to do something was the worst. The silence was bad, and the emptiness, and the endless snow, fighting us with that soft, inexorable insistence every foot of the way. But waiting for him to do something was the worst.

"What a stupid organization, the Mounted Police," he said. "They send a sergeant-major like you five hundred miles after a man, with orders to bring him in, alive and well, and half the time you Mounties come back crazier than the man you haul in. You have to feed him and nurse him and keep him happy, like he was a baby, and all the time he's just waiting for your first slip so he can kill you and get free. And even when he does make the break, you have to keep yourself from killing him."

I thought: *Maybe you think I don't want to kill you?* I squatted by the fire, kneading the grease and water and dough together for the bannocks, gritting my teeth, keeping my face turned away from him. *Maybe you think I don't want to, Dubrois. More than anything in life.*

He waited a moment for me to answer him, and then laughed. "Oh, you don't have to humor me any more, Graham. I've got the manacles on, haven't I? You don't have to try and keep it from me. I know you think I'm crazy. *Voila!* Tell me what keeps you from doing it, then, Graham. After you've been goaded and baited and maddened twenty-four hours a day the whole three-hundred-mile run by some man you think is crazy . . . what keeps a Mountie from killing him? An ordinary man couldn't stand it. They say Constable Walsh was as crazy as the man he brought in last year. Yet he brought him in alive."

It was hard to realize he was unbalanced; he talked so rationally, so intelligently, even if there was that sly undertone to his words. But all I had to do was turn enough to see his eyes. I had seen the same thing in the eyes of a trapped wolf. Cunning. Waiting. That was it. Waiting. He was waiting. I was waiting. The whole world was waiting. . . .

"All right," I said, and my hands shaped the kneaded dough into the frying pan with quick, jerky gestures. "All right. Not one prisoner has died on this patrol since Nineteen Oh Four."

"Ah." His voice was mocking. "Tradition. That's it. The force. Bigger than one man. Or all men. But why say *this* patrol, Graham? You won't offend me, I assure you. Why not the lunatic patrol?" He stopped a moment, and I could feel him watching me. "I don't think that's it, Graham. Maybe that's part of it. But not enough. Not enough to keep you from killing me when you want to so bad you cry in your sougan at night."

"Never mind." My grip on the handle was so tight it hurt as I stood the frying pan face up toward the fire to brown the bannocks, and I was driven to it, somehow. "You're a sick man, Dobrois, that's all, and I have no right. . . ."

"Ah, a sick man. *Voila!* That's even better than a homicidal maniac. That's the best one I've heard." Dobrois's face was mostly beard, and all I could see of his mouth was the shadowed white line of his teeth showing in that artful grin. Then the grin faded, and he frowned. "A sick man, *hein?* It

84

seems somebody told me that before. Or a sick mind. *Oui,* that was it, a sick mind. It wasn't you, was it, Graham? *Non.* Somebody else. Some girl. . . ."

"Shut up!"

The dogs stopped their restless whining, staring briefly at me now, instead of Dobrois. The echoes of my shout rang down the somber lanes of black poplars that were so stunted by the short summers up here north of Lac la Martre. There was a surprised look on Dobrois's face.

"You're touchy about that, Graham? What is it? Your pet theory? A sick mind."

My teeth were grinding again as I stared at him. Surely he must know. He was just baiting me. Then I smelled the bannocks, and whirled to pull the frying pan away from the fire. They were burned on top. My hand shook, scraping the crust away, spilling the ashes over my caribou-hide leggings. He was still frowning when I carried the folding tin cup of tea and the bannocks over to him.

"Somebody told me," he said. "A sick mind."

"Don't tell me you can't remember. Don't try and make me believe that, Dobrois."

The tone of my voice brought his eyes to my face, and they were as guileless as a baby's. "Remember what, Graham?"

"Ben Shovil down on the Moose Jaw, for instance."

"Non, non." His voice was sharper. "Why do you keep insisting I murdered him? I'm not a lunatic, Graham. You are. I never knew any Ben Shovil."

"Or Laurent Duprez?" I was bending tensely toward him. "Or Jean Fontaine, or . . . ?"

"Or who, Graham? Go on." He was watching my face with a certain, growing calculation.

I couldn't believe he didn't remember. It was so inconceivable to me that it shouldn't be in his mind, as bright and bitter and hateful as it was in mine. I shoved the tea and bannocks at him and caught the sudden cunning flash of his eyes, and tried to jump back from it. But the tea was already in my face, scalding and blinding. I heard my own shout of pain as I jumped backward, fumbling beneath my parka for my Webley. Then I stopped, without pulling the gun out. Vision had returned to me, and, holding my free hand over my burned face, I could see him through my fingers, still sitting cross-legged where he had been, the empty cup held in his hairy, manacled hands, grinning slyly up at me.

"What's the matter, Graham, *hein?* What's the matter?"

South of Lac la Martre, the noise we made only seemed to accentuate the silence, lying as thick and intense and malignant as the snow, all around us. This was the lonely, empty country that had driven Dobrois mad, and so many others brought back on the lunatic patrol. The spruce runners on my big Cree police sled made their monotonous crunch through the slush, and, when I thought I couldn't stand it any longer, I would shout at the dogs.

"Mush, Eric, mush . . . !"

"Whoa, Eric!" shouted Dobrois. "Whoa, whoa!"

"Mush, Eric! Shut up, Dobrois!"

"Shut up, Dobrois," the half-breed mocked me. "Whoa, Eric!" Then he threw back his shaggy head to laugh wildly. I couldn't help the spasmodic way my hand went out toward him. The frozen fingers of my mittens touched the lazyboard, and I stopped myself, hoping he couldn't hear the small, strangled sound I made. How many times had I reached for him like that? How many times had I wanted to kill him?

Nous irons sur l'eau. . . .

86

He had started the song again, staring straight ahead with a crazy smile on his face and muttering in that maddening sing-song voice.

Nous y promener, nous irons jouer dans l'ile. . . .

"Dobrois, stop that!" I shouted at him.

He turned abruptly, that vacuous leer on his face. "What's the matter, Graham?"

Jogging beside the sled, I tried to find any calculation in his face, and couldn't. His eyes were bright and empty, and he began to gibber the song again.

"Dobrois, where did you learn that song?"

His smile was guileless. "The *chanson*, Graham? I don't remember. I think I heard a girl sing it. Célie? *Oui.* Célie, I think."

He *did* remember! At first I thought it was the runners across the ice, that shrill, broken sound. Then I realized it was I. The desire to get my hands on him swept me with such a bitter force I couldn't see for a moment. *You do remember, you dirty cross-breed liar! All that was just baiting me, before. Where did I hear that, Graham? I don't remember. Some girl? Oui. All baiting me, and.* . . .

Maybe it was Dobrois's shout that brought me out of it. He was jerking from side to side in the sled as we ran through a stand of stunted poplars, laughing as the cariole rocked dangerously.

"Dobrois," I yelled, making a grab for the bobbing tail line. "Dobrois, stop that. You'll tip the sled! Whoa, Eric, whoa . . . !"

My grab at the line missed, and the cariole rocked over on the other spruce runner, swinging the stern around to pull the whole team into the trees. Eric rammed head-on into a

87

spruce, the other dogs piling up behind him. I heard his agonized howl as the overturning toboggan smashed in on the whole yapping, snarling bunch of them. I ran up to heave the heavy police sled off the dogs, tearing at their writhing, furry bodies to free Eric. Either the weight of the other dogs had done it, or the sled itself. Eric lay there with both hind legs twisted under him, looking up at me, and his big dark eyes knew how it was, just the way I knew.

I must have been cursing even then. I whirled away from the lead dog, my head jerking from side to side until I saw where Dobrois had been thrown out of the sled. He had rolled out of the cariole and brought up against a snowbank, and was sitting cross-legged there with that empty grin on his face.

"Whoa, Eric," he said, laughing inanely, "whoa, whoa."

"Damn you, Dobrois, I'll have to kill that dog. You've broken his back legs, and I'll have to kill him, do you understand? I'll have to kill him, kill him, kill him. . . ."

With my hands around his neck and his heavy, stinking body jerking and fighting against me, I stopped myself, realizing it wasn't Eric that had driven me this far. It was still in my mind, somewhere—*nous irons sur l'eau, nous y promener. . . .* But the other was there, too, coming up through my terrible blind passion—*a sick mind, Graham, a sick mind, and he's not responsible. No matter what he does, he's not responsible.*

It was a moment before Dobrois could get back his breath, choking and gasping. Finally he managed to sit up again, and the blood returned to his face. He looked up at me where I stood above him, and I could see no anger in his face, not even pain now. Just that blank leer. He raised his manacled hands, shaking them till the chain rattled, and giggled at the sound, like a baby amused with his rattle.

"Whoa, Eric," he babbled. "Whoa, whoa."

★ ★ ★ ★ ★

I stared into the darkness. Feeling the strange, breathless fear that rises in a man, sometimes, when he is awakened abruptly in the night. I lay sweating, my fists clenched in the heat of my blankets, fighting the reasonless panic.

"Graham." It came again, and I realized that this time I hadn't dreamed it. I grabbed for my Webley where it lay by my side, and rolled over, pulling out the sougan till I could sit up with my legs still beneath the blankets. I could see him now. He was still in his blankets, dog chain holding his wrists to the stunted poplar.

"Graham," he said. "My neck hurts. What happened?"

"Go to sleep."

"I want some tea."

"You had your tea."

"Graham"—his voice was soft with cunning, and I realized some lucidity must have returned to him—"Graham, I want some tea. If you don't get me some tea, I'll start yelling and cursing and wake up the dogs and cause a hell of a *veillée*. You've got to take care of me. I may be crazy, but you've got to take care of me like I was a baby and feed me and nurse me and make me happy, and if you don't. . . ."

"All right, Dobrois, all right!" In desperation, I got out of the blanket roll and began to build a fire with numb hands. When the tea was made, I had to unhitch his dog chain so he could raise up and drink. He kept rubbing his neck. He asked me again what happened. I didn't answer, and that speculative light came into his eyes.

"Did I try to get away, Graham? Why won't you tell me? It feels like somebody choked me."

"You know what happened."

"But *non*, I don't."

I studied his face. "You really don't remember?"

89

He shrugged. "The last thing I remember is throwing tea in your face before we went to bed this evening." He laughed suddenly, slyly. "Does it still hurt, Graham?"

I couldn't believe it yet. "That wasn't this evening. That was two days ago. We're thirty miles south of Lac la Martre now."

His surprise seemed genuine enough, and he rubbed his neck. "Two days? You're lying, Graham. You just don't want to tell me what happened."

"You smashed up the sled and broke my lead dog's legs, and I had to shoot him. You didn't even try to get away."

He studied his handcuffs a long time, then he looked up at me, laughing craftily. "Never mind, Graham. Next time it will be different. Sooner or later, I'll get away. It's a hundred miles more, and you've only got four dogs left, and you're about to crack under the strain. How much longer do you think you can stand it, Graham? Where do you think Constable Walsh cracked? The first day? The twentieth? They say he was as crazy as the man he brought in."

He stopped, chuckling as he saw how I was leaning forward. I tried to relax, unable to reconcile this lucidity with his periods of utter idiocy. I didn't know enough about insanity to tell if it was logical. Yet, if he really didn't remember upsetting the sled. . . .

I lowered my head so he couldn't see I was watching him, and then began to hum the song:

Nous irons sur l'eau, nous y promener. . . .

"When were you on the river, Graham?"

It wasn't the reaction I had wanted, or expected. "The river?"

"That's an old *voyageur chanson,*" he told me innocently.

"I didn't think many white men knew it. The rivermen used to sing it when they poled their York boats up the Athabaska. Where did you learn it?"

"Don't you know?" I said.

Again his surprise seemed genuine. "*Sacre bleu,* how should I?" He began to sing it, waving his manacled hands back and forth to the time.

> *We shall go on the water for a boat ride,*
> *we shall play on the island. . . .*

"Will you shut up?" I whirled on him, fists clenched.

He chuckled, and that cunning was in his eyes. "Is it just the strain, Graham, or is there something special about the song?"

"Never mind." Trembling, I turned around and walked stiffly to the team, and unhitched my butt dog from where I had chained him to the tree. "Morning star's coming. No use going back to sleep now."

"Where did you learn the song, Graham?"

I had myself under control now. "Where did you learn it, Dobrois?"

He hesitated a moment. "I don't know exactly."

"Or don't remember?"

"It seems to me a girl was singing it."

"And she said you had a sick mind."

His head raised. "How did you know?"

"And you weren't to blame no matter what you did. You had a sick mind, and you weren't to blame. . . ." I clamped my mouth shut over it, dragging the reluctant butt dog to the sled and attaching the heavy moose-hide traces to the toggles on his collar. I went back to get the next dog and was unhitching his chain when an agonized howl from the sled whirled me about, my hand on my Webley. Dobrois stepped back from my big Chippewayan butt dog, grinning at me. The animal was lying on its side, tugging feebly at the traces, howling in dismal pain. I saw his right forepaw, and I couldn't help the way my gun came up.

Dobrois grinned at it. "You can't kill me, Graham, remember? You're not just a man. You're a policeman. Tradition, Graham. The force. You shouldn't have told me how Eric got his legs broken. It gave me ideas."

"Get in the sled," I said, and my voice was shaking. "Dobrois, get in that sled!" The gun was trembling in my hand, and he saw it, and climbed into the cariole. I got some *babiche* lashings from the birch-bark rogan in the bow and tied the 'breed in till he couldn't move. Then I went over the other side of the fire and retched.

"Does it make you feel sick, Graham?" he said. "*Mon Dieu,* I never wanted to kill a man that bad."

It started to storm before noon. I had been forced to kill the butt dog, and soon the drifts were piling up so heavily in front of us that my three remaining dogs were unable to haul the heavy sled without aid from me. Finally we struck a slope, and I got them going at a fair pace.

"*Cha, you klis, cha!*" I cried, turning them left from a bank in front of us.

"*Euh!*" shouted Dobrois from the sled, "*euh!*" and the dogs turned right again.

"Shut up, Dobrois," I called desperately. "*Cha, cha, cha!*"

"*Euh, euh,*" laughed Dobrois, and the dogs turned right once more, and went head-on into the drift before I could turn them away. Dobrois lay in the cariole, laughing gleefully as I shoved the heavy sled out of the bank and undertook to untangle the dogs. A trace had caught in one of the toggles, and it was a maddening job getting it out with my frozen hands. Finally I finished and went back to the sled, getting a Hudson's Bay four-point from the bow. Dobrois watched with bright eyes while I cut a strip from the blanket. Suddenly he began to sing.

Nous irons sur l'eau, nous y. . . .

It was the blanket that stopped him. I jammed a wad between his teeth, trying to hold it there and tie another strip over his mouth. But he spat out the first wad and bit me. I yanked my hand away, shouting hoarsely.

"Nous irons sur l'eau," he howled, jerking his head from side to side and laughing crazily, *"nous y promener. . . ."*

I wanted to kill him. I had both hands on the edge of the rocking cariole, gripping it so tightly I couldn't feel the pain of my bitten hand. I was trembling as violently as the sled, and the tears began to slide down my cheeks past my mouth before they froze. God, I wanted to kill him!

Nous irons jouer dans l'ile, nous irons jouer dans l'ile.

I was still crying when I had finished gagging him. The storm had grown more violent, and the dogs were so exhausted by now that I fastened myself into the harness and pulled with them. In the white, swirling snow and cutting ice I couldn't tell when night came and only stopped when I could run no farther, seeking an uplift of some kind so I could pitch camp in its lee. By the time I found the rise, all I could do was throw myself down with the dogs and lie there, still in the harness, with the snow piling on top of me.

Finally, moving in a stupor, I managed to get up and cut myself loose. I groped through the snow till I found some timber, chopped off some high branches of the stunted spruce, and stumbled back to camp.

Then I went to get my Marble axe from the cariole. There was snow on Dobrois's face, and I wiped it off, and then was sorry I had, because I could see his eyes. He lay there motionless in his tight bindings beneath the snow-mantled musk ox robe, the lower part of his face hidden by the gag. But the way his eyes were fixed on me, I knew he was grinning, and they were filled with that cunning intelligence, and I knew it had started once more.

Going back to the wood, my whole body was taut with a sense of waiting for Dobrois to do something again. He was bound and helpless in the sled, yet my jaws ached from gritting my teeth, and waiting.

I chopped up the branches, then put the axe aside to get my knife and carve away the wet outer wood. I shifted a little to get more shelter from the rise above, and built the fire. I was bent over the first blaze, shielding it from the snow, when I thought of the axe. There was no reason to think of it that way. But I did.

"The cariole was coming apart, Graham," he said, when I looked up and saw him standing close to me. "I've been working my way out of that *babiche* all afternoon." And then he yelled hoarsely and swung at me with the axe in both manacled hands.

I hadn't been able to throw myself back far enough, but, when his body struck me, it wasn't the way he had gauged the blow, and I screamed with the stunning pain as the blade struck my cheek at an angle instead of cleaving my skull. The best I could do was roll blindly aside beneath his next blow, still gripping the knife in one hand. The axe struck the snow beside my head with a dull thud, and I tried to catch his arms while they were still down there.

"I waited, didn't I, Graham?" he panted, struggling back up. "All the time you had to run while I was resting, and I waited. Two hundred miles, Graham, and pulling the sled yourself these last two days, and I waited. And now you're so tired you can't even fight me, and I'm going to kill you, Graham, I'm going to kill you. . . ."

I could see that lucidity was leaving him, as it must have left him when he had murdered Shovil on the Moose Jaw, and the others. He tore free of my feeble graspings with a wild shout, and the cunning was swept out of his eyes by a maniacal lust. He rose up, straddling me for the third blow, and I knew it would be the last. It was all I could do to lurch up beneath him and paw groggily for the chain on his manacles. He pulled back to tear my hand away, and it threw him off me with my fist still around that chain, yanking me across his body as he rolled to the side.

I was over him now, holding his arms above his head with the grip of the chain. My free arm rose with the knife. He must have seen my expression, because his scream held a sudden, animal fear.

"*Non,* you can't kill me. You can't!"

The palisaded walls of Fort Simpson stood on the island at the mouth of the Laird, and the river was frozen over enough so I could drive my sled across to where Inspector Arden and a few of the others were waiting for me at the edge of the ice. The welcoming twinkle left Arden's blue eyes as he saw the mess the axe had left of my face.

"You've had a rough time, Graham."

I fumbled beneath my coat for the patrol sheet, not wanting to talk about it now. "Your original report had three people murdered in district D. I found a fourth."

We kept check on the white settlers, and the paper contained a list of the people in my district. Arden's glance ran down the line, lips forming the names that were crossed out.

"Fontaine, Duprez, Shovil. . . ." He stopped on the fourth one, and the blood drained from his weathered face. "Graham . . . you've got Célie Lanier."

"He found her by the river." It came from me in a hoarse, driven way. "She was singing that French *voyageur* song her father always sang when he was drunk. She even tried to argue him out of it. She told him he had a sick mind and wasn't to blame for what he did. She promised him we wouldn't kill him. . . ."

"Dobrois confessed?"

"No." I hardly recognized my own voice. "He doesn't remember any of them. I thought he did at first. I thought he was baiting me. But he has periods in his right mind, and then he goes out of his head completely."

"But if he didn't tell you," asked Arden, "how do you know? The song, I mean . . . trying to argue him out of it?"

"It was the same thing she told me, Arden." It tumbled out of me hoarsely, almost incoherently. "I was up at her cabin when I got orders to report down here for my patrol sheet, and we both knew it meant the lunatic patrol, and she told me. A sick mind, she said, and he wasn't to blame for what he did. No matter what he did, he wasn't to blame. She made me promise, Arden. She said it would drive me crazy if I didn't remember. It was the only thing that kept me from killing him. No matter what he did, *she* wouldn't blame him. She'd want it *this* way, wouldn't she? She wouldn't blame me . . . ?"

"Of course not, Graham, of course not." He had his hand on my arm now, and there was understanding in his face. He had been on the lunatic patrol himself. "Célie would be proud of you."

Dobrois had been brought up in time to hear Arden. "Célie?" he said.

The inspector turned to stare at him. "You really don't know?"

Dobrois had been lucid these last few hours, and he shrugged, grinning. "Know what?"

Dully I felt Arden's sinewy hand tighten on my arm. "Célie Lanier was going to be Graham's wife, Dobrois."

"*Bon,* Graham, *bon.*" Dobrois's face was as guileless as a child's. "When is the wedding going to be?"

THE LOBSTICK OF CHARLIE GIROUX

All morning long I had noticed this man hanging around the Hudson's Bay buildings across the street from my barber shop. It was a cold autumn day for this part of Alberta, but all he had on was a tweed suit and a snap-brim hat. A few minutes after Teddy Melbourne left the shop, the man crossed the street and came in. He was not tall, but that coat was cut for shoulders so broad I could have worn it comfortably. He came in, closed the door softly behind him, and stood with his back against it, both hands in the pockets of his coat. He kept the lids almost shut over his eyes, and there was a faint smile on his lips.

"Shave, *m'sieu?*" I asked him.

His voice was like the hiss of silk through the fingers. "That was Teddy Melbourne who just left, wasn't it, John?"

It was natural that he should know my name. Everybody in Athabaska knows French John, the barber. "You a friend of Teddy's?" I asked.

"Just call me George," he murmured. "What does Melbourne come here for, anyway? You never give him a shave or a haircut. That beard of his looks like a brier patch."

"Maybe he likes to play checkers with me," I said. "Or have a drink of Chambertin and just talk." I stopped, as the new thought struck me, and I felt foolish for not having seen it before. "Are you of the police, *m'sieu?*"

"What makes you think that?" He smiled.

"Look," I told him. "Almost everybody in Athabaska comes to this barber shop sooner or later. I hear many things. Superintendent Allison at the barracks must have told you how often the police confide in me, or you wouldn't be here. Do you have a problem, *m'sieu?*"

He chuckled softly. "All right, John. You know how rare a sea otter pelt is. Only a few hundred a year come from Amundsen Gulf. Their migration started last month, and Hudson's Bay should have got their quota from the Eskimos by now. But none is coming through."

"Sounds like big-time poachers."

He nodded. "Charlie Giroux's name is being mentioned again."

I turned away to hang up a towel so that he would not see that I was disturbed. It gave me a glimpse of my face in the mirror, and I saw that it was pale. I have been told that it is a sardonic face. The bones are heavy, but they join at oblique angles, giving the brow and jaw a narrowing, sharpened look. Even the beard I have grown these last years fails to change the line. It has always struck me funny that the gray should appear in the beard first, when my hair is still black.

"Why should they bring up Giroux?" I asked. "The man's been dead for five years."

"It's the kind of a job he would do," George said. "In fact, he was carrying a load of sea otter pelts when he was killed, wasn't he?" When I did not answer, George shrugged. "No matter. These poachers have their outlet in Ottawa. They must take the pelts down there by sled before the thaw. Our agents in Ottawa spotted one of them, but couldn't nab him in time. They figure he'll be heading back by river, now that the snow's gone. His description was sent to Edmonton, and I was assigned. I've narrowed it down to a few possibilities. Teddy Melbourne's one."

"Why don't you arrest him, then?" I asked.

"We want to be sure he's the one. That's where you come in. I want you to come with me and shave off Melbourne's beard."

I stared at him, and then I could not help laughing. "You make the joke, *m'sieu*."

"I admit it sounds funny. But it's not. Melbourne may be traveling with companions. We get him away long enough to tap him on the head and shave off that beard, but we may not have much time to work in. If I tried to do a quick job myself, I might hack up his face so much I couldn't get positive identification. I need a man who knows his barbering."

It still seemed almost funny to me. I laughed again, deep in my chest. "*Non, m'sieu.* I cannot do that. I cannot go chasing all over Athabaska with you to catch a man and shave off his beard."

He walked over to study the row of shaving mugs on the shelf. "I've saved something till the last, John. I hoped I wouldn't have to use it. You're supposed to know everything that goes on around Athabaska. You're even supposed to have known Charlie Giroux very well."

"Yes," I said carefully, "I did know Charlie Giroux. You will not find his kind in Canada today, *m'sieu*. He was the last of the old-time *voyageurs*. Not a man he couldn't whip, not a woman he couldn't have, not a stretch of white water he couldn't run. A rogue. A magnificent rogue."

"I understand you're the only one left who ever saw him."

"He was a wild one," I said. "The woods knew him. The Indians. That was all."

"Killed trying to run Murderer's Shoal ahead of a Mountie, five years ago," he said.

"That's right," I said. "The lobstick they cut for him is still there."

"And they never found the body," he murmured.

I shrugged. "It was probably cut to bits on those rocks."

"On the other hand," said George casually, "what if Giroux lived? What if he was swept on downstream, out of the Mountie's sight, and escaped? What if it was such a harrowing experience that he decided to turn straight, and he grew a beard and came to Athabaska and took up a trade he had learned from his father, becoming a barber? French John, the barber?"

The blood was so thick in my throat I thought I would choke. My whole body was trembling. I stared at him, unable to speak for a moment. "That is a dangerous supposition, even for a policeman," I said.

He turned toward me. "You said the Indians knew Giroux. We have one prisoner down at Edmonton. He stole some Hudson's Bay goods. I talked with him. Giroux's name came up. He said he had a story about that. I promised him clemency for the story. I got it. He can identify Giroux."

"He lies," I said gutturally. "Charlie Giroux is dead."

"There are half a dozen counts the police would like to get Giroux on," he said.

"*M'sieu,*"—I could hardly speak—"you cannot do this."

"The Indian may well be free in a couple of weeks," George told me. "Help me with this, John, and I will see that he doesn't tell his story to anybody else. I will see that I forget his story."

I stared at him a long time, still trembling. "Very well," I told him at last. "Let us go and shave Teddy Melbourne."

At the docks, we learned that Melbourne was aboard the Hudson's Bay scow that had left for the north a half hour earlier. There would not be another boat till tomorrow, so

George hired a farmer to drive us through Twottenny Hills to Wendell's Cove. From the heights, we sighted the scow, and pulled ahead of it late in the afternoon. The cove was no more than a sandpit thrust out into the river, with a cutbank deep enough for a boat to pull in against.

The scow came around the turn of the river, forty feet of spruce-wood boat, built like an oversize punt, with decks fore and aft and a crew of six pulling at the sweeps in the middle. The cargo was stored under the decking, and the passengers sat back of the oarsmen. Captain Fred Storie stood at the tiller, and, when he saw us waving at him, he worked the scow into the cutbank. He was such a heavy man that, when he jumped off into the sand, he sank in to his ankles.

"You picked a good place to board, John," he said. "We might as well eat supper here as any place. Where you bound?"

I waited for George to answer, but he just kept watching me with those half-closed eyes, and finally I said: "Upriver, Captain. This is George."

"I'll pay the fares," said George. "How much is it to Fort Chippewayan, Captain?"

I did not hear Storie's answer, because the passengers and crew were all climbing out, and the last one to step over the thwarts was a woman. I know of nothing as black, as mysterious as the river at midnight. Her hair was like that. And her eyes. She had a big, white Mackinaw covered with Indian quillwork that hid her figure, but that didn't matter. I knew too well what it looked like. George was transacting his business with the captain. The man who had helped her out of the boat had climbed back in for something, and I had that moment to speak with her alone. She saw me, and her chin lifted a little in surprise.

"Kitty. . . ." The blood was so thick in my throat I could

102

scarcely get it out. "Kitty."

"If you followed me to apologize over that little spat we had last night," she said, "I'd already forgotten it. I didn't leave over that. You knew I was going to spend the winter with my uncle at Resolution."

"I didn't exactly follow you to apologize," I said. "I'm taking the boat, too. But I do wish we hadn't fought. If you could only understand, Kitty. . . ."

Her lips tightened impatiently. "Let's not talk about it any more, John."

"But if you could only see. . . ."

"What more is there to see? It looks simple to me. You like a beard, and I don't."

"It goes deeper than that, Kitty."

"Of course, it does," she said. "As much as I abhor a beard, John, it's only a small part of the whole thing. I guess it's become a symbol of the real issue. It only serves to emphasize the difference in our ages. Every time I see it, I think of you spending eighteen hours a day in that barber shop, with those cronies of yours, all old men, growing fat on checkers and wine."

"Good French wine. Napoléon himself would have nothing but Chambertin."

"You miss the whole point, don't you?"

"Not at all, *ma petite*," I told her sadly. "Is there such a great difference in our ages, with you past twenty-five, and me not really much older than forty? If you could only overlook a few little idiosyncrasies a bachelor develops through his lonely life. . . ."

"That's just it. Your beard makes you look older . . . you live older. Why, to see you mooning around in that stuffy little shop of yours, anyone would think you were fifty years old."

"Is the old man bothering you?" asked someone, from behind us. It was Wapiti Lamont, the man who had helped her out of the scow and then climbed back for his Mackinaw. I had seen him going around with her a lot while she was in Athabaska Landing this year, and he and I had already exchanged ideas about that. He laid some claim to being a trapper, but I had never seen him carrying any pelts.

Whenever it came up, he was so vehement about his pure French descent that I had begun to look for a little Indian blood in him somewhere. He did walk with his toes pointed straight ahead, and once, when he was smoking a pipe in my shop, it smelled very much like the *kinnikinnick* those Chippewayans use for tobacco.

"If you like the idea of the old man," I told him, "it has always been my impression that the young should not speak until spoken to."

His face was the color of mahogany and narrow as a hatchet, and the smile did not lend it much humor. "That's a little old-fashioned," he told me.

"Would it be old-fashioned of me to ask you to leave until I'm through talking with Kitty?"

"It would be an insult."

"It's about time one of us insulted the other," I said. "In my day, I've kicked the head off men much more worthy than yourself."

His grin was more of a leer now. "I've always heard the very old live in the past. Hasn't anybody told you that savate went out of style with the beaver hat? It's considered unsportsmanlike to fight with the feet now."

"Perhaps you would like to see how unsportsmanlike I can be."

Wapiti leaned so close to me I could smell the Indian *tiswin* he had been drinking. "Let's quit talking about it, John.

Leave us now, or I'll forget your age."

"Oh, let's not go that far, Wapiti," George said in a soft voice from behind us.

Wapiti turned sharply to stare at him, a strange look crossing his face. Then he stepped back from me. Kitty was looking at George, too, standing there so short and broad, with a hand in the pocket of his coat.

"My father was fifty-two when he started traveling with a bodyguard," she said.

After the painter was made fast to a stake driven in the sand, and they had started kneading the dough for bannocks, Fred Storie called for someone to go and get the wood for a fire. On a trip like this, the passengers do their share of the work, so Melbourne started off toward the timber. He was a tall, lanky man in corduroys and a canvas Mackinaw, and I had to admit he might have looked younger without his beard.

His eyes were young and bright, like a kit fox's, with a ceaseless motion to them that picked up everything about him. He was lost in the dusk before he reached the timber. Then I saw George get up, his eyes on me, and there was nothing to do but follow him. Nobody took any notice of our departure, probably thinking we meant to help Melbourne with the wood.

The nearer we got to the trees, the more reluctant I grew.

"Go right up to Melbourne and keep him busy while I get around behind," George told me. "All I'll do is hit him on the head. I want that beard off before we go any farther."

"Any farther? What do . . . ?"

"John!"

"Very well, *m'sieu*, very well," I said quietly.

All the berries had fallen from the saskatoon, and the dry

bushes rattled like old bones as I pushed through them. Teddy Melbourne straightened up from where he had been tugging at a big piece of driftwood.

"I came to help you," I said.

"After that last game of checkers?" he chuckled.

"I don't hold that against you," I told him. "You're got to win sometime."

He bent down again to pull at the wood. I tried to place George but couldn't hear anything. For a moment, I had the impulse to tell Melbourne about this and try to escape in the darkness. But if he were mixed up with the sea otter poaching, that would link me with it, too. It would be foolish.

I bent to help him, making a lot of noise to cover whatever sounds George might cause. Then, behind Melbourne's bent form, I saw George. He had a little Mauser 7.65 out, and one more step would bring him close to Melbourne.

A sudden clatter in the saskatoon at the edge of the timber made me jump.

"Melbourne!" Captain Storie called. "What are you doing? We're ready for the wood."

Melbourne straightened abruptly. He saw me looking over his shoulder at George, and turned that way. The lump in my throat was so big I thought my heart had jumped up there. Then I saw that George had slipped the gun away before Melbourne turned.

"Thought you might need a little help," George smiled.

"Did you now?" asked Melbourne.

Something was gagging my throat, and I felt sick. It wasn't the shock of thinking Melbourne had seen the Mauser. It was realizing, suddenly, that George had held that gun, not as if to strike a man, but as if to shoot him.

Up by Murderer's Shoal, the river begins to reek of tar.

The land is stained with it, the cutbanks carry channels of it right down into the water, even the trunks of the trees are turned black and slick by it. We reached this stretch of the river two days after boarding the scow. Captain Storie's untimely entrance had kept us from doing anything about Melbourne that first evening, and since then we had had no other chance. But I had plenty of chances to think. George had been going to shoot Melbourne. I knew that now, for sure. And it had suddenly ceased to be amusing to me. It had become very terrible.

The story George had first told me had seemed plausible enough on the surface. I could understand that a novice might well hack a man up, if he shaved him fast, so identification would be difficult. But I could not see a policeman shooting his fugitive in cold blood. Did that mean that George was not a policeman? Then how had he gotten that information about Charlie Giroux? Maybe the Indian he had talked with was not a prisoner. That still did not remove the threat. If there was an Indian around who could identify Giroux, I was still caught in this, whether George was a policeman or not. So I stayed with it till we reached that shoal water on dawn of the second day.

Within a mile of the shoals, the water became so rough that the passengers had to get out on the bank and *cordelle* while the oarsmen stayed at their sweeps and rowed. They unshipped the hawser from beneath the forward deck, and cast it ashore for us.

"You can stay in the boat if you want to, John," said Storie. "We might be able to get away with three on the tow rope."

"I am not an invalid, Captain," I answered. "I have pulled my share of the *cordelle*."

What is this? I thought. *Have I really become such a venerable institution in that barber shop that they think of me only as an old man huddled near the heat of the stove with his cronies, growing fat on Chambertin and checkers?* Sacre!

The trail led up over high, rocky banks, through timber that was already beginning to show the effects of the cruel winters. Here and there we passed those dwarf spruce you see up in the Barrens, where no tree is over four or five feet high, standing like little hunchbacked gnomes among the taller timber.

Finally we came in sight of a tall pine, standing alone on the bluffs above the shoal. The branches had been shaved off the trunk till there were only a few of them left at the top, shaped like an arrow.

"Charlie Giroux's lobstick?" asked George.

"Yes," I told him. "It is the way we commemorate things up here. They cut it for him after he went down in the rapids. The police were too close behind for him to stop and portage. He lost out at Phantom Rocks. The foam there makes it impossible to tell how many rocks there are."

"Doesn't he know a lot about Charlie Giroux, George?" asked Wapiti, who walked ahead of me, between grunts at the rope. "Is that not a distinction? Giroux was such a famous man. A stupid half-breed nobody ever knew, who never did anything more than get killed trying to run some rapids nobody else was ever foolish enough to attempt."

"You sound so bitter, Wapiti," I said. "Are you ashamed of your blood?"

The flesh across his sharp cheek bones shone like wet leather. "I am of pure French descent, and you know it well."

"Is that what gives you a taste for the *tiswin* these Indians think is liquor?" I asked. "No self-respecting Frenchman could stomach it."

He let go the rope and wheeled toward me. "You've taken

refuge in your age too long, grandpa."

I dropped my eyes to his boot. "A *bess-hath*, perhaps. The Coppermines use that kind of knife, I understand."

He made a sound deep in his throat, but, before he could move, George was between us again.

"Why don't you pick up the rope again, Wapiti?" he said mildly. "We wouldn't want any trouble right now, would we?"

That strange look swept Wapiti's face once more. Then he bent over to pick up the hawser, and we started pulling again.

At the head of the rapids, Hudson's Bay had built a tramway along the bank, by which a boat can be portaged as well as cargo, for not even an empty hull could be towed through that shoal. By the time we reached there, I was so played out I had to sit down on the bank.

They made the scow fast and unloaded it, and started packing the cargo down the tramway to the other end of the rapids. George and I were alone for a moment, and he squatted down beside me.

"I heard Storie put Melbourne on boat watch," he said in a low voice. "You just keep on being too tired to move until everyone's out of sight on the trail. When Melbourne comes down, get his attention on something so I can come in behind."

I saw Kitty looking at me from where they had piled the cargo, and the expression on her face was very clear. Disgust would have been better, or contempt. But it was pity. If I looked as old as I felt in that moment, I could understand it. I bowed my head and tried not to think how it was going to be in the years ahead, without the music of her voice, or the scent of her, more poignant than the bouquet of Chambertin.

When I looked again, she was gone. The women do their share of the work up here, and she must have strapped on a light packing board and followed the others up the trail. Only Melbourne was in sight, coming down to the boat from the cargo.

"If you're too done in to take the portage," he said, "why don't you take the boat watch and let me carry a load?"

I saw movement in the trees behind him, very close, and raised my voice a little. "Before you go, see if you can force those port strakes back into place. They are loose, and I'm afraid the tramway will jar them open."

He climbed in, glancing at me before he squatted down to look. Then his head dipped below the level of the thwart. I tucked my head in, so the movement of my mouth would not be visible from the trees.

"Listen," I said. "George is after you."

"I figured that," he said. "How do you tie in?"

"He made me come with him. He said he was a policeman, and that they suspected you of being mixed up in this otter poaching. He wanted me to shave off your beard for identification."

"That's almost funny," he said. "I'm Lieutenant Melbourne. I've been following George clear up from Ottawa. We spotted him trying to unload otter pelts down there, and wanted to find out who else was in it with him."

"Keep your head down," I said. "He can't see you from the trees. Do you trust me?"

"I guess I'll have to," he said. "My gun's in my duffel. I thought they'd suspect me if I wore it."

I understood now why George had wanted me all along. They knew Melbourne was with the police. If Melbourne and another man were found dead together, and it looked as if they had killed each other in a gunfight, and, if that other man were eventually identified as Charlie Giroux, it would be a closed case. George would be free of the officer who had followed him, and could go on with his poaching, with no connection between him and Melbourne's murder.

"Keep down," I told him softly. "He's coming."

The thwart was high enough so that, as George stepped from the trees, he still could not see Melbourne. It was three long paces from the timber to the boat. George was pulling his gun from his pocket as he took the first one, his feet making no sound in the sand. His eyes were on the thwart, watching for Melbourne to rise up.

The thole pins were set loose in their sockets, made to come out with the oar when one lifted it. By the time George took his second step, and the gun came out, I had the oar off the thwart. I heaved it the way a man would throw a spear underhanded, putting all my two hundred pounds behind it. The blade struck him in the stomach. He gave a retching cough and doubled over and fell heavily into the sand.

Just as he fell, I heard a sound behind me. I whirled to see Wapiti, coming up over the bow. He must have been creeping in behind us all the time. He was pulling that knife from his boot as he leaped. It was a *bess-hath,* as I had thought, the crooked knife those Indians use up on the Coppermine. Before I could wheel, Melbourne was on his feet and lunging past me to meet Wapiti.

The half-breed came in over the thwart and landed with both feet on a seat, taking a wild swipe at Melbourne with the knife. Melbourne tried to dodge, his knee caught on the edge of the seat, and he pitched headfirst over this into the bottom of the boat. His head made a sharp, cracking sound against the strakes, and I knew he would not get up.

As Wapiti jumped off the seat at me, I stooped low. That way I was under his knife wrist. He made the mistake of driving down from above with the *bess-hath.* I shot my right hand up to catch his wrist in the saddle of my thumb and forefinger, then surged up against his body, grappling with him, keeping his knife above our heads. The scow rocked back and forth under the violent shift of our weight as we fought. That's what must have started the stern sliding off the beach into deep water. The boat pitched and the current caught the stern so violently that the whole hull lunged against the painter. The rope snapped, and we were swirled away from shore.

Wapiti made a strained, mewing sound in his throat, and surged against me. I had to admit that the youth of him was telling, that I could not hold up much longer against his strength.

"It is too bad you only fight with your hands nowadays, *m'sieu,*" I gasped.

I shifted my weight over to my left leg. He thought I was giving up, and shouted triumphantly. Then my right leg came up. In the old days, I could kick the pine cones from a branch three feet over my head. Even in this confined position, his ribs were easy to reach. My heavy boot made a dull, cracking sound against them. The pain stamped itself into his face. His whole body stiffened. I stepped back far enough for another kick.

"*Touché,*" I said.

The toe of my right boot caught him on the point of his chin. The whole scow shuddered when he struck the deck.

Then I looked up and saw Melbourne, farther up, clinging to the thwarts and staring at the foaming white water directly ahead of us. It was too late to jump, too late for anything but to stay with the boat.

"*M'sieu,*" I said, "it looks as if you and I are going to run Murderer's Shoal."

I jumped onto the poop deck, grabbing for the tiller. Now came the delicate distinction. If I turned too loose, our stern would swing into the rocks before we were past them. If I turned too late, we would run full-on by the bow. There was only one spot, where the current parted around the rocks.

"Look out!" screamed Melbourne. "You'll run head-on into that rock."

In that last moment, the foam seemed to have parted, revealing the first fangs of the river. I saw the bow sucked in by the splitting current, and put my whole weight against the sweep. Our speed and the force of the split current of water fairly bounced us away to one side. We shot past the rocks into a stretch of water as black and slick as an otter pelt.

Then the roar of the rapids drowned us. My clothes were drenched and foam covered my beard like shaving lather. I was laughing and shouting and singing "Alouette" and all the other songs, and I didn't care if Melbourne heard me or not. That's the way it gets you, to ride the white water.

Then the lobstick of Charlie Giroux was ahead of us on the bluffs, right above Phantom Rocks.

"The wind whips the foam around so much here you can't tell where it's breaking on a rock and where it isn't," I shouted at Melbourne. "Giroux was past his fifth rock when he thought he saw another dead ahead. It made him swing out and carried his stern into the one he'd just passed."

The first rock leaped from its veil like a cat from a tree. The bow bobbed into the suction of parting current. At the last instant I lunged against the sweep. We whipped out, the rock flashed past. Then another. The bow dipped again. I leaned into the sweep. We were whipped out so violently I almost lost my footing. Was it four now? Five? I was sick at my stomach with the knowledge that I had lost count. Another one jumped at us, and I barely caught it in time.

Then, as we were still turning out from that one, a huge, black nightmare of a rock seemed to burgeon out of the spray,

113

dead ahead. My whole being contracted with the impulse to lunge against the sweep and turn us out from it. But that would swing our stern right into the rock we were passing. Was this the one, then? My eyes ached as I watched the water directly in front of the bow, waiting for the current to part before the rock. Melbourne stared, transfixed. In another instant, we would smash full against the rock, or. . . . Still no parting of the turbulent current. Then we went right into it. I stiffened for the shock. There was none. We shot through the foam and came out into a clear run of water. Behind me the spume closed over the immense black hole that had looked so like a rock. I hung against the sweep, too weak to guide us ashore for a time. Finally I began working the scow over through the quieter water to the beach.

They were all there, waiting for us. Storie said George was still back at the other end of the tramway, so sick from that blow in the stomach he could not move. They were all asking questions, and Melbourne told them as much as he could.

Finally he turned to me. "I still don't see why they got you in on it."

"I think they meant to kill me, also," I said. "If you and I were found dead, as if we had killed each other in a gunfight, would it not appear that you had found your poacher?"

"Perhaps you're right," Melbourne murmured. "But why you, John? I should think they would have picked someone who had a known criminal record."

I shrugged. "Perhaps that was one of their mistakes."

"I suppose so. It leaves you with quite a distinction, you know. You're the only one besides Charlie Giroux who ever ran Murderer's Shoals." He smiled at me, with those quick, bright eyes that never missed anything, then moved off.

There was a lot of cargo still to be portaged, and, when Storie got the crew quieted down enough to go back and get

George, it left only Kitty, standing there, looking at me.

"He was wrong, wasn't he, John?" she asked in a tremulous little voice. "Charlie Giroux is still the only one who ever ran Murderer's Shoal."

"Is he, *ma petite?*"

She was suddenly in my arms, face against my chest. "Was Charlie Giroux really so bad, John?"

"He was a rascal, Kitty. Maybe even a thief. But perhaps he got off on the wrong foot, and nobody ever taught him different. Sometimes something can change a man like that. I'm sure if Charlie Giroux had happened to be near Fort Resolution one day, and had seen you standing in the doorway of your uncle's house, that one glimpse of you would have made him renounce his former ways and try to achieve something worthy of you."

"Forgive me for not understanding." She was almost crying now, and her fingers were touching my beard. "It's a wonderful beard. You should never shave it off. And I'll never think of you as old again. You were young down there on the rapids, wild and young and magnificent."

"Like Charlie Giroux?"

"Like Charlie Giroux."

"A magnificent rogue," I said. "A magnificent rogue."

A MAN DOESN'T WHIP HIS DOGS

Athabaska's main street was filled with a milling crowd of tipsy Cree bucks, Chippewayan squaws in dirty Hudson's Bay blankets, and fur-hatted *voyageurs* who had put their York boats away for the winter. François Voltaire trotted through the mêlée disdainfully.

"Voltaire," I told him, "you are leading a team that has won the race for five years. This time we have competition. They say Pebos Ardal is down from the Yukon." I gave him the order to swing right—*"Euh!"*

There had been earlier races in the season, but this was the biggest run, arranged by the Hudson's Bay Company, and it seemed as if everybody in Canada had gathered on the flats beyond the boat yards. I had found a choice starting place by the river, when the crowd of yapping dogs and cursing drivers made way for a man who came careening through them, riding the runners of a long Cree *odobaggan* that had been stripped to its skeleton for the race—and his dogs!

There were eight of the coal black Siberians running in a gang hitch, and each of them must have weighed at least a hundred and fifty pounds. White-tipped fox tails bobbed from the blue tapis covering their saddles, and bells jangled from their collars. He lashed them with a long dog whip, shouting in Cree.

"Chanipson," he yelled, *"chanipson!"* and the runners threw up a dirty spray as the team wheeled to the right and halted. He had been to the Landing some years before, Pebos Ardal, making the long trek down from the Yukon, where they all drive their dogs in a gang hitch. The silk embroidery on his moccasins marked him for a French half-breed.

Have you ever seen the walk of a timber wolf? There is something about the lithe, effortless flexion of each muscle, something in the sinuous swaying ease of its every movement that distinguishes the singular evil in the beast. Pebos Ardal walked this way. He stepped off his sled, and his shoulders made him look top-heavy. "You seem to have made a mistake about your position, Charlevoix," he said.

Alexandre Dumas was my butt dog. He began to growl. "Please don't come any closer, Ardal," I asked.

But he came on. "I said, you made a mistake, Charlevoix. This is my starting position. I chose it last night."

Alexandre Dumas jerked my sled around with him as he lunged at Ardal.

"Sacre bleu!" Pebos dodged aside, lashing out with a long leg. His foot struck my butt dog in its throat. With a choked howl, Dumas somersaulted backward. The traces caught him short in mid-air, and slammed him down, pulling Anatole France back on top of him. Snarling, Dumas scrambled to his feet, jerking the whole team with him as he lunged again.

Pebos already had that whip curling out from his mittened fist. It exploded in the dog's face. Blood spurted from Dumas's nose—he howled and tried to cringe back and escape the next lash. I had reached Ardal by then, and he almost fell when I caught his arm and spun him away.

"I'll whip your damned dog's face off!" he shouted, floundering backward in the snow.

But Teddy Faber came through the crowd in his red

Mountie coat. "You, there," he said.

Ardal stood a moment with his whip trailing the ground. Then he pulled the long lash of caribou hide to him and began to coil it up. That is the kind of policemen the Mounties are.

"What's the trouble?" Teddy Faber asked.

"Nothing, Sergeant," said Pebos. "Nothing. It's all settled now. Charlevoix is going to start from here. Sure, go ahead, Charlevoix. It won't help you. You can whip your *giddes* till their blood melts the snow, and. . . ." He stopped and looked up, and his smile wasn't nice. "Ah, but I forgot. You are Charlevoix. You are the man who doesn't use a whip on his dogs. You just talk to them."

"There are things a man doesn't do," I said. "He doesn't beat his dogs, or his woman."

Ardal's voice was thin. "I whip my dogs. Would you say I am not a man?" For a moment, I thought he would use the whip again. "You will wish you had whipped your *giddes*"— and Pebos Ardal curled his lips around the word—"when this race is finished."

He turned and swung onto the stern of his *odobaggan* and lashed his huge Siberian Huskies away through the crowd.

"Sorry that man came south this winter," said Faber.

I shrugged. "Those elephants of his look imposing. But you know it's the big dogs that drop out first on a forced run."

"I wasn't thinking of the race," said the sergeant. He had to set us off with his gun from Otter Point, and he left before *she* came through the crowd.

Have you ever seen a wet beaver *plieu?* That was her hair. Drawn over the back of her head as sleek and black and glossy as a prime pelt, hanging in thick plaits against the shoulders of her beaded capote. Watching her come, I wondered if pretty soon, perhaps, they would no longer have their joke about me—Teddy Faber and the others here at Athabaska.

I don't remember when it started. Perhaps it was that I had become a fixture at the Landing, after so many years with the Hudson's Bay Company, and the men were always ribbing me: "*Tiens!* Charlevoix, when are you going to get a squaw?" My answer was always: "*Oui,* I know how men get their women up here. Maybe trading for dogs up in the Mac-Kenzie Basin, and they find out the chief will include his daughter if they throw in another pair of Hudson's Bay blankets, and they decide they need someone to carry that extra load of beaver down to Athabaska anyway. Or maybe they get drunk the night before the races and wake up the next morning married to a squaw. Not that for Charlevoix."

But now I realized how many years I had been sitting there in that big, dim trading post with its musty smell of beaver and Lipton's Tea and sour leather. Maybe soon Teddy and the others would have to find another joke. A trapper named Pierce was at Athabasca this year, with his daughter. I told you about her hair, those shining plaits on the shoulders of her capote.

"*Bon jour,* Céleste."

She stood there at the stern of my sled. "*Bon jour, M'sieu* Charlevoix."

"Have you come to watch the races?" That was stupid, wasn't it? I guess they are right about me being that way about women.

She had big, dark eyes that smiled softly with her lips. "*Oui, m'sieu.* I have come to watch the races."

"You seem surprised at something."

"I expected someone else," she said. "He told me he had picked this starting position."

Teddy Faber shouted from the higher ground of the Point. I wanted to say something else, but there was no time. The sergeant's gun made a flat, hard sound.

"*Ma-a-rche!*"

At first it was the running, slithering confusion of fifty teams, and then, farther on, the Indian racers' mongrel *giddes* dropped behind, and the better dogs fought for position. At Pelican Village, where we made our turn back to Athabaska, I was running second. Pebos Ardal was somewhere behind me, whipping his dogs for every foot of gain.

The Eskimo ahead of me was driving a fan hitch—all right in the open for which it was designed, but tricky to handle through the roughs or on a sharp turn. When he wheeled around the lobstick that was our turning point, his king dog stepped over its traces and fouled his mate.

I called to my dogs. "*Euh!*"

They wheeled right with perfect precision, and my sled was out in front going back. I held the lead for a mile through the timber south of the village, running ahead of my team to break trail. We had reached the open when I heard the crackling of a whip behind me.

Pebos Ardal was riding the stern of his *odobaggan* as he swung by me, and he leaned far out from the lazy-board, lashing my butt dog with his whip. Alexandre Dumas howled and swerved aside. I put all my weight on the tail line to keep the sled from turning over. Throwing his head back to laugh, Pebos raced past, driving his dogs with that snapping lash. I got the sled righted, and rode the runners for a time, steadying my team.

The street was full of whooping Indians and trappers as I topped the Twottenny Hills and ran down into the Landing. Teddy Faber was at the finish line to meet me.

"Too bad, Charlevoix. But there's always next year."

Pebos Ardal had been in long enough to empty a bottle. He shoved his way through the crowd. "Who is the man now,

Charlevoix?" he said. "Tell me, who is the man now."

Céleste was with him. I couldn't understand at first, then I saw the way she looked up at him. Pebos grabbed the side of my cariole, shaking the sled. Alexandre Dumas snarled and tried to jerk around in the traces.

"I said . . . tell me who is the man?" yelled Pebos.

I was still watching the girl. "Winning a race changes nothing. That does not make a man. I say a man does not beat his dogs or his woman."

"Ah, his woman," said Pebos, and caught Céleste and swung her around so that all I could see was her glossy hair as he kissed her. Then he shoved her away and hit her across the face. "You mean like that?" he laughed.

I saw her stumble against the stroud leggings of a *voyageur*, and fall to her knees. I saw Pebos Ardal's face as I smashed my fist into it. That was about all. The crowd made a lot of noise when I went down. I got up once, but the blood in my eyes blinded me, and, when I went down that time, I knew it was for good. I heard Teddy Faber blowing his whistle, but Pebos was using his feet on me. I lay there and saw Céleste going away with him, hanging on his arm.

Canoe season came and lichen spread its golden blanket over Twottenny Hills above the boat yards, and the Richardson owl came out at night to sing its love song in the black poplars across the river. The factor thought I hadn't recovered from the beating and kicking, and he tried to send me to Edmonton for a rest. Pebos and Céleste had gone north after the races. Now and then a *courier du bois* or a trapper brought news of Pebos. The half-breed had got drunk at Fort Smith and knifed an Indian, or he had whipped a *voyageur* half to death on the MacKenzie. More than once, Teddy Faber said: "Wish that 'breed had stayed in the Yukon. Sooner or later, we'll have to pick him up."

Winter had come again, and Teddy was making his circuit. They brought him back on the police sledge, and the worn-out dogs lay down in front of the barracks across from the Hudson's Bay Company. The sergeant was wrapped up in a four-point blanket. He was able to talk, but that was all, when they carried him in.

"Joe Flint caught Pebos poaching his beaver lines on Lac la Biche," he whispered. "Pebos killed Flint. I was at Fort Smith. I caught up with Pebos a day's run north of the Dog Rib village on Athabaska Lake. That Forty-Five-Ninety of his. . . ."

"Take it easy, Teddy," the captain told him. "We'll have that 'breed."

Teddy shut his eyes. "The man is close to the MacKenzie . . . his country. The Indians will cover his trail. There isn't a team in the Territories that could catch him now. I wouldn't have known where he was if I hadn't found his woman, Céleste, in a teepee, beaten, almost killed."

"That will be another," said the captain, but I was already running to my house.

I found Céleste in a Dog Rib teepee near Athabaska Lake. An old squaw was with her. It was hard to believe that a man could have done that to a woman. Céleste didn't recognize me at first.

"Don't try to move me," she said. "The Dog Ribs here told Pebos the Mountie was following us. Pebos got drunk that night. You know how strong he is . . . my man. When he found out I was . . . too sick to travel in the morning, he went on without me. The Mountie came a day later. I heard that Pebos shot him. Is that true? I don't want Pebos to get in trouble. He is my man."

I sat there the rest of the night, coughing from the smoke of the fire in the teepee. Once I ran my hand through her hair, sleek and black like a prime *plieu*. The dogs had begun to howl when I shoved the flap aside and stumbled out of the teepee.

There was that Loucheux buck from Fort Smith, north of the Dog Rib village, sitting across the fire outside and licking the grease from his fingers. "You must be crazy, Charlevoix. Nobody can catch Pebos Ardal now."

"Maybe the Indians will hide his trail from the Mounties," I said, "but have you forgotten how you used to come down to Athabaska every winter, when you were a papoose, and play in my store and get sick on my candy?"

After the Loucheux buck, there were others who would tell me what they would tell no Mountie, and it was thus I followed Pebos Ardal.

The tribes had gone south and soon even the hunters had left the country north of Fort Smith, but by that time I had closed with Ardal enough so that I could follow his trail myself.

The day came when I had fed the last whitefish to my dogs. After that I began to boil my leather. And then, the only leather left was in my Cree webs and the harness, and we couldn't eat that, so we ran on empty bellies.

It was that day that I found where Ardal had killed his first dog. Everything of him had been eaten—hide, hair, and bones. There was not even a spot of blood on the snow, licked clean by the starving Huskies, but I knew the signs.

"Ha," I told my dogs, "we are gaining on him. Maybe Pebos could win a race with his whip, but this is a different kind of race."

Muskeg is the Cree word for swamp. It is more than a swamp. In winter it is hell congealed. The undulations leave huge waves that drop off into furrows thirty feet deep in some places.

Perhaps it was one day after we found where Ardal had killed a dog that we reached the muskeg south of the Great Slave Lake. Perhaps two days. I was running in a daze by then.

The muskeg had been covered by the snowfall of the night before. The white blanket on the ridge tops had softened and then frozen slick as ice. It was a constant battle to keep the sled from going off into one of those deep gullies and smashing up, and, by the time we had traveled a mile into the muskeg, I was crying like a baby with exhaustion.

I was staggering blindly when I hauled François Voltaire up out of a furrow onto that last ridge. I yanked on the tail line to straighten the sled and turn it to run along the top of the *arête*. Then, half a mile ahead, I saw him, riding the back of a long Cree *odobaggan*. When I drew breath to speak, it coursed through me like a snow knife.

"You have done it," I cheered my team. "Now I ask one more effort. Hereafter you shall sit in the post by the stove and eat caribou quarters. Never again shall you feel the saddle on your backs. But give me this one last run."

They gave it to me. They had been running with the down brush that tells how near a dog is to being finished. But now their tails drew taut. They raced like a fresh team, along the slippery top of that *arête*. Whatever sound we made was swept away behind us by a wind blowing in our faces.

To get close enough to him for one sure shot, that was what I wanted. It had to be close, for snowblindness was on me. And it had to be quick, before he saw me, for he had his .45-90, and he was a better shot than I was.

"On, on!" I shouted to my dogs that had never known a whip. "On, François! On, Alexandre! Give me this last race."

124

And they galloped like a fresh team despite their empty bellies. The ice flew from their claws, and we ran down on him as if he were standing still.

Then, when we were closing on him, he turned and saw us. Quickly he reached into his cariole for his rifle, but instantly he had to give all his attention to his sled or it would have been off into the deep gully. Then, he turned again, as if desperate, to look behind him. He shook his head and swept his mitten before his face, and I saw that he was snowblinded, too. He could not stand and trust to a shot. Standing on the runners of his *odobaggan,* he turned and lashed his team. The howling of his curses was blown back to me by the wind.

So we two half-blinded men, with exhausted teams, raced along the crest of the *arête* that stretched far before us in that ice hell of frozen muskeg. The teams flew. You have never seen such a finish!

At first the Siberians pulled ahead, but there is a limit to what the whip can do. I called to my dogs. "On, on, my children! Don't fail me. On, François, on, Honoré!"

And they closed the gap. We were into him. Then Pebos turned and lashed at François Voltaire. My lead dog took the biting caribou hide again and again in the face, but his furred throat pushed forward without faltering, to the stern of the *odobaggan*. The Siberians had checked when Pebos stopped whipping them. His sled was at a standstill, and my dogs mounted up on Pebos like a wave.

It was but a second. François Voltaire leaped for his throat. The others were tearing his parka from him. So great was Pebos's strength that he shook them off and seized his rifle, but he never fired a shot. They were all over him again, and his sled and mine, with all the dogs, rolled off the ridge and down thirty feet into the hollow. I slid and rolled after and was in among them with my knife in hand, but I did not have to finish the man. He was covered with blood, but what killed him was striking his head against a frozen hummock at the bottom. His inflamed eyes were wide-open and already glazed. His mouth was agape, and his teeth were white in his black beard. I laughed in his face.

Around the shattered *odobaggan,* his dogs lay, unable to move. They had been run to death by my team that never tasted a whip. I killed them one by one.

The meat of these *giddes* would take us back to the Landing.

So we left him there, for the wolves to take his body, and the devil to take his soul.

It is such things that make a man a savage. I have never taken a woman. I sit here, growing old, in the Company store, and I think of that night, stroking her hair in the Dog Rib teepee. He beat her almost to death, but she loved him. I am not a savage, I am a man, and a man does not beat his dogs or his woman.

IN THE LAND OF LITTLE STICKS

I

Division G covered northern Alberta with headquarters at Edmonton, and the superintendent's office here had the usual, nebulous austerity reflected in most official quarters of the Royal Mounted Police. The inevitable maps formed their precise geometric pattern on the wall behind Superintendent Corbett, who sat at a broad desk with no more papers on it than was necessary. He was a small man with careful, reserved eyes in a face scored deeply by former duty in the seasons of this land.

"Glad to have you, Inspector," he said, standing as Napier entered. He offered a firm, brief grip, then made a meager inclination of his head toward the sergeant major who had risen from a chair by the window. "This is Sergeant George Sallybrook. We needed someone who wasn't known in this section, so we brought him in from E Division to work with you. Sallybrook, this is Inspector Victor Napier."

"Of C.I.B.," finished Sallybrook, before holding out his hand. It was an impersonal addition, almost as if the man had spoken to himself. But, in the faint flash of light that crossed the sergeant's chill, blue eyes, Napier saw the antipathy.

"Haven't you ever worked with the Civil Investigation Bureau before, Sergeant?" Napier asked.

"You'll have to remember it's a rather new department," muttered Sallybrook. But Napier could see it now. Old-line was stamped so deeply into the sergeant major that the impeccable Stetson in his hand should have been a spiked white helmet. No telling how many horses had gone into the bow of his booted legs, or how many blizzards had etched their cruel history in his ruddy, seamed face. The leg-of-mutton cut to his trousers was faultless, and the polish of his Sam Browne harness reflected things like a mirror. The faint sound Corbett made clearing his throat brought Napier's gaze back to him.

"This seems to be centered around Fort Resolution," Napier offered.

Corbett nodded. "That's where the tribes gather every year to get their treaty money, of course. We don't know exactly when the counterfeiting started. The country's flooded with it now. You can see what a ticklish problem that presents. Counterfeit can't be explained to an Indian. Either the government bills are good, or they're not. It's not the amount of money so much. It's what it stands for. Those peace treaties are the work of centuries . . . literally. Any change in the *status quo* would entail enormous loss of face for the government. If the Indians lost faith over this, it would take years to restore the balance. I wouldn't go so far as to predict an uprising. But we'd have our hands full with some of those wilder tribes."

Napier dug into his pocket for a pipe. One of the main reasons he had been chosen for this job was his knowledge of the Chippewayan tribes. He felt a little incongruous, somehow, in his casual, single-breasted pepper-and-salt. There was something sardonic about the quizzical arch of his sharp, black brow, lowering its bony prominence over the brooding pools of his black eyes. The outward thrust of his long jaw to take the pipe in his mouth only accented its sense of restrained belligerence.

"Surely the Indians must sense something funny is going

on," he put in, when Corbett finally paused.

"As long as we keep honoring the money, they'll play along," shrugged Corbett. "Furs are about the only thing worthwhile for the counterfeiters. They pay the Indians in counterfeit treaty money for pelts that would otherwise go to Hudson's Bay or some other legitimate trading company. The Indians naturally head for the nearest Hudson's Bay post to spend the money. The government's ordered H.B.C. to honor the money and, in turn, has to redeem it."

"I understand Hudson's Bay has had a thirty-five percent drop in their fur trade this year," nodded Napier, sucking on his pipe to light it. "Which would indicate that we not only have counterfeiters to deal with but fur smugglers as well."

"E Division's watching that," Sergeant Sallybrook offered. "They've had two unidentified craft in the Sound already. We figure they're sending the furs on sleds from here to the coast."

"As good a supposition as any." Napier waved out the match, flicked it into a glass tray on the desk. "Ottawa's given up the idea that the money's being printed outside and shipped in. I think that corporal's disappearance up near Resolution was what convinced them. Richards . . . ?"

"Richardson," Corbett corrected. "We don't know exactly what happened to him, Napier, but he was working on the case. That's why we need an undercover job now. It's obvious you won't get near them in a red coat. Corporal Richardson left a few patrol sheets and some interviews with traders he took down in shorthand, if you're interested."

"I'd like to see your whole file on the case," Napier said.

Corbett's about-face belonged on parade. The files must have been in the next room on the far side, for his footsteps went out of earshot in there. Napier dropped his hands casually into coat pockets. Rocking back and forth on his heels a little, his eyelids drew together. He was apparently studying the wall charts.

"Ever run on drum ice, Sergeant?" he asked abruptly.

Sallybrook's surprise stirred him in the chair. "Plenty, I guess. I've filled out a lot of patrol sheets up there."

"Echoes like hell, doesn't it? So many reverberations you can't tell the bad spots from the good ones."

"You don't like shaky running?" asked Sallybrook.

"Little dangerous, isn't it, when two men will probably be depending on each other for their lives?"

"See any rotten spots?" asked the other.

"You don't care for C.I.B." It was a statement from Napier.

Sallybrook's heavy jaw muscles bunched. "I've broken in a lot of recruits, Inspector, and one of the first things I try to beat into their heads is how many times they'll have to subordinate personal feelings to the demands of the service."

Napier removed his pipe, studying the bowl. "What are your personal feelings?"

"If a man's an officer, he shouldn't be ashamed to wear the uniform any time, any place."

"It's not a matter of pride," murmured Napier.

"Maybe I didn't use the right word," said Sallybrook. "I just never liked to sneak around the back door when I made an arrest."

"And kicked like a green mule when they changed the spike helmet for the Stetson," said Napier.

Sallybrook's shrug was dogged. "So I'm an old mossback. You'll find a lot of us in the service."

"In any service, Sergeant." Napier's pipe had gone out, and he set about relighting it. "There's always a clash between the old and the new. And always something to be said for each."

"The methods I've worked with for thirty years have kept the provinces cleaner of crime than any other given territory," asserted Sallybrook.

"But you've got crime now. Not just some settler going crazy and murdering his wife, or a couple of fur poachers on the Coppermine. Organized crime, Sergeant, and your red coat methods haven't handled it." Napier stopped as he saw the antipathy still lurking turgidly beneath the surface of those chill eyes. He shrugged. "You can beg off this duty, if you want."

Sallybrook's chest filled his coat like a barrel. "I've never shirked an assignment yet."

"What if I requested it?"

"Inspector . . ."—a flat, uncompromising tone filled Sallybrook's voice—"I don't think you'd better request that of me, or of any of my superiors."

"Is that a threat?"

"I just mentioned it."

Corbett came back through the door, closing it carefully behind him. There was no expression on his face as he glanced from Napier to Sallybrook. He put a manila folder on the desk, opened it.

"Richardson's reports and patrol sheets," said Corbett. "The only notable thing we could gain from them was mention of some woman in an interview with the Hudson's Bay factor at Athabaska Landing."

The patrol sheets were made out for the sub-districts with the name of every settler, so the patrolling constable could check each one, and Napier picked up the sheaf of these, thumbing through them. His question was an idle one, even in his own mind, at that instant. "Some woman?"

"Yes," said Corbett. "Richardson doesn't even mention her name. Why do you ask?"

131

"Yes." Sergeant Sallybrook was staring at Napier with a new interest. "Why do you ask?"

It must have been some subtle alteration of Napier's face. As Corbett had said, the name hadn't been mentioned in the reports. Neither was it underlined on this patrol sheet, to separate it from all the other names there. Guillaume Dumaine, it said, Great Slave Lake. And after that, Charlotte Dumaine.

II

The train ride from Edmonton to Waterways took two uneventful days in which Napier tried to acquaint himself with Sallybrook without forcing anything. The man had not tried to hide his resentment at being forced to change from his uniform into civilian clothes, and Napier was constantly aware of that undercurrent of antipathy.

At Waterways they boarded one of the stern-wheelers making its spring run up the Athabaska River to Fort Chippewayan. At Chippewayan they got a Peterboro canoe and supplies, and started the long haul up the Slave River to Fort Resolution, the last outpost before the dread Barren Lands. Spring lay in deceptive beauty over the land, and the first few days seemed an idyll to Napier. Sometimes they were borne for hours without paddling down the swift currents running in against a chocolate cutbank; sometimes they spent days gliding in among leafy Acadian islands where stillness from another world reigned. Wild ducks covered the shining, white drift logs in amazed rows, but the muskrats, squatting in secluded spots along the bank, scarcely looked up from stuffing their mouths full of rat grass, as the canoe drifted past.

Beneath the idyll, however, like silt waiting to be stirred from the river bottom lay the dank cruelty of the land. The fangs showed four days out of Chippewayan. They chanced a run of white water they should have portaged, and the canoe sliced itself apart on a shoal of sharp rocks. Sallybrook laid the flesh of his head open pitching from the ripped craft, and Napier had to haul him ashore in an unconscious state.

As soon as Sallybrook revived, however, the stubborn sergeant insisted on helping Napier salvage what they could. They got the canoe ashore, along with one duffel bag full of food. Wading in the shallows below where the accident occurred, Napier found a sleeping roll wedged in the rocks. It was ripped at one end, and something red was sticking out. He carried it ashore, tugging in puzzled, growing anger at the scarlet cloth. Finally the brass buttons of a tunic came free.

He did not try to hide the anger in his face as he raised it toward Sallybrook, where the man had been sitting in the white sand, bloody head between his hands. Slowly the sergeant stood up, a defiant pallor in his face. There were a lot of things Napier wanted to say.

"Build a fire," he told Sallybrook. "We'll burn it."

"Inspector!"

Sallybrook's one word held everything he couldn't have said in a thousand. There was an intense plea. And at the same time, that sense of flat, latent threat his voice had carried when he told Napier not to ask that he be dropped from this job.

Napier had read it before as stubbornness in the man. Now he saw his mistake. Now he saw it as a pride so intense it could be painful. The red coat to Sallybrook was a symbol of a service he had devoted his life to, and would give his life for, if necessary. Napier realized how completely he would alienate the man by destroying it.

"You know what it will mean if anyone sees it," he told Sallybrook finally.

Sallybrook's chest lifted with a sharp breath. "I'll take the responsibility, Inspector."

"See that you do," said Napier, tossing the duffel at him. "Now, let's build a fire."

They had not yet gathered enough wood when the Indian appeared from the trees. He came without sound, appearing abruptly from the spruce. Napier saw the startled suspicion in Sallybrook's lifting face.

"*Wachee,*" said the Indian.

Napier answered the universal greeting cautiously. It was impossible to tell the man's tribe by his dress. He had a caribou-hide shirt dyed yellow and fringed with moose-hair, and the inevitable rawhide *assian,* a strip of leather passing between his legs and through a belt at the back and front, to hang down a foot or so behind and before. He must have had quite a standing in his tribe, for there were half a dozen garters holding up his leggings below the knee, covered with fancy quill work.

"*Szi, tsel twi,*" he said, his grin digging greasy creases in the swarthy face.

"What is it?" said Sallybrook.

"Chippewayan," Napier said. "Might be a Dog Rib or a Hare. He wants some tobacco."

"Tell him we haven't got any," said Sallybrook. "We can't afford to lose any more of our supplies. Let him come any closer and we sure as hell will. I never saw one yet who couldn't steal the webbing right out of your snowshoes."

"You forget what we're here for," said Napier. He turned to the Indian. "*Quanachi,*" he murmured. "We'll all make a little fire."

"Will you give me some tobacco then?" asked the man in Chippewayan.

"I'll trade you something for it, then," Napier told him, and started hunting for dry kindling. Grudgingly the man pretended to kick around in the driftwood, but by the time Napier and Sallybrook had found enough to burn, the Indian still had not come up with any wood.

"Damn' lazy maggot-eaters," growled Sallybrook.

Glancing at the sergeant, Napier wondered how much chance he was taking in trying to deal with the Indian. He could appreciate what state Sallybrook was in. He himself was jumpy with exhaustion, and the flies weren't helping any. He built a smoky fire and stuck his head in it to try and escape them momentarily. The Indian sat cross-legged before it, blandly ignoring the insects as only a man of his race could.

"What do they call you?" Napier asked, pulling his head out of the smoke.

"Bess-Hath," answered the man.

"Crooked Knife," Napier translated for Sallybrook's benefit.

"And I bet he'd put it through your back if you turned around," growled Sallybrook.

Napier let that grin twist his lips. "Take it easy, will you, Sergeant? We're going to have to deal with a lot of these people." He took a twist of tobacco from his pocket and showed it to the Indian, asking him in Chippewayan what he would trade for it.

"The pelt of a *tha*," the man answered.

"I don't want a marten pelt this time of year," Napier told him.

The man stared enigmatically at the tobacco in Napier's palm. Firelight glittered across eyes as unreadable as wet black stones. But Napier knew what was going through his

135

mind. Tobacco was priceless in this land where so little was to be had. If an Indian would give his right arm for a beaver tail, he would give his soul for a twist of tobacco. Finally he reached beneath his caribou robe and drew forth his medicine bag. There was something deliberate about the way he pulled his war cap out. Perhaps he wanted them to see it. There were many tribes making up the people who inhabited the country around Great Slave Lake, and most of these tribes had a practice of attaching a plume for every man killed in battle. There must have been a dozen plumes on the cap of Crooked Knife. He paused, as if waiting for some reaction from them. Finally he pulled something else from the bag. It was three dollars in treaty money.

Napier heard Sallybrook's thin inhalation. "Find out where he got it."

"Take it easy," Napier told him. "He can read you like fresh tracks in the snow."

Sallybrook settled back with a soft curse. "He's not that smart."

It took Napier half an hour to trade the man out of one bill. Then, while the Indian broke off part of a twist and jammed it into his pipe, casting a covetous eye on the rest of their soggy supplies, Napier slipped the bill to Sallybrook. "It's counterfeit, all right," he told the sergeant. "They don't try to do a very good job, do they?"

"Why should they?" said Sallybrook. "It's only the Indians they have to fool. They'd do it with rocks if the Indians would take them. They know the spot they've got the government in. Find out where he got this, Inspector."

Napier asked Crooked Knife, knowing how foolish it was. He saw that suspicious glitter in those eyes again as the man answered that he had gotten it on Treaty Day at Fort Resolution.

"Liar as well as thief," growled Sallybrook. "If I only had my coat. . . ."

"He'd close up like a bear trap," snapped Napier. "Maybe a red coat can stop a riot, but I've yet to see these *Tinneh* talk if they don't want to."

"I could make him talk," snarled Sallybrook, wiping a vicious hand across his gnarled cheek to come away with it covered with blood and black with mashed flies. He leaned toward the sun, all the tension of these last hours filling the line of his body in a rigid culmination. "Where did you get that stuff, damn you?"

The man grinned inanely at Sallybrook.

Napier told the sergeant: "He doesn't understand you. Will you take it easy? You're not in the barracks now, and you can't use the same methods up here."

"He understands me," said Sallybrook in a burst of rage he might have controlled under less strain. "I'm asking you, Crooked Knife, where did you get it?"

The man still only grinned at him, and it goaded Sallybrook beyond control. Napier had been watching for this, but he could not reach the sergeant before Sallybrook had leaped across the fire to grab the Indian by the front of his robe.

"Now, talk, you thieving Dog Rib maggot-eater . . . !"

"Illa, teotenny," grunted the Indian, surging up against the sergeant's grip and trying to tear free.

"Let him go, Sallybrook," called Napier, reaching out and trying to pull the man off.

"When he tells me where he got that counterfeit money," gasped Sallybrook, shaking the Indian like a terrier in a rage. "How about it. You know what I'm saying like it was in your own language. Where did you get that treaty money?"

With a grunt, the Indian dipped his head, sinking yellow

teeth into Sallybrook's hand. The sergeant yelled, jerking his hand free. Napier caught his elbow, spinning him around and away from the Indian. Sallybrook's eyes were blank with rage as he wheeled back, and Napier saw he was going back in, blindly, and that only one thing would stop him. He ducked in under one clawing hand and sank a vicious blow as deeply into Sallybrook's solid belly as it would go.

The sergeant jackknifed and went to the ground. He lay there, doubled up, and the sounds he emitted, trying to get breath, made Napier gag slightly. He turned to the Indian and told him to get out. The man stared sullenly at Sallybrook, then picked up his war cap and put it carefully back into his medicine bag and faded out into the forest.

Sallybrook was retching when Napier turned back to him. When he finished, he sat up.

"I told you we'd never get anywhere with those anti-quated, spike-helmet methods of yours," Napier said. "Now every Indian north of Chippewayan will know there are two men in the province who want to find the source of that money badly enough to fight for it. I'll eat sour bannocks if that doesn't add up to the Royal Police."

III

Fort Resolution was rather a pompous name for such a meager scattering of buildings on the southern shore of Great Slave Lake. Promise of early snow already chilled the air when Napier and Sallybrook reached the place, pulling their battered craft up among the motley collection of birch-bark canoes on the rocky shore. The only sound, as they walked through the glistening lodges of caribou hide scattered across the beach, was the yapping of dogs. It was incessant, and it drowned all other noise.

138

They passed an Indian shouting to be heard above it, and could not distinguish his words. A mob of naked children descended upon the two men, emulating their elders in the plea for tobacco. The two men could hardly keep themselves from beating the little animals off. Finally they were through, and made their way up the trail to the store.

"Here before God," murmured Napier wryly, in that ancient joke of this country mocking the white H.B.C. on the flag of the Hudson's Bay Company that flaunted its tattered banner on a tall pole above the slanting roof. They climbed to the porch and into the reek of *kinnikinnick* tobacco, sweeping from the pipe of a man leaning against one of the unpeeled supports. Napier had the impression of a pudgy, greasy face, turned blue around the jowls by a beard, and the bright interest of black eyes following him into the store.

The inevitable odors of sour leather and stale fur and tea assailed him. There was a long, solid counter, rounded and whitened down the length of its outer edge by the contact of bodies and hands and belt buckles through innumerable years. A clerk in a shirt of wool plaid stood behind this, stooped a little so that the overhead oil lamp shone on his bald pate. Napier had thought it was an Indian woman, at first, standing in front of the counter. The skirt looked Cree, fringed with moose hair, fastened by the stiff, quilled belt behind. The hair was black enough. But it held too much wave. And then she had turned from the counter, stopping the breath in him.

It had been on his mind, of course, all the way up from Edmonton. Ever since he had seen the name on that patrol sheet. Wondering when it would come? And where? An outsider would look upon it as outrageous coincidence in such a vast country. But, in reality, there were so few places for a white man to be, unless he cast off from the settlements.

139

Three or four, at most, this far up. And here it was.

"Vic," she said in a throaty voice. Even in surprise, it still held the old invitation.

"Charlotte." His voice was flat, dead, with the restraint he was putting on himself. But he couldn't keep his eyes from taking it in. The mouth. Rich and full and pouting, putting the thought of a kiss in a man's mind. It seemed made for nothing else. And the strange gauntness to the hollows beneath the high, oblique cheek bones, shading the face with a vague, piquant sense of mystery. And the incessant, restless movement of something just beneath the surface of her big, black eyes.

"You're a long way out of Ottawa," she said. Her voice held a small, puzzled hurt at his stiffness, but already her glance was taking in Sallybrook behind him. A certain misunderstanding raised her brow faintly. She allowed her eyes to focus for an instant on the plain hide shirt Napier wore. "Not with the police any more, Vic?"

"What do you think?" he said.

That lifting brow. "I'm sorry, Vic."

"Forget it," he said. "I don't owe them anything. They don't owe me anything."

"It was different, then," she murmured.

"I was younger, then," he said against clamped teeth. Half a lifetime of developing a poker face did not help now. She'd always had such a rare discernment of every nuance in him. And there was so much going on now. The coals of an old fire stirred to a new glow. And something else inside him he could not define. It was not the same, somehow, as he had imagined it would be, meeting her again. Part of it was the same. But something was different. And all the time, this sparring was made doubly difficult by his consciousness of Sallybrook, right behind, taking it all in.

"Your partner?" she asked, dipping her head in Sally-brook's direction.

"We're running trap lines to the north," Napier told her.

"We might see each other," she said. "Dad is angling for a Hudson's Bay post up by Old Graves."

She hesitated, seeming to wait for something. His throat twitched with the words pushing up in it, but what he wanted to tell her he couldn't in front of Sallybrook. Finally she lifted one shoulder in a vague shrug, and, smiling lamely, circled him and went out. Napier moved over to the counter and took out the draft Corbett had given him on the Edmonton Hudson's Bay office. It was signed by the chief factor down there so as to clear them of any police connections, and the clerk nodded his bald head in acceptance.

"We'll start with a couple of rifles," Napier told him. "We lost ours in an upset downriver."

"I've got a couple of good Remington-Hepburns," the man offered.

Napier glanced at Sallybrook. The sergeant nodded. "Suits me, long as they're Thirty-Thirty." He leaned against the counter with a comfortable sigh, watching the clerk make his way into the back room. "Charlotte Dumaine?" Sallybrook said softly.

Napier had known it would come, sooner or later. He nodded silently. Sallybrook scratched his nose carefully, studying the tinned food on the shelf.

"That was the name on the control sheets. Guillaume Dumaine's her father? French. Ottawa French? That's where you knew them, Inspector?" Sallybrook paused, taking in Napier's nod with the tail of his eye. He licked his lips. "Ottawa isn't too far from Big Quill Lake, is it?"

Napier felt himself lift up against the counter. "Drum ice again, Sergeant?"

141

The man chuckled deeply within him. "Not many of us ever get known in this service, Inspector. We go along, do our duties, get shot up or drowned or killed, maybe. Nobody ever hears about us but our mess mates, and they forget too soon. Only a few names really stand out. I was surprised to find you such a young man. You've built a reputation quick. I guess it really started with the Big Quill Lake affair, didn't it? You weren't with the C.I.B. then."

"That's right," Napier said stiffly. "I had a red coat."

"And were proud of it . . . the way she spoke," smiled Sallybrook, without much humor. "Why should she think you weren't in the service any more?"

"I wasn't wearing the uniform."

"I got the impression it was something more than that," said Sallybrook. "She was sorry. For what? Did she think you'd been booted out?"

"You and I differ on a lot of things," said the C.I.B. man. "The one thing I thought I'd never have to ask you is to mind your own business."

"If it's police business, it's my business," said Sallybrook. "The Big Quill Lake affair was police business. Almost eight years ago, wasn't it? What were they doing? I forget the details. I remember your name. Smuggling, wasn't it? Furs or something?"

"They got their"—Napier was surprised at the savagery of his own voice—"smuggler."

"Yes," murmured Sallybrook, "you did send a couple of men to jail, didn't you?"

"Sallybrook," said Napier, wheeling toward him. "I told you. . . ."

The clerk cut him off, coming back into the room. In stiff reserve, they chose the rest of their equipment and then asked about dogs. The clerk said the man on the porch had some animals for sale. He was still there when they emerged, and Napier got a fuller impression. A big beast of a man with the full, sensuous lips of mixed bloods, his shoulders and chest threatening to burst the threadbare flannel shirt, a gut inclined to be sloppy unless held in by the broad, beaded belt that also supported his corduroy pants.

"Sure I got dogs," he told them, waving his pipe. "Hundreds dogs. None of this Indian *gidde* they try for sell you down on the beach, either. Come wiz Portage Marquette."

The kennels were in sight behind a nearby cabin, and he harangued them all the way over. "If you are going down over the old canoe route, you need good guide to show you the portage till the snow come, *hein?* Why you think they call me Portage Marquette? Don't answer. Look." He thumped himself on the chest so hard it echoed like a *hali-gali.* "A bear. See?" He beat eagerly against the back of his bulging neck. "A bull moose. Who can beat me with a packing board? Nobody."

"We don't need a guide," said Napier, as the man opened the kennel gate for them. "How about that MacKenzie River with the docked tail?"

"You never find better moosher," said Marquette.

"Too big," Sallybrook scowled. "Get us something that won't shape up over eighty pounds when it's full of winter feed. How about that one with the blue spots?"

"Good king dog," said Marquette. "He's Yukon River Husky crossed with MacKenzie malamute. I get him, *hein?*"

He kicked his way through the cringing, yapping, snarling mass of them to where the dog was hitched, and Napier spoke to Sallybrook. "You don't like them big?"

"Big man, big dog, it's always the same," muttered Sallybrook. "They'll wear out on the trail first, every time. It's their soft spot."

"It's difficult to find a man without a soft spot some-where," said Napier.

"I suppose so," said Sallybrook. "Some it's liquor, some it's gambling. What's yours, Napier? A woman?"

Napier turned sharply toward him. "Will you forget that?"

"How can I?" said Sallybrook. "If you can't? You know, Napier, I thought I'd build a grudge against you for that time with Crooked Knife. But I don't have to worry. I told you it was the same with a man or a dog. If they've got a streak of fat, they'll wear out sooner or later. The country will take care of them. It'll get you in your soft spot sooner or later."

With great effort, Napier halted himself from answering, as Marquette came back leading the mangy-looking dog. "I got him from big Norvege. That's why his name is Trofast. It means trustworthy in Norvege, or something, I don't know. Little starve-looking now, but wait till you feed him up. And with me for guide. *Sapristi!*" He made vicious, stabbing mo-tions at the ground with an imaginary gee pole. "Moosh. Haw. Gee. What a driver! Hundred mile run in one day. You don't believe? I prove you." He spread his hands out, rolling his eyes upward. "*Sacre nom,* how can any man be so *marveilleux?* Don't ask me." He drew himself up. "I'll take two dollar a day. No less."

Napier was busy feeling the animal's ground wool. Not a very heavy *pelage* there. "I told you we don't need a guide."

The man turned a sly eye down toward Napier and let out a chuckle or a burp; it was hard to tell, the sound came from so deeply inside him. "I would even take the pay in treaty money," he leered. "If anyone were to question."

IV

With dogs and equipment loaded in their Peterboro and another canoe they had gotten at Resolution, Napier and Sallybrook headed west along the lake shore, hunting for a campsite from which they could work. Napier wanted to lay the trap lines as far afield as they could, and thus come into contact with as many Indians as possible, establishing at the same time their own identity as trappers in this land.

About fifty miles down the lake from Resolution they built a cabin, and caught and smoked enough fish to last the dogs. They spent some time hunting to fill their own larder. And then winter was upon them.

Napier had already made his acquaintance with a few Indian camps, passing out gifts and making arrangements with some squaws to make him a fringed shirt. He was on speaking terms with several chiefs, but knew how foolish it would be to push anything or question them too closely about the money. It was about two weeks after the first snowfall that the two men set out separately for their trap lines, agreeing to return that evening. Napier found a few martens on his line, and returned in darkness to find the cabin empty. He gave Sallybrook till dawn and, with the first light, started out on his trail.

It had not snowed in two days, and it was not hard to find the tracks. One by one, Napier found the man's traps. At the third one, he was surprised to find a white fox. Then, at the fifth, he found Sallybrook.

He could not help but feel a stab of admiration for the crusty old sergeant. It looked as if it had been done very deliberately. The sled had been chopped up for fuel, and had been fed so carefully to the fire that coals were still warm. The dogs crouched around in a whining semicircle, staring with puzzled, cocked heads at Sallybrook. He sat against a tree wrapped in all the blankets and the canvas cariole covering, with only one leg out, the ankle held in the vicious jaws of a heavy bear trap.

It took Napier half an hour to pry it loose, and, by that time, Sallybrook had come out of his stupor. After doing what he could for the mangled ankle, Napier made a pot of strong tea and some bannocks.

"Damned thing was made fast with such chains I couldn't budge it," muttered Sallybrook. " I knew I wouldn't last long if I lost my head and started thrashing around. Tear that ankle so bad I'd pass out from loss of blood and freeze to death. Lucky I was close enough to the sled to reach it. I figured you'd be along sooner or later. So I just wrapped up and sat tight."

Napier looked at the ugly, bloody trap. "Isn't one of yours."

Sallybrook nodded on down the little gully. "That's mine with the white fox in it. This was set right where I'd pass going for it. I almost stopped the sled on top of it. So much snow drifted over it, I didn't even see the thing."

"Or was piled on top," said Napier. "You wouldn't have lasted another night out here, even keeping your head that cool."

"Do you suppose it was that Frenchman?" asked Sallybrook.

"Marquette?" Napier shrugged. "Just because he grins and mentions the treaty money? You'd have arrested him right there if I'd let you. I don't know who it was, Sallybrook. All I know is you've got to get back to Chippewayan or Athabaska Landing."

"It's a good month to Chippewayan. If it doesn't kill me, it should heal by then."

"I can't let you stay up here with that," said Napier. "There isn't a decent doctor this side of Chippewayan. It's liable to infect."

"Inspector"—the tone of Sallybrook's voice raised Napier's head sharply—"you know as well as I do you're working against time. Your main chance of finding the source of that money is through the furs bought from the Indians with it. The *pelage* starts getting mangy come spring. They won't be buying any pelts after that. Your best, and probably your only, lead will be gone by the time you get back from Chippewayan. Even with the best of luck, you can't possibly make it down and back in under ten weeks. You'll lose this whole year. Probably the whole job."

The logic of it was too complete. But that wasn't what struck Napier the deepest. The same tone had been in Sallybrook's voice when Napier had found that red coat. Napier was seeing the man's intense pride again. He was seeing what it would do to Sallybrook to be shipped back in such ignominious defeat.

"You know what a spot you put me in," he told the sergeant. "It's in my hands to take you back, and, if I don't, and something happens to you, I'll be responsible."

Sallybrook remained silent, his pride preventing an actual plea. But it was in his eyes, like a dog begging to be included.

Napier had a brassy, tarnished taste in his mouth. "What do you want to do?" he said, dropping his eyes.

There was an eager lift in the sergeant's voice. "Get that can of lard we use to fry the fish in. Mix it with gunpowder for a poultice and wrap the ankle up tight. Then stuff me in your sled and track down the trapper that laid this bear trap."

It was a remedy the trappers had used up here for a hundred years for everything from gunshot wounds to broken legs. They got going in half an hour, with Sallybrook poulticed and bandaged and tucked in the cariole, his dogs trailing loose. The man had obscured his trail with great skill in the vicinity of the trap, but by making an ever-increasing circle Napier finally picked up shoe tracks where the man had quit trying to cover himself.

The trail led north toward the Barren Lands, coming into a country criss-crossed by caribou trails, almost as ancient as the land they marked, and forming a veritable maze of ditches and sloughs in the snow until, in some places, it was like traveling over the wave of a wind-blown lake. It was late afternoon when they came in sight of the tall, pointed poles driven into the ground in a circle. It was an Indian grave, with more of them farther on, austere and lonely atop a low hill. And then it struck Napier like a blow at the pit of his stomach. Old Graves?

He had to force himself on. They hit the glare ice of a river and were almost upset by a rising wind. Skidding into the snow of a bank, they rose over this and dropped down a slope that overlooked the group of buildings. It looked like a trading post, with a few tattered Indian dwellings of reeds and mud gathered around the three log structures. Napier swung the sled in a great arc from the slope onto the flat, jamming his foot on the claw brake to spit a white froth up behind. The native dogs were already yapping wildly and lunging at their chains. Napier had a battle to gather Sallybrook's loose team up and chain them to the sled. The door in the main building had opened by then, and Charlotte Dumaine stood there.

Her hair seemed to have caught the blackest midnight and held it. Her eyes could catch a man the same way. Her fawnskin skirt was so white it looked as if the snow covered it, and the crimson sash binding her waist only made the swell of her breasts more noticeable.

"Vic," she said. "You *did* come."

"My partner got his foot caught in a trap," Napier told her.

"Is it bad?" Her voice held genuine concern. "Bring him in. Can we do anything?"

"No more than I've done already, unless you've got a doctor around," said Napier. Sallybrook was already climbing from the sled, and Napier was forced to turn and help him. With assistance from Charlotte Dumaine, they got the man to the door. Napier noticed, before stepping inside, that the shoe tracks they had followed went on past this building and disappeared among the Indian lodges.

It was a big, well-built room, boasting a rough wainscoting of pine. Charlotte's father stood aside to let them put Sallybrook in a chair. He had the girl's vivid face, Guillaume Dumaine, with a heavy, lustrous head of black hair, despite his fifty-odd years.

"Caught his foot in a trap, you say," he murmured. "How could that happen?"

"He had a light trap planted farther down the gully," Napier told him. "Somebody put this bear trap right in the spot he would have to cross to reach his own trap."

"They covered it with snow," offered Sallybrook. "And baited my own trap with a white fox to draw me in."

"They say the white fox comes when the lemmings migrate," smiled Dumaine softly.

"That so?" Those heavy, somnolent lids had dropped over Napier's eyes, giving them a hooded, disturbing look, as he stared at Dumaine. "You have a trading post here, Guillaume?"

"Yes." The man inclined his head southward. "Charlotte

told me she met you at Resolution. We were down there laying in supplies."

"With Marquette?" said Napier.

"Portage?" Dumaine chuckled huskily. "Did you meet him? Modest little fellow, isn't he?"

"Is he around?" said Napier.

The man's raised brows made a washboard of his forehead. "He seldom comes here, Napier."

"That's funny. I got the idea he worked for you."

"Why don't you make Vic's partner comfortable, Dad?" asked Charlotte. "I'll fix something to eat. Help me, Vic?"

The little switch of her hips made fawn-skin seduction of that skirt, leading him into a kitchen with the walls blackened by smoke behind the sooty pipe of an iron stove. She thrust in some fresh kindling, building the fire, and then put a teapot on to boil. From this, she faced toward him, something breathless in her voice.

"Tell me the truth, Vic. Are you up here with the police?"

He smiled wryly. "Is that why you were so distant at Resolution?"

"Did you want it any different?" she asked sharply. "You weren't much warmer than an iceberg yourself. I was just meeting you on your own ground, Vic. It was that man with you, wasn't it?"

"My partner?"

"Yes." She was staring intently at him. "Why didn't you want him to know how it had been between us, Vic? If the police had found out about me, they *would* have suspended you, wouldn't they? Or worse. Is that it? You're still with the police, and they don't know about us at Big Quill."

"Why do you keep harping on the police?" he said. "What's eating you, Charlotte? Are you mixed up in something here?"

A withdrawing speculation narrowed her eyes. "What could I be mixed up in?"

"The counterfeiting."

When her words finally came, they were in a whisper. "You *do* know."

"Everybody north of Chippewayan knows about that," he said disgustedly. Then the flesh of her upper arms was warm and resilient in the grip of his corded hands. "Charlotte, what are you getting at? What's going on?"

"That trap was obviously not set in your partner's path by accident."

"You speak as if you know," he said.

"I don't, Vic, I don't. Only, your partner would have died if you hadn't reached him in time. You can see that."

His grip tightened till she winced. "You *do* know, Charlotte. What is it you're trying to tell me?"

"Only that you're in some kind of danger, Vic. You can see that yourself. . . ." Her voice still held that denial, but the focus of her eyes had changed, even in the pain of his grip, till her attention, for a moment, was beyond him, toward the door.

"Your father?" he said in a husky undertone.

"Don't be a fool!" The heat of her words brought her hard against him. For a moment she stared into his eyes, then her nostrils fluttered with the breath she let out, and she sagged against him, saying in a barely audible, pleading way. "Vic, I don't know what's going on. All I know is you're in danger. If you're not still with the police, somebody must think you are. If you're only trapping, why don't you get out? There are other places. Saskatchewan. Peace River. Why not Peace River? I could meet you there. . . ."

"You said that last time. Quebec, then, wasn't it?"

"And who was it who didn't come?" she flared. "How long

151

do you expect a girl to wait? Do you think I didn't try to get in touch with you?"

He knew a vague, youthful sense of guilt, and could not hide it completely. That switch from regular service to C.I.B. had come just at the wrong time, preventing any trip to Quebec. And how many times afterward had his loyalty to the service been threatened by his feelings for this woman? Some of the tortured desperation he had known then must have showed in his eyes now, and the sense of guilt he could not hide, for she was looking up at him with a vague, indulgent triumph. Then it was something else in her eyes.

He saw it coming. He knew the danger of it, knew how much reason it had robbed him of before. But it was the only way he could tell. He had waited for seven years, and he had to know now. It started soft and tender, and ended hot and savage.

Finally she pulled her mouth away just far enough to speak, breathing heavily from the kiss. "Now, will you go, Vic? Peace River, just you and I?"

She waited his answer, arched back over his arm, staring up at him from eyes heavy-lidded as a freshly awakened child's. Then the strange expression on his face must have made its first impression on her, for she stiffened abruptly, asking in a strange, almost frightened voice: "Vic, what is it?"

"Oui, mes enfants," asked Guillaume Dumaine from the doorway. *"Qu'est-ce que c'est?"*

V

Sallybrook sulked in the cariole on the way out from the Dumaines' place, with the snow spitting in sullen sympathy from beneath the runners. Napier was still filled with the turmoil that kiss had left. He trotted behind the sled in silence.

For seven years he had looked forward to that meeting, to holding her, to kissing her. Yet, now, there was something in him still unresolved. It had been different from what he had expected. He was not naïve enough to expect it to be exactly as he had dreamed, for so long. The difference lay in something other than that inevitable gap between dream and reality. Had Guillaume's breaking in like that cut it off too soon? He shook his head, unable to answer that, feeling that if he could only have it again, for a moment, he would know what was wrong.

"You should have taken the whole pack into custody"— Sergeant Sallybrook's voice broke in on Napier's thoughts— "because those tracks led right up to the post."

"They were lost in the other tracks among the buildings before they reached Guillaume's place," said Napier. "It could just as well have been one of the Indians."

"Fat chance. You didn't find out anything from them, did you?"

"Not much," Napier told him. "They're a sullen bunch. Most of them wouldn't let me in their lodges."

"You still in love with Charlotte?" Sallybrook asked.

The abrupt transition took Napier off guard. He held his answer as they reached a smooth, downhill run, stepping onto the runners for the ride, where they could talk more easily. Then he spoke in a careful tone.

"What makes you think it was ever love, Sallybrook?"

"I'm not blind. She was mixed in with the Big Quill Lake affair, wasn't she? Why don't you tell me about it?"

Napier was silent, and finally the sergeant spoke again. "I'll tell you then. A bunch smuggling furs into the States from Big Quill. Charlotte and Dumaine mixed up with it in such a way that you couldn't tie them in clearly. You fall for the gal, and she convinces you she's clean. You arrest a couple of small fry to close the case, and let the Dumaines get away. And now you're doing the same thing here. You're getting soft, just the way you did then."

"I'm not getting soft, and you know it. We would have been stupid to put anybody in custody now. We have no proof of anything."

Napier halted himself with an effort, realizing how vehement his voice had become. He jumped off the runners and dropped back, watching the back of Sallybrook's head, wondering if he were smiling.

They spent the rest of the trip in silence, reaching the lodge on the Slave River about dusk. It was the dwelling of an ancient couple Napier had been cultivating. They were outcasts for having broken some taboo of the tribe, and their lodge was several miles north of the main Dog Rib village. They had been extremely appreciative of Napier's attentions and gifts, and he felt safe about leaving Sallybrook with them.

Sallybrook put up a big fuss about being left with them, but he was weakening from his wound and the exposure, and subsided once Napier got him inside, finally falling into a heavy sleep.

The days that followed were full of grueling routine for the inspector. He continued to string his trap lines and expand his contact with the Indians. There was much excitement over the appearance of white foxes this far south, and the possession of a white pelt or two was *entrée* into any camp. The Indians would give a dozen marten pelts for one fox fur, with plenty of talk in the trade. He soon found out the tribes were saving their pelts rather than turning them in to the Hudson's Bay post at Fort Chippewayan. They could get more, they said, from a traveling factor who paid them in treaty money instead of trade goods. When this man would appear, none seemed to know, or where. But Napier was sensitive to a growing tension in the country, and knew it would be soon.

He tried to see Sallybrook every day, but once in a while was drawn so far away from the lodge there on the river that he was gone for two or three days. After one of these longer intervals, he returned to find the old man not in his accustomed place by the fire. He asked the woman where he had gone, and she mentioned the village in a vague way. The wound had apparently been healing nicely. Napier moved over to talk with the sergeant where he lay on his bed of robes, with no intent of examination. But there was a ruddy glow to Sallybrook's face, and that made him feel the man's cheek.

"You've got fever," he said, startled by its heat.

"It's hot in here, that's all," growled Sallybrook.

"Teotenny!" It came from the woman, over by the great brass trade kettle spitted above the fire. It meant white man in their language, and the tone of her word held a dark, whispered portent that wheeled Napier to her. He saw the troubled darkness of her eyes, in a face of seams and furrows, and he moved over to her.

"I thought he was getting well, but the wound is infected," she murmured. "He will not admit it, but he is growing very weak. I put a new poultice of black root on it. I don't know if that will even draw the swelling out."

"Don't listen to that old squaw," called Sallybrook from the corner. "She'll have you burying me tonight."

He stopped as the Indian *giddes* started their canine chorus outside and Napier's own dogs joined in. The old man entered to this insane babble, stamping the snow off. He nodded greeting to Napier, speaking to the old woman.

"I did well at the village. A man is there paying treaty money for pelts. I got five dollars for our white fox."

It jolted Napier like a physical shock. Trying to hide the

reaction, he heard Sallybrook's violent movement behind, and turned to see the sergeant halfway out of his robes already. An eager light filled the man's eyes, and his mouth was open to say something. Then his eyes passed to the Indian, and he closed his mouth sharply. He did not sink back, however. His glance swung again to Napier.

"I'm going," he said, trying to get up the rest of the way. "I'm going with you."

"You're too sick," Napier told him, and moved swiftly to stop the man.

"No." Sallybrook was on his feet, struggling with Napier. "We've got to do it now, Napier. This is our chance. Forget about me, will you? I'm all right. I'm going with you."

There was just enough strength in the sergeant to carry Napier backward, gasping at him. "Damn you, Sallybrook, don't be a fool. It would kill you."

"I haven't got a soft spot. I'm going. I'm going . . . !"

Napier had seen that blank look in the sergeant's eyes before, and knew only one thing could stop him. It was a short blow to the button. Sallybrook raised up onto his toes. Then he fell back into Napier's arms, limp. Napier carried him back to the bed, covered him, took a last, reluctant look at that stubborn face. The two old people were staring at him, puzzled.

"Keep him here till I get back," he said, waving a hand at Sallybrook. Then he turned on his heel and stooped through the opening, untying his sled from a tree and mushing his dogs off.

For a while, the whispered crunch of Napier's snowshoes and the hissing spit of spruce runners were the only sounds. The pristine sentinels of timber fluttered by like the shadow pattern of a picket fence. Napier followed the old Indian's trail toward the village and was so intent on what lay ahead that the furtive movement through the stunted trees on his flank startled him. He started to call to the dogs, but they had already run free of this timber into a gully that lowered rapidly down a slope. Any abrupt halt in this would pile the sled on top of the dogs unless he had hold of the tail line from behind. He dove after the bobbing strip of *babiche,* meaning to grab it before shouting the order.

This took him right into the upper end of the gully. Bent over as he was, reaching for that tail line, the drifts piled up on either lip of the cut were several feet above him. He only had a dim impression of violent movement up there, and had turned part way toward it when the man came plunging down on him. It was the Indian they had met down on the Athabaska when their canoe sliced itself open on the rock, and in his hand was the wicked, crooked-bladed *bess-hath* that gave him his name.

Napier could do nothing but throw himself forward, twisting on around to try and block the knife with an upflung arm. That succeeded in deflecting the blade into the deep fur fringing the hood of Napier's parka, as Crooked Knife's leap carried him right on top of the inspector. Then both of them were rolling down the steep gully after the yelping dogs.

Napier caught the knife arm in both hands, pinning it in against his body as they rolled. He clung to it in battered desperation as they went over and over clear down to the bottom. Here, as they rolled to a halt on level snow, Napier came up on top. Crooked Knife tore his arm free and lunged for the guts. Napier jumped up and away, and this carried him with his back into the steep bank of the gully. All he could do here, before the Indian could rise after him, was kick the man in the face.

Crooked Knife fell back with an incoherent sound. Napier followed him over, putting his foot into that face again, with all his weight, and again, and again.

When it was over, Napier stepped back, breathing heavily. Crooked Knife's medicine bag had been torn off and the contents spilled all down the gully. The varicolored feathers of that war hat looked pathetic, somehow, mashed into the snow.

"That's one plume you won't put into your bonnet," muttered Napier, and turned to stumble after his dogs.

Napier stopped pushing his team within sight of the main village. The lodges were hardly recognizable as human habitations, so covered with snow they looked like a scattering of hummocks along the riverbank. Most of the village seemed to have gathered around a pair of sleds just free of the black timber. As he drew closer, Napier saw an Indian step from the crowd with a load of furs and dump them into one of those sleds. The man at the lazy-board of the sled bent to sort through the pelts. Napier was close enough to hear his voice now.

"Blue lynx. A hundred. White fox. Fifty."

The muttering started among the Indians as soon as Napier halted his sled, but it did not reach the man sorting the furs till he had straightened and pulled a sheaf of bills from his pocket to pay the Indian. By that time, Napier was in the front ranks with his Winchester.

"I'll take that money, Portage," he said. "In the name of the Royal Police."

For a moment Portage Marquette stood there with an inane leer on his face, making vague, childish gestures with his hands. Then he made a sound. It was hard to tell whether it was a chuckle or a burp.

"So you *are* with the poleez?"

"I am," said Napier. "Did Crooked Knife find that out for

158

you down on the Athabaska?"

A bestial suspicion drew Portage's little eyes together. "Crooked Knife?"

"You've got the idea,' said Napier. "I met him out on the trail. Only he wasn't quite as successful this time as he was with Corporal Richardson."

"Corporal"—that fatuous wave of the hand—"Richardson?"

"You know who I mean," Napier said.

"*Hein!*" The man grinned. "Maybe I do. Maybe he was the one who come all dress up in his red coat, hunting for the counterfeits. How foolish to come all dress up in his red coat. He didn't get half as far as you. I had the puzzle about you. I almost let it go too long, didn't I?"

"No almost about it."

"You are so confident," grinned Portage. Then he lifted his voice, speaking in Chippewayan to the restless Indians. "Did you hear this *teotenny?* He met one of your brothers down the trail. Bess-Hath . . . he met. They have fought. Now where is Bess-Hath? Killed, maybe?" The muttering grew louder among the Indians, and one buck called out something hoarsely. Portage wiggled his head from side to side, grinning at Napier more broadly. "What if I don't believe you are poleez? What if I ask for your proof? The red coat, maybe."

"You'll see plenty of them at Edmonton. Drop that money in the snow, Marquette, and step back. Then we'll go to where you've got the printing press."

"No red coat?" That guttural chuckle again belched from the swinish lips. Portage cocked his head to one side. "Something else to prove. A commission, perhaps."

Napier did not answer, staring at the man, seeing the sly intent growing in his black eyes. That sullen, ever-expanding sound and movement from the Indians made Napier realize what that intent was. He hadn't thought it would come from them, somehow. He had thought of them as a passive, neutral factor.

"No commission?" Portage tipped his head back the other way, his grin spreading. "It would be no matter. These Dog Rib cannot read. How foolish of you to do this with no proof of poleez."

"Listen, Marquette. . . ."

"You hear what this man says?" Portage had turned to the Indians, raising that sheaf of treaty money. "He killed your brother along the trail and comes here with the rifle for your money. Police, he says. Make him prove it."

Someone plucked at Napier's parka, and he whirled involuntarily. The buck cringed back from the Winchester, but there was more than fear in his face. There was a puzzled, growing anger, a hatred. And Napier could hear the words now. *Teotenny*. How scornful they could make it sound. Or *taislini*. "Devil," to them, had infinitely more odium than its English equivalent. Or *nezonilly*. Or worse. There was an insidious viciousness to the sound, like the growl of a savage dog behind a closed gate, that raised the hair down the back of Napier's neck. He realized Marquette would not have to whip them up much longer. Marquette was shouting at them again.

"How could he be the police? Police work for the government. The government gives you this money. She wouldn't send a man out to take it away again. This is your money, and he's trying to take him from you. How could I pay you for the furs then? He tries to take your living? You'll starve? Are you going let him? One man with a little rifle . . . just *one* man."

The restraint broke with an inundating babble of voices. A buck hooked one of Napier's arms from behind. He tried to

160

whirl free. Someone tripped him. His face went into the harsh surface of a parka. He had his gun against a body, but he knew a terrible reluctance to shoot. Then even the weapon was gone. His arms were pinioned from behind. A kick in the groin brought a sick, retching nausea. Then a commanding voice was speaking to Portage in Chippewayan.

"What shall we do, *Tingisuethli?*"—that one word revealed the influence Portage had with them, and how he must have gained that influence. It meant "white-man-who-has-turned-Indian."

"What do you do with your own *nezonilly?*" asked Portage, "your own evil ones?"

"The land takes care of its own," answered the chief. "If Chutsain sent him, Chutsain will take him back."

By the time the import of that reached Napier, they had his parka off and were tearing at his leggings. They were screaming and yelling like a pack of animals now, filled with the conviction that their most hereditary, inalienable rights had been violated. Napier had a last impression of Portage's greasy, leering face as the man turned to mush his dogs. Then that was gone, and they were lifting the inspector's nude, struggling body into the cariole of another sled, getting out whangs of rawhide to lash him in.

"Shut up, shut up, you filthy maggot-eaters, before I bring the whole Royal force down on your heads!"

The shout came from somewhere far off. Napier did not understand at first. All the screaming and yelling ebbed from around him in a dying tide. His body was no longer torn from side to side in that constant battering motion. He heard the strained breath close in through cut lips. Vision returned slowly. Finally he saw.

Sergeant George Sallybrook, at the edge of the village, in the proud scarlet tunic of the Royal Northwest Mounted Police, so sick and feverish he could hardly stand erect, holding the mob of them with the sight of the crimson coat that superseded their aboriginal gods in their respect and awe.

"Now, untie him and get him out of that cariole," Sallybrook said, swaying like a drunk with his fever. "And give me that rifle."

By the time they had lifted Napier out of the sled, the chief himself had picked up the Winchester and carried it over to Sallybrook. Napier groped around for his clothes, as the sergeant started his precarious trip to the sled. Something inane and obvious always came out at a time like that. Napier heard the words babble from him amid silly laughter.

"They were going to tie me in and take me out on the Barrens naked."

"You wouldn't have lasted long," offered the sergeant.

"I guess I should be grateful you're so damned stubborn."

"Gratitude's for old squaws. How did you get in this mess?"

"Portage Marquette," said Napier. He had his leggings on now, and some lucidity had returned. "Must have had a lot of influence with them. Whipped them up like this when I couldn't prove I was a policeman. He's got about ten minutes' start on us."

"You know where he's going?"

The sergeant's voice held a quiet portent, and Napier met his eyes for the first time. "I think so."

"You got the guts to do it?"

"I'm going after him, Sergeant," said Napier. "Can you make it back to the lodge?"

"No," said Sallybrook. "Couldn't walk another step." The cariole shrieked shrilly with his weight dropping over his side, and then his voice drowned that. "Now, by God, if you don't take me, I'll strip off this red tunic and then let them finish what they started."

162

VI

Napier did not feel the outside things too much. His perceptions were still too dazed for that from the beating he had received. He knew he ran, and rode the runners when he could no longer run. He knew a wind had sprung up, and it made a mournful sound through the timber. But, mostly, it was the inside things. It was the poignant, twisted pain somewhere in the spirit of him, running toward something he should have run away from, killing something, step by step, that he had tried to keep alive all these years since Big Quill Lake.

The Indians were gathered around the door of Dumaine's post when Napier pulled up. He got the Winchester and shoved his way through their stench. He went through the open door, shoving a shell into the magazine with a snap of the finger lever. The place had a cyclonic appearance. Furniture was overturned and trophies down off the wall. A trap door was open in the kitchen floor. The stairs led to a basement dug out of the earth. He wasted no time here, going outside again.

"They left the printing press in the basement," he said. "It looks like they've gone tripping with their pelts."

They left the chattering bunch of Dog Ribs behind and picked up the trail of three heavily laden sleds heading westward. The wind was rising and picked up the snow that sputtered from beneath the runners to lift it in great, powdery plumes behind. Napier tried to spare the dogs by again running himself. Each breath he took was like a cold knife blade cutting out his lungs. But that wasn't the greatest pain. Because he didn't know, he still didn't know!

"They're on that glare ice ahead." It was Sallybrook's

voice. Napier squinted his eyes to make out the three sleds crossing a broad expanse of ice-covered river swept bare and shiny as a mirror by the wind. He put the dogs into a slide down the bank, and the sled ran onto the ice with a clattering, banging sound.

The wind caught it like a sail, whipping the stern around. Napier grabbed for the tail line, trying to straighten it. But he slid on the ice and went off his feet. The rest of it was madness. The wind was rapidly becoming a gale, and, if he let go of that tail line, the sled would be blown right over. Yet he could not get onto his feet without letting go. For a long stretch, sliding, rolling, battering across the ice, he fought to regain his snowshoes without relinquishing his grip. But it was no use. The sled was going like an iceboat, with that wind on its quarter, and the dogs had all they could do to keep ahead of it.

Napier could see the three sleds ahead were caught up in the same thing. The lead outfit had already overturned, and the driver had thrown himself free to slide across the ice into the slush of the riverbank. Napier caught the ruddy flash of Portage's grizzly pelt coat as he regained his feet. Then the other two outfits were crashing into the first one with a crackle of spruce and a yelping of dogs.

Napier lost the rest of what was happening as his own outfit went into the bank. He made one last, wild effort to keep the sled from going over and dumping Sallybrook. But the wind came up from beneath and dumped the sergeant out on his belly.

From the bank, Portage was already firing at them. Sallybrook had the Winchester in his hands, and he struck the ice in a perfect, prone position—legs spread, elbows cocked beneath the rifle. All he had to do was let himself swing around toward Portage in his slide across the ice, and fire as his rifle muzzle crossed the target. It only took that one shot, and Portage went flinging backward.

Dazed by his own crash into the snowbank, Napier wobbled to his feet and started fighting through the slush. The other two drivers had already abandoned their outfits and were on the bank above, disappearing into timber. Napier stooped as he passed Portage's body to pick up his rifle. The man was lying on his belly and moaning, with his blood staining the snow beneath him.

The rifle was an old Krag-Jorgenson. Automatically, as he ran on, Napier pulled the bolt back to see if there was a live shell left. Fresh brass glittered at him, and he plunged into the timber, listening for the two ahead. When he heard the soft pump of their snowshoes, he called out.

"Guillaume, stop now! I don't want to start shooting! For Charlotte's sake, don't start shooting . . . !"

His answer was the crack of a rifle. The bullet ricocheted off a spruce behind him. He dodged on through the trees. Then, abruptly, he broke from the timber and saw a gully below. They must have met it as unexpectedly, and plunged down into the depression before realizing how exposed it left them. Guillaume was already half turned back toward Napier, his rifle coming up. Napier threw himself forward onto his belly in the same position Sallybrook had fired from back there on the river. It was the most accurate way. And Napier did not want to kill.

Guillaume's bullet puffed snow off the ground a foot to Napier's left. Napier's bullet caught Dumaine in the shoulder and spun him around and dropped him heavily against the steep, opposite bank of the gully.

Wide-eyed, Charlotte stared at her father for an instant. Then all the sand seemed to go out of her. "Vic," she gasped weakly, turning toward him, and sank to her knees. "Vic, oh, thank God, thank God. You *were* the police. I didn't know. I wasn't sure. I was so afraid you weren't."

He had reached her now, caught her elbows, lifting her up. "What are you trying to say, Charlotte?"

"Don't you know yet, Vic?" she said. "Didn't you understand back there at the post?"

"You weren't very clear."

"How could I be with Dad in the next room? I thought you understood."

"What? Understood what?"

"You don't know how hard it's been." Her face was against his chest. "All these years, Vic. I tried to stop him so many times. He got brutal toward the last. How could I do anything else, Vic? My own father. How many times I wished for your help. Your strength."

"You mean he was forcing you in on this?"

The shocked look to her widening eyes excluded any other possibility. "Vic," she said, clinging to him, "you're the only one who can understand. The rest wouldn't. Your partner's a policeman, isn't he? You know what he'd think. It *can* be Peace River now, Vic. I'll wait for you there."

"Will you, Charlotte?"

"You know I will." The throaty seduction filled her voice, and she started lifting her face to him that way. He let her do it, because it was the only way he could tell, really. When she finally pulled her lips away from the kiss, his eyes had that hooded look.

"You can't take all the sleds back with you," she said huskily. "I'll go on about a mile. Then, when you've left, I'll come back for one. With good weather, I can make Peace River. You know me in the woods, Vic."

"You're not going to Peace River. You're turning back with us."

166

It escaped her on a whisper. "What?"

"You're in this just as deep as your father, and you know it," he said. "As deep as you were back on Big Quill Lake. You didn't love me then any more than you do now."

"Vic, no . . . !"

"I guess I really should have known when you kissed me back at your father's post," he went on heavily. "There was something wrong. It didn't do what it used to. Unconsciously, I guess, I did know. But consciously I was still hanging onto a dream I'd had for seven years. I had to have it this way again to really know, Charlotte. Now I know I've been trying to keep something alive that wasn't ever there. Something that happened to a kid, back on Big Quill. You can't do it that way again, Charlotte."

"I'm glad to hear that," said Sergeant Sallybrook. Napier wheeled to see him sitting on the lip of the gully with the Winchester in his lap, a weak, feverish grin on his face. "I was afraid she'd find that soft spot in you, Napier. I thought maybe that streak of fat was still there. But I guess the trail's worn it off you. You're all nails now."

"You've got a lot of gravel in your own craw," said Napier. "Think you can last a few more miles?"

"Clear to Edmonton," grinned Sallybrook. "This wound ain't as bad as that old squaw would have you think."

"The wound's as bad as we thought. You're just tougher than we thought. I'll be proud to turn in this report with you, Sallybrook."

"I never returned a compliment before," the man grunted. "But I'll take my coat off to you and C.I.B. any day."

SKAGWAY'S SEAL

Skagway lifted his beer glass off the table and stared blankly at the wet ring it left on the oil cloth. Then he set it down again. He glanced over to where Blackie Karne and Martia Bennet were dancing, and the leathern skin of his face tightened till a network of seams appeared about his eyes. He looked away quickly as the music wailed to a stop. Blackie said something to the woman and headed for the bar. Martia came over the table and sat down.

"I thought you liked George's beer," she said.

Skagway shrugged. His eyes lifted from the full glass momentarily. The soft lights caught richly in her chestnut hair. Her large blue eyes held a subdued sparkle in a faintly flushed face.

"There's a waltz on now."

"I don't even do that," he said. "All I can do is sing a halyard shanty."

She put her elbows on the table, leaning forward. "You're always so short with me, Skagway. What is it? You won't even look at me."

He held up his hand, starting to say something. Then he looked over at Blackie Karne, his skipper on the Bureau of Fisheries boat, and let the hand drop. "I just can't see you on a B.F. boat. It's no place for a woman."

168

"I missed the regular run to the Pribilofs, and I've got to reach Saint Paul before the new term, that's all. Those kids haven't got anyone else to teach them." Martia ran her finger around the wet ring his glass had left on the tablecloth. "Or is it that?"

"Is it what?"

"Under ordinary circumstances, you wouldn't object to a woman on the *Chatinika*. You took me across last season. Are you expecting trouble this time?"

"What are you tacking toward?" he said.

"Blackie thought Tabor might show up here tonight."

That brought his head up. "He told you. . . ."

Whatever else he might have said was stopped by the slam of the door. Skagway twisted slightly in his chair. Then he turned to look. It was Tabor.

The big Aleut half-breed's mukluks made a soft, sighing noise against the sawdust of the floor as he advanced toward the bar. The hood of his Kotic parka was lined with dirty fox fur that framed his brown, fat, bland face. The grease on his beardless chin was so thick it looked ready to start dripping off any time.

"Blackie!" He grinned. "Look what we got . . . *hi yu* whisky tonight!"

Blackie had started from the bar with three fresh beers; he turned back and set them down with a loud clink. "Yeah," he said. "Plenty of whisky tonight. How's the halibut fishing, Tabor?"

Tabor went on up to the bar in his paddling walk, followed by three stolid Aleuts as bland and prodigious as himself. They ranged themselves along the rail without taking their eyes off Blackie.

"Four whiskies, George," said Tabor. "Halibut fishing would be fine if the Bureau of Fisheries didn't keep running

169

their survey boats back and forth across the banks all the time. What's the B.F. here for tonight?"

Blackie put one elbow on the bar and leaned his weight over against it. He drew his lower lip back against the fine white line of his teeth, and ran a thumb across the stubble of blue-black beard covering his outthrust jaw. "We heard you shipped aboard two dozen kenches for seals in Seward," he said.

The Aleut grinned. "Somebody's been feeding you herring bait."

"The Bureau of Fisheries doesn't get its bait from a halibut boat, Tabor," said Blackie. "We also heard you took on a thousand pounds of salt in Valdez."

Martia Bennet was leaning forward across the table toward Skagway, her eyes on the men at the bar. "Does he have to talk so loud?" she whispered.

"Maybe he wants them to hear," muttered Skagway.

Grinning, Tabor downed his jigger. "Maybe I'm salting my halibut instead of icing them this year."

"In kenches?" Blackie's voice sounded like anchor chain scraping a rusty hawse hole.

That bland smile was still on Tabor's glistening face. "You B.F. men get to thinking you own the whole Bering. Whether I shipped a half a ton of salt or a hundred tons wouldn't make any difference to you, Blackie. I got my clearance from the Navy."

Blackie's weight shifted toward Tabor. "You don't leave Kodiak harbor till you dump those kenches, Tabor. There'll be no seal poaching."

Martia was squeezing the edge of the table with both hands, and her eyes were squinted as if in pain. "Oh, Blackie, do you have to shout?" she whispered. "That's no way to handle them."

"My boat's in the harbor, Blackie," said Tabor. "I'm shipping anchor as soon as I leave Greek George's here."

"The hell you are!" yelled Blackie. "You're dumping that salt, Tabor, hear me, you're dumping that salt!"

"*Patrioti,*" said Greek George. He stood behind the bar, wringing his hands in a dirty rag. "*Patrioti,* let's not quarrel in Greek George's."

Tabor downed his drink and turned away. His three men moved to do the same.

"Tabor!" yelled Blackie, jumping after him to grab his shoulder. "I told you. You're not leaving!"

Martia's hand caught Skagway's arm. "Can't you do something . . . ?"

Skagway put both hands on the table and leaned forward. His face was turned toward the bar, but he had already spotted the half-empty bottle of Old Forester on the next table. It was tall and had a long neck.

"*Patrioti!*" shouted Greek George.

Tabor did it so fast Skagway could not see exactly what kind of blow it was. He saw the Aleut whirl back toward Blackie and lunge forward. Blackie's wind left him with a sick gasp, and his hands opened spasmodically off the other's fox-fur hood as he slid down the bar, trying to keep his feet. By the time he had lost his balance completely, Skagway was going for the bottle of Old Forester.

Blackie shook the floor with his falling, and Tabor leaped after him with one hand dipping beneath his parka. The mukluks of the three other Aleuts made a swift, shuffling sound against the sawdust as they spread out behind Tabor. They had knives in their hands.

"If you want to fight, Blackie . . . ," said Tabor, and the rest of it was lost in the tinkling crash the bottle of Old Forester made against the table as Skagway struck downward.

His whirl away from the table put him between Tabor and Blackie Karne. All four of the Aleuts stopped when they saw the broken bottle in Skagway's hand.

"Yeah," Skagway said, "let's fight."

The following sea lapped at the *Chatinika*'s stern like a hungry cat. The Wolmanized hull trembled faintly to the steady throb of the motors. Skagway's heavy, plaid Mackinaw made him top-heavy, and the slight roll to his bowlegged walk only accentuated that.

> Oh, Reuben Ranzo was a tailor,
> Ranzo boys, Ranzo,
> Oh, Reuben Ranzo was no sailor . . .

"Who was Reuben Ranzo, Skagway?" Martia Bennet interrupted.

He came to an abrupt stop at the end of the companionway. The seams in his leathery cheeks tightened up about his faded blue eyes. He let his gaze fall on Martia's face where she stood in the doorway of the wardroom. "Some say a Dago named Lorenzo," he said uncomfortably. "But that ain't a Dago name, and whoever heard of a Dago named Lorenzo? I met an old square-rigger once claimed it was Ronzoff, and he came from Poland. I learned it when I was. . . ."

"Go on," she said. "When you were what?"

"Nothing."

A faint smile caught at her mouth. "Why do you always stop that way with me, Skagway, as if you felt you were talking too much?"

He shrugged, turning to the gleaming Monel rail. On their port quarter, the twin helmet peaks of Bogoslov Island played hide-and-seek with the green swell. Martia moved to the rail beside him. "That broken bottle sort of soothed them down last night," she said finally.

"Nothing like it to put a damper on a fight. No use in all that blow, anyway. Blackie had no authority to make Tabor dump those kenches."

"How long have you been playing nursemaid to Blackie?" she wondered.

He turned to her involuntarily. "Nursemaid?"

"Blackie was making all the noise."

"I've seen Blackie handle worse than that," said Skagway.

"By yelling at them?"

"Why do you keep pulling on that shroud?" he said irritably. "Blackie can hold his own anywhere. He wouldn't be a skipper if he couldn't."

"Is that what he tells you?" She saw the look in his eyes and laughed softly. "I'm sorry, Skagway." Then she sobered. "How about you? Don't you ever want to be a skipper?"

"Maybe some men just don't have the capacity."

"I suppose you got that from Blackie, too."

"What are you tacking toward?"

"How long have you been with him? Since that time he saved you from drowning, Skagway?"

He pulled away from her hand on his arm. "Big blow off Nome. I went overboard with a swell. Blackie was the one that got me. I would have been dead if he hadn't."

"But how?"

"With a gaff," he said impatiently. "How else?"

She was silent so long he looked at her. "I don't know," she said. "I had a different idea. I mean, considering what's between you."

"No use diving into ice water, when all you have to do is reach outboard and hook your gaff on a man's pants as he goes by."

"I suppose not," she said. "I just had a different idea."

"That ain't the point," he growled. "I been with him a long time, that's all. A lot of things happen. A woman can't understand. He's master and I'm mate, that's all."

"Is it?" There was a restrained intensity in her voice. The lines of her body were taut against the wind. "I don't think so. I think you've been under his domination so long you've lost something. He talks a good boat, and you're ten times the sailor he is. I know, Skagway. I've taken enough runs from Kodiak to Saint Paul with you. You could be a master if you wanted to. If you quit listening to him and. . . ."

"I got to check the Fairbanks-Morse," he said, turning away.

"Skagway,"—she caught his arm—"why does it always have to reach this . . . with us?"

"You brought it up."

"Not just this. Everything. You're always trying to get away from me."

"Look,"—he met her eyes—"I'm just an old sailor. . . ."

"Thirty-five?" She started to laugh. But she was still looking into his eyes, and she didn't laugh. Her lower lip grew soft as she stared at him. "Thirty-five isn't old, Skagway."

"I didn't mean that." He moved his head from side to side, not looking at her now.

"Blackie?" she said.

"No!"

"Yes!" Her head raised sharply. "Yes." Her head dropped again, and her weight settled back on her heels. She let out a slow breath. "Even for a woman, then. I didn't think it went that far, Skagway."

"What do you mean?"

"Between you and Blackie," she said. "Even a woman."

"What about him and me?" asked Blackie Karne.

Skagway had not heard *Chatinika*'s skipper come down the companionway.

Blackie Karne stood there grinning, his lower lip pulled in flat against his teeth, rubbing a thumb across the stubble on his outthrust jaw. He dropped his hand and laughed. "You aren't trying to cut in on me, are you, Skagway?"

"Is it funny?" asked Skagway.

Karne threw back his head and roared. "Funny?" Still laughing, he jerked his thumb at Skagway and looked at Martia. "An old sea dog like you with bowlegs and a walrus head for a face. . . ." Karne stopped abruptly.

Martia had not answered his laugh. The breeze whipped up her thin wool skirt against the curve of her leg. She had been looking at Skagway, and her eyes were big and dark.

Karne glanced from the sober woman to his mate. His mouth relaxed from the laughter. "Wait a minute," he said.

"I gotta go check the fresh water system," said Skagway.

"I told you to wait a minute!" Blackie grabbed his arm as he tried to whirl away. Karne stood there, holding Skagway by the coat sleeve. He looked at Martia again. "Maybe it's not as funny as I thought. What's going on between you? You're not really trying to cut me out, are you, Skagway?"

"What do you think?"

"Don't talk to me that way," growled Karne. He grasped Skagway's lapel and jerked him around square. "Answer me. What kind of course are you charting with this woman?"

"Don't do that, Blackie. We been together a long time. . . ."

"That's right. We've been together a long time." Karne yanked Skagway in by the lapel until their faces were almost touching. Skagway could smell the oil and sweat of Blackie's body. "We've been together a long time, and, when I picked you up, you were nothing but a puking, dying little wharf rat

175

living on herring chum the canneries wouldn't even feed to the fish. If I hadn't come along and given you a berth on the best B.F. boat in the Bering, you'd have been chum for the fish yourself right now!"

"Blackie. . . ."

"No!" Karne whirled him around and slammed him back against the wardroom so hard the whole structure shuddered. "Just because you can hang onto the wheel, you think you can be a skipper? You saw what was between me and Martia. You've known all along. What right have you to do this? A stinking, chumming, little wharf rat like you. What right?"

Rigid against the wall of the wardroom, Skagway could see Martia's face over Blackie's shoulder. She had been up on her toes, staring at him. But as Blackie held him there, shouting in his face, she dropped back, slowly. Her eyes narrowed, and her mouth twisted in some expression and then thinned. She put her hands on the Monel rail and leaned back, watching woodenly.

"I ought to dump you off right now," said Blackie. "I ought to. . . ."

His mouth was still shouting the words, but Skagway could not hear him. The other noise drowned it out. It was a wild, screaming sound. The boat rocked and shuddered.

The steady throb of the diesels turned into a clanging, crashing roar. Then that stopped, and there was a muted screech dying below decks as the boat wallowed in a soundless sea.

In the abrupt, awesome silence, Blackie released Skagway and whirled toward the end of the wardroom. The clang of someone scrambling up the ladder from below entered Skagway's consciousness. The engineer's hands appeared on the edge of the engine room hatch. Oil beneath his nails formed ten black half-moons at the tips of his fingers. His greasy face rose above the sill.

"Piping from the Fairbanks-Morse got torn loose somehow and dropped in the shaft alley of our port engine," said Kickup.

"How much damage?" Blackie asked him.

"Nothing permanent," said the engineer. "Threw all the pistons out of line. Made a mess of the shaft bearings. Take a helluva long time to fix."

Blackie's eyes hardened. "How long?"

Kickup wiped the back of an oily hand across his face and only succeeded in smearing more grease on his cheek. "We'll be a couple of days late striking the Pribilofs, if that's what you mean."

"That's what I mean," said Blackie.

The Pribilofs were garmented in summer livery, a pastel riot of grasses and moss covering the slopes and casting limpid, green shadows in the hollows. The beach seethed and heaved with one, solid, shimmering mass of barking, croaking, bellowing seals, and a mob of bachelors was frolicking out through the surf to meet the dory as she pulled away from the *Chatinika*.

They said he was a lubber, Ranzo boys, Ranzo,
And they made him eat whale blubber, Ranzo . . .

"Will you shut up, Skagway!" shouted Blackie from the bow, "and get us out of these crazy sikets!"

Skagway leaned hard on the tiller, veering the double-ended boat away from the cavorting animals. "They won't hurt anything," he muttered.

Huddled over her luggage just behind the oarsman, Martia twisted toward him. "They will, Skagway. I've seen what can happen. Last year a couple of Aleuts in a baidarka were trying to separate a bachelor from the herd. One of them got excited and speared him. When the others smelled blood, they stampeded and turned the boat over and killed . . . ."

"That's different," he said. "The blood crazes them. I saw an old bull down on Bogoslov go wild when he smelled blood. He stampeded the whole herd right into the water."

The double-ender ground its bottom on the sand, and Skagway jumped over the thwart. Green brine foamed around his sealskin mukluks as his feet churned the sandy bottom, running the dory onto the beach. After beaching the boat, Skagway hoisted Martia's two suitcases. They had searched the beach for a boat without sighting one, but Blackie stood now staring across the writhing bodies on the beach, running his thumb across his jaw.

"I told you that was crazy about Tabor," said Skagway. "Poaching is out of date. That piping must have just worked loose and fallen into the shaft alley."

Blackie did not answer him, but Martia turned momentarily. "Are you going with me and Blackie across the island?"

"No, he's staying here!" Blackie's voice was harsh. He whirled around and picked up the suitcases. "It's a good two-hour walk to the village. Somebody's got to stay here and start taking census." He turned toward the bluffs, throwing this last over his shoulder to Skagway. "I told Kickup to take her offshore a couple of miles. That wind coming up is liable to blow him on the rocks if he stays in too close."

Once, before they reached the bluffs, Martia turned to look back at Skagway. He started to wave, then dropped his hand. He took a black book and pencil from his coat and started toward the first seals. The early sealing had been so profligate that it actually threatened the extinction of the animals, and so, to prevent this, a treaty had been made between

Japan, Great Britain, Russia, and the United States whereby the sealing would be controlled by the governments interested. Since 1911 the Bureau of Fisheries had taken annual census of the herd and selected the surplus males among a certain age group to be killed for their hides.

Kickup was already pulling the *Chatinika* away as Skagway stopped at the first harem to take count. The bull was a great, hoary old sultan that must have weighed six hundred pounds. He raised up on his lava throne, grumbling a warning at Skagway, and his harem of shimmering brown cows shifted nervously about him, barking and squealing. The *Chatinika* was out of sight in the fog lying off St. Paul, and the wind had risen to a dismal howl by the time Skagway found the kench.

The wooden, trough-like structure was in a deep cove between two lava shelves and would be visible only from this narrow area at the open end of the cove. Skagway put his pencil and book away and worked through the seals toward the kench, looking down. The leathery skin tightened about his faded blue eyes till a network of seams surrounded them. The kench was full to the brim with salted hides.

"No, Skagway, don't go back to the dory for your rifle."

Skagway stopped his motion toward the boat. Then he turned back. Tabor stood on the rising shelf above him with an Enfield .380 in his hand.

"How did you get aboard to loosen that piping?" Skagway asked finally.

"If you'll remember," grinned Tabor, "a bunch of Aleuts were paddling around in their baidarkas the day you hit Kodiak. Kickup shouldn't have let them aboard to trade for that tinned beef. In the confusion, my man got a chance at the piping on your Fairbanks-Morse. He assured me it would delay you four or five days. The Coast Guard cutter on this run doesn't pass until next Sunday. It would have given us

179

plenty of time. How did you repair it so fast?"

"Maybe Kickup's a better engineer than your man fig-ured," said Skagway. "You know what kind of head wind you're bucking?"

"I do," said Tabor. "The return is worth it. I've already got my contacts on the mainland. I'll make more on this one deal than I would in ten years off the halibut."

Skagway turned in the direction Tabor waved the Enfield and climbed up the shelf. He heard the shuffle of Tabor's mukluks as the man started up behind. A flock of black auks startled Skagway, whirring into the air with loud, scraping cries as the two men climbed the lava. The breeze had been coming from the sea, and that was why the stench had not reached Skagway before this. As he topped the rise, his mouth twisted with the nausea of that first fetid odor. Then he could see the carcasses.

Tabor's men had driven a herd up from the beach and were separating it into pods of twenty or thirty. A pair of Aleuts, working in a pod already separated, were in the act of stunning a young bachelor with a blow to the head. As the seal grunted and sagged, the man with the knife stabbed him in the heart. Then with swift, skillful strokes he made a cir-cular cut around each fore flipper. The skin came off like a bag with two holes where the flippers had been. Tabor waved the revolver again to one side. Skagway's jaw dropped a little when he saw them. Then he moved heavily through the soggy mess covering the bluff.

"Walked right into them," said Blackie Karne. He was sit-ting on the side of a half-filled kench.

Martia Bennet's eyes met Skagway's. They held a wide darkness. Tabor called one of his Aleuts over and handed him the Enfield, speaking to him in their own language. The men had finished skinning and salting the hides of this herd, and they followed Tabor down the lava shelf to get another pod of bachelors from the rookeries there.

"They drive them up here to kill so it won't be visible from the sea," said Martia. "That's why we didn't spot them from the boat. Tabor didn't expect us to get here so soon, but he wasn't taking any chances. As soon as Kickup pulls far enough away, Tabor's going to bring his boat in on this side of the cove where they can't spot her from the *Chatinika*, and load on the skins."

"That's taking a big chance on smashing against these rocks," said Skagway.

"Hasn't he already taken some big chances?" Her lips were pinched and white. She searched his face for something. Then she waved her hand vaguely at the Aleut guarding them. "You don't think . . . ?"

"No," said Blackie, raising his head. "They'll load the furs and shove off, that's all. We have nothing to worry about."

"Why not face it?" said Skagway. It turned both of them toward him sharply. He shrugged, looking at Martia. "Trying to spare you would only be silly. You can see it as well as we can. Tabor's got to have time to get away. If he leaves us here, we'll jump for the *Chitinika*'s radio the minute Kickup pulls back in. There's a dozen B.F. and Coast Guard boats between here and the mainland. Do you think Tabor's going to have that, after going this far?"

"But"—Blackie turned part way toward Martia—"a woman . . . ?"

"Indians don't look at a woman the same way we do, Blackie."

The blood had drained from Martia's face. Her lower lip trembled slightly. She clamped her mouth shut. She looked from Blackie to Skagway; then her eyes passed across to the Aleut. She drew a thin breath between her teeth. "He doesn't speak English very well," she said.

Skagway waited a minute, watching Blackie. The skipper met his gaze momentarily, without saying anything. Then Blackie's eyes shifted. Skagway licked his lips, turning to Martia.

"You game?" he said.

"It's better than waiting for it," she said.

"Then start bawling," said Skagway. "Make a big fuss over her, Blackie. Get her away from this kench."

Martia sniffed a couple of times. The Aleut glanced at her closely. Then she started crying loudly.

Blackie slid down the kench toward her. "No, no," he hissed at them. "He's right on top of us with that Enfield. He'll blow the hell out of us the minute we move. We can't do anything, Skagway. . . ."

"Get her off that kench," Skagway said between his teeth.

Blackie made a half-hearted gesture toward Skagway with his hand. Then he saw Skagway's eyes. He put his arm around Martia's shoulder and helped her up. The Aleut took a step forward, grunting something. Blackie and Martia stumbled away from the kench. Skagway couldn't tell whether it was the woman pulling Blackie or not. She was bawling louder than ever. For that moment, all the Aleut's concentration was on them. The Aleut took another step forward, shouting something. Skagway stooped over and grabbed a salted hide. He had whirled with it before his motion caught the Aleut's attention. He hit the Aleut full in the face as the man fired.

Skagway felt a blow on his leg that almost knocked it from beneath him as he threw himself at the man. He struck the Aleut's face. Skagway saw the man's finger squeeze the trigger again, but no sound came except a hollow click, and the gun wasn't pointed the right way anyway. Skagway had the .380 torn from the man's hand before they hit the ground. He straddled him and raised up and struck with the gun butt. The sealskin was still across the Aleut's face as Skagway got to his feet. He took a lurching step and fell down again.

"I guess I shipped one," he said.

Martia was on her knees beside him. "Skagway."

He broke the gun open. "This won't do no good. The first fired shell jammed in there. That's why it didn't go off the second time."

Martia took the .380 from him, tore her nails in a desperate attempt to rip the shell out. "Blackie, can't you do something?" she panted, shoving it at him. He tried to eject the shell without much success. Tabor's men had gathered down among the harems and were starting up the lava shelf.

"You and Martia get going," said Skagway. "You might make the village."

"Don't be a fool," said the woman.

"You going to throw away the only chance?"

"We're not leaving you," said Martia.

"But he's right," said Blackie. "This is our only chance, Martia. We could make the village."

She turned toward Blackie without saying anything. His eyes dropped before hers.

Skagway shifted painfully. "There's one other way."

"What?"

"There's still a lot of seals between us and Tabor."

It struck them about the same time. "Don't be a fool," said Blackie. "It'd be suicide. If the seals didn't get you, Tabor would. They've got guns."

"You're talking as if Skagway could do it," said Martia. "How could he get down there with a hole through his leg?"

They were both looking at Blackie now. He took a half-step backward. An odd, putty color was beneath his beard.

"Think I'm crazy?" he said.

"It's the only chance, Blackie," said Skagway.

"No," said Blackie. "Don't be crazy. There isn't a chance!"

Skagway looked up at him for a moment. Then he got a clasp knife from his pocket and opened it. He got to his knees; his face grew white and twisted. He stumbled forward, catching the kench to keep from falling. The woman caught at him.

"Skagway . . . !"

"Get her, damn you," Skagway bawled at Blackie. "Get her."

"Don't be crazy, Martia." It was Blackie's voice behind him. "You'll never get out alive. Let him go. They've got guns."

"Skagway, Skagway, please, Skagway!"

He stumbled on down the shelf with her yelling behind him, and then lost her voice in the other sounds. Some of them were his own. He kept grunting in pain. Some of it was Tabor's. They shouted and began firing. The harems began to stir restlessly as the noise of the shots reached them over their own bedlam of barking.

He spotted the first big bull and lurched toward it. The rest was a crazy madness of running and stumbling, fighting the pain, going down the lava with Tabor and the Aleuts shooting and screaming and coming up toward him. Skagway threw himself directly toward the bull. He felt his knife blade sink into its throat, and ripped downward. The bull's bellow changed to a scream of pain. Then the heavy body struck Skagway. His hand was torn off the knife, and he went to the ground with the sense of an infinite pulsing, heaving, screaming weight bearing him down. The deafening sound enveloped him.

He lay there in a stunned eternity beneath that black convulsion. It took him a long time to become aware the throbbing had changed to the region below his body. Hazily he rolled over, and saw it. The stream of blood the bull had left led down the lava shelf to the beach, and there the animal, still gushing from its crimson throat, was flopping toward the sea. The scent of its blood and its crazed behavior and frenzied bellows had set the other harems off. Skagway could not see Tabor and the other men. The beach was not visible. It was hidden by a solid, shimmering carpet of writhing, crawling, maddened seals, all heading for the sea. It took a long time for Skagway to make out Tabor and his men. There were many bodies of the seals strewn on the beach, trampled by the others. Finally Skagway could see Tabor. He lay in a twisted, motionless heap.

"Skagway. Skagway. Skagway."

She said it three times like that, in a muted, husky whisper. She was kneeling by him, her hands touching his bloody face hesitantly.

Her lips were against his, and that chestnut hair was soft on one side of his face before he realized what she was doing. He took a heavy, shaky breath.

"Don't take on so. That bull might have cracked a couple ribs, rolling on me like that. No more." Past her head, he could see Blackie Karne, just coming down the lava shelf. Suddenly he laughed. "You know," he said, "I think I'll take a stab at those master's papers when we get back to Kodiak."

HARD-ROCK MAN

When the log began to spit, Kurt Shaeffer instructively reached out to shove it farther into the fire. He stopped himself with a muttered curse, looking down at his wrists, where the flickering light played ruddily over the bright metal of the handcuffs.

Sitting across the fire, his back along the long Cree sled, Eugene Cowle put out a moccasined foot and worked the log into the flames. It stopped spitting.

Shaeffer raised his shaggy head, voice coming through his black beard like the growl of a surly bear.

"I still don't know how you figure in it. This is Mountie country."

"We might have left you with the Northwest Mounted if you'd just blown up the building," said Cowle. "The guard you killed was a U.S. deputy marshal."

He was a big, broad-shouldered man, this Shaeffer, his craggy face half hidden by the beard he had grown fleeing into Canada. He wore a thick Mackinaw coat and duffels under his heavy, laced boots. Turning so he could look directly at Cowle, he grinned. "The sucker died then?"

"Your bullet punctured his lung. He didn't last the night," said Cowle, almost inaudibly. "I sat up with him. . . ."

He trailed off. He was a short, square-built man, much smaller than Shaeffer. The hood of his jacket was lined with white fox, and the hair falling from beneath it showed streaks of gray. His wind-burned face was shaped by the deep lines that come to a man in later life, yet his clear blue eyes, gazing into the fire, were young enough.

He didn't see the crackling flames, or the dogs chained to the spruce trees beyond, or the endless Canadian night that had closed in about them. He saw viscid, red blood spreading from beneath a body that lay among the blasted bricks and mortar, the old bank building near the water that Kurt Shaeffer had dynamited.

"You've done some mean and low-down things in the thirty years I've known you, Kurt," said Cowle suddenly. "But this is a new low."

Shaeffer hunched forward sullenly, pulling his Mackinaw coat tautly around the tremendous bulk of his shoulders. "Hell! I just make a play for money anywhere I can get it, that's all." Shaeffer's bloodshot eyes widened. "Don't tell me it was you staked out in that hotel?"

"Some of your outfit have been working Seattle for a long time," said Cowle. "The gold steamers coming down from Nome, the returning prospectors bringing back dust and nuggets. But you couldn't have known that old brick building you blew still happened to belong to the government. It hadn't been sold yet to Wells Fargo, so naturally the gold you were after wasn't there. That's why the government spotted a marshal to guard its property."

Shaeffer laughed. "I figured there'd be some sort of a guard in the place. I planted the detonator in a little room at the back. He was a damned fool to come blasting out that way."

"He got a good look at you, Kurt. When he described you, I knew who'd shot him."

"Well, I didn't get a good look at *him*."

"Of course not," growled Cowle. "The light from the open door was behind him."

"But how'd you know I'd be at that hotel?"

"I told you some of your outfit had been working up there a long time. We rounded up most of 'em after you did your job. They talked enough. They told us where you would come to collect for your job, and when."

"You government tin stars couldn't trap a fool hen sitting on a limb," laughed Shaeffer. "I bet you still don't know how I gave you the slip."

Cowle said: "We heard the laundry chute bang."

Shaeffer glanced at him from beneath heavy, black brows. "You must be close to fifty, Cowle. How is it you've got such a man-killing job as this? Didn't you have any younger men?"

"Not with my background," said Cowle. "And I sort of asked for the assignment."

Amazement crept into Shaeffer's voice. "Asked for it! You mean you *asked* 'em to let you trail up here into this god-forsaken corner of hell?"

"Something personal, Shaeffer."

Shaeffer's bloodshot eyes were puzzled for a moment; then he threw back his head and began to laugh. "You don't mean to tell me you've been waiting all this time to get back at me for Sheila? Not eighteen years, Cowle! I always knew you were a queer duck. But eighteen years! All for a cheap little cheat like Sheila."

Cowle bent forward suddenly, face twisting like a man whipped. His mittened hand tightened around the Winchester in his lap. For a moment he was held that way. Then he relaxed, and his shoulders sagged, and his voice had a weary sound. "Sheila wasn't a cheat, Kurt. She was a good woman. I wouldn't expect you to realize that. I'll admit I wanted to kill you at the time. But I never really blamed her.

A woman can't help something like that. Maybe if I hadn't married her first, she would have married you. And, as you say, it's a long time ago. No, I didn't come out here after you because of Sheila."

He rose stiffly. An axe leaned against the sled. Beside it was a pile of spruce Cowle had cut. He didn't put the Winchester down. He had seen the gleam in Shaeffer's eyes.

"I heard you weren't with her when she died, Kurt."

"Sheila?" said the other. "I didn't know how bad she was. And Keslinger was going to climb Kinchinjunga again. You know I couldn't miss that. I was even expecting you to show up."

"I figured a man should stop climbing mountains when he got married," said Cowle, shoving the log into the fire. "And after Sheila left me, there were other things."

"Yeah, yeah. She told me you had a son."

Cowle drew a black wallet from the inside pocket of his Cree jacket, and handed it to Shaeffer. The black-bearded man glanced momentarily at the small silver badge pinned to one flap, then at the picture of the smiling boy. Cowle watched his weathered face for a sign of recognition. There was none.

"Sheila named him," Cowle finally said. "Paul. He was two years old when she went away with you."

"Makes him about twenty now, doesn't it?" said Shaeffer. "Did he inherit your wanderlust?"

Cowle's voice was hardly audible. "He went into government service."

"The hell you say! Another little do-or-die tin badge, eh? Just like his dad." Shaeffer looked up at Cowle, and his voice was malicious. "Got Sheila's eyes, too."

Cowle opened his hand and held it out for the wallet. His jacket was open in the front. Instead of handing back the wallet, Shaeffer poked him in the belly.

"Getting soft around there, Cowle," he said, grinning, then nodded toward the jagged, black peaks of the Caribou Mountains on their back trail. "Too soft to follow me if I got over the mountains into the Barrens."

"Why," said Cowle indifferently, "do you think I planned to intercept you on this side?"

Shaeffer's laugh grated on Cowle's nerves.

He took the wallet and put it inside his jacket. His hand slipped across the cold butt of the .45 Colt through his belt. It was the gun he had taken from Shaeffer.

The sled was a Cree *odobaggon,* a canvas cariole shaped like a bathtub and lashed to a spruce frame between the runners. Cowle moved over to get the sleeping bags. He bent into the cariole, free hand curling around the *babiche* lashings that held the bags in their roll. The movement took his eyes off the other man for just that instant.

He heard Shaeffer grunt as he leaped.

Cowle dropped the bags and whirled. Shaeffer was big and blurred, charging in on top of him, cuffed hands raised to form a vicious bludgeon. Cowle threw himself desperately to one side, and Shaeffer's blow missed him. As the big man crashed on by, Cowle hit him a wicked a backhand blow that caught Shaeffer on the neck just below his ear, sending him falling heavily against the sled. The spruce frame snapped beneath his hurtling weight. He rolled off into the snow and lay there groaning.

Cowle stumbled, looked at the big man in the snow. "Did you really think I was that soft, Kurt?"

Day began before the morning star was dim. Cowle had slept with his head beneath the cariole. He awoke to find that it was the only part of him not buried under the blanket of snow that had fallen in the night. Shaeffer's head was protected by a shelter formed of four stakes driven into the ground, supporting the sled cover that was stretched over them.

Because the dogs would have gnawed through leather or rope, they were hitched at night by chains, each to a separate tree. Cowle had used a dog chain on Shaeffer, attaching one end to the handcuffs, hitching the other around a spruce. It was long enough for the man to sleep with his hands inside the bag.

From time to time, Shaeffer glanced at the Caribous, bright in the morning sun, snow saddles gleaming brilliantly, rock faces harsh, cruel, and magnificent.

"Maybe you couldn't have gotten over them anyway, Kurt," said Cowle. "The snow's pretty deep, and you didn't have a sled. You'd have had to take a few rock faces."

"I've climbed enough rock faces in my time," Shaeffer said.

"Did you?" asked Cowle softly. "I seem to remember one on the Matterhorn you fumbled. Then there was Mont Blanc. Why won't you ever admit you're no good on the rock, Kurt?"

Shaeffer's face darkened; his voice was thick. "I can take any rock face you name."

"Kronstadt didn't think so," said Cowle, tossing a chunk of fish to his big Chippewayan butt dog. "Remember what he told you that time in Zurich?"

Shaeffer half rose, mouth twisting. "Kronstadt didn't know a rock face from a sérac. He was an old fool."

"He was the best mountain climber we'll ever have the privilege of knowing," said Cowle. "He said you fought the rock instead of climbing it, remember? He said you didn't belong on the mountain because you didn't understand the rock. And because you didn't understand it, you were afraid of it."

Shaeffer jumped to his feet. His voice was almost a scream. "I'm not afraid of anything, damn you, Cowle! I tell you there isn't a rock face in the world I can't take. I'm not afraid. . . ."

He stopped suddenly, looking around, mouth still open. The dogs were watching him with a peculiar intensity in their bright eyes. Then his heavy breathing was the only sound. He closed his mouth. His bloodshot eyes swung around to meet Cowle's.

"You shouldn't let it get you like that, Kurt," Cowle said. He jerked his Winchester toward the sled.

Shaeffer got the two butt dogs first and hitched them to either side of the trace, Nome-style. He didn't speak again until he was through with the leaders. "I still think you came after me because of Sheila."

Cowle hunched down inside his fur-lined jacket, feeling suddenly very old and tired. Couldn't Shaeffer understand that eighteen years was too long for a man to hold a hate? No, Shaeffer couldn't, because he was the kind of a man who would hold that hate, cherishing it, fanning it higher through the years.

His mouth drew down bitterly, and his voice had a dull sound. "I don't care what you think, Kurt. Get in."

The sled trembled as Shaeffer settled his weight into it.

On the flat lazy-board Cowle had rigged a sling for the Winchester. He wanted his hands free to drive. It was out of Shaeffer's reach. He slipped the .30-30 in, bent inside it to strap on his snowshoes. Then he rose and uncoiled the long dog whip.

"Mush!"

A last line of foothills lay between them and the level

country around Caribou Lake. Cowle tried to take a snow saddle through, but the fall had been heavy the preceding evening, and slush continually popped up from beneath the runners into his face. He caught Shaeffer watching him from the corner of his eye.

The sides of the ridge were steep, and, when they reached the top, the snow saddles on either side were far beneath them. Cowle wouldn't need the whip till they reached the bottom. He jumped onto the rear of the sled, let the long lash settle into the back of the cariole.

"Kurt! Stop!"

Screaming that, Cowle lurched over the lazy-board in a futile effort to grab the man. Shaeffer already had the long whip howling out over the dogs.

"Mo-o-sh, you black Cree devils!"

The dogs knew they were mushed by a master. They burst into a dead run, flattening out down the steep ridge. It took Cowle that long to comprehend Shaeffer's intention, the sled quivering beneath him with the speed of its suicide run. Cowle let go the lazy-board and tried to fall away backwards, kicking free.

But Shaeffer had thrown himself from the cariole even before he was through yelling. He hit the snow running. As he went down, he gave the sled a shove.

The tail end switched around. Cowle's snowshoes weren't yet off the rear when a runner slid from the ridge. The sled tilted violently. Cowle's right shoe caught slantwise between the spruce runners. The butt dog slipped, pulling the others with him. When the whole outfit rolled over into space, Cowle was carried with it.

His last conscious act was to jerk forward and wrench the Winchester from its sling, throwing it far out ahead of him so it would hit in the deepest part of the drift below. Then Cowle hit against the steep side of the ridge for the first time, and the heavy sled came down on top of him with the howling, yapping dogs, and that was all he knew.

Cowle regained consciousness with a sense of soft, white suffocation. He was lying deep in the snow, a smashed runner holding him down. His head throbbed like a Chippewayan medicine drum.

With his bare hand he could feel the blood caked over his head and on the fox fur of his hood. He remembered the sled falling on him. All that blood would make a man look dead enough. Maybe that was why Shaeffer hadn't bothered to finish the job.

Cowle felt inside his jacket. He had put Shaeffer's gun in his belt. It was gone, of course, and also the keys to the cuffs. Sudden panic went through him. His hand slid up to the inside pocket. Then he relaxed. What would Shaeffer want with his wallet?

Cowle crawled painfully out of the snow, using the broken runner to pack it down beneath him. He saw Shaeffer's footprints coming down from the ridge. He felt confident the man hadn't found that Winchester. It would have sunk down.

Five dogs lay dead in their traces. Two of them Shaeffer had butchered for meat. What did he have then? A .45 automatic, a pair of snowshoes, an axe.

Cowle looked northward to the jagged Caribous. That was where Shaeffer had looked. The Barrens were beyond. Once in the Barrens, a man like Shaeffer would be safe. Cowle reached inside his jacket and drew out the wallet. The federal badge gleamed as he opened it.

With the eyes of a man whose whole life had been built around his son, he looked for a long moment at the picture of the smiling boy, Paul.

★ ★ ★ ★ ★

Eugene Cowle sighted the man he was following on the second day. He had constructed crude snowshoes from the sled. The Crees lashed their *odobaggons* with *babiche*—untanned strips of moose hide. Cowle split the spruce runners down until they were thin enough to warp. He used the *babiche* for webbing and foot straps. Already the makeshift webs were coming apart.

Shaeffer hadn't left him a knife, and raw dog meat two days ago was the last food he had eaten. He had traveled the night without sleep. His moccasins had gotten wet and were frozen to his feet. He felt sick and dizzy and weak. But all that ceased to matter the moment he sighted Shaeffer.

Shaeffer had climbed enough mountains. He knew the dangers of those drifts. With a sled he might have chanced it, but he had no sled. He was working across on the higher slopes. The rock face ahead of him was unavoidable if he wished to stay out of the drifts below. Cowle saw him cross a narrow plateau and stop before the sheer rise of granite.

Cowle smiled thinly, murmuring: "You'd be a fool to take that snow on my shoes, Kurt. And you said you weren't afraid of the rock."

He caught a movement that might have been Shaeffer's head turning to glance at the drifts below him. The man's diminutive figure seemed reluctant, working out onto the granite. He hadn't seen Cowle yet. He climbed cautiously.

Cowle let him get well out onto the face, then he slung the makeshift webs over his shoulder and broke into the open. He was halfway across the level when Shaeffer caught sight of him.

Cowle had hoped to get closer before the man spotted him. But it had to happen sooner or later, and he had known exactly what he was facing. He was light-headed from lack of food and sleep, and from the altitude, and the gun didn't hold the threat for him it should have. He grinned thinly. A man who was afraid didn't make a very good shot anyway.

Shaeffer had quit moving across the rock, and was waiting. He kept shifting nervously, bracing his feet anew every few moments, looking up the sheer face, then down at the snow névé so far below. He held his fire till Cowle had crossed the plateau and was working out the first of the rock.

The shot echoed down into the snow-filled col. The bullet went wide. Cowle saw Shaeffer lift the Colt .45 again and take careful aim. He found a fissure and slid into it; the slug plucked at his sleeve. It ricocheted off the granite behind him and screamed into space.

Beneath the sound, Cowle heard Shaeffer's curse, bitter with rage. Then Shaeffer began shooting in a wild, crazy way, bullets coming out as fast as he could squeeze the trigger. The thunder of shots and the screaming whine of lead glancing off the granite deafened Cowle.

Then the sounds died, and there was a painful moment of intense silence. Cowle recalled the scene back at camp when Shaeffer had suddenly stopped screaming that he wasn't afraid, and had looked around him with his mouth still open, realizing how far beyond control he had allowed his rage to carry him.

Finally Shaeffer's voice came across the rock face, sounding high-pitched. "Thought you were dead back there, Cowle. So much blood on your head. You haven't got a chance here. Show your face and I'll knock it right out of your hood. Tell you what. Give me your word you'll quit and go back, and I'll give you mine not to fan your tail with lead."

Cowle climbed out of the fissure. "I don't think you have any more bullets left, Kurt."

He wasn't close enough to see the expression on Shaeffer's

face. He only saw the dark sprawl of his body against the rock. Then there was a clanging, metallic sound that diminished down the granite face toward the bottom. Shaeffer had dropped his empty gun.

The axe blade flashed in the sun as he began hacking at the granite. There was another plateau above. He worked toward it.

But Shaeffer was the one cutting the trail, and Cowle had only to follow. He closed in on the other, surely, inexorably. The Matterhorn and Mont Blanc and all the other mountains Cowle had climbed were far behind him. All the old skills were dim, half-forgotten things that came back through the veil slowly. Yet they came, and, as he moved upward, his work became more sure, more deliberate.

He felt his age. His belly was soft against the harsh stone; his breath came in swift, short gasps. He had tugged off his mittens, and the rock cut his hands deeply with every fresh hold. It was agony at first, his fingers curling spasmodically with pain. Then, the cold numbed his hands, and the only way he could tell of a fresh wound was by the blood on the rock, wet and red.

But there was something far greater than physical strength driving him. He had known that for a long time. He felt it surge up like a flame inside him every time he bellied down against the rock and could feel that hard squeeze of the wallet pressing into his chest.

Shaeffer looked back, and Cowle could see the expression on his face. He had never been one to hide his feelings. There was rage, and fear.

"Kronstadt was right, wasn't he, Kurt? You know he was right, now, don't you? You're afraid, aren't you, Kurt?"

Shaeffer's voice came down to him in a hoarse pant. "Shut up, damn you! I'm not afraid of anything! Not anything!"

"Then why run away, Kurt? Why not stay and fight? You wanted to fight in camp. You jumped me. The only difference now is that we're on the rock."

Cowle jerked suddenly aside. The big wedge of granite Shaeffer had thrown at him bounded past and on down the face of the rock.

Shaeffer began hacking at the stone again, moving up. But he was fighting it, and he was afraid. The ring of the axe had a frantic sound. He was hurrying too fast. His foot slipped, and he cried out.

"How is it, Kurt? How is it to know you don't understand the rock . . . to know you don't belong? How is it to be afraid?"

"If you don't go back, Cowle, I'll kill you! Go back. Sheila isn't worth it. I know you're doing it because of her. She wasn't worth it!"

"Maybe because of her . . . in a way," Cowle called to him. "But I told you a man couldn't hold a hate for eighteen years."

Shaeffer looked down at him, his bearded face twisted. He had been traveling laterally across the face, using the natural fissures and crevices to help him.

"I'm coming, Kurt," Cowle said, and he was coming. "Are you afraid, Kurt?"

With a hoarse shout, Shaeffer began working madly upward in a vertical line. Moving blindly. Moving too fast. Fighting the rock. Afraid.

Then Cowle heard a sound he knew well enough. It was a man's foot slipping from a toehold, a dry, scraping, ominous sound. Shaeffer screamed hoarsely, and Cowle looked up. Shaeffer's right leg was jerking spasmodically, seeking the toehold it had lost. The man tried to sink his axe in above him. But he had no leverage. The blade glanced off. Then his jerking leg pulled his other foot out of its step.

Cowle lay flat against the rock as Shaeffer fell past him. The man screamed all the way down. Cowle looked, finally. Shaeffer was sprawled, small and black against the snow névé so far below. That was the way Paul had looked, grotesque and twisted and pitiful, somehow, his blood spreading from beneath his body and darker on the broken, blasted red bricks of that ancient building nearly out into Puget Sound. Cowle wondered suddenly if Shaeffer, in those last few moments, had guessed why he died.

DEATH RULES THE WILDERNESS

I

The muskeg below the Peace River post was a weird, haunted bog at best, and the humid spring day drew ghostly pennants of steam from the Arctic vegetation lying in thick, scarlet mats on either side of the game trace leading through it. Céleste Manatte had been frightened by the place before. She stood there, slim and lithe in her ten years, dark head cocked to one side, her big, liquid eyes filled with the nameless terror peculiar to a little girl whose feminine senses reach far beyond those of sight and hearing. Out of the bog at her left a yellow rail began its troubled *kick-kick,* and then stopped again, and the silence it left seemed only more physical, pressing in on Céleste till her heart beat against her ribs like a frightened sparrow's. Then, trying to smile at herself, she clutched the handful of white ledums she had been gathering for her mother and started up the trail toward the Hudson's Bay post her father ran here at Peace River Landing, its hoary logs standing staunch and adamant on the higher ground above the bog. Almost out of the muskeg, Céleste stopped again. This time she could hear it plainly. Horses?

They came at a trot down the Peace River trail that led back through the Whitemud Hills, five of them in single file. Enough men came that way to the post every year, and Céleste knew a growing anger at herself for feeling this apprehension. Yet, there was something in the way they rode that drew her again into a run toward the buildings. The man in the lead forked a roan with chest and hocks that might have meant a little Percheron somewhere, and he had a straight military seat in the saddle, his gaunt, dark face turning ceaselessly from side to side. His eyes caught the girl, coming out of the muskeg, swinging to her, so bitter and black, they stopped her as if he had reached out a hand. He hauled his horse to a stop and swung off without any lost motion.

"I'm Kamsack Carter," he said, and his voice held the same feral restlessness Céleste had heard in the howl of a wolf from the Whitemuds. "Is your father inside?"

"Yes," she said faintly, still held by his bitter eyes. "Inside."

Carter dropped the reins over his horse's head, moving beneath its neck and throwing his words to the Indian behind him. "Bring her along."

The Indian leaned forward, tilting his head to one side. *"Ka-qui-oko?"* he asked in Cree.

Kamsack turned fully toward him, speaking louder, anger making his voice harsh. "I said bring her along."

"Ah, *taboi,*" said the Cree, dismounting stiffly, and turned toward the girl. He had an ugly, seamed face, and his gnarled scarred torso was bare to the waist. "Come here, *me-u-no-gwon.* Come here, beautiful. They call me Namotawacow, but I can hear things men less deaf cannot."

"No," said Céleste, dropping the ledums and darting around him toward the door. But Kamsack Carter was there, and he caught her with one hand before she could get by, his other hand still holding the rifle. The crushing weight in the long, sinewy fingers drew a gasp from Céleste. Her black hair jumped with the abrupt dip of her head as she bit him.

"Damn you!" shouted Carter, his fingers opening spasmodically and jerking off her.

"Don't talk to my daughter that way, Kamsack," said Georges Manatte from the doorway.

Carter whirled to the man, still shaking the hand Céleste had bitten. Céleste darted around Carter to her father, one small hand hooking into the broad, black belt around his tree-trunk middle, and the fear in her was wiped away by the solid warmth of his leg against her trembling body. He was her god, Georges Manatte, a great, towering mountain of a man, well above six feet tall, his hair still jet black above the lithic granite of his heavy-jawed face, although he was past fifty.

"Daughter?" said Carter, glaring at Céleste. "She's a little animal. Where are your *engagés,* Manatte?"

"They've taken my furs down to Athabaska Landing," said Manatte. "Won't be back for several weeks."

"That's what we figured," said Carter. "Let's go inside."

"I don't think I want you inside," said Manatte.

"I think you do," said Carter, and he did not have to shift the muzzle of his Stevens much to bring it to bear on Manatte.

The pungent odors of new fur and old leather and black-strap sorghum and Lipton's Tea that filled the big front room of the Peace River post had always represented home to Céleste, but now, somehow, they gave her a nameless suffocation. Still clinging to her father, she backed into the room, Carter following, the others crowding in behind. Manatte's great grandfather had come to the New World with Montcalm, and Georges himself had never seen France, but he had the volatile Gallic temper of his blood, and Céleste could feel him begin to tremble with it now.

"Carter. . . ."

"Never mind," said Carter. "Wight Reddington was due here a week ago. What happened to him?"

"How would I know?" said Manatte, his face dark.

202

Carter pushed the Stevens against Manatte's solid belly. "You know. You've done something to throw us off the trail. What's Reddington done with it? They were going to bring it upriver to your Peace River post this year instead of Fort Resolution. What's happened to Reddington?"

Céleste was watching her father's face carefully. "Oho," he said softly, as if understanding something fully for the first time. "Oh."

"Don't try to act dumb." Carter's mouth was beginning to work at one side. "We don't care how we find out. This way or another. This way will be easier on you. I'll give you one more time. Where's Reddington?"

"Perhaps something held him up," said Manatte.

"Not a whole week," said Kamsack. "We rode the river as far south as Lesser Slave, and there wasn't a sign of him. What did you and Reddington cook up, Manatte? I want to know."

Manatte shrugged his big shoulders.

Kamsack Carter stared at him a moment longer, lips working faintly. Then he turned his head a little. "Belcarres, get a big chair. A good solid one. And some rope."

Belcarres was so square he looked shorter than he actually was, wearing a canvas parka with the hood hanging behind his head, belted around a waist not much narrower than his shoulders, moving in a quick, catty way, his pale blue eyes opaque and impersonal as they swept across Céleste and her father. He shoved her father's big, hand-hewn armchair away from the potbellied Kisling stove by one of the huge supports in the center of the big room and went behind the counter stretching down one wall, clattering through the cans of tinned beef, tossing aside a bale of beaver furs, finally coming up with some five-eighths hemp Manatte kept for the lanyard of the H.B.C. flag out front. Carter indicated Manatte should move to the chair. The big Frenchman backed up, Céleste still hanging onto his arm, her eyes widening as she understood what they meant to do. Then she saw Carter's gaze shift to the doorway behind the counter that led to the stairway.

It was Tipiscopesum, Moon Woman, Manatte's Cree wife, standing there, dark and silent. She was a large, statuesque woman for an Indian, and her striking beauty hinted at what might be expected of Céleste in a few years. She wore a pure white bolus of doeskin fringed with black horsehair, belted about her waist to limn the arresting lines of her figure, her own hair falling in two raven braids down either side of her smooth, aquiline face, something haunting in the black depths of her luminous, faintly oblique eyes.

Perhaps it was the startling beauty which held them spellbound there in that instant, or perhaps it was the surprise of her utterly silent appearance. Either way, Manatte took that moment for the chance he undoubtedly knew would be his last, flinging Céleste aside with the arm to which she still clung and knocking aside the muzzle of the Stevens while Carter's gaze was yet on the woman. The gun exploded toward the ceiling, and Manatte's shout came at the same time.

"Get out, Tipiscopesum," he bellowed, "get out!"

Céleste was thrown heavily against the counter, the pile of tinned beef falling about her with a clattering crash, and she saw her father through a dazed pain, catching the rifle in both hands and using it as a lever to thrust Carter backwards. Unable to release the gun soon enough, Carter was shoved into Namotawacow and the other two men, knocking down the deaf Indian. Carter tried to keep his feet, but Manatte let go the rifle and slugged him in the face. Carter's head snapped back, and he shook the floor, falling. Namotawacow caught Manatte about the knees from where he had been knocked down, and the other two men leaped in, grappling Manatte's arms so the big man could not strike with them. Raging in their grasp like a wild animal, Manatte twisted around, tearing one leg free and lashing out to kick one of the men in the groin. Over the man's scream, Manatte's roar came again.

"Take our daughter and get out, Moon Woman. I order you, I order you . . . !"

But Tipiscopesum had already reached them, moving like a big, silent cat, her eyes black and burning, a crooked-bladed *bess-hath* in her hands. She caught the other man hanging onto Manatte from behind, her breath coming out in a hissing sound as she struck. The man stiffened, pinned between Manatte and his wife, then began to slide down. Tipiscopesum leaped backward, whirling toward the deaf Indian as he tried to rise, a knife in his hand, too. Céleste was on her feet now, swaying, still dazed by her fall, and it was then the shot came. Tipiscopesum was turned toward Céleste. The girl saw her mother's mouth open slightly. The Indian woman made a soft, strangled sound, her eyes wide with pain, or surprise. She dropped the bloody *bess-hath* she held. Then she fell forward across Namotawacow, the deaf Cree.

Céleste stared at her mother, her mind blank, refusing to comprehend it, and the shock must have held Manatte the same way. His face twisted and dead white, he stood with his great shoulders thrust forward slightly, watching Namotawacow squirm from beneath the woman's body. Belcarres stood over by the counter where he had been getting the rope, the gun still smoking in his hand. Carter was getting to his feet, shaking his head, bleeding over one eye where Manatte had hit him. He picked up his rifle, stepping across the groaning man Tipiscopesum had stabbed, bending over the woman.

"Did I . . ."—Belcarres hesitated a moment, his lips pulling back from his teeth, and that impersonal opacity was gone from his eyes—"did I . . . ?"

Carter had turned the woman over, and he rose, nodding. "Yes. You did."

"Killed her." Tears had begun streaming down Georges Manatte's weathered cheeks, as he mumbled it, a terrible agony creeping through the shocked glaze of his eyes. "Killed her." He took a step forward, his big hands jerking out, his voice rising. "You killed her!"

Instead of moving toward Manatte, Carter moved so the Stevens covered Céleste. "Unless you want your daughter to get the same thing, you'd better sit down in that chair."

For a moment, Manatte's heavy, hoarse breathing was the only sound in the room. Then the stabbed man began groaning again. Manatte stared at him, then at his own hands, still held out that way, finally at his wife. At first Céleste did not know where the sound came from. It sounded like an animal, broken, guttural, muffled. Then she realized it was her father, his whole body trembling. Carter jerked his thin head toward Belcarres.

"Tie him up good."

Belcarres was still looking at the dead Indian woman, and did not seem to hear. Carter's anger caught at one corner of his lips, twitching them, and he turned toward the other man. "Tie him up, Pengarth."

Pengarth was the one who had been kicked in the groin. Still holding his hand across his belly, he moved across the room, a heavy, black-bearded man with a shaggy mane of hair beneath his wolfskin hat and a dirty red Mackinaw, patched across the back with greasy buckskin. Still unable to believe her mother was dead, Céleste took a step toward Carter.

"Please," she said in a hollow voice. "Don't, please. . . ."

Carter jerked his head toward the deaf Indian. "Take care of her."

As Namotawacow moved to grab her, Céleste threw herself at Carter, catching his arm. "Please." She was crying now, a little girl filled with terror and fright, her face wet with tears. "What are you going to do? You can't. He's my father. Please. . . ."

With a snarl, Carter threw out his free arm, open-handed. The blow struck her fully across the face. She fell back across the room, smashing into the counter, and her head struck its edge. There was a stunning pain, and she knew nothing after that for an indeterminate time. Finally she rose through a mist of vague agony, hearing someone groaning. When she was conscious enough to realize it was herself, she stopped. She seemed to be lying beneath the counter, her head swimming. She knew a dim impulse to move, and could not answer it. The sounds about her were becoming coherent.

"All right, Manatte, where is he? You and Reddington rigged something up. What happened to him? We can keep this up all night. He was going to bring it here instead of Resolution. What happened to Reddington?" There was a pause. "All right, Namo. . . ."

The hoarse groan gave Céleste the abrupt, painful impulse to move again. Her fingertips were tingling now. She could see them somewhere beyond her head, lying among the scattered cans of beef she must have knocked down when she struck the counter. She was conscious enough to realize the blow on her head must have stunned her. The tingling sensation was climbing her arms now, and she could wiggle a fingertip. Feeling was returning to her whole body in waves of pain. Dimly she perceived the slight movements in the room about her. Carter stood lean and stoop-shouldered directly before her, blocking out the chair where she guessed her father was tied. They had put more wood into the potbellied stove, and Namotawacow had just turned from the stove with a live coal held in a pair of fire tongs. When he thrust them forward, they disappeared behind Kamsack Carter's figure, and the agonized groan came again.

"Where is Reddington, Manatte? What did he do with it?"

"No." Georges Manatte's voice had a shrill, cracked sound, and Céleste realized how long she must have been unconscious, for a man like her father would not have broken in a few minutes. "No, no, no, no. . . ."

It trailed off in a guttural moan. Pengarth came from the door behind the counter, and Carter turned to him. "Well, Indi?"

"Nothing upstairs," said Indi Pengarth, not looking directly toward the chair in which Manatte sat. "I ripped up all the beds and dumped everything he had stowed."

Belcarres was standing at the other end of the counter, his head shifting nervously toward where the dead Indian woman lay, and Céleste guessed he had looked that way more than once before. "Listen,"—he wiped his mouth—"can't we move that or something. No use sitting here and looking at it. Can't we . . . ?"

"You did it, Johnny," said Carter. "Why don't *you* move it?"

Johnny Belcarres turned toward him, opening his mouth to say something, then closed it. The sweat made his pallid face gleam. He wiped his mouth again.

The fifth man was hunkered down against the far wall, now and then rubbing tentatively at his head where Manatte had struck him. He was a youth with a lean, avaricious face and black eyes that kept shifting around the room, bright and quick like the weasels Céleste had surprised in the storeroom upstairs last winter. He wore a capote of caribou hide, belted with the bright red L'Assumption sash about his lean waist, and his shoes of buffalo skin dressed in the hair made no sound on the puncheon floor as he rose, moving over to the chair.

"You never get anywhere this way, Carter. I learned a few tricks with a knife down in Durango. I never saw anybody stand up to them."

"All right, Rodriguez," Carter told him. "They better be good tricks."

Rodriguez pulled a long knife from beneath his caribou capote, his eyes taking on an eager, sadistic light. His thin lips pulled back from his teeth, white and sharp as a wolf's. He hunkered down in front of the chair, only his left shoulder and side visible beyond Carter. Céleste could move her arms now. She wanted to cry, but she bit her lips to keep from doing that. She wanted to jump and throw herself at them, and she trembled with the effort of holding herself back. She knew she was helpless against them. Her father's groan stiffened her, and she felt tears begin to roll down her cheeks.

"No, no, no, no. . . ."

"Where's Reddington?"

"No, no, no. . . ."

"What did Reddington do with it, Manatte? I know he was bringing it up here. The Indians know it. Where is it?"

"No. . . ."

It was a shout, and it ended in an agonized sound. There was a moment of silence, and Rodriguez stood up, both his hands empty, looking at the chair. Carter bent forward, reaching out with his free hand. His breath erupted in a curse.

"You've killed him. Damn you! You cut too deep."

"No." Rodriguez's voice was strident. "He lunged up against me."

It rang through Céleste's head like a tocsin. Completely conscious now, she could see them all, the picture stamped in her brain so she knew she would never forget. Namotawacow inclined his scarlet head toward Carter.

"Ah?" he asked.

"I said Rodriguez killed him!" shouted Carter, turning toward the deaf Indian in a rage. "Killed him, damn it, killed him!"

"Ah, *taboi*," said Namotawacow, looking toward Manatte. "Truly."

Céleste realized what she had to do now, if she wanted to stay alive. She knew a terrible lust to kill that would have sent her screaming into their midst, but overriding that was the knowledge of how useless that would be. She drew a careful breath, and rose.

"The kid!" shouted Belcarres.

But Céleste was already behind the counter, running for the door. Her feet made a hollow thud on the stairs that led to the second story, and she could hear the scramble they made to follow her, Carter shouting something, another man cursing the tinned beef as he stumbled through it with a tinny clatter. The upstairs bedroom overlooked the roof above the front porch. Céleste ran through the mess Indi Pengarth had left, Hudson's Bay blankets torn from the bunk beds Manatte had built. Tipiscopesum's trunk of white doeskin dresses was dumped onto the floor, a leather-bound Bible lying past that, some of its pages torn. With the men running up the stairs, Céleste tore the bar from the sockets and threw open the shutter of the bedroom window, crawling over the high sill and dropping onto the roof. She slid down the shakes, tearing her dress, and hung from the slanting roof long enough to drop to the ground. It was a long fall, and it twisted her ankle. She was rising and turning toward their horses when Kamsack Carter appeared in the window above.

"She got out front!" he shouted. "Get her, Indi!"

There was a movement from inside the lower floor, and

Indi Pengarth ran out onto the porch. Knowing she could never reach the horses in time, Céleste whirled the other way, running with a painful limp down the meadow toward the river. The haunted *kick-kick* of the yellow rail came to her from the muskeg. Behind her, Indi Pengarth had mounted a horse, and Kamsack Carter and the others were streaming out the front door. She took one of the trails into the bog, so narrow in some places it was only discernible to her because she had traveled it so many times before, treacherous mud sucking at either side of the solid ground. She was hidden from them by the rabbit brush and spreads of cloudberry bushes, but she heard their hoofbeats growing nearer. Then Johnny Belcarres's voice came, easily recognizable.

"I'm in a bog, Kamsack. This ain't solid over here. Kamsack, I'm in a bog . . . !"

"Don't tell me about it, you damned fool. Get off your horse. Your weight just makes him go down faster."

"I can't get off, Kamsack. I'll get stuck in the mud, too. Help me, Kamsack!"

"The hell with you!"

She was out of earshot then, nearing the river, and she took a secret delight turning through a mass of chokecherry, overgrown with rotting yellow dodder, and plunged deliberately into a stagnant bog, covered with sickly green caribou moss. Hanging to the stout bushes, she allowed herself to sink into the ooze. She had known it was shallow enough here for her to crouch on her knees on the solid bottom, head hidden completely in the bushes, and she could watch the viscid mud suck at her footprints leading in, slowly obliterating them so that her trail had completely disappeared by the time Kamsack Carter came into view.

They passed by, cursing and swearing, the horses moving slowly down the treacherous way. Johnny Belcarres was black with mud up to his knees, and the muck was dripping off his gray Mackinaw. A frog boomed from the muskeg farther out, and Rodriguez straightened nervously in his saddle, staring that way. Kamsack's eyes swept the bog on either side of him, black and bitter, and, when they dropped over the bushes hiding Céleste, she grew rigid. But they passed on.

Clouds of bulldog flies rose to torture her, and she wiped them from her face impatiently. She was still trembling with fear, but there was something else growing in her. The men passed her again, going back, hunting over trails through the bog, Belcarres muttering angrily.

"I tell you she took to the river. She's probably on the other side now. Nobody could. . . ."

"Oh, shut up," snarled Kamsack Carter. "She's in this bog, and I'm going to find her. We can't let her stay alive after seeing that. It'd just be tying a rope around our necks."

They passed on, and Céleste crouched for a long time in the eerie boom of frogs. Once or twice she heard the men farther out, plunging through the muck, rattling the bushes. Finally, as dusk was falling, she saw them pass her for the last time.

"I'm getting out, Kamsack," Belcarres muttered. "I ain't bustin' around this muskeg at night. One slip and you're through."

Carter slapped viciously at a fly. "You're staying till we find her."

"Belcarres is right, Kamsack," growled Pengarth, hunching deeper into his dirty red Mackinaw. "We don't stand a chance of finding her in here at night. I don't even think she's here now. Anyway, she can't live very long up in this country, a little girl like that."

And as she heard the direction they took, and realized they were heading out, Céleste knew what was inside her, now, drowning the fear and horror—a cold, bitter hatred, crystallizing in her till she could feel nothing else. Her black eyes were mere slits in a face mottled with swelling bites of the bulldog flies, and her mouth twisted malevolently around her soundless words.

I'll live long enough, Indi Pengarth. I'll live long enough to make you pay for this, like no murderer ever paid before.

II

"There's a dive up at Athabaska Landing run by a woman known as Spanish Lou. Trappers, Indians, *voyageurs,* miners, Crees, Irishers, Canucks, Spicks, they all strike the Diamond Ring sooner or later, and they all see Spanish Lou, and she knows more about that country than any woman has a right to know. If you want to find out something, that's where to go."

Standing there in the doorway of the Diamond Ring, he couldn't remember where he had first heard that. Montreal maybe, or Nicolet. It didn't matter much. He moved on into the dingy barroom, a tall man in immaculate dark broadcloth, a thick streak of gray through the jet black of his hair giving him a distinguished look, something mordant lying in his black eyes, behind the veil of the heavy blue lids. He moved detachedly through the jostling crowd of men, past a bunch of corduroyed Canucks listening to a derby-hatted house man with a cigar beat out "The Ballad of Sleeping Joe" on the tinny piano.

He reached the bar and set his suitcase down beside a pair of trappers with snow still in their beards arguing the merits of a jump trap for beavers.

"I am Janeece Arcola," he told the bartender.

"I am Badger Bates," said the bartender.

Arcola ignored the mockery there. "Is Spanish Lou around?"

Badger Bates was a singularly evil-looking specimen with a perfectly bald pate and a revolting, puckered scar running across his face from above his right eye. "Lou ain't in."

"Not even to her brother?" questioned Arcola.

"Not even to her brother," said Bates. "What'll it be?"

Janeece Arcola put a hand on the bar, long fingers spreading pale and slender against the dark mahogany, and his blue lids opened more widely around his eyes. "I have come a long way to see the woman known as Lou. I'll go a bit farther if I have to."

Bates seemed suspended that way, bent toward Arcola, staring blandly into his eyes. Perhaps it was what he saw there. He jerked his bald head up abruptly, taking a quick, fumbling step backward, reaching behind him till his horny hand closed around a bottle of bourbon on the shelf.

"Look, friend, I don't want trouble. Either order your drink or get out. Lou ain't in."

Arcola gazed at him a moment longer, then turned without any perceptible change of expression across the dark aquilinity of his face. He lifted his suitcase, and his pointed black shoes made a deliberate, unhurried sound across the sawdust-covered floor. There was a roulette game, but he passed that because it would take too long, and passed the half dozen poker games at the deal tables, and reached the man in a seedy, blue pin-striped suit standing by the rear door.

"I'd like to hustle a few," Arcola said.

"What makes you think we've got any of that here?" asked the man.

"Badger misinformed me?"

The house man took a minute to wonder how the five

dollar bill had gotten into Arcola's hand, then he glanced over toward the bar where Badger was busy filling jiggers, shrugged, opened the door for Arcola. The room was blue with smoke, and the bare walls reverberated to the incessant shuffle of feet and the constant buzz of voices.

They had an old pool table for the game. The house man stood at the head of the table with stacks of colored chips in front of him, the stick man beside him, raking in the dice with a little curved stick after they had been thrown and shoving them back to the shooter. There were perhaps a dozen men crowded around the table, three or four women in cheap dresses, smoking cigarettes or hanging onto the arm of their man. Arcola bought a stack of chips and waited his turn. He didn't have to watch the shills work long to find out this one was not very complicated. The stick man had at least twenty pairs of dice in a glass bowl, allowing the customers to pick the ones they wanted, and, knowing the house would not risk having that many fixed cubes, it would have satisfied the average hustler. But Arcola saw what kind of chance the stick man had when he raked in the thrown dice and gave them back to the shooters. For just an instant, the cubes were in the stick man's hands, and that was the tip-off. When it came Arcola's turn, he reached for the bowl.

"Oh, sorry," he gasped, and his hand clumsily shoved the bowl over, and a dozen cubes spilled onto the green felt. The house man gave him a surly glance and began gathering in the dice. Helping him, Arcola palmed two of the cubes, slipping them into his pocket when the house man's eyes were off him. When the bowl was filled again, Arcola chose a pair of dice out of it, moving them between his sensitive fingers to see that all sides were perfectly flat, then rolling them in a cup between his palms to see if they were loaded. Apparently they had given him a fair throw. That meant the cubes he had pocketed were probably legal, too. He took his first throw, drawing nine for his point. He made his point on the third throw, and left the pot in, adding a dozen more blues from his own stack to make the bet heavy enough to encourage a move from the house. He came out again and got ten for his point. The stick man raked in the dice as usual after the throw, handing them back to Arcola. Arcola allowed his fingers to slide around the surfaces again without drawing notice from the shills. He felt a momentary impulse to smile, and knew a grudging admiration for the stick man. He had been watching the man closely, and had not been able to detect him switch the dice. Yet they had been switched. A pair of six-ace flats had been given Arcola in place of the fair cubes, and, with these, it would be impossible to roll his point with a normal throw. Arcola ran his tongue across his lower lip.

A newcomer shoving through the crowd behind caused the shift that gave Arcola his chance. With two or three hustlers jostling against him, he allowed one heavy-set man to block him partially from view of the shills and the house man and, in that instant, got the dice he had palmed out of his pocket, switching them for the six-ace flats, and dropping the six-ace flats into his pocket. Then he worked the legal cubes around in his fingers till they were set for a Greek shot, and made his throw. The stick man reached out automatically to rake the cubes in, then stopped, with the rake above the dice, and his voice held a hollow surprise. "Ten?" he said.

Arcola smiled blandly. "Ten."

A look passed between the stick man and the banker. The banker shoved out the chips Arcola had won, watching him narrowly. Arcola shoved all his own chips into the pile, still smiling. The stick man gave him back the dice. Arcola felt the cubes. They were fair dice again, allowing him to get any point on his throw. It did not matter to him now, anyway.

The only reason he had palmed the first pair was so he could switch them for the fixed cubes when they appeared, and now those fixed dice were in his pocket. As far as the throw went, he could gain his point with good cubes or bad, using that Greek shot. His point this time was four. The stick man raked them in and handed them to Arcola. Again the man had switched good cubes for a pair of six-ace flats. One of the shills was watching Arcola's hands now, and the banker was watching his face. Without any perceptible shifting of his fingers, Arcola set the dice, and threw.

"Four," said the stick man, and this time there was not so much surprise as anger in his voice. Thin-lipped, the banker matched the pile of blues Arcola had stacked on the table. One of the shills drifted back through the crowd, and Arcola heard the door open, and close again. The mob pressed in, and the heat of the room was drawing a faint perspiration from Arcola. He could feel himself tightening up, knowing it was coming soon now. He tried to relax, making his next throw. His point was a ten. He got another pair of six-ace flats, when the stick man handed him the dice for the next throw. He threw a trey the first time, just to make it more interesting, getting a certain enjoyment from watching the nervous tension build up in the house man. The stick man's hand was trembling as he raked them and handed them back. Still the six-ace flats. This time Arcola threw his point. The stick man made an effort to rake them in. Arcola felt a tap on his shoulder.

"You're wanted on the phone, Mister Arcola." It was Badger's harsh, grating voice. Arcola shoved his chips toward the banker to be cashed, but Badger spoke again in his ear. "We'll cash in for you when you come back."

Arcola shrugged, moved through the crowd toward the door, Badger beside him. The man in the pin-striped suit was there, his thick, bucolic face mirroring a heavy anger. Badger nodded to him, and he opened the door.

"You're getting off easy," Badger told Arcola. "Just leave now and we won't make no trouble."

"You must be very versatile," said Arcola.

"Henry takes care of the bar whenever anything like this comes up," said Badger.

"I'll have to cash in before I go," said Arcola.

Badger's weight settled forward till he was standing on his toes, and the singular breadth of his shoulders became even more apparent beneath the house man's white coat. "I think you understand better than you let on. We don't like crooked hustlers. Are you going to leave, or would you rather see what we have in the back room?"

"I don't think you could get me into the back room before I inform your customers here what kind of dice you use when you don't want them to make their point," said Arcola. "I have a pair of your six-ace flats in my possession."

The man in the blue suit looked startled, then let go the door to grab Arcola, but Badger shoved his bulk between them. "Take it easy, Al, we don't want no trouble," he said. His breath was hot and fetid in Arcola's face. "What's the hitch?"

"Is Lou in?" said Arcola.

"I guess maybe she is," said Badger.

Spanish Lou had the bold, voluptuous beauty Arcola had expected in a woman of her reputation. She was standing with her back to the window when they ushered him in from downstairs. The draperies matched the rug, their dark richness accentuating the alabaster of her bare shoulders. Her luxurious brown hair was done up in a chignon on her head, and could not have been more effective.

"You played your cards all right up to that last deuce, Mister Arcola," she said, and the huskiness lent her voice a certain sensuous attraction. "I'm surprised you should make such a simple mistake. There aren't any customers in here to see what happens. You would have been better off playing out your hand in the dice room."

"That isn't exactly the point," he said. "I don't particularly care what the customers see, or don't see."

"He asked for you when he came in," Badger said.

The woman's plucked brows raised slightly, and she seemed to understand for the first time. "You pick a roundabout way to gain my attention."

"Your man was reluctant to give me an audience with you," said Arcola. "I thought maybe this would work."

"Frisk him," said the woman, and her voice held an edge.

Arcola made a slight turning motion, and one of his hands had raised slightly toward his coat pocket before he saw the weapon Badger had pulled from beneath his coat. Arcola turned back, allowing Al to run this thick fingers down his coat. Al reached inside and got the long knife from its sheath beneath Arcola's left armpit, handing it and his wallet and the dice to Lou.

"That's an odd weapon for a man like you to carry," she said.

"*Klewang,*" he said. "Natives in the Indies use it."

"Is that where you learned to roll the dice?" she said idly.

"A man in Suez showed me that one," he said.

"You get around . . . ," she cut off, her body stiffening perceptibly as she sorted a paper out of the others in his wallet. "The Royal Northwest Mounted. . . ."

"Police," he finished, smiling faintly. "Department of Intelligence."

Spanish Lou made a violent gesture with her hand. "Look

here, Arcola, I haven't. . . ."

"Don't worry, don't worry," he said, laughing softly. "I'm not here for anything like that. It's rumored, all the way from here to Ottawa, that you know a bit more about Alberta then any other person living in the province."

"The police have a post here at Athabaska," she said. "Why don't you go to them?"

"The things you may know might be a little different than the things they might know, if you see what I mean."

She ran one scarlet-nailed hand down her shimmering gown of green velour. "I don't think I care to see what you mean, Arcola. I don't think a confidential agent would be carrying his credentials around openly like this where anyone can see them."

"Perhaps I wanted someone to see them," Arcola told her.

"Well, now they've seen them," she said. "And you've seen me. I don't know anything that would help you, I'm sure. I just run the Diamond Ring and I keep my nose out of other people's business and I think you'd better go now."

"Inspector Burke has K Division here," said Arcola. "He might be interested to know how so many of Athabaska's upright citizens are getting clipped at your dice tables."

"If you can prove anything without the dice, go ahead. Show him out, Al."

Badger lifted his Mauser, and Al shifted to open the door. It must have been the very simplicity of the expedient that allowed its success. All Arcola did was take a step that placed him in front of Al, putting Al between himself and Badger. Badger tried to jump aside so he could fire without shooting through Al, and Al dropped his shoulder. His scarred face looked like it had come from the ring, and that dropped shoulder gave him away. Arcola blocked the punch without much effort, catching Al's wrist while it was still out there and using the outflung arm as a lever to swing the man around.

"Damn!" shouted Badger, and staggered back as Al crashed into him, the gun going off at the ceiling. Badger was carried back into the wall beneath Al's weight, his gun arm knocked out flat against the buttoned plush. Arcola stepped after them, kicking Al aside to catch Badger's arm still against the wall that way. He jammed a knee against Badger's elbow and caught the gun from Badger's fingers. Arcola stepped back.

"Now," he said softly, "*you* get out."

Al was bent forward, holding the wrist Arcola had grabbed, a strange, dazed pain on his face, as if he could not believe what had happened. He looked at his wrist, then at Arcola's long, pale fingers. Lou stood stiffly with her back against the drapes watching Badger get up. Both her men were looking at her now. She made a jerky effort with her hand, starting to say something. Then she closed her mouth, nodding toward the door.

When the men had gone, Arcola set the safety and pulled the slide back, releasing the magazine and pulling it out. He put the unloaded gun on the table along with the clip, picking up his *klewang* and slipping it back into the case beneath his coat. Then he took the dice between his fingers musingly.

"Six-ace flats," he murmured wryly. "Rounded just enough on four sides to give the house a great advantage without being noticeable. Flat on the six and one. A person doesn't need to be a physicist to see how many more times those flat sides would come up than the rounded sides. You could seven-out with these, but it would be next to impossible to throw a ten, wouldn't it?"

Spanish Lou had been studying him narrowly, and suddenly she laughed.

Arcola squinted his eyes in a faint distaste. He had never

221

liked a loud laugh in a woman.

"You're smooth," she said. "Nobody ever spotted those dice before. They're always looking for loaded cubes, but no busters like this. My stick man tells Badger you made your point after you'd been given the fixed dice. I didn't think that was possible."

"I used a Greek shot," he said.

"The one you learned in Suez?" she said, and he saw how she was watching his lean, mordant face now. He was used to his effect on women. Maybe there was something about his strange, glowing eyes. Or the sad cynicism in the droop at each corner of his mouth. He didn't know what it was exactly. Lou turned away abruptly, as if angry at being caught watching him that way. He smiled softly, moving to the ivory spinet at one side of the room and sat down on the bench, his slender, supple fingers weaving a brooding bit of "Solvejg's *Lied*." It helped, too. He saw the stiff line of Lou's bare shoulders relax, and she turned back.

"About fifteen years ago," he said, the Grieg forming a somber undertone to his cultivated voice, "a man named Wight Reddington left Athabaska Landing *en route* to Peace River Landing, purportedly to find an new winter route to the Hudson's Bay Peace River post. Somewhere between Fort Chippewayan and Peace River Landing, the whole party disappeared. The police have always been interested in what happened to Reddington."

"I know the story," she said.

"They're still interested."

She looked at him narrowly. "That seems an awful lot of fuss to make over a man who was just hunting a new winter route to Peace River."

He rose from the piano and went to the table, hunting a cigarette. "What else?"

Her green velour gown made a silken rustle, moving across the room to him. The table was paneled, and she lifted one panel to show him a built-in drawer containing cigarettes. He let her take one and sit on the sofa, lighting it for her with the gaudy, gold-chased table lighter.

"A lot else," she said, blowing twin streams of blue smoke from her nostrils. "Other men have disappeared up there and been forgotten in a month. Why should Reddington cause such a stir? There was something else people connected to his disappearance. The factor of the Peace River post and his Indian wife were found murdered that same year. Manotte, I think. Manatte. Something like that. When his body was found, there were marks of torture."

Something passed through Arcola's eyes. "What do you think?"

"How do I know?" she said, crossing her legs. "Furs?"

"If Reddington was carrying any furs, they would be rotted by now."

"Would they?" she said.

"Why should Reddington be carrying them north anyway? The only way furs come is south from up there. I mean . . . any big shipment."

"He could have reached Peace River and been coming back," she said.

"You're conjecturing, my dear. I can't go on conjecture." He put his cigarette down to take out his wallet, slipping a sheet of paper from an inner flap. "Here's something you missed when you were going through my credentials. It is not conjecture. It's a sheet of Wight Reddington's log. It takes him from Athabaska Landing here as far north as Wabiskaw Lake. Intelligence figures if we can find the other sheets of his log, it would take us up to the time of his disappearance."

"I don't have them," she pouted.

223

He laughed indulgently. "I got this from an old, deaf Cree down at Edmonton. He said he found it in an Indian camp near Loon River. The chief had it among his fetishes."

"You take that to mean Indians hit Reddington?"

"If it does, wouldn't it stand to reason the rest of his log might be in evidence somewhere up there, among an Indian's war coups?"

"Isn't that a little far-fetched? A book . . . like that?"

"No," he said. "It's quite logical. You know what reverence the Indians hold for anyone who can read. They think a white man can forecast the future or control the weather by reading out of a book. Anything like Reddington's log would be a great coup. They'd think its possessor was endowed with magic powers."

"Why come to me?"

"I can't just go up and ask the Cree for the rest of the log," said Arcola with a heavy patience. "I don't know the country. The people."

"Neither do I."

Anger at her petulance put an edge on his voice. "Everyone from here to Great Slave Lake hits the Diamond Ring sooner or later. You must know someone."

"You can hire guides for two dollars a day from Hudson's Bay."

He realized evidence of his own anger had only heightened her antagonism, and he waited a moment before speaking again, taking a careful drag on his cigarette, modulating his voice deliberately. "I don't mean just anyone, Lou. If I'd wanted an ordinary guide, I could have gone to H.B.C., of course. But I don't mean just anyone, you know."

"You mean someone who won't be too particular what happens along the way?" she said. "Or maybe who wouldn't be averse to taking a little bonus for not being surprised if you find out Reddington was going up there for something more than just a new winter route to Peace River Landing?"

"You still don't believe me, do you?"

"I'm afraid I can't tell you anything," she said, crushing out her cigarette with an abrupt, decisive gesture. "You've thrown your Greek shot for nothing."

"Maybe I have. It was just a shot in the dark, anyway. I thought you might know of someone. But maybe my reason for wanting to see you wasn't entirely business." He seated himself on the settee, reaching for the dice. "Speaking of the Greek shot, maybe you'd like me to teach it to you."

He had known it would touch her, and with her immediate interest aroused it was easy for him to take her hand in his, putting the dice in her fingers. "Hold the dice in your right hand, so, hmm? Resting on the two center fingers. That's it. Bring your little finger and index forward till they form a cup. When you close your hand and shake, the dice knock around violently without changing. Suppose you want a ten. You set the dice with two fives on top, so, one cube on top of the other. That's it. Throw them level with the table instead of dropping them. They spin instead of turning over and over, your fives always on top. No, you dropped them too far. Level, so they spin. That's better." She gave a pleased laugh as the dice spun to a stop with the ten. He put the dice back in her hand, wrapping her fingers around them. "You should do well with that shot. You have the hands for it. Velvet? No." He took a breath, turning toward her. "No, softer than that. Softer than anything I've ever touched."

"You aren't going gallant on me now?" she said.

But the mockery in her voice was not convincing, even to herself. He could see it in her face. The struggle of more than one emotion, beneath the surface, was changing the planes of her cheek, the line of her mouth. He had seen it enough other times, in enough other women.

"That's the trouble," he said, letting his index finger slide up her hand onto her forearm, and then grasping it. "There have been so many other men, with so many other lines. You don't know when it's real."

"Don't I?" she asked. The struggle was still going on, but she had not tried to pull free of his grasp. Something in his eyes held her gaze. Her lower lip dropped, glistening. He had seen it enough other times.

"No, Lou, you don't."

Her eyes were closed when he finally took his lips away. She took a heavy breath, not raising her head from the settee. When she let the breath out, her words came with it. "They don't come often . . . like that . . . up here."

He kissed her again, more easily this time, sure of his ground, allowing his lips to slide across her cheek till he could murmur in her ear. "You know, if Reddington had been doing something besides hunting for a new route to Peace River Landing, something, say, that could be remunerative, financially, to anyone who found out what happened to him, and if I were the one to find out, and someone up here had helped me to some extent, I wouldn't mind sharing whatever arose from that discovery."

She started to soften against him. "Arcola. . . ."

He kissed her again. "I wouldn't mind sharing it with you, Lou. Surely you know someone. They all come here. You or Badger. Someone who knows things no H.B.C. guide could ever know. It's always that way in a business like yours, Lou. The authorities never get on the inside, really. The Mounties, H.B.C. But you must know."

"There's a man called Glengariff," she said faintly. "An Irisher. Works the York boats during the summer. Drunk most of the time. But he knows a lot."

"Maybe," said Arcola. He ran his long forefinger across her cheek, something calculating entering his eyes. "There was someone I heard of. Thought you might know. A woman. They say she knows more about the Peace River country than any."

"Céleste Manatte?" Spanish Lou had opened her eyes.

He tried to keep his voice easy. "That her name?"

"She's part Indian," said Lou, and some of the dazed look was gone. She pulled away slightly, as if wondering how it had happened to her. "Lived with Dog Ribs for a while, I guess."

"Any relation to the Manatte who was murdered on Peace River?"

"His daughter, I think," said Lou.

"I understand she's rather nebulous. People don't see her for years on end, and such." Arcola bent forward slightly. "I imagine you would know where to contact her."

"Badger could." Spanish Lou pulled completely away, putting her hands against his chest to hold him there, staring into his eyes. "Arcola, suddenly I'm afraid."

"Lou, honey,"—his voice caressed her—"you know I wouldn't hurt you."

"Not afraid for myself," she said in a strange, hollow voice. "Céleste Manatte."

III

The York boat had docked at one of the short piers extending out from Athabaska Landing's boat yards, and the woman with five white dogs had been the first passenger to disembark. There were a dozen *engagés* of Hudson's Bay working on an H.B.C. scow in the first way she passed. The one to look up must have

227

been of French descent. He dropped the thole pin he had been setting.

"*Sacre nom,*" he said. "Céleste Manatte."

The man next to him glanced around, and quit cleaning shavings from the strake he had cut in the thwarts. The sound of the whipsaws ceased. By the time the woman was halfway up the muddy path leading toward town, there was not a man working in the whole crew.

The only resemblance, perhaps, between the Céleste Manatte of today and the frightened, bitter little girl of fifteen years before was the intense luminous blackness of her eyes beneath their arched brows, and the shimmering midnight brilliance of her long hair. She had fulfilled the promise seen in her Cree mother's beauty, taller than the average girl, something statuesque in the lines of her body, yet something lithe and quick, too, in the way her hips swung to her walk. She was hatless, wearing a man's checked flannel shirt tucked into the belt of her caribou-hide leggings that gleamed with daubs of grease that were no marks of slovenliness among those who spent most of their time on the trail and had not napkins to wipe their hands on after a meal of marrow bones or bear steak. There was an untamed quality to the dark aquilinity of her face, the proud line of her straight, rather prominent nose. Moving with all the unstudied grace of a wild animal, she passed by the grinning row of men, one arm swinging with a coiled dog whip at her side.

Maybe it was because they did not see too many women in this wilderness outpost, or maybe it was her startling beauty; either way, it held them spellbound till she was almost gone. As she stepped onto the wooden sidewalk leading down the street in front of the police barracks, she could hear the remarks begin.

"She ain't been down this far in four years."

"I think I'll knock off for today."

Then they were out of earshot, and the plank walk clattered softly beneath her moose-hide moccasins. There were not many people in the street at this hour of the day, a few trappers who stopped to stare at the tall, black-headed girl walking down the sidewalk in the midst of her five pure white dogs, a couple of degenerate ration Indians across the way in front of the R.C. mission. She reached the Diamond Ring and pushed through the batwing doors.

The first sound striking her was the piano. It was a tinny, battered old instrument, and there was a glass of whisky set precariously on its scarred top that slid an inch or so toward the edge every time the piano shuddered to the man striking the discordant keys. He was a short, square, red-headed Irishman in a faded blue denim shirt, open across the chest to show the heavy woolen sweater beneath. The slight upward tilt of his eyebrows gave a mischievous cast to his face, and his blue eyes were glazed with drink.

"La Connach molta da mbeinn im'thost," he sang, and the lyric sweetness of his voice drew Céleste. *"Connach aoibinn gan aon lacht. . . ."*

Badger Bates was behind him, pulling at his shoulder. "Come on now, Glengariff, you gotta leave. You know Lou won't have you in here since the last time. You get drunker and you'll be breaking up the place again. Please, Glengariff."

The Irishman threw out one thick arm, knocking Badger back against the roulette table. "Lemme be, Bates. You got the only piano in town, and I'm in a singing mood. *Ta or le faighail ag lucht aithris rann. . . ."*

"That isn't Cree," said Céleste, moving toward the piano.

He glanced her way without focusing his bleary eyes, and his long, mobile upper lip moved around the words half angrily, half caressingly. "Have you ever heard Gaelic? That's Gaelic. A man's got a right to sing his own tongue, ain't he? Who's gonna stop me? I'm a Connach man and no Black and Tan."

"Sing it again," she said. "So I can understand."

He stared at her, and something entered his face. Sadness? She wouldn't have looked for that in such a face. Abruptly he turned back to the piano.

" 'Connach is praised, though I were silent. Beautiful Connach without one fault. There is gold to . . .' "—he brought both hands down in a smashing chord suddenly, drowning out his voice, sitting there a moment to stare blankly at the keys, chest rising and falling with the heavy breath passing through him. Then he rose, knocking over the piano stool as he whirled about, stumbling toward the bar. "Gimme another drink. I'm a Connach man, and I can't disgrace the boys by going back to Athlone sober. Never a Connach man that doesn't stagger down the road going home." His voice had risen steadily, and the last was a wild roar as he lurched into the bar. "Gimme a drink, Badger. I'll never go down the road to Athlone . . . I'll never go back to Shan Van Vocht. Erin's dead, and every Connach man with her . . . gimme a drink!"

Badger gave the word to the barman behind the mahogany, then turned to Céleste, shaking his ugly head. "The police'll be coming for him, if he don't get out of the Landing. I never had so much trouble with one man in all my life."

Céleste was still staring after Glengariff, her lower lip tucked under her teeth. "One of your ration Indians hit Fort Resolution last week. Said Lou was looking for me. Something important."

"That's right," said Badger. "Lou sent the word out. We didn't know exactly where you was. I think Lou's in her

rooms now. You want I should take your dogs?"
Her brows raised slightly as she turned toward him. "You
know better than that, Badger."

It had been years since she'd seen Lou's apartment, but
the odor of perfume was as strong as ever. Badger ushered her
in, leaving and closing the door behind her, its buttoned
plush lining muffling whatever sound it made. Lou was
dressed in a peach negligee with too many ruffles. She came
forward eagerly enough.

"I'm glad to see you again, Céleste. We've been hunting
for you pretty hard. It was good of you to come all the way
from Resolution." Lou became aware of how the man who
had risen from the sofa was staring at Céleste, and the
warmth left her voice abruptly. She turned halfway toward
him. "I'd like you to meet Janeece Arcola, Céleste. Jan, this is
Céleste Manatte."

Arcola bowed with a faint smile. Céleste measured the
height of him and the breadth beneath the tailored shoulders
of his pin-striped morning coat, and then he had straightened
fully again, and she was looking at his face. Something indefinable passed through her. He was handsome enough, in a
smooth, sardonic way, blue-shadowed eyelids almost closed
over the slumbering blackness of his strange eyes.

"What is it, Miss Manatte?" he said, in a soft, cultured voice.

"I . . . I don't know," she said, and she didn't. It was an effort for her to take her eyes from his face. She turned to Lou.
"Your Indian said you needed my help in something."

"And would pay you well for it," said Spanish Lou absently, still looking from Arcola to Céleste with a speculative
narrowness to her eyes. Then she turned to Céleste, taking a
decisive breath. "Yes. Sit down, Céleste, won't you? Arcola
will tell you."

The man had moved nearer, and one of the dogs began to stiffen up, growling. "Kitch-eo-kemow," Céleste told him, calling him Chief in Cree, and the big white spitz settled back, the growl dying reluctantly in his thick-furred throat. Céleste took a seat on the couch, declining the cigarette Lou offered her. Arcola had taken credentials from his wallet.

"Department of Intelligence, Miss Manatte. I suppose you know their interest in Wight Reddington."

Céleste tried to keep anything from showing in her face at the name, and nodded. "Fifteen years is a long time to hunt for a man. No one ever did know what made him so valuable."

Arcola's laugh was deprecating. "The police haven't actually been hunting him that long. But they don't forget a thing like that. And what has lately come to our attention revived their interest in finding out exactly what happened to Reddington. He had kept a daily log of his trip, and last March one of the pages from that log came into our possession, found among the fetishes of a Cree chief up on Loon."

"You think the Indians attacked Reddington?"

"You can see the implications," said Arcola.

Céleste nodded. "They do keep trophies, all right. It's possible the rest of the log may be in existence somewhere up there. It's rather a long shot."

"That's why we wanted someone like you," he said. "You can get us places no ordinary guide could. If not the log, at least the knowledge of what happened to Reddington, and where." She was looking up at his face again, and he smiled softly. "Your recompense will be equal to your worth, naturally."

Lou was watching what lay between them again, and there was an edge to her voice. "He means you'll be paid well. Cigarette, Jan?"

Arcola spoke without looking at her. "No. No, thank you, Lou."

Spanish Lou was about to say something else when the knock came on the door. Her negligee made an impatient rustle to the portal. The gaudy, buttoned plush of the walls and door must have acted as soundproofing to some extent, for, when she opened the door, the sound burst in on them. Someone was shouting, and that was drowned out by the splintering crash of furniture striking the wall, and then the jangle of breaking glass. The whole building shuddered, and a man screamed from down below.

"It's Glengariff!" shouted Al, at the doorway, one side of his pin-striped suit torn completely away, his hand cut and bleeding. "Badger tried to put him out, and he got mad. He's wrecking the place, Lou. Nobody can stop him. He'll have the Mounties here in a minute."

Céleste followed Lou out the door, Chief and the other dogs after her. There was a short balcony here, overlooking the bar, a stairway leading down at either end, and, as they ran to the one in the front, they could see the carnage below. Badger Bates was just rising from behind the bar. It looked as if he had been thrown bodily over the bar itself and crashed into the mirror, for the big glass was broken, and a whole shelf of bottles lay smashed on the floor. Badger's bald head, lacerated badly, was covered with blood. The piano lay on its back across the room, and, out in front of it, Glengariff was struggling with a knot of house men and customers. The croupier lay across his roulette table, holding his head and moaning.

"Won't let a man sing about Ireland?" bellowed Glengariff, and a white-coated barman staggered out of the milling crowd, weaving across the room blindly and finally sinking to his knees. Céleste saw his face then, and it looked like he'd put it under a pile driver. "Won't let a man sing about his own Shan Van Vocht!" And the whole bunch of them were shifted by the wild, red-headed cyclone bellowing in their midst, leaving another man lying on the floor. "I'll sing you a rann you'll never forget. I'll show you what we did to the stinkin' Tans on Easter Monday."

She saw what it was then. He had pulled his shillelagh from his belt. Cursing and roaring, he whirled this way and that in the crowd, wielding the short club with a deadly effect. A poker dealer jumped on his back and caught him around the neck, while the stick man from the roulette table whacked Glengariff viciously across the face with his rake. Glengariff threw himself back against the wall, smashing the dealer to the boards with all his weight, and then jumped out again, the dealer dropping off his back, stunned. He caught the stick man's rake across his left forearm and went on in to crack the stick man across the face with that shillelagh.

"*Arragh,* I'll sing you a rann all right!" Roaring drunkenly, Glengariff whirled to catch one of the lumberjacks who had been playing roulette, smashing the man back through the crowd with a blow from his shillelagh. "I'll sing you the Royal Blackbird. 'On a fair summer morning of soft retreating, I heard a fair lady a-making a moan. . . .' "

His wild paeon ended with a grunt as he caught another man across the head. The crowd was scattered now, leaving him swaying and roaring there with three or four men lying about him. Badger Bates had gotten a broken bottle from the mess on the floor behind the bar, and was climbing over the mahogany.

"That's right, Badger!" bellowed the Irishman, kicking free of the feebly grasping roulette croupier and jumping across an unconscious lumberjack toward Lou's barman. "Come at me, Badger!" He smashed the bottle from Badger's hand with one blow and caught Badger across the brow with the backward sweep of it. "With sighing and sobbing and sad lamentation, Badger, I'll sing my ranns till the aurora borealis stops turning red, and nobody from here to Erin can stop me."

Badger had stumbled backward across the littered floor, losing his balance to crash up against the stairs just as Lou and Céleste reached the bottom. "Stop him, somebody!" screamed Lou. "Badger, stop him! Glengariff, you're crazy drunk!"

"Damned right, I'm drunk!" bellowed Glengariff, reeling to the bar and sweeping his arm across it to knock all the remaining bottles and glasses in that section to the floor. "Drunk as hell, Lou. You can't stop a drunk Connach man. Come and try it. All of you. Come on and try it. I'll sing you a rann."

He picked up one of the bottles with its top broken off and threw it at Badger as the man got up from the stairway. It struck the wooden riser on the bottom step, broken glass flying in every direction. This startled the dogs, and their weight thrusting against Céleste from behind pushed her and Lou off the stairs onto the floor. At this moment a pair of trappers who had been working around toward one end of the bar came at Glengariff from that side, and Badger got on his feet and jumped the Irishman as Glengariff turned toward the trappers. The two men went into Glengariff hard, knocking him back into Badger, and all four of them reeled on back into Lou and Céleste and the dogs. Roaring in the midst of the men, Glengariff began slugging with his shillelagh, knocking one trapper back against the bar. The other one tried to catch his arm while Badger gave him a rabbit punch from behind. Glengariff went to his knees beneath the punch, catching the remaining trapper about the waist. By now the excited dogs were a swirl of white fur and pricked ears about the struggling men, yapping and snapping at the men and each other.

"Pe-is-su!" shouted Céleste, tearing her wheel dog, Thunder, away from Badger, and then caught at her number two animal, but, when they got excited like this, nothing short of a club would stop them. Glengariff had pulled the trapper on down with him by now and was dodging aside beneath another of Badger's blows. He rose up, smashing his knee into the trapper's face, catching Badger by the wrist and pulling Badger's arm over his shoulder. Then he heaved, and Badger flew bodily over Glengariff's head.

"Dogs, too, is it!" howled the Irishman, blood streaming down his face, blue shirt torn almost off his black sweater. "They even set their dogs on me. Do ye hear that, Michael Collins . . . they even set their dogs on me. That's what a man gets for his I.R.A. card. Dogs. Damn you howling white *giddes!"*

He was snarling like one of the animals now, whirling this way and that in the swirl of their leaping white bodies. Chief leaped at him, and Glengariff let the dog strike him, ripping his arm from elbow to hand, and caught the animal by both forefeet before it could leap away, swinging it up over his head.

"Glengariff!" shouted Céleste in sudden anger. "Stop that! Leave my dogs alone. You fight them and they'll kill you. I'll get them off, Glengariff!"

"Leave them alone, is it?" howled the Irishman, and swung Chief around in a circle above his head and let go. "That's how I'll leave them alone. Dogs or men, it doesn't matter to Glengariff. Man or beast. That's how I'll leave them alone."

He whirled to catch another dog as it leaped at him, roaring drunkenly. Face flushing darkly, Céleste straightened

236

from where she had been trying to pull one of the animals free. She still had the long dog whip in one hand, and she sent the six feet of caribou lash flying back over her shoulder with a vicious movement of her arm, then brought it back with a flick of her wrist. Glengariff was still bent forward to catch that second dog when the lash caught him around one arm, pulling him straight with a violent jerk. While the caribou hide was still wound about his arm that way, Céleste heaved backward with all her weight. The Irishman couldn't stop himself. He had to come toward her in a stumbling run to keep from falling. She waited until one more step would have crashed him into her, then jumped aside, her red mouth twisted, her black eyes flaming.

She freed the whip from his arm, as he lurched by, and had it whining out behind her again, and, as he took two or three steps more and was about to recover himself, she lashed out with it again. This time it caught him about the arms with his back turned to her, winding around and around him and pinning his arms to his sides. With the weight of him against it, holding the whip around him like that, and his own momentum giving the impetus to start it off, Céleste swung him around on the end like a pendulum. He made a complete half circle around her before the whip unwound. It released him like a rock from a slingshot, and he spun across the room to crash up against the wall so hard the whole rickety building shuddered.

Glengariff slid down the wall to a sitting position, and Céleste leaped through the carnage after him, long black hair flying. She stood above the man, eyes hot, checked shirt rising and falling with her breathing. But he made no sign. His head had fallen forward on his chest, and his legs were thrust out slackly before him.

"Well," said Arcola, finally, from where he had stood on

the stairway through it all, "twenty men in the place and it takes one woman to stop him. Don't tell Glengariff that when he wakes up. He'll never be able to look another Irishman in the face, if you do."

IV

A pair of weary Percherons were trying to draw an old Studebaker wagon loaded with dirty hay through the muck of the street, and the day in the boat yards must have been over, for the town was filling with laborers, going home for their meals or pushing through the batwings of the Diamond Ring and other saloons, and a party of trappers was coming in for the evening's gambling from their camp in the Twottenny Hills, above the Landing. The bell in the Catholic mission began its lonely tolling as Céleste and Arcola and Lou left the Diamond Ring. Glengariff had gone an hour before, and Badger and the other house men had succeeded in cleaning up the barroom to some extent.

"I don't see what you want to go out now for," Lou said petulantly, drawing her mink wrap closer about her shoulders. "It's already beginning to get cold. Couldn't we do it in the morning?"

"No use in getting any dogs down here," said Céleste. "They've got plenty of good teams at Chippewayan. But we'd better hit Hudson's Bay for the other supplies right now. It's awfully late in the summer to start the upriver trip and expect to hit Lake Athabaska before the ice comes."

Chief had not been hurt too much when Glengariff threw him, and he limped along behind the three people, with the other dogs following him. Arcola took Céleste's elbow as she stepped off the plank walk to cross the muddy street, and she pulled away instinctively.

"You *are* the wild one," he murmured. "I was only going to help you off the curb."

"I guess I can manage," she said.

"It's just what a gentleman does," he smiled.

"Is it?" she said.

He had been bent toward her, speaking that way, and she saw a momentary irritation pass across him, as if he had expected a different reaction from her. He straightened, perhaps sensing for the first time how they were both in the street, and how Lou had not yet descended. "Excuse me, Lou," he said, and that cultivated tone was in his voice again as he reached back for her elbow. Anger plain in her smoldering eyes, Lou stepped into the street. Arcola waved his free hand slightly, trying to cover the *faux pas*. "That Glengariff," he said.

"A crazy drunken Irishman," spat Lou, staring cat-eyed at Céleste. "Belongs to the I.R.A. or something. Always spouting about it when he's tight."

"The Irish Republican Army?" said Arcola. "De Valera outlawed them in 'Thirty-Six. I was there at the time."

Lou glanced at him. "You really have been around, haven't you?"

Arcola shrugged. "A man travels."

"All for the Mounted Police?" asked Céleste.

Arcola laughed amusedly. "How does Glengariff manage here? If Glengariff was forced to flee Ireland because he belonged to the I.R.A., it must mean he'd violated some part of the Treason Act. Couldn't they extradite him on that?"

Lou shrugged. "If they catch him. The Mounties had him once down here, but he got away. He was crazy to come into the Landing today. I know he's tried to get into the States, but the quota business kept him from that. I don't even think he got into this country legally."

Céleste could make little sense of what they said, and didn't care much. To think of Glengariff, for her, was only to remember the sudden, ineffable sadness that had appeared in him, so out of place, somehow, in such a mischievous, devilish face. Arcola was careful to help them both up on the sidewalk this time, and they were passing Alden Tone's little shop on the way to the Hudson's Bay post when Arcola stopped them.

"I might as well pick up a gun while I'm at it," he said. "That *klewang* is an amazing instrument, but it has its limitations."

"That *what?*" said Céleste.

"I understand Tone is quite famous for his guns," Arcola told them, entering the dim little clapboard building. The gunsmith sat over a vise at the rear end of a long, battered counter, a green eyeshade on his graying head, stooped and gnarled in a black leather apron. He left his high stool reluctantly and shuffled toward them. Arcola leaned on the counter, glancing at the rack of rifles. "I'd like something in a repeater, good and heavy, for all-around work north of here."

Tone shoved his visor back and scratched his head, contemplating the guns, finally removing one with tender hands. "Got it about a week ago. It's Winchester's Holland and Holland Magnum. Some amateur sportsman brought it up here and got discouraged when his scope sight was smashed up a little on a sleigh ride. That's the only thing wrong with it, and I got a Malcomb scope here that'll do just as good."

It was a beautiful rifle, the Circassian stock done in two colors, all the carving on the pistol grip and forearm obviously hand work. The way Arcola handled it, shooting the bolt a couple of times and testing it for balance and feeling for the trigger pull, Céleste decided he knew some about guns.

"A Thirty-Thirty or a government caliber would be better," she suggested. "You aren't going to find many Three-Seventy-Five slugs up around Chippewayan."

"I like the gun," said Arcola. "We'll take plenty of the Magnum shells to last. How about that Malcomb scope, Tone?"

The old gunsmith brought out the telescopic sight. Arcola squinted through it, nodding, and handed it to Céleste. She turned toward the doorway, closing one eye to look through the reticule, then shook her head.

"The magnification's too great. I don't use a scope myself, but you don't want over a four power scope for hunting. This is at least eight. You magnify body movement that much more. Your gun will look like it's jumping all over the woods in a snap shot." Arcola couldn't hide his surprise, and she put down the Malcomb, shrugging. "My father was a gunsmith. I learned a few things. Besides the magnification, this Malcomb couldn't stand the recoil on your Three-Seventy-Five. Haven't you got a Mossberg scope, Tone? That Seven C should fit this gun."

"I got a Seven C," said Tone, reaching into the drawer, "but you only got a field of view of twenty-seven feet at a hundred yards."

"We aren't shooting bulldog flies," she told him, taking the rifle up so she could fit the scope. "This base will fit all right. Your gun's tapped for a Lyman Alaskan, and Mossberg fitted his sight to sit on a Lyman or a Fecker base . . . or any of them."

Arcola was watching her with a small grin. "You would advise me to use this on the gun, then?"

Sensing the mockery in his voice, she put both scope and rifle down, turning in a flashing anger. "Maybe you'd rather have someone else take you north."

241

"No, no!" he said, catching at her arm. He shrugged apologetically. "I'm sorry. You know I wouldn't. It's just that I'm not used to having a girl . . . a woman . . . tell me what kind of a gun I should take along, and in such detail."

She shrugged off his hand. "Well, that's it. Take it or leave it, I don't care. I think a Thirty-Thirty would be better, but, if you want the Three-Seventy-Five, that Mossberg's the scope to use."

"Of course, of course." Arcola turned to Lou, holding out his hand. "You don't mind writing a check, do you, honey? That draft on Hudson's Bay should come through soon."

Spanish Lou had stood there all the time, and Céleste could see the anger that had been building up in her at being left out of this. "No," hissed Lou, drawing herself up. "I don't mind writing a check. I don't mind at all." She whirled to the gunsmith. "I'll send it over with Badger this evening. Is that all right?"

"Sure, Miss Lou, sure."

The woman spun toward the door, her long skirts making a swift, impatient rustle down the plank floor, and Arcola turned after her. "Lou . . . ?"

"When you two get through talking over your little *business*," she flung over her shoulder, "I'll see you in the Ring."

Arcola looked after her till she was in the street, then turned to Céleste, shrugging. "Now what makes a woman act like that?"

"Don't you know?" smiled Céleste faintly. Then she undid a button of her shirt and unbuckled a specie belt from inside and pulled it out. "I'll take five hundred Thirty-Thirties while you're getting those Magnums."

Tone brought out a case of shells, stacking them on the counter, and Arcola opened one of the cardboard boxes, taking out a .375, turning it in his fingers as he spoke. "You must know Lou pretty well."

Céleste was opening a box of her caliber. "Not very well, why?"

"You came a long way after hearing she needed your help."

"Not so far."

With his fingernail, Arcola idly scraped a little of the wax from the .375. "Farther than an ordinary guide would have come for a job. Are there other reasons than just appear on the surface?"

"I don't understand."

He slipped the cartridge back in the box. "You are the daughter of Georges Manatte, the factor of Peace River Landing who was tortured and murdered in Nineteen Twenty-Three?"

Her head came up swiftly. "It's a common name in this country."

"But everyone does not have it who has lived with the Indians or has run wild in the woods most of her life, orphaned at ten by the killing of her parents."

Her eyes flashed. "You know more than what might be good for you."

"It's all in the police files," he shrugged. "I just put two and two together. The Mounties never got the murderers?"

"No," she said simply.

"Yet Pengarth was found dead up north of Edmonton in Nineteen Thirty, and a Dog Rib who saw it claimed he had seen a woman follow Pengarth from the post when he left with his team for the trap lines." Arcola saw how she had begun to breathe more heavily, staring at the wall, and he went on softly. "There are some . . . a few police among them . . . who find some vague connection between Wight Reddington's disappearance and your father's death. Is that why you came down here?"

"You've put a lot of twos together," she said. "You had better stop adding. As far as motives go, we could just as well inquire about yours. Why did you come here?"

"You know."

"Do I?" she said. "When I first came into that room, I was struck with the strong feeling that I had seen you before." She turned toward him. "Arcola, just who are you?"

V

The cranberries were gone from the saskatoon and the balsam poplars were beginning to turn brown and the first Lapland longspurs were migrating southward from the Barrens with their haunting *chee-chup* echoing across the Athabaska River north of Twottenny Hills. It made Sean Glengariff shiver a little as he stood there on the high bank overlooking the water. He hated the winter. He liked the summer here, when he could roar down the white water with his *voyageurs* shouting on the thwarts and the thole pins thumping to the shifting beat of his sweep; but he hated the winter, when every night brought a wish to be back in Connach with the peat fire snapping softly on the flat hearth and the soft Gaelic of ancient Erin warming his heart. *Arragh,* he would never see that again. He turned up the bank and kicked his way morosely through the backbrush toward Twottenny Hills.

He couldn't remember the time he had been able to enter a town without slinking through the streets in fear of some kind of authority tagging him. The Royal Irish Constabulary. Scotland Yard. The Mounties. He had been a fool to get drunk in Athabaska yesterday. They would be looking for him again now. He scratched the pink stubble of his beard morosely, pulling a pint from his pocket. It was bitter rotgut, and he emptied what was left in one long pull, grimacing violently as he heaved the bottle away. How many had that been this morning? He didn't remember exactly. He'd gotten a couple of extra pulls from the 'breed who'd sold him the pint. What was the difference? Drink your breakfast, drink your lunch. He spat, shoving dirty hands in his pockets, to stand there looking out over the murky river and trying to remember exactly what had happened in the Diamond Ring yesterday. When he had come to, Badger had said something about a woman. A woman? *Arragh,* no woman could have done that to a Connach man!

Glengariff turned as he became aware of two figures making their way to him along the bank. Spanish Lou's bold beauty was awkward and out of place, somehow, in a bulky Mackinaw and heavy corduroys and black, laced boots. Badger Bates was with her, in a canvas coat. Lou stopped before Glengariff, looking at his bleary eyes.

"You been drinking again, or is that from yesterday?"

Glengariff spat once more, glaring at Badger, and started to turn away. Lou caught his arm. "Wait a minute, Glengariff. I'll forget what happened in the Ring yesterday, if you'll sign on my boat going upriver. I'm having trouble with my *voyageurs.* I knew you could settle it if I could find you. You've worked with most of the crew before, and they respect you. I'll put you on the sweep, if you can get them to shove off today."

Glengariff stared at her a moment, shrugged. "Where's the scow?"

It took them half an hour to walk to the boat yards, and, as they neared town, Glengariff became filled with the hunted feeling again, looking about him for a red coat behind every bush. The Hudson's Bay scow was already loaded, run bow

245

foremost into the bank, and the crew of Canuck *voyageurs* stood sullenly together near the secured painter, apparently arguing with Arcola and Céleste Manatte.

"I'm glad you're here, Lou," said Arcola. "Can't you do something with these men?"

"Maybe Glengariff can," said Lou.

Céleste turned angrily. "I won't have a drunken man on my sweep."

"You won't find a better man on the river, drunk or sober," said Lou.

"What seems to be the trouble with the men?" Glengariff asked Céleste pointedly.

She turned away, apparently not meaning to answer, then, drawing a frustrated breath, she turned back, waving her hand. "Hudson's Bay didn't have enough flour to last upriver."

"We ain't going to live on soda biscuits," said one of the French-Canadians. "We ain't going without flour for our bannocks every day."

"Gentlemen," said Glengariff, moving toward them somewhat. "You know me. You're going to live on soda biscuits and like them. They're just as good as bannocks, and they ain't as greasy. Now, get on board."

They shifted uncertainly, glances passing among them. Then they turned, one by one, climbing over the bow into the boat.

"I told you he was the best man on the river," said Lou, smiling in some sense of petty triumph over Céleste.

Céleste looked from Arcola to Glengariff, shrugged, swung aboard. The Irishman and Arcola helped Lou in, Arcola following. Then Badger and Glengariff unhitched the painter and shoved off. She was a heavy scow, some forty feet long with a twelve-foot beam, bow and stern square and sloping like a punt. The rowing was done by eighteen-foot sweeps working in thole pins, three sweeps to a side, the rowers rising from and falling back on the seats with each stroke. Glengariff ran a practiced eye over the craft as he made his way aft, pleased that she had been put together so neatly. The cargo was stored on garboards instead of flat on deck, free enough of the bottom to keep dry no matter what water they shipped, strakes beneath the thwarts to take care of heavy water or rapids. There were a couple of steel rods along the bottom to save wear on the timbers in striking rocks, and Glengariff spotted pumps in the bilges.

"A veritable luxury liner," Glengariff grinned, climbing to his spot on the short afterdeck where he was to steer with another sweep. There were five Canucks, and Badger took his place in the sixth spot at the oars, the two women and Arcola sitting just beneath Glengariff to keep the weight in the stern.

There was the somber threat of rain in the gray overcast, and the wind had beat the water into ugly whitecaps north of Athabaska Landing. Glengariff did not realize how much the liquor had affected him till they came to the first rocks about a mile north of the Landing. He let the boat drive straight for the submerged boulder and put his weight against the sweep at the last moment. The scow was suddenly shuddering to the crunching scrape of granite along its bottom, and Badger was thrown back into Arcola and the women with the violence of his sweep slamming against the boulder.

"Glengariff," shouted Arcola, "what are you doing?"

The boat scraped off the rock and dipped into deep water with a groan, and Glengariff eased his weight from the sweep. "Faith, it's no use trying to point her around them boulders. The suction will take you right into them. We have to go straight for them and catch the division of water on the rock, and it carries us clear. . . ."

He trailed off as he saw Céleste looking up at him. He tried to keep from wiping sweat off his face, but couldn't, and she saw that, too. Well, what if he had run it a bit too close? He'd catch the next one. He saw the boiling water after a bit and spread his legs a little. He could feel the indecision in the oarsmen now as they pulled, their mistrust of him causing them to lose unison as they neared the eddy. He tried to see where the water divided on the rock. He blinked his eyes. *Arragh,* what was wrong with them? There didn't seem to be a division. Or were there two? Or three? Suddenly, he threw all his weight against the sweep, and the scow turned violently. The three *voyageurs* on the left were thrown across the seats into Badger and the others. Lou fell hard against the thwarts, crying out. Glengariff clung desperately to his sweep to keep from being thrown outboard as the stern of the scow smashed into the rock.

As they rode free, he caught Céleste looking up at him again, and forced a grin. "What did I tell you . . . a *vourneen deelish* . . . just catch it on that division of water and you ride free every time. I've been running the Athabaska more seasons than I care to remember now, and I've never foundered a boat yet. It's like punting on the Shannon only you got a bigger. . . ."

The full comprehension in her big eyes made him trail off again, and then, in an uncomfortable bluster, he shouted at Badger: "Ship your sweep there, do ye want to ram the bank?"

They were in quiet water again now, and, after Céleste turned back, Glengariff clung glumly to his own sweep. What was the world coming to when an Irishman couldn't have a little drink now and then? It began to rain before noon, and the water became more choppy. The men at the sweeps huddled dismally into their Mackinaws, rising and falling in grim accord, fighting the current with every stroke. The black poplars reeled along the banks before Glengariff's vision in tipsy ranks. When he thought nobody was watching, he shook his head, trying to clear it. He was beginning to feel sick, and the dizziness was increasing. Faith, it had only been a pint! A pint couldn't more than make a Connach man warm around the gills. He became aware that Badger was calling to him.

"Aye?" he said.

"We passed the Hudson's Bay marker already!" shouted Badger over the beat of the rain now falling against the deckboards. "We'd better pull in and portage White Rapids!"

"Don't be a puling *lanabh!*" the Irishman called back. "You're riding with Glengariff now. No use portaging on a little four-foot drop like that. We'll ride it over."

"You can never make it over in this rain!" Badger howled. "You can't even see where you're going. Pull her in, Glengariff, before it's too late."

Céleste was climbing up onto the rear deck. "Give me that sweep, Glengariff."

"Get off my deck," shouted the Irishman. "I'm the pilot up here."

"You're drunk," she shouted back. "Lou, why did you ever let him come aboard in this condition?"

"I didn't know he had taken on so much," Lou called, something frightened in her voice. "Please, Glengariff, turn us in."

"I'll not turn in!" he bellowed, struggling with Céleste as she sought to get the sweep. Her long, wet hair swung around in his face as she turned, blinding him. "You're riding with Glengariff now."

The grinding crash drowned his voice, and the stern tilted violently. White water shot up around Glengariff, and he had the sensation of falling swiftly through foam. The sweep was

249

torn from his hands, and the deck shot from beneath his feet. He realized he was sliding down the garboards, and clutched wildly for some hold.

"Arcola! Arcola!" he heard Lou scream.

A heavy body crashed into his, and he got an instant's impression of Badger's scarred face. Then water closed black and icy over him, and all sound was blotted out completely. Something slammed into his feet from above, sending a shock of pain to his hips. He came up once in the foam to see the scow tilted over on one side with three of the *voyageurs* working madly at the sweeps to get it out of the rapids before it turned over completely. He didn't remember when he had struck his head, but the pain there made him wipe his hand across it, and his fingers came away red with blood. Maybe that was what Céleste saw, from the scow. Through a daze, he caught sight of her still clinging to the stern sweep, and realized it must have been the only thing that saved the boat from upsetting completely. She shouted something, pointing toward Glengariff. Helpless, stunned, Glengariff was swept into a bunch of rocks, smashing about among them and going beneath the water once more. He came up that last time too weak to fight, and barely heard what Arcola shouted from the scow, before going down again.

"Céleste!" screamed Arcola, "don't go into that white water, you'll never come out alive!"

The rain had stopped, and the poplars stood dripping dismally about the flickering campfire there on the bank above the Athabaska. The *voyageurs* were eating cabin biscuits and bacon, and a big kettle of Lipton's was coming to a boil above the flames. Céleste had changed her clothes and was drying her hair over the fire when Lou called to her from where they had laid Glengariff. As Céleste walked over, the Irishman opened his eyes, staring up at Lou, where she crouched above him, then turning his head until he could see Céleste.

"Faith," he groaned, "first she tries to kill me with a dog whip, then she saves my life."

Arcola had been standing behind Lou, and he allowed a faint disgust to show in his face before turning away and walking toward the fire. Biting her underlip, Lou rose, moving after him. Glengariff sat up dizzily, feeling for the thick bandage they had wound about his head. His blue eyes were clear now, and he sat there staring at the ground.

"I was drunk," he said finally.

"Why?" she said.

He looked up in some surprise. "Because I put a pint of whisky down me, that's why. Why else?"

She sensed his belligerence was aimed at himself more than at her, and she shook out her long hair, moving nearer. "I don't mean that, Glengariff. I mean *why* do you drink? Were you a drunkard before you left Ireland?"

His head turned up sharply, and she saw that strange sadness cross his face, so out of keeping with the devilish arch of his bushy brows and the puckish mobility of his mouth. She felt a sudden compassion for this strange man, and dropped to her knees beside him.

"I wasn't past stopping into O'Falleron's for a sip now and then," he grumbled.

"But not the way you do it now," she said.

"No." He shook his head. "I guess not."

"Why is it so bad?" she said. "What is it makes you do it this way? Arcola said something about the Irish Republican Army and De Valera outlawing you or exiling you or something."

251

"Yes,"—a sudden bitter intensity had entered Glengariff's voice, and his face seemed to take on a gauntness—"I'm I.R.A. That's what they do to you. Fifteen years you fight for your land, and then they make you an outlaw. If Michael Collins was alive, he'd be right here along with me. . . ."

"Michael Collins?"

"Aye, and Arthur Griffith and Eamonn Geannt and Patrick Pearce and all the others, right . . . ," he looked up suddenly, realizing what she had meant. "You don't know Michael Collins?" He slumped back, staring at the ground. "Of course, you don't. The greatest man the world ever saw, and ye don't know him, and not many others do, either. Dead a scant sixteen years, and already forgotten. Not only general of the I.R.A., but leader of all Ireland. I was with him when the I.R.A. was the Sinn Fein Volunteers. I guess I saw him run his flying columns into the Tans a hundred times. A thousand. . . ."

"Tans?" she said.

"A bunch of *Dubh Gaills* sent over by England to help the Royal Constabulary fight us. They wasn't even official army. That's why we called them Black and Tans. The uniform was a mixture of British army and civilian. They couldn't stop Collins."

She had heard little of the world outside this frozen north country, and there was something about the way he talked that enthralled her. "You were fighting England, then."

"That we were," said Glengariff. "We still are. The I.R.A., that is."

"Arcola said something of a treaty."

"That's it, that's it," said Glengariff, flushing, jerking his hand. "De Valera signed a treaty. We're a dominion like Canada. Do you think we fought for that? Half of Ireland belonging to England complete, and the other half tied to her by a dominion status chain. Free State? That makes me laugh."

"But if you signed a treaty, how can you still fight?" she said.

"The I.R.A. never signed any treaty," he said.

"Oh." She said it softly, because she was beginning to understand. "And that's why this De Valera outlawed you?"

"Who do you think put him where he is today? Who do you think made him prime minister? So he outlaws us. Where's Sean Glengariff? Oh, you mean that machine gunner who saved my life in the Easter Monday Rebellion? I had to outlaw him. He belonged to the I.R.A. We would have hung him if we could have found him."

His bitterness beat against her in an acrid wave, but she could understand it, and she was beginning to understand that sadness she had seen. "And you can't go back," she said.

"Do you know what that is?" he said, and his eyes held that desolation. Then he shook his head. "No, you wouldn't know. You didn't even know Michael Collins. You don't know Erin. How could you?" He was looking beyond her now. "Sometimes of a night, I get to thinking of it. Or almost anytime. That's when I get to drinking, mostly. The way the lilacs bloom in Athione. An ass coming down between the blackthorn quicks with a creel of turf bowing his legs. Irish yews as tall as heaven." He was holding her raptly again, as if she could see it through his eyes, not so much in what he said, as the way he said it, his expressive lips stirring caressingly around the words. "And the songs."

" 'The Royal Blackbird?' " she said, caught up in it.

"Aye, and 'Granuaile' and 'Molly Baun' and the rest. The only time I ever hear them any more is when I sing them, and that's only when I'm drunk."

She was silent for a moment, the compassion deep within her. Then she moved her hand vaguely. "But if it's over, if you can't go back, why not start again? You're young and strong and. . . ."

"Where?" he said, and looked emptily about him at the dripping poplars under the black sky. "Here?"

She straightened slightly. "Why not? What's wrong with here? It's a good land. It's a beautiful land. You would have seen it if you hadn't been so blinded by your own bitterness. The way white water roars over the falls in the spring. There's nothing so clean looking. The feel of snowflakes on your face with the first fall of winter. So soft, you think it's angels reaching down to touch you. The fresh, green smell of piney woods and the way the cones crunch under your feet, and the baby beavers sliding down a mud bank when you catch them unawares, and a funny old black bear rooting around through the pine needles for onions. And we have songs, too." She inclined her head toward the *voyageurs* where they had finished their meal and were huddling, wet and disconsolate, about the fire, trying to raise their spirits with a feeble "Alouette." "Listen."

" 'Alouette, gentile Alouette, Alouette, petite plumerai,' " they sang, one after the other joining in, voices becoming stronger and more boisterous as they went on, the song warming them as much as the fire. "Je te plumerai la tête, je te plumerai la bec, je te. . . .' "

Glengariff listened for a minute, something crossing his features, and then turned toward her, his face twisting in some nameless expression. Holding the blanket around him, he stood abruptly, walking away from her and down toward the river where they had beached the scow.

Arcola came over to Céleste. "Well," he said, and he was

254

talking of what had happened to the scow, "did Glengariff learn his lesson?"

Céleste was watching the Irishman go, and she did not mean the same thing Arcola meant. "Maybe he's beginning to learn," she said.

VI

The buildings of Fort Chippewayan stood white and substantial on the rocky point of Athabaska Lake's north shore. The most important northland mission of the Roman Catholic Oblate Fathers, it was also practically the northern boundary of the Cree Indians and the southern line of the Dene Nation, that extended northward from Chippewayan to the Arctic. Céleste was first out of the scow as they beached it, helping Badger and the *voyageurs* to haul it up on the sand. Glengariff was busy unshipping the sail they had used across the lake, and Céleste got the packet of mail they had been entrusted with by the. H.B.C. factor at Athabaska Landing and headed for Chippewayan's dozen log cabins overlooking the beach. The factor of this Hudson's Bay post was a crisply thatched Scot named MacDougal, who offered them drinks and told them of a French half-breed living north of the post who had several good dog teams he would like to sell. This was what interested Céleste most, as the first snow was due any day.

"I don't see why we have to go look at them right away," pouted Lou wearily. "Can't we rest a day or two . . . now we're here?"

"The longer you put off getting the dogs, the more you'll pay for them," Céleste told her. "The Indians and 'breeds up here are just as careless of their dogs during the summer when they don't need them for sledding, as they are of their boats during the winter when the water's frozen over. From May to September the dogs just get along the best they can, starving and getting mangy and sick. Buy them then and you get them for a song. About now the Indians start paying attention to their teams again, and the closer it comes to the first snow the more their value rises."

"You go, then," said Lou. "Jan and I will stay at the post."

"I really think we'd better go, Lou," said Arcola. "After all, we're going to depend a lot on those dogs from here on in. I'd like to see what we're getting."

"Jan. . . ." Lou held out her hand angrily, then stopped, looking from Arcola to Céleste. Her eyes narrowed momentarily. Then she took a deep breath. "Oh, all right. I'll send Badger along with you."

"Has he any money?" asked Arcola.

Lou's hesitation mirrored her annoyance. She looked at Arcola without answering for a moment, then turned in an irritated way to Céleste. "How much will it be?"

"We should have two full teams besides my own dogs, and two sleds," said Céleste. "Several hundred dollars, at least."

It was about a mile to the half-breed's cabin, over a low range of hills just back of Chippewayan. The spruce stood around the swart building of undressed logs, sighing softly in the wind, and the dogs began yapping madly even before Céleste could see them. A huge, black Husky loped toward them with yellow fangs bared as they stepped from the trees, followed by two or three gaunt spitz. A bearded man erupted from the cabin, waving his arms and shouting at the beasts.

"Whoa, Voyageur, whoa!" he bellowed, but the dogs did not stop till Céleste uncoiled her whip and snapped it in the air. The black brute slid on his haunches and began circling her, his throat rumbling. *"Bon jour, bon jour,"* called the half-breed. "Forgive my *chien* . . . he is hungry. I am Petit Pierre,

256

an', if you come to buy dogs, I welcome you, but, if you come to eat my bannocks, you better go back to Chippewayan."

"MacDougal told us about your dogs," said Céleste. "He seemed to think they'd be better than the ones we could get at Chippewayan."

"Merci, merci," said Petit Pierre, and waved his hand at the dogs gathering from behind the house, snarling and growling in a dark hostility. "How you like Hector over there? He's MacKenzie River. I got him in four-dog hitch pulling a thousand pounds two years ago."

Céleste glanced perfunctorily at the huge, brown animal with its docked tail, and shook her head. "I don't want any work dogs. MacKenzie Rivers are all right on heavy loads, but they'll wear out on a long run. How about that spitz?"

"That's Bigriver. He pulled Sebat the Black eighty-five miles in a twenty-four run with only two fires. Come here, Bigriver, come here."

He went among the dogs, shoving them aside with his legs. Bigriver snapped at him, and he jerked aside, slapping at the black muzzle. The dogs were half wild with hunger, having foraged for themselves all summer, and it was like playing with a bunch of wolves. Pierre dragged Bigriver nonchalantly over to Céleste, and she squatted down, more careful than the French half-breed had been.

"Ninety pounds in good condition, maybe a little light now," said the man, squatting beside her. Then he was looking at her with a certain calculation in his eyes. "You want them for a long run, ah? Peace River, maybe."

She sensed Arcola stiffen behind her, and looked narrowly at Pierre. The man was gripping the dog's rear legs. "Look at the second thighs here. I bet you look a long time to find bigger ones. Made for pulling, ah? Good king dog, I say."

"Peace River?" she said.

"Nice coat, too. With ground wool like that, how you ever get any mange?" He pulled at the long master hair. "Yes, things travel, *mam'selle*."

"Nobody outside our party knew. Even some within it didn't know."

"There was an Irishman," said Pierre, pursing his lips. He likes his *vin,* no? *Oui.* Once he talked with some Indians down at Fort Smith when he had drunk a little *tiswin* they were making. The Indians arrived here sometime before you did, on their way north. I talked with them, you know."

"I know," she said.

"Reddington?" he said.

"You seem to know," she told him.

"Nice light spring in the pasterns, too," he said, running his hands down Bigriver's forequarters. "There's a man here you might be interested in. He's been waiting around Chippewayan for some time. He has something of Reddington's he might like to sell to you."

"How much is the dog?"

"Twenty beaver, ah?" said Pierre.

"I'm paying cash."

"Oh, sixty dollar."

"Give you forty," Céleste told him.

"What, and a neck like that on him? He'll pull twice as long as any you get. Fifty."

"His feet are soft. Forty-five."

"He is yours."

"Now, how about a wheel dog to work with him?" said Céleste.

Pierre tied Bigriver to a stake, away from the others, and got hold of a mangy-looking Husky. Céleste ran her eye over the hindquarters and saw the strength in the stifles. She ran her hand through the coat for mange.

"We're only interested in one thing of Reddington's," she said.

"This one . . . he is deceptive. He looks like he's dying, but there's more left in him than most are born with. He's only five." Pierre squatted down, studying the dog. "It's a piece of paper with writing on it."

Céleste saw the expression on Arcola's face. "What writing?" she asked.

"I don't read," he said.

She looked up at Arcola, and he nodded. "Maybe after we finish with the dogs. How much?"

"Fifty dollars," said Pierre. "He ain't camped far from here."

"He's getting old. Thirty-five dollars."

It went on like that till they had the two teams out of it. Pierre had the ten dogs tied apart, then he got an old Springfield .30 out of his cabin and swung off toward the timber. It was about a mile through poplars and spruce over a low swell of hills and down into a shallow valley where a stream ran into the lake southward. There was a tattered birch-bark canoe beached on the sand of a mucky inlet, and the bulldog flies hung in maddening swarms above the sere buffalo grass. There were two men seated at a small fire drinking Lipton's from empty cans that had once held tinned beef, and Petit Pierre stopped within the woods.

"Johnny's sort of jumpy. You liable to get a slug through your tripe if you come on him sudden," he explained, then called to the men in the open. "Ho, Johnny. Is little Pierre. I come in, ah?"

One of the men at the fire had leaped to his feet as the half-breed called out, his hand diving for a big Webley. He held the .455 pointed up till Petit Pierre stepped from the trees, then shoved it back inside his canvas parka.

"I brought *M'sieu* Arcola," said Pierre. "And a couple others with him. Johnny, I like you to meet. . . ."

"Céleste Manatte," said the woman, stepping into the open behind Pierre.

Johnny Belcarres stood there with his mouth open. His pale blue eyes were blank in that moment.

Céleste had her dog whip, and her eyes were wide and black and waiting for his reaction, knowing what it would be when it came, wanting it. "Go on, Johnny," she said finally, taking a breath through her nose that fluttered her nostrils. "Do you know how long I've been waiting for this? Do you know what it is to see your mother and father tortured and murdered? Go on, Johnny, go on." She took a step forward, her voice a hissing intonation now. "I've thought of it often, Johnny. I've thought of what I would do if I ever met you again. Go on. . . ."

He did. With a sudden, choked sound, he went for the Webley. His eyes were no longer blank or pale, but filled with a violent, fearful resolve. At the same time, her whip snapped to life, back and forward, and the long lash of caribou hide caught him with his gun just past the lapel of his parka. The .455 went off when the whip snapped around his wrist, and his arm was yanked outward, pulling him forward. It was then Céleste heard the faint singing noise past her ear. Her lash was still around Belcarres's wrist when he jerked violently erect, his weight lurching backward against her whip and stretching it taut. He hung that way for a moment, glassy-eyed, the hilt of a big knife protruding from his chest. Then he dropped his gun, and fell face forward onto the ground. Céleste stood there, holding her whip, feeling frustration. Arcola stepped to Belcarres, turned him over, pulling the knife from his chest. Then he saw the expression on Céleste's face, and he seemed suddenly surprised.

"He would have shot you," Arcola said.

"Would he?" she said.

"Did it mean that much to you?" he asked her.

"Faith, and he never would have got a chance to squeeze the trigger on her," said the other man, standing by the fire now. "The way she had that whip on him, the banshees was already singing his *caoine*. You didn't have to throw that blade, and you know it, Arcola."

"Glengariff," said Céleste blankly. Her attention had been so taken up with Belcarres she had been aware of the man by the fire only as a dim background figure until now. "What are you doing here?"

"Sure, and I came to sup a bit of *poteen* with an old friend of mine."

Pierre was kneeling by Belcarres. "I did not know it would be this way. *Sacre nom,* I would not have brought you if I'd known. Now the red coats get us all, and I can't sell dogs no more or anything."

"Red coats, nothing," said Arcola. "I'm from Intelligence at Ottawa. That's all the officiating you'll need here. He pulled a gun on us, that's all. Your name needn't even be mentioned when I turn in my report at Athabaska."

"Oh, *merci, m'sieu, merci,*" said Pierre, almost crying. He jumped slightly as Belcarres moved. "*Bon Dieu,* I think he lives!"

There was something empty within Céleste now. The terrible, bitter hatred she had carried for Belcarres all these years was suddenly gone, leaving an emotion she could not define, a vague sensation akin to regret, or a remnant of that first keen frustration she had known when she realized Arcola had taken the vengeance out of her hands. Belcarres was trying to say something, and she went to her knees beside him, trying to tell herself this was the way she had wanted it, the way it should be.

"Didn't know it was you," Belcarres gasped, clutching the bloody wound in his chest. "Thought you had gone south. That's what they told me. Wouldn't have come back if I knew it was you. We all know you haven't stopped looking. Got Pengarth down in Edmonton, didn't you?" He tried to take a breath, and it made a ghastly, gurgling sound. "Didn't know it was you. Pierre said a man named Arcola. . . ."

"*Botte* it was," said Pierre. "That's what those Indians said. They got it from the drunk Irisher."

"Who's drunk?" said Glengariff.

"Shut up," said Céleste. "Pierre just said something about Reddington."

"Yeah,"—Belcarres tried to laugh ruefully, but it came out with that other sound again—"want to buy it? Page from his log. That's what you want, isn't it? You got one. I got one."

"Where?" Céleste didn't realize she had hold of him.

The pain in Belcarres's sweating face grew more intense. "I got mine from an Eskimo up in Dawson. Said he'd gotten it off a Loucheux he killed. You know how those Eskimos go at it with the Indians. Somewhere on the MacKenzie. No telling why the Indian kept it. Fetish or something, maybe. Like scalps. The Eskimo knew white man's writing. Thought somebody in Dawson could read it. I read it. Want to buy it?" He tried to laugh again. "Make a deal with you. Split fifty-fifty with you when you find it."

"Find what?" said Céleste. "What will this log lead us to? That's what you and Kamsack wanted when you killed my father?" Her fingers were white on his arm. "Tell me, Belcarres, tell me. . . ."

She stopped at the strange pallor that had come into his face. She realized he had been staring at something above her most of the time. Beneath the pain in his eyes there had been a faint speculation that came and went. Now it was gone, abruptly, and a terrible, stunned comprehension was there, wiping away the pain. His eyes grew wide, staring beyond her, and his mouth opened without any sound coming at first, and then his voice was filled with wild surprise.

"You," he gasped. "You!"

He remained that way an instant longer. Then his head lolled back with the eyes still open, but they were blank and empty, and the weight of his body sagged heavily against Céleste's leg. It was a moment before she realized he was dead. She turned to see at whom he had been looking. Arcola stood just above her, staring down at Belcarres.

"What did he mean, Arcola?" she said. "Where did he know you . . . before?"

VII

The first snow came to Chippewayan on October the Nineteenth, four days after the scow had arrived there, descending like a soft, white hand through the waiting poplars about the dozen log buildings of the post. It filled Arcola with a sense of relief as he stood down by the lake shore, once the snow had stopped, the heavy, checked Mackinaw giving his slim figure a bulky look. It was all Céleste had been waiting for, and they would start now. The sleds were loaded and the dogs waiting restlessly on their picket chains where Céleste had pitched camp, up from the beach in a grove of spruce. Arcola was walking back toward camp now, and, as he neared the trees, he became aware of another figure on the lake shore, square and blocky in a tattered Eskimo parka. The man turned, the stringy wolverine fur lining his hood forming a dirty fringe above his blue eyes.

"Watching something?" asked Arcola.

"Nothing particular." Glengariff kicked absently at the snow. "Funny."

"What's funny?"

"When it comes down," said Glengariff, "when it falls on you. Like angels reaching down to touch you."

"The snow?"

"You wouldn't look for it in a woman like that, would you, now?" Glengariff seemed to be talking to himself more than to Arcola. "A wild wight of a thing like that. But that's what she said. Like angels." He toed the snow again. "I never thought about it that way, did you?"

"Can't say that I did," said Arcola.

This facet of Glengariff's nature did not surprise him so much as it had surprised Céleste. Arcola had spent enough time in Ireland to know the dreamy mysticism that lay in every Irishman. He had seen that vagrant sadness in Glengariff's eyes, and had marked it for evidence of the Gaelic romanticism that lay beneath the Irishman's bitter, cynical, volatile exterior. Glengariff seemed to become aware of how Arcola was watching him, and pulled his head up, as if snapping out of a dream. His eyes dropped to the Holland & Holland cuddled in Arcola's elbow.

"Like it, don't you? Been shooting?"

"Practicing a little," said Arcola.

"That Mossberg scope stand the recoil?"

"Like a rock," said Arcola.

"Never took much to a scope sight myself."

"You were doing mostly snap shooting in Ireland," said Arcola.

"That I was. But I can shoot the eye out of a yellow rail at fifteen hundred. Maybe you'll need a man like that along."

Arcola didn't understand it for a moment, then he laughed

without much mirth. "You? When you could spend the winter in glorious, bibulous bacchanalia here at Chippewayan. Don't be absurd." A suspicious discernment entered his eyes. "Why?"

"Because there's been too much blather about Reddington. He was doing something more than just trying to find a new winter route to Peace River Landing. Whatever it is must be big enough to cut me in. I've come this far. I don't want to stop now."

"Don't be absurd," said Arcola. "I know what makes you think that. We wouldn't take you along, anyway, whatever the circumstances."

"Wouldn't you?" A slyness curled Glengariff's mouth. "That police commission of yours, Arcola. Signed by Joseph Longworth in June of Nineteen Thirty-Seven. Yet you said you were in Ireland when De Valera outlawed the I.R.A., and that was in June of the same year. It's not only a mathematical improbability. It's also a temporal and geographical impossibility."

Arcola failed to hide what that did to him, and it drew an irritation through his voice. "I said I was in Ireland when De Valera outlawed the I.R.A.. You forget that first happened in Nineteen Thirty-Six."

"Did it?"

"What are you driving at, Glengariff?"

"What Belcarres meant when he saw you just before he died."

Arcola felt his fingers tightening around the rifle. "You're drunk."

Glengariff leaned forward slightly, his clear blue eyes staring into Arcola's. "Am I?"

Arcola looked at him a long moment, controlling the anger that beat insistently through his body with an effort. "No,"

Arcola said finally, "you're not drunk."

"Céleste already wonders what was between you and Belcarres," said Glengariff. "Now, if I were to drop a word or two about the little temporal discrepancy you allowed to slip in between the date of your presence in Ireland and the date of Longworth's signing that commission . . . ?"

Arcola bent forward, speaking through thin lips. "I told you Nineteen Thirty-Six."

"That's what you told me," said Glengariff. "What did you tell Céleste?" The Irishman waited, while Arcola stood there, his breathing hoarsely audible. Finally that Gaelic smile caught up Glengariff's flannel mouth. "You don't remember, do you? You don't remember whether you told her you were in Ireland in 'Thirty-Six or 'Thirty-Seven. How unfortunate, Arcola."

"Glengariff. . . ." Arcola couldn't help the jerky way he raised the .375 till its end caught against the Irishman's parka.

Glengariff stood without moving, still grinning. "They can see you from the post here, Arcola. It wouldn't help." He waited until Arcola let the muzzle of the Magnum drop. "You swing a lot of weight with Spanish Lou. Just a word dropped, and I could be included in your little trip."

Arcola's words came out with a hissing intonation. "All right, Glengariff, you're cut in. But it's the biggest mistake you ever made in your whole misbegotten, rum-soaked life."

Arcola found Céleste feeding the dogs their evening meal of whitefish where they were chained to the trees, hidden somewhat from the main portion of the camp. The wild litheness of her body, crouched there, caught at him, as it always did, and he stopped, drinking in the rich, black abundance of her hair half obscuring the curved line of her smooth cheek.

Had he thought Lou possessed a certain beauty? It almost made him laugh now. Céleste felt his eyes on her and turned, smiling when she saw who it was.

"You'll have a good king dog in Bigriver. He already knows me. All you have to be careful about is not making any fast moves near him."

Arcola leaned his rifle against a tree, coming to hunker down beside her while she went on gaining the spitz's confidence. "You're a strange woman, Céleste. You have such a way with dogs. You have such a deep affinity with this country. Seeing you when you're wild, like that time you took the whip to Glengariff, one would think that's all you were, living up here all your life, as crude and untamed as the Indians. Yet, you possess a refinement, a sophistication that constantly surprises me."

He had allowed his hand to drop on her arm, and she turned toward him, nothing in her eyes. "What do you mean, Arcola?"

He let himself move in till his leg touched her hip, and his voice had taken on that vibrancy. "I mean I've traveled all over the world, Céleste. . . ."

It was an old game with him, and he was expecting a stereotypical reaction to his hesitation, and, when it did not come, he knew an abrupt irritation. He was looking into her eyes, and he waited for that blank veil to leave them, the way it had left Lou's, and so many others'. But Céleste's eyes remained devoid of any expression he could see, and her breathing was barely audible.

"I've been all over the world," he was forced to say finally, "and I've never found a woman like you, Céleste."

She withdrew her arm from his hand, rising. "That's a nice compliment, Arcola."

"Don't you understand what I'm saying, Céleste?" He realized his voice sounded harsh, shrill, and he stood stiffly, trying to regain that suavity. All the times in the past it had been like this. So many other women had come so easily, and yet this one. . . . He closed his hands tightly, moving toward her again, lowering his voice deliberately. "You do understand what I'm saying. You're avoiding the issue. All the way up from Athabaska you've played cat and mouse with me. Changed the subject and put me off, and pretended you didn't see how I felt. You're going to stop pretending, Céleste. No other woman ever did this to me."

Céleste met his eyes with that disturbing gaze. "Didn't she? I've finished with the dogs here, Arcola. I'd better go see about the sleds. We're starting tomorrow morning, you know."

Arcola took a spasmodic step after her, as she turned toward the fort, then halted himself. Someone else was standing in the beeches. Céleste was going in the opposite direction, toward Chippewayan, and, as she disappeared through the sumac, Spanish Lou stepped from the trees.

"Won't she play, Arcola?" Lou asked.

He could not help noting how awkward she looked in the heavy plaid Mackinaw and buckskin leggings, and he did not try to hide his anger. "You were listening."

"That's right." She came up to him, a hissing intonation to her voice, little pin points of light catching in her eyes. "I've been watching for weeks now. I'm through watching, Arcola."

His voice softened abruptly, and he tried to touch her. "Now, Lou. . . ."

"No!" Lou took a step away, her eyes dropping to his hand, her mouth twisting in repulsion. "You can't do that to me again, Arcola. I don't understand why I let you do it in the first place. I don't understand why I didn't see how you were using me. You've used every woman you've ever known, haven't you? Let me go, let me go!" She was almost screaming now, twisting out of his hands. "You've used every woman. And now you come up against one you can't use, and you're lost. It's almost funny to watch." She tossed her head back in what was meant to be a mocking laugh, but it sounded more hysterical. He could see the tears streaming down her face. "Have you tried the soft technique on her yet, Jan? Did you tell her she was the softest thing you'd ever touched? That's what got me, wasn't it? Only she's wise, isn't she? Just a little half-breed ta. . . ."

"Don't call her anything," Arcola snapped, "that you'll be sorry for," and took another step forward to catch her arm again.

She writhed in his grip without tearing loose this time, her face turned up to him in a twisted way. "I will call her names. She's just a dirty little *métisse*. What you see in her I'll never understand. I could have given you anything you wanted, Jan. I did, didn't I? All you had to do was snap your fingers, and I was there. And you threw it away, Jan. You threw it away for a dirty, stinking, cross-blooded little. . . ."

His hand made a sharp crack against her face, knocking her backward in the snow.

She stood there with her hand on her face, a hoarse, guttural sobbing rising and falling through her chest. "You do have a case on her, don't you?" she choked, and it seemed an effort to force her voice out. "How does it feel, Jan? How does it feel to want something you can't have? How does it feel to see her laughing at you when you turn on the goo?" She saw what that did to him and laughed again. It had a cracked sound. "Yes, laughing at you. We're all laughing at you, Jan. Even that drunken Irisher. You're making a fool of yourself."

His fists were clenched, white-knuckled at his sides, and

he felt as if he were beginning to tremble. "Get out, Lou, get out."

"I thought we had something, Jan. I was thirty, and there's been a thousand men, or a million, I don't know, and still, when you came along, I thought we could have something. I was a fool, wasn't I? Like a schoolgirl. And I couldn't help it."

"I told you to get out!"

"I'm getting out. For good. I'm going back to Athabaska, Jan."

That drew him up slightly, as realization leaked through his anger. "I don't mean that, Lou. The dogs."

"Maybe Céleste will buy your dogs for you," said Lou, backing away. "Why don't you ask her? You've made a big enough fool of yourself already."

"You know she won't," said Arcola. "We can't go on without them, Lou."

"Can't you?" said Lou. "Then you're stuck here, aren't you? You should have thought of that before."

He moved toward her. "Lou. . . ."

"Don't start that again. Don't talk to me. I'm through, and I'm going."

A strange, feral glow came into his eyes, and he kept moving toward her and saw the way her face contorted with a sudden fear. "Are you, Lou?" he said.

Hoar frost formed a delicate coating over the clumps of reindeer moss on the hummocks, and frozen cranberries hung in clusters from the saskatoon all about the clearing. The dogs stood impatiently in their moose-hide traces with their breaths steaming the chill air. Céleste finished knotting the off trace into the collar toggle of her king dog, and stood erect as the two men came into the clearing from Chippe-

270

wayan, and she could not keep the surprise out of her voice. "Glengariff!"

"Yes," smiled Arcola. "Lou has decided to wait for us here at Chippewayan, and, naturally, Badger won't be going with us. I thought we'd need another man."

Céleste studied Arcola. "That's very strange."

"Glengariff can run with the best trippers," said Arcola.

"I wasn't thinking about Glengariff."

"Oh," Arcola shrugged, "you know Lou. Soft lights and velour gowns and good rye. Thought of all this snow was too much for her."

"Was it?" said Céleste. Finally she turned to Glengariff. "I won't have you drunk."

"The cry of the morning be upon me if I touch a drop of *poteen*," said Glengariff. "Anyhow, where would I get it?"

"You'd find something to get drunk on where the devil himself would fail," Céleste told him. "Now, if you're driving the Cree toboggan, you'll have to use Chippewayan on Bigriver. He doesn't work under English. Shall we start?"

Glengariff had brought his old Krag .30 along, and she saw him unsling it and stuff it into the cariole of his sled before she turned to her own outfit. Her white dogs rose from where they had lain in the snow, sensing her intention, moving forward till the heavy moose-hide traces were taut, bushy tails raising in an eagerness to be off. Without using her whip, she started them.

"Ma-a-arche!" she called, and the first withy collar creaked against furred throat as Kitch-eo-kemow leaned into his pull, and the hide cariole shuddered to each succeeding jerk as the other dogs followed suit, and then the hickory runners chuckled against the snow, and Céleste knew a sense of freedom she had not experienced since catching the boat south of Athabaska. She set the pace a little slower than what

they would keep later on, wanting to warm the dogs into it the first day or so, her medium-size Seauteaux shoes leaving a steady track behind her.

It was the second night out she saw Glengariff looking at the trees. Peace River was frozen over, and the beeches that formed a row of skeleton sentinels along the bank and farther back the banksian pines bowed beneath the first weight of winter snow. They had made their camp back from the cutbank, and Arcola went nearer the river to hunt some dry wood. Céleste was through chaining her team up for the night when she became aware of Glengariff. He was standing beside his sled holding a dog chain in one hand, and looking up at a white spruce, towering well over a hundred feet above them. The utter silence struck Céleste abruptly, and the immensity of the mystery around them, and she took a quick little breath, sensing what must be passing through Glengariff's mind. He must have felt her eyes on him, for he spoke without turning.

"They *are* tall, aren't they?" he said. "Like they was reachin' up for Saint Patrick's blessin'."

"Is that what you say of the yews in Connach?" she asked.

He turned toward her, and a smile started to lift his mouth. Then it faded, because their eyes had met.

"Why did you come, Glengariff?" she asked.

"Maybe because you were right about me," he said. "There's beauty to this country, if I wasn't too blinded by my own bitterness to see it. The song. . . ."

" 'Alouette?' "

"How did it go?"

She smiled faintly. "You're slipping, Glengariff."

"No. Really. How does it go?"

She turned and began kicking the snow away for a spot for

the fire. "You've heard it enough," she said, embarrassed, suddenly not able to sing. Then, angry at her own shyness, she began to hum it slowly, melodiously.

" *'Alouette, gentile Alouette.'* " It was Glengariff's liquid Irish tenor beginning it, his faint brogue lending the French words such an odd accent, Céleste had to laugh, and, when he got stuck, she helped him out, and soon they were both singing, working in time to the music as they cleared the snow away.

" *'Je te plumerai le cou,'* " sang Céleste, touching her neck.

" *'Je te plumerai le cou, et le bec, et le bec, et le bec,'* " laughed Glengariff, patting his nose and kicking up a little jig.

They were like a couple of children, for a moment, and it must have struck them both at the same time, for Céleste stopped almost the instant Glengariff did. They stood there, sobered abruptly, staring at each other. Then Glengariff moved his hand in a strange, apologetic way.

"It's not a bad song," he said.

"I never heard you laugh before," she said.

He shrugged, and Céleste saw in his eyes, before they dropped, the same embarrassment she had felt.

The Caribou-Eater camp Arcola sought was at the head of Loon River where it ran into the Peace, a huddle of the dome-shaped Cree lodges set in a clearing surrounded by naked spruce, a week's run from Chippewayan. As soon as the three sleds made their appearance, the forest was filled with the vicious baying of a hundred Indian dogs rushing out to surround them. Céleste had already run ahead of her own team, uncurling her dog whip.

"Illa, illa!" she shouted, beating at the ferocious mob of dogs descending on them from every side, her lithe figure

273

swaying back and forth, the long lash leaping and curling like a snake in spasms. "Glengariff, help me with these *giddes!*"

He was beside her, then, snarling as viciously as the dogs, not with any whip, but laying about him with his shillelagh. "Go on, you *cua gombeens,* you've got Glengariff to bark at now. I'll split every skull among you . . . !"

The dogs cringed back from the two crazy, shouting figures, and by that time the Crees had gathered. The chief came, pushing his way through the crowd of bucks, kicking a dog casually out of his way. The dominant command of his beaked nose and heavy brow was turned ugly by deep smallpox pits in the thick brown of his face. His dirty parka had once been white caribou hide, and leggings of H.B.C. stroud were wound as high as his knee.

"*Wachee,* Musk-quaw," Céleste greeted him.

"*Wachee,* E-shim," said Musk-quaw, The Bear, speaking Cree. "We heard you were coming north from Athabaska. Welcome to my *me-ke-wape.*"

The *me-ke-wape* was twenty feet in diameter, its framework of alder wands bent into a permanently arched shape and covered by caribou hide with the hair on the outside. The deep layer of spruce boughs on the floor gave springily to Céleste's moccasins, and she seated herself on the coverings made of rabbit skins sewn together. She saw the nauseated expression cross Arcola's face as he stepped through the door behind her and caught his first sniff of the mingled odors of boiled dog and perspiration and fetid blanketing and rotting caribou hide that filled the lodge. Céleste had carried in a bundle she had brought from Chippewayan, and she untied the thong from around it and rolled the trade goods out of a strip of tarp.

"I brought three wolverine furs to my *e-stays,*" she said,

"my elder brother," and saw the pleasure in his black eyes, for wolverine was prized highly by the Indians, as it was the only fur upon which breath would not congeal in cold weather and form icicles, and Céleste had seen a buck trade a good Winchester and five hundred rounds of ammunition for one pelt of the *carcajou*. But the pleasure was tempered by a certain speculation in The Bear's eyes as he fingered the three prime plews.

"My E-shim is good to me," said the Indian. "And now, let us eat and drink. You must be hungry after such a long run on bannocks and tea."

He growled something to his squaws, hovering in the background, and they began scooping a stew from the big trade kettle slung on spits over the fire in the center of the large lodge. Other bucks had taken their places around the circle. The Indians ate mainly with their fingers, using their knives to cut at the joints of meat.

Glengariff dipped greedily into his plate of stew, and soon his face was dripping as much grease as the Indians'. Arcola tried to keep the disgust from his expression as he picked up a chunk of meat between a long, pale finger and thumb.

After the stew, they were served a pudding, and, after tasting it, Arcola turned to Céleste. "The stomach of a caribou," she told him, "and its undigested contents, mixed with liver and blood and boiled intestines."

Arcola made a sick sound and shoved the bowl away, and Glengariff threw back his red head, laughing boisterously. "What's the matter, Arcola, have you got a weak stomach? That's a very tasty morsel among these *dubh-gaills*."

Then they began pouring the *tiswin*. Eagerly Glengariff accepted the cupful of corn brew, raising it to his lips. Then he stopped, and over the rim of the cup Céleste saw his blue eyes swing to her. He put the cup down and waved his hand dis-

275

gustedly. "*Arragh,* it's a mess o' *shebeen* anyway. Not even a Dublin man could partake of that foul corn."

He dipped back into the pudding almost angrily, scooping up the caribou and its undigested contents with an ardor that drew a sick look to Arcola's face. Céleste kept lifting her cup of *tiswin,* although she managed to spill the bulk of it outside her rather than inside.

The Indians' voices rose in ratio to the amount they drank. Two or three times she saw Glengariff's eyes slip around to that full cup before him, and then jerk away, and she couldn't help the small tingle somewhere inside her. The speculation in Musk-quaw's eyes disappeared before the fog of inebriation. The men began reaching for their *appits,* smoking bags hung at their waists, and soon the hot, fetid lodge was becoming filled with acrid black smoke from a dozen twists of Brazilian tobacco stuck into pipes or wrapped in shucks.

Céleste had hidden her real intent beneath an easy flow of small talk about the happenings in Athabaska and the state of Indians met on the way, but now she thought they were drunk enough. "For many winters I have heard from Ta-cullies to the east and Chippewayans to the north of your prowess in war, Musk-quaw," she said.

Trying to hide the pleasure the compliment gave him, The Bear tugged uncomfortably at his parka, sweat streaming down his face, and growled for more corn brew.

"I have heard you have over thirty scalps in your collection," said Céleste.

Musk-quaw's shoulders rose toward his greasy ears in a defensive shrug. "That was many years ago, when I was a young man. We no longer make war as we used to."

"They must have been wonderful times," said Céleste, and saw the intensity that had come into Arcola's face as he realized her purpose. "Is that one of the coups?"

The Bear's eyes raised to a rotting war club hung from the wall, nodding. "A Ta-cully weapon. My medicine bag holds more."

He jerked his head toward one of the squaws, and she unhooked a big buckskin rogan from one of the alder wands, handing it to him. He opened the bag and took out the scalp of an Eskimo, highly prized among these Indians, deadly enemies of their northern neighbors, and several other fetishes.

"Surely there is only one warrior greater than you on the Peace," she said.

"Who can that be?" he asked indignantly, eyes bleary.

"The *a-ye-nu* who counted coup on a party of white men on the Peace fifteen years ago."

"I am that man," he shouted, half rising and thumping his chest in a burst of primitive egotism. Then he dropped back, a surprised look crossing his face, as if realizing he had made a mistake.

"Surely the red coats have forgotten it by now," she said. And he was mollified somewhat. "Yet it will never be forgotten among the Indians. It is too much to expect that you brought back any coups. Not even as great a warrior as yourself could. . . ."

It had goaded him enough, and he fumbled in the bag, and what he brought out stopped her. Céleste stared at the scalp of long blond hair and the little black leather tobacco pouch, and the torn, partly burned book, trying to keep any expression from her face.

"Does that prove it?" The Bear almost shouted. "Do you doubt your *e-stays* now? It was south of Resolution."

"So they were going to Resolution, after all."

Céleste turned to Arcola. "What?"

"Nothing," he mumbled.

"The year before, a party of white men had raided our village, and killed a dozen women and children and stolen our furs," Musk-quaw stated. "We sent warning to Athabaska that no more whites would be tolerated north of the Peace. We came upon the track of this party led by the yellow-haired one in *Nis-ka-o Pe-sim,* the Goose Moon."

"April," Céleste almost whispered, and remembered how the muskeg had smelled that spring so many years ago at Peace River Landing.

"We followed them and killed them all," went on The Bear, carried away now by his own drunken boasting. "I took these coups and many more. A year ago we were feasting with a Cree named Namotawacow, and I showed him the trophies. We came upon him trying to steal my medicine bag. He got away with some of the sheets from this book, and I have had word that he died a violent death in Edmonton only three months ago."

"Namotawacow," said Céleste, "The Deaf One."

Suspicion glittered through Musk-quaw's eyes. He settled back, panting, staring at Céleste. "You knew him?"

"You can bet your medicine bag she knew him," said someone from behind Céleste, and she turned to see him standing tall and stoop-shouldered against the flap of the doorway, his eyes so bitter and black that they drew Céleste up sharply before she recognized him, and it had been so many years that it took that long, and then her jaw dropped slightly, and her voice had a hollow sound.

"Kamsack Carter," she said.

VIII

The snapping of the fire had been the only sound in the smoky *me-ke-wape* for a long time. Finally Glengariff began shifting restlessly where they had lashed his hands above his head to one of the alder wands.

"A fine *lanabh* I turned out to be," he said. "Just sit there and let them tie you up, Glengariff. They're only going to boil you in a kettle with their dog meat."

"Oh, be quiet, Glengariff," said Céleste irritably, from where she was tied. "If you'd made one move, Kamsack would have blown your head off with that Stevens."

Glengariff looked toward Arcola. "Finding that commission on you didn't help much. They don't like the idea of a Mountie knowing they got those coups from Reddington."

"I still can't figure out how Carter knew I was attached to the police," said Arcola, tugging futilely at his bonds.

The flap rustled, and Carter stooped inside, squatting on his hunkers just within the doorway. He looked around at them, glaring in an evil, relishing way.

"You were discussing me?" he said at last. He laughed shortly, glancing at Céleste. "Petit Pierre told me Arcola was from Intelligence in Ottawa. I struck Chippewayan just after you left. Belcarres had contacted me in Montreal and told me to meet him at Fort Chippewayan. Said he'd gotten a page from Reddington's log from an Eskimo in Dawson, and was on the trail of the rest of it. He must have thought Arcola had it. I can't figure any other reason he contacted you. I guess Johnny didn't know you were with Arcola, did he, Céleste? When Petit Pierre told me what had happened to Johnny, I left Chippewayan on your trail."

Les Savage, Jr.

Carter turned, still squatting there. For a long time he studied Arcola. He rubbed his lean, brown, unshaven jaw, squinting one eye. The alder wands that formed the lodge's framework were sunk into the earth, and Céleste had slid her hands down the one she was lashed to until her fingers touched the ground, digging patiently at the hard earth. She already had a small hole formed around the base of the wand, and a sense of growing urgency drove her to risk Kamsack's detection as she heard the sound from outside. Her movement caught his attention suddenly, and he turned from watching Arcola.

"What are they doing out there?" she said swiftly, to cover up.

His smile revealed broken, tobacco-stained teeth, and Céleste realized for the first time how the fifteen years had aged Carter. "Deciding your fate, beautiful," he said. "They don't know exactly what to do. I tried to help them by suggesting a few choice methods of disposal. But it ain't the old days. I guess Musk-quaw's sort of rusty on this type of work. Him and the elders are having a big powwow in the medicine lodge. I sort of hope the majority rules. It will save me the trouble of getting rid of you."

He broke off to move over where they had tossed Arcola's wallet and knife. Kamsack took up the long *klewang*, turning it over in his hands. Then he turned toward Arcola again, and understanding wrinkled the seamed, leathery skin of his gaunt, dark face.

"I been trying to figure it out. You've changed so much. But you was just a kid then, wasn't you? Fifteen years can change a man plenty. But when it changes a kid into a man, that's even more, isn't it? I guess I wouldn't have caught it except for this knife . . . Rodriguez."

"Rodriguez?" It came from Céleste in a hollow disbelief.

280

"Yes," Kamsack said, turning to her. "Esteban Rodriguez. The Mexican boy I had with me that day. I don't wonder you didn't recognize him. I never seen anyone change so much. But this *klewang* is the knife he used on your father at the Peace River post."

Céleste realized now what had made her stare at Arcola the first time they had met in Lou's apartment, filled with a nebulous sense of having seen him somewhere before. She knew a momentary rage at herself for not having recognized him. Yet she had seen him so fleetingly at the Peace River post, and she had been but a little girl. Fifteen years drew many clouds across the memory. Even Kamsack had had some trouble recognizing him.

Dogs outside the lodge began to set up a din, howling and yapping and baying, and Kamsack Carter dropped the *klewang,* his Stevens swinging as he bent through the flap. She heard him say something to the Indian sentries Muskquaw had posted outside. One of the Crees answered, having to shout now to be heard over the din.

"Something's happening out there," said Glengariff.

"The dogs would only make that much fuss over a newcomer," said Céleste. She stared at Arcola a moment longer, and it was in her again. The same bitter, driving hate she had felt rise up at the first sight of Belcarres, and Kamsack. Arcola! She still thought of him as that, and not Rodriguez. With a savage decision, she renewed her digging about the pole again. She had dug deeply enough so that it was jiggling back and forth. Outside, the shouting of Crees had been added to the baying dogs. The lodge shuddered somewhat, and Céleste stopped digging for a moment, thinking it was Kamsack returning. But the door flap did not raise. It was the hide wall at the rear of the lodge. The hides twitched and jerked. There was a ripping sound, and she saw the tip of a knife come through, sawing at the rawhide lashing the hides together. Arcola and Glengariff were watching, too. A man's hairy, blunt-fingered hand caught a piece of the hide he had cut loose, tearing it out. Then his head and shoulders came through.

"Badger Bates," said Arcola.

"Yeah." Badger's whole body was inside now. His bald pate was hidden by a ratty parka hood. That puckered scar over his brow had a livid look against the pallor of his face, and his eyes burned in a feverish way. He licked his lips, rising off his knees to a crouch, and pulling his Walther from beneath his parka. His glance swept the room until they settled on Arcola. "Yeah." He licked his lips again and stood up, going toward Arcola. "Did you think you could do that, Arcola? Did you really think I wouldn't find her like that?"

He was breathing heavily, and Céleste stared at him in a strange fear, not yet realizing what he meant, yet sensing the terrible intent in him now. Arcola drew himself up against the alder wand he was tied to, and the sweat on his face gave it a greasy look. His voice had a tight, grating sound.

"Don't be crazy, Badger. You'll never get out of here alive. The minute they hear the shot the whole camp will be in here."

"I don't care about getting out." Badger's voice was hoarse, driven. "I got in. That's all I care about. I cut my own dogs loose just outside of camp. That kept the Indian dogs busy so I could circle around and come in from behind." He leaned toward Arcola. "Al would have done the same thing, Arcola. He and I been working for Lou a long time now. We ain't the kind she'd go for, and it didn't matter how we felt about her, but we felt that way anyhow, and Al would have done the same thing if he'd found her all cut up that way, and knew why. He would have followed you to hell, Arcola."

"Badger. . . ."

"Yeah?" It was in that same flat, heavy way, coming out hoarsely on his breath. He bent forward a little more, and his thumb slid the safety up with a small, snicking sound. "Yeah, Arcola? I haven't slept in four nights, Arcola . . . you'll have to speak a little louder. I haven't eaten since I left Chippewayan. Not since I found her back there in the clearing, stabbed to death."

"I said you'll never get out alive." Arcola's voice caught on it.

"I told you I don't care about getting out alive." Badger was bent until his face almost touched Arcola's, his lips pulled back off his teeth. "Can't you understand that, Arcola? I guess not. You never felt that way about a woman, did you? You just played them for a while and then dropped them, and, if they broke, that was their hard luck. I been with Lou a long time, Arcola. Here's one thing you *will* understand."

"Badger. . . ."

Céleste stiffened for the shot. But as Badger raised the Walther, the flap in the door rustled, and he could not help turning that way. Kamsack Carter stooped through the door. There had never been anything dull about Kamsack, or slow, and the moment he lifted his head and saw Badger standing that way, he must have understood, and realized he had no time to raise the Stevens and shoot. It had taken Badger that long for reaction, and his gun jerked around toward Kamsack about the same time Kamsack threw the rifle with both hands. It struck Badger with its full length, knocking his gun toward the ceiling as it exploded. Kamsack dove for Badger's legs. Badger tried to pull his 9mm. back down as he went backward under Kamsack's tackle, but his second shot went above Kamsack as they both smashed into the opposite wall.

283

Céleste tore madly at the loosened alder wand, trying to pull up on it and free the length that was still left embedded in the ground. The rawhide lashings tore her wrists, and her hands became sticky with her own blood. Biting her lips, she jerked from side to side. The lodge shuddered to the thrashing, struggling men across the way. The Cree sentry stooped through the flap, rifle leveled. Badger's pistol whipped Kamsack across the face, blinding him momentarily with the slashing blow, Badger rolled free. The Cree yanked at the lever of his Winchester. Badger came to his knees and saw him and twisted around to bring his 9mm. into line. They fired at the same time. The Cree hugged his Winchester into his belly in a spasmodic jerk, grunting, and fell face downward across Glengariff's legs where he sat tied at one side of the door. Badger stayed there on his knees for a moment. Then his face twisted with the awful effort of will it took to force himself toward Arcola. The Walther seemed too heavy for him to lift. He grabbed it with his other hand, trying to raise it.

"Damn you," he groaned, "damn you," and the gun was almost in line with Arcola's chest, "damn you," and then Badger fell to one side, dropping the gun beneath him.

Outside, the camp was in an uproar, and Céleste could hear feet pounding toward the lodge. Carter was pawing for his Stevens with one hand, wiping blood from his eyes. It was about then Céleste felt the alder wand jerk behind her. It had come free of the earth at last. She slid her hands down to the butt end and was loose from the lashings. Kamsack must have caught her movement, because he started to rise, dropping the hand he had been wiping his eyes with and jerking up the Stevens. Her bloody hands still entangled in the slackened lashings, Céleste threw herself at Badger, scooping up the Walther. It was a double-action piece, and she didn't even have to thumb the hammer back. She squeezed out the shot lying full-length across Badger. Kamsack jerked and took a step forward, his eyes squinting. Céleste fired again, and again, and Kamsack dropped his Stevens, and again, and Kamsack made a last sick sound, and his eyes closed tightly on his pain, and the weight of his body falling on Céleste made her cry out. Squirming from beneath him, she tried to rise, but was beaten back down by a blow on her head. She came over onto her back, firing point-blank at the sweating, brown face above her, rolling violently aside as the man fell.

More Crees were shoving in through the door, and the lodge shuddered to their press. Kamsack and Badger had dislodged some of the alder wands on the opposite side with their violent struggle against the wall, and Céleste had pulled one up on this side, and the Crees rushing in caused the whole structure to sway and groan, pulling it completely out of plumb, giving Glengariff and Arcola the chance they needed to tear free of the alder wands they were lashed to, in the same manner as Céleste had, pulling the weakened stakes from the ground and sliding the rawhide bindings down to the butt end and off.

Céleste emptied the Walther into the mob of Indians pouring through the narrow door. Two or three went down in the forefront, and those coming from behind tripped over them. Then Glengariff was among them.

"The cry of the mornin' be on you," he bellowed, and that wicked shillelagh was going. "It's Glengariff you've got to contend with now, you devil-ridden *dubh gaills*."

Apparently the Crees hadn't known what they were coming into, but, once inside, there was no retreat, as that narrow doorway was blocked by more trying to push in. Three or four had tripped over the ones Céleste had shot, but were on their feet again. Glengariff brought his shillelagh around in a vicious arc that caught one Cree on the bridge of his nose, dropping him like a poled ox. But another Indian ducked past Glengariff, yanking that Ta-cully war club off the wall. He whirled toward Céleste, and she saw it was Musk-quaw, The Bear, his pockmarked face fiendishly twisted. She squeezed the trigger. It clicked on an empty. Musk-quaw jumped toward her, and she threw the gun at his face. He dipped sideways, and the Walther flew past him, striking a wall with a *thump*. Another Cree staggered through the crowd, crossing in front of The Bear.

"*A-wis-se-tay,*" Musk-quaw shouted, "out of my way," and knocked the Cree aside with a backhand blow, and Céleste dodged the downward swing of that war club, and her shoulders struck the alder wands supporting the lodge and would go no farther. She stared up wide-eyed at that last instant at the varicolored arc the painted club made coming down and knew it would be the last thing she saw.

"*A-wis-se-tay,* yourself!" someone bellowed in her ear, and a red blot flashed between her and Musk-quaw, and the club seemed to jerk in mid-air, and, when it did strike her, it was only with the force of its own weight falling, for Musk-quaw's hand was no longer gripping it, and then the club dropped off onto the rabbit skins.

"*Na-maw!*" shouted Musk-quaw, "no!"

"Yes!" yelled the man between her and the Cree, "yes!"— and then Musk-quaw's pockmarked face dropped abruptly from her sight, and the red-headed Glengariff was standing spraddle-legged in front of her with that shillelagh in his hand.

"*Acushia,* I haven't hit a skull that hard since the Tans tried to keep me at Wellington Barracks," laughed Glengariff. "Where are you going? That ain't the way out."

"The log," shouted Céleste, stumbling against a shouting

Cree who was reeling back from something in the middle of the lodge.

"And what do you think it is Arcola's got?" yelled Glengariff, cracking the Cree across the head as he stumbled on past.

It was then that Céleste saw what the Cree was trying to escape from there in the middle. Musk-quaw had carried his medicine bag with him when he left the lodge for council with the elders, and must have still had it with him when he rushed back in with the other Crees. Arcola stood in the middle of the lodge, the medicine bag in one hand, his *klewang* in the other. There had been half a dozen Crees still on their feet on that side of Céleste and Glengariff, but now they were scattering wildly backward before that terrible figure whirling this way and that in their midst with the long blade. Arcola was transformed with that *klewang*, all the careful, deliberate suavity of him swept away before a wild bestiality. He made a soft snarling sound, jerking this way and that, crouched forward on springy legs, bent deeply at the knees, his black hair down over his face, those strange black eyes blazing with a battle lust.

"Arcola," shouted Céleste, "Arcola, over this way!"

He stiffened, head jerking toward her, as if snapped from a trance. Then he jumped across the body of a Cree toward Glengariff and Céleste. It brought him into the press of Crees again, and Céleste saw the blade flash among them.

"*Ne-pa-how!*" screamed a Cree, reeling back with his hands held across a bloody parka, "*ne-pa-how!*"—and Arcola whirled away from him, still coming forward, and caught another man with a vicious, slashing stroke.

Arcola had forced three or four of them into Céleste and Glengariff, stumbling, slugging, kicking, trying to wield whatever of their own weapons they could find about the lodge. One of the Crees fighting to escape that awful blade staggered into Glengariff.

"A *vourneen deelish*," said Glengariff, and his shillelagh made a sharp crack against the man's head, and the Cree started going back the way he had come, and fell on his face. The Irishman caught Céleste's arm and shoved her toward the flap covering the door. A Cree threw himself at her with the sweat dripping on his twisted face. She ducked beneath his outstretched arms and let the full weight of his body crash across her bent back, and then heaved up. His own momentum carried him on over her. The hides gave with a ripping sound as he crashed into them, and an alder wand collapsed, and he went clear through the wall, leaving a gaping hole. Then Céleste burst through the door, with the shouting Irishman at her heels.

The camp was in a bedlam. Patently none of the Crees outside had known exactly what was happening inside, and there was no organization in the crowd passing in through the door.

They fell back as Céleste ran against them, and, before they could close on her, Glengariff came in behind with his deadly shillelagh, whacking from one side to the other in wild abandon, and then Arcola was in the open, adding his long knife to the Irishman's club. They had cut their way through the crowd before the Crees knew what had happened, and ran toward their three sleds, the dogs still in harness.

Glengariff beat madly at the mob of Indian dogs that rushed them, yapping and baying, and Arcola was like a fiend, slashing right and left with that deadly palm-up stroke. In a madness of shouting Indians and howling dogs and Gaelic curses they reached the sleds.

"*Ma-a-arche!*" shouted Céleste, "Kitch-eo-kemow, *ma-a-arche!*"—and the white dogs lunged into their collars with a series of spasmodic grunts, tearing the sled out of the snow even as Céleste bent into the cariole for her snowshoes. She hopped along after the sled to slip her right Seauteaux shoe on, stopping momentarily to jam her moccasin into the rawhide lacing of the left footgear.

A Cree came fighting his way through the Indian dogs as Céleste straightened up, a bright marble axe flashing above his head. Her only weapon was that dog whip, and she was whirling toward the man with the lash swinging back over head when the shot rang out. The Cree stumbled with a wild cry of pain, and went down. For a moment Céleste could not tell where the shot had come from. Neither Arcola nor Glengariff offered a possibility. They were too far behind, trying to start their sleds through the howling mob of Indian dogs. Then she saw Arcola had gotten his .375 from his sled, and remembered that Mossberg sight. At that moment, Arcola quit trying to fight his sled out of the camp, and beat his way through the dogs on his snowshoes, firing to the right and left from his hip. Céleste realized Glengariff would never make it unless she did the same.

"Glengariff!" shouted Céleste, "forget the sled. You'll never get through with it. They're getting guns. Glengariff . . . !"

"Chanipson!" he roared, *"chanipson!"*—and Bigriver made a valiant effort to answer the command, lurching to the right against the press of Indian animals.

Scattered firing began breaking out among the lodges now. Céleste had fought her way through the dogs almost to the edge of the village. Another Cree ran from between two lodges. He had an old .30-30, snapping the lever on it. Running after Céleste in his Ungava shoes, Arcola turned and fired from the hip. The Cree ran on toward Céleste without faltering, and his lever snapped home so loudly she could hear it through the other sounds. At first she thought the shot was his. Then, as he fell forward with his .30-30 unfired, she realized it wasn't.

"There's your snap shooting for you, Arcola!" shouted Glengariff. "You don't need a Mossberg scope on that one."

The Irishman had left his sled and was running through the Indian dogs after Arcola and Céleste, and his Krag was swinging at his hip, and it was curling smoke, too. It was then it happened, with the three of them strung out like that, Arcola closing in behind Céleste, Glengariff fighting after him. Céleste never knew exactly which shot it was, the firing was becoming heavier all the time. She saw Glengariff stumble, and catch himself, and she thought he had merely struck heavy going. Then he went down.

"Glengariff!" she called, and then, *"ja!"*—and her team wheeled sharply to the left, and then, "whoa!"—and the butt dog steadied down on his forefeet to halt.

"No!" shouted Arcola. "Céleste, no, we can't stop now. He's done. That shot took him square. Stop now and none of us will get out alive. *Ma-a-arche,* Kitch-eo-kemow, *marche!*"

"We can't leave him here!" she cried, not yet quite stopped. "We can't leave him."

"Ma-a-arche!" screamed Arcola again, running up beside the dogs, and they continued to run forward in a half-hearted run, bumping into one another in their confusion.

"No, Arcola."

"Yes, Céleste."

She looked down the muzzle of that .375 pointed at her belly, and the eyes above it, cold and implacable now, and her face twisted in a bitter, frustrated way. She took a last look back before turning away. Her voice held a small, choked sound.

"Glengariff."

IX

The pale birches stood like timid ghosts along the cutbank, brooded over by the somber majesty of the barren elms standing farther back in the pristine silence of the forest. The fire was burning low, and the dogs crouched about it in a nervous, waiting way, watching Arcola out of large, bright eyes, feverish with exhaustion. Céleste, her hands lashed together, was watching him in the same way. Only there was nothing nervous or feverish in her eyes. They were big and black, something primitive in their depths. Perhaps that was what gave her the look of affinity with the dogs. Her face seemed darker, more impassive, more Indian. It was the same way her mother's face had looked that instant she had stepped in the doorway of the Peace River post so many years ago, realizing what the men were doing to her husband.

Arcola had been going over Reddington's log, and he began reading aloud from it again. " 'April Twenty-Second, four days southwest of Loon River on the Peace. It looks as if the Crees are going to attack us. A big war party has been following us ever since we left the headwaters of the Loon. I have talked with Croix, and he thinks it advisable to cache the treaty money. . . .' "

"Treaty money?"

Arcola raised his head, smiling faintly. "Yes. You wondered why so much fuss was made over Wight Reddington's disappearance? I thought that you, of all people, would know, Céleste."

"I was only a little girl. . . ."

"I still thought you'd know," he said, "till I'd been with you on this trip long enough to see your ignorance was genuine. You know what treaty money is. The practice has been in operation up here for a number of years. Once a year the tribes who have made a treaty with the government gather at Fort Resolution to be paid five dollars a head for their co-operation. Multiply that by several thousand Indians and you have enough money to make it interesting to a lot of people. Enough money, for instance, to set up a man for life in this kind of country, if he got it all in one chunk."

She was bent forward. "And that's what Kamsack Carter . . . ?"

"Was after when he killed your father," answered Arcola. "There had been several attempts to get the money in preceding years, and the police knew Carter had been active up here that year. In order to preclude any trouble, they sent the money north with Reddington rather than the regular messenger, letting it leak out that Reddington was hunting a new trail to the Peace River post for Hudson's Bay. Kamsack decided that your father was in on the deal. As this log proves, Reddington never planned on striking the Peace River post at all, but going on to Resolution with the money. But when Reddington realized Musk-quaw and his Crees were trailing him, and knew they were out for blood, Reddington finally had to cache the money rather than be caught with it on him. Apparently there were no survivors in the Reddington party."

They had been tripping four days through the frozen wastes since leaving the Cree village, following the Peace southwest from the Loon, but the emotion still kept beating up from beneath Céleste's weariness, a strange, poignant grief for Glengariff that she could not explain or define, only knowing she had left some part of herself back there with the red-headed Irishman.

"Rodriguez?" she said bitterly. "Esteban Rodriguez."

His smile was ironic. "Does it gall you, Céleste? It took

Belcarres a long time to recognize me, and Kamsack, and they had known me well. You only got a glimpse of me, and you were but a child then. A man changes in fifteen years, Céleste, especially when he lives the way I have. I've seen the world. And as much as I've seen, Céleste, I promised myself that someday, sooner or later, my travels would bring me back here, and I would have a crack at this money. The real Arcola did not recognize me on the train from Montreal, but I recognized him. I had some official dealings with him when I worked with Kamsack, and knew he was connected with the police. I knew I couldn't return to Alberta under my own name. What better than with the credentials of an Intelligence officer in the Royal Northwest Mounted? You'll have to admit it gave me marvelous access to things. As soon as I struck Alberta, I began hunting up my old friends. Namotawacow in Edmonton. He was in his dotage, and one had to shout to make him hear, and to his dying breath he didn't know it was his old friend who got that sheet of Reddington's from him." Arcola got up, pacing restlessly about the fire, glancing into the trees. "A poplar, Céleste."

She would still think of him as Arcola, despite herself now. "What do you mean?"

"On the log, here," he began to read, and she realized why she had noticed him glancing around ever since they had stopped. " 'April Twenty-Third. This morning we made the cache. We built it like a fur cache, digging in the soft ground above the cutbank at the foot of the largest poplar in the vicinity. From the campsite, one can look true south through a pair of beeches on the riverbank and see between them the notch of Caribou Pass through the Indianheads below Peace River. The poplar stands some forty yards back of the river due north from this spot.' " Arcola took a step sideways, staring out over the river. "There are the beeches, and I can see a notch in those mountains. They must be the Indianheads." He turned halfway around till he was facing away from the river. He stood that way a long time, looking into the forest, holding the log up several times, speaking finally. "It says poplar here, but I fail to see one."

Céleste felt an excitation despite herself, an excitation arising from fifteen years of waiting and searching and remembering. So many men had died for this, through the years. She couldn't help speaking. "Look at the moss on that fir to your left."

He turned that way. "What do you mean?"

"As long as you can see it from where you're standing, you haven't got true south."

He moved to the right a few paces, then looked through the beeches. "The notch," he said, and turned halfway around once more, and drew a breath. "The poplar."

He took a quick step toward the forest, then halted himself, turning around. With a soft smile, he took the step back to the fire and picked up his rifle. Céleste stood bent forward that way a moment longer, toward the gun, her breath caught in her with the frustration of it, then she straightened up and moved toward the poplar. When they reached the gray, ridged trunk of the tall tree, he waved the Magnum at her.

"Sit down with your back against that cedar," he said. He leaned the Magnum against the tree and began breaking up the frozen ground before he started to dig. He had been repressing an excitement in himself up to now, but, as the work drew a sweat from him and the frozen crust gave way to black, loamy soil beneath, Céleste saw his eyes begin to shine. He stopped to rest, breathing heavily, and removed his parka. Back at the dead fire, the dogs had begun to move about restlessly, their chains tinkling. Céleste's fingers were intertwined, and her lips made a straight, tight line. Fifteen years.

So many men. Kamsack. Moon-woman. Namotawacow. So many memories.

Arcola started digging again. Céleste was so intent on it she did not realize, at first, when the dogs stopped shifting and whining. The shovel made a clinking sound against something. Arcola stooped and pulled a rotting branch from the loose earth, then another.

"Like a fur cache." His voice held a shaking edge. "They always line their fur caches with boughs this way. That's what he said, wasn't it? Like a fur cache."

His digging became more feverish. Then Céleste sensed the dogs' silence. She glanced toward camp. Her whole team was standing, pricked ears straight up. Chief began to raise his black muzzle. Arcola dropped his shovel abruptly and stepped down in the depression he had dug, kicking at something. Then he bent over. Only the bowed portion of his back was visible to her, and, in that instant, Kitch-eo-kemow started baying. Céleste was on her feet by the time Arcola had jumped from the hole. He whirled to scoop up his gun and run toward camp, his hand closing over the bolt as he ran. He came to an abrupt stop before he had reached the fire, glancing back at Céleste. Then he began backing up till the trees screened him again from the open campsite.

"Go on, bay, you bane banshees. I might have known you wouldn't let me come up without raising a *caoine* like that."

It came from the forest, and rang through Céleste's head like the clang of the mission bell at Athabaska, and the name was in her mind, like a deafening shout, before Arcola said it.

"Glengariff?" he called, and his voice held a shrill note.

"Damned right it's Glengariff," came the answer. "You didn't think a bunch of *dubh gaills* like them Crees was going to stop me, did you? I'm coming, Arcola."

"Don't, Glengariff," called Arcola. "You'll only be

hurting Céleste. I've got Céleste, and. . . ."

"No, you haven't!" screamed Céleste, throwing herself at a thicket of chokecherry growing beyond the poplar. She crashed into the bushes with the deadly crack of a rifle behind her. The slug kicked dirt in her face as she rolled through the thicket. That sent a spasm of animal panic through her she could not help answering, coming out of the roll onto her feet and breaking in a wild, bent-over run through the bushes past the poplar. Again, Arcola's Magnum smashed through all other sound. The bullet clattered through the bare cherry bushes, and something plucked at her parka hard enough to jerk her sideways in her run. She had one glimpse of Arcola through the brush, bent forward, with one hand tugging at the bolt for a third shot at her, and then, if he would have tried for her again, it didn't matter, because the hard ground beneath her gave way, and in that last, flashing instant she realized she had taken the direction toward the river, and then she was sliding feet first over the cutbank in a small avalanche of her own making.

She struck at the bottom, going helplessly end over end until her head banged against the ice with a stunning impact. Lying there at the foot of the bank, through a roaring blanket of pain that engulfed her, the full knowledge of what she had let Glengariff in for struck Céleste. At least, Arcola did not have her presence as a threat to hold over the Irishman. But he had something far more deadly. As the first agony subsided in her, she felt a bitter disgust with herself. She had run away. It had been a thoughtless, spasmodic reaction, engendered entirely by the circumstance, and, if she had stopped to reason, she would probably be lying dead up there now. Still she had run away. There was no other way of looking at it. And now, up there, alone, Glengariff—the Irishman who . . . .

With a strangled sob she forced her will on muscles lethargic with pain, getting to her hands and knees and crawling toward the bank across the ice of the river. She was with Arcola, now, in her mind. She could almost feel that Circassian stock, the way it felt in his hands. The nine and a half pounds of the gun seemed to pull against her shoulders. The reticule of that Mossberg scope loomed before her eyes.

Don't, Glengariff, she thought, clawing her way up the steep bank, *oh, please don't. This won't be snap shooting now. Just waiting for you, Glengariff, just sitting there and waiting for you with that scope right in front of him. You'll be sitting right on the end of his barrel, Glengariff. Two hundred yards away. Three hundred. It doesn't matter. Right on the end of his barrel.*

"Was that Céleste, Arcola?"

It was the Irishman's voice, coming muffled and dull from the woods somewhere above, and Arcola's answer.

"What do you care, Glengariff?"

"Arcola, if you've hurt her. If you have. . . ."

"That's right, Glengariff, come on . . . come right ahead."

"If you've killed that woman. . . ."

Don't, Glengariff. Not with an old .30 Krag. You can't do it. Please don't try. Her hands were cut on the ice now, and the blood ran down inside her sleeve, and she didn't even feel the pain. Her breath made a hoarse sound, and she tried to control it for fear Arcola would hear. *Not with an old Krag, Glengariff. He's got that Magnum. Don't you know, you fool? You won't even be able to get within range. Four power Mossberg, Glengariff. You saw it. You know. Right on the end of his gun. Three hundred yards away, you'll be right on the end.*

"I'm coming, Arcola."

She stopped, almost at the top of the bank, when Glengariff called that. She seemed to hear a rustling in the trees beyond. Or was it the dogs? She could hear one whining now, from the camp. And Arcola? *Oh, God, Glengariff, no, no, no . . . !*

She bellied over the lip of the bank, and there he was. Arcola had remained just outside the clearing where the poplar was, screened by the cherry bushes from the woods farther in, visible, undoubtedly, only from the position of the river formed by this bank, invisible from any other section of the terrain. He was crouched, facing away from Céleste, and the rifle was at his shoulder, and she knew instantly what it meant. *Right on the end of his gun, Glengariff!* And in that same instant, still gripped with this impotence, she saw the movement some three hundred yards away through the trees, higher on the slope above the river. She started to shout, and it died in her throat, knowing how little that would help, with the Irishman so big in that reticule. The rest arose from sheer desperation. Her action resulted from no conscious thought she could have identified. It was the only thing left.

The rocks on the bank were covered with ice and snow, and she had already stooped for one and torn it from its position and straightened again, flinging it before conscious thought could enter it. The rock must have struck Arcola at the moment he pulled the trigger. It knocked him forward with a shout, and the Magnum exploded. Running toward the man, Céleste did not know whether the rock had struck soon enough until Glengariff appeared, coming down the slope through the trees in a driving gallop.

"That's how much good them fancy sporting sights do you, Arcola!" he shouted. "Here's a real snap shot for you."

He must not have caught sight of Céleste yet, directly behind Arcola and in the line of fire, because his Krag bucked at his hip. The crash of the rifle was still alive as the scream of a ricochet broke into being, and Arcola's yell of agony mingled with the other sounds. He seemed knocked backward, jumping to his feet to keep from falling, and dropping the Magnum. Céleste saw reason for that ricochet then. The beautiful Circassian stock of the .375 was shattered, only a shred of its whitened wood yet clinging to the Winchester proof steel of the barrel. The stunning impact had numbed Arcola's hands, and he held them out before him in a surprised way. Glengariff continued to come on through the barren trees in that run.

Arcola's face lifted, and Céleste couldn't help but admire the cold nerve of the man in that instant. "Go ahead," he said.

Glengariff's run slowed, and finally he was walking, and he dropped the Krag with a grin. "What do you think this is, an arsenal? Springfield only made these old breech loaders to hold one slug at a time."

Arcola's thin lips opened to form a soundless O, and then he reached his right hand beneath his parka and drew out that *klewang*.

"Glengariff," shouted Céleste, "he's going to throw it!"

She heard the Irishman's shouting laugh as he broke into the run again, yanking something from his own parka, and then she had leaped at Arcola. The man tried to jump aside and throw the *klewang* at the same time. She caught his knife arm at the elbow as her body struck him, and they went down together. Her hands were still lashed together, and she could not hold his arm. Rolling from beneath her flailing legs and writhing torso, he jerked to his knees, slashing viciously. It caught her across the stomach, ripping her parka open, and she gasped with the pain. Then he was on his feet, whirling to meet Glengariff, and she saw what it was the Irishman had pulled from his parka. Glengariff ran straight at Arcola, and his shillelagh clanged against the *klewang*, knocking it aside. Their bodies met with a fleshy thud. Arcola staggered back,

299

tripping over Céleste, trying to roll away as he saw the Irishman was not going to stop.

"Just like the Athione taproom when the boys had taken on too much *poteen*," laughed Glengariff, and threw himself bodily over Céleste onto Arcola, and the two of them rolled crashing into the chokecherry. Céleste tried to get on her feet, stomach burning where Arcola had ripped her. As the torn brush closed about their bodies, she saw Arcola's knife flash upward. But they were still rolling over and over like a pair of cats, and, by the time Arcola grunted with the force of his thrust, the chokecherry screened them. Céleste stumbled after them, clawing her way through the bushes, brought up short as she burst into the clear. They were on their feet again, facing each other. Arcola's thrust had sliced Glengariff's face from forehead to jaw, laying the flesh open to the bone, and the Irishman swayed on his wide-spread legs, bent forward a bit, his hand white-knuckled around the shillelagh.

"Come on," panted Glengariff, "come on and get your skull split."

"Glengariff," sobbed Céleste, and made a small, abortive shift toward them, and then they had met again. The Irishman had come in, aiming his shillelagh to knock the *klewang* aside as before, but this time Arcola feinted, and drew back as Glengariff swung, and Glengariff was lurching in hard when Arcola's real lunge came. The Irishman saw his mistake and tried to jerk aside in that last moment. Their bodies met with that same fleshy thud, and Glengariff stiffened, and threw his head back and screamed. Céleste heard her own broken sound beneath his voice, as agonized as if she had taken that wicked palming thrust through the center of her own belly. Then, with both men together like that, Glengariff recovered enough to grab Arcola by the hair. The knife must have still been in the Irishman, for Arcola grunted, his far elbow jerking backward as if trying to yank the blade free, but with his grip on the man's hair Glengariff kept them locked together, pinning the long *klewang* in his own body. His face contorted with pain, he raised the shillelagh.

"Glengariff!" shouted Arcola hoarsely, and then the short club had struck his head.

"Aye," gasped Glengariff, and raised the shillelagh once more. Arcola struggled to free himself. The club descended again. Arcola fell backward, pulling Glengariff on top of him. Sprawled over the man, Glengariff raised up, and struck once more. The dull, cracking sound held a hollow finality. The Irishman lay there long enough for Céleste to stumble over, tugging at his arm.

She was surprised at his ability to get on his feet. The *klewang* was still sticking in him, and he pulled it out with a ghastly, sighing sound, dropping it on the ground. He stared at Arcola, gripping one hand over the bloody wound in his side.

"Michael Collins would have liked that fight," he said.

X

The ice was breaking up on Athabaska Lake now, and the Lapland longspurs were already coming back through the poplars for an early spring, and Céleste and Glengariff stood on the shore below Fort Chippewayan, staring out over the lake. It had been several months since Glengariff had met Arcola back there on the Peace, and the Irishman's wound had healed nicely. In that last instant, he had managed to jerk aside from Arcola's belly thrust, and the *klewang* had penetrated his side just beneath the ribs, missing the vital organs. It had been an old

301

voyageur's remedy, lard and gunpowder for gunshot wounds or any other kind, and the poultice had worked so well that by the time they returned to Chippewayan, the doctor had nothing to do. They had brought the treaty money back with them, still stowed in the rotting moose-hide bags Reddington had used fifteen years before. Now, Glengariff turned to watch Céleste's face as she stared pensively at the dark line of poplars on the lake shore. Her dog team stood restlessly in the traces behind her, the *odobaggan* loaded light for but one person.

"You know why I came along," he said.

"Arcola thought you wanted a cut out of whatever they were after."

"You know what I wanted," he said, and it brought her eyes around to meet his, and he was speaking more intensely now. "At first, down at Athabaska, it was just a way to get out of trouble there. But it was five weeks on the river from Athabaska to here, Céleste. You and I were thrown together a lot during that time. Maybe it really dated from that time you pulled me out of the river. I didn't realize it then, but something began to change in me. You caused that change. Nothing else. Part what you said. About the country. About a man." He stopped a moment, searching her eyes. "I didn't go with you and Arcola for a cut in what they were after, Céleste."

"I know." She met his gaze. "I've been drawn to you, Glengariff. More than I've been drawn to anyone."

His hand tightened. "Then . . . ?"

It must have been the way she pulled back that stopped him. "Are we ready for that?"

"What do you mean? I'm ready. Erin doesn't hold a colleen that compares with you"—his blue eyes raised upward momentarily—"Saint Patrick forgive me if that's blasphemy, but it's true." Then he was looking at her again. "And I'm a man who knows what he wants when he sees it."

"Is that enough . . . just knowing what you want? You say you've changed. Have you, yet? Can a man change a lifetime in a few weeks? Have you forgotten Michael Collins completely? Or Connach? Or the Easter Monday Rebellion? What would happen, for instance, if you meet a man you knew had been a Tan?"

His fists clenched, and he bent forward. "I'd. . . ."

He stopped abruptly, and she waited for its significance to penetrate fully before she spoke again. "You see what I mean? Maybe you've changed a little. Maybe you've come to see some beauty in a country outside of Connach. Maybe you can even sing 'Alouette' now. That isn't everything. You still belong to the I.R.A., Glengariff. It will take longer than this to wipe it out."

"You could help me," he said, almost inaudibly.

"It isn't only you who would have to change," she said. "I still get restless when I hear a lobo howling out in the night. I'm restless now. It will be a long time before I'll want to stop my sled for good."

"Céleste. . . ."

"No, Glengariff. You know it as well as I. Both of us have to live a little more before anything like that. Maybe we'll meet again. But for now . . . good bye."

He took a small step after her as she turned, then stopped, seeing the proud will in the supple line of her body, knowing how useless further argument would be. Without turning back again, she mushed her dogs and swung onto the spruce runners of the sled, swaying a little as she rode down the steep incline toward the poplars. Just before she entered the trees, she turned on the runners and lifted a hand. Then she was gone, the eager baying of her five white dogs carrying her into the infinite mystery of the country to which she belonged.

303